THE PROPS MASTER 1

Ritual Reality

First Print Edition
ISBN 978-1-939275-71-4

THE PROPS MASTER 1

Ritual Reality

DEVON LAYNE

ELDER ROAD BOOKS
BELLEVUE WA

Contents

Prologue

I F YOU grew up in America during the '60s like I did, you are probably still humming Beatles tunes and wondering whatever happened to the good music. You might even have spent hours running the *Abbey Road* vinyl backward to hear the message "Turn me on, dead man." You may have fought in Viet Nam or narrowly avoided the draft. Either way, it affected you and you knew people who were killed or wounded there. You were probably old enough to understand what happened when Kennedy was shot, to have joined the world in sadness when Pope John XXIII died, and may even have been on the streets protesting during the 1968 election campaign or when Bobby Kennedy was shot. You knew segregation, integration, the Great Society, busing, and the words of Dr. Martin Luther King, Jr.'s, "I have a dream."

Maybe more than any other generation, growing up in the '60s marked its progeny deeply with the culture of Woodstock, whether you were there or simply heard about it later. Even if you didn't participate in all the drugs, sex, and rock & roll, you knew it was happening. The pill launched the sexual revolution. Women's Lib promoted the burning of bras in the same fire some of us burned draft cards. We all had a glimmer of an idea that Haight-Ashbury was a Mecca for potheads, we'd been told to never trust anyone over thirty, and we knew the peace sign and were ready to fight over it.

We'd also seen race riots in Watts and Detroit that nearly burned cities down. With our long hair, beards, beads, music, and braless tits we went out to change the world.

Maybe we weren't as successful as we wanted to be. Maybe we've forgotten the fervor and passion we once had. Maybe we didn't use all the right methods. Maybe there were some people who were working toward other ends who knew the power that lay beneath our feet and to whom goddess-worship and magic were more than hippie fads. When we were standing on the pavement holding signs protesting carpet-bombing in Cambodia, the invasion of Laos, and the draft, maybe we should have been chanting spells around a fire as we did a naked spiral dance.

That's the world Wayne lives in. Your typical, everyday theatre student, he is drawn deeper into the pagan cult that draws its power from the earth and uses it to repair and heal.

Of course, where there are good witches there are wicked witches. The whole thing just changes the battlefield.

While I tried to be as true to historical events as possible, keep in mind this story is fiction. But you'll find a lot of things that ring true and you might get sucked into the magic the same way you get sucked into an enchanting performance on the stage.

If we shadows have offended,
Think but this, and all is mended,
That you have but slumber'd here
While these visions did appear.

Now on with the show! The play's the thing wherein I'll catch the conscience of the king.

Vocabulary

SOME RITUAL WORDS are used in this that may be unfamiliar.

Tools:

Athamé: is a knife or sword—a blade—sacred to the workings of magic and representative of Air and the East. The ritual *Athamé* of Coven Carles is named Creüs and was in the keeping of Ryan McGuire, The Blade.

Wand: may be a short wand (think Harry Potter) or a full staff (think Gandalf), sacred to the workings of magic and representative of Fire and the South. Usually, but not always, made of wood. The ritual wand of Coven Carles is named Iäpetus and is sometimes referred to as the 'Staff of the Vagabond Poet'. It was in the keeping of Doc Heinrich, The Flame Keeper.

Cup: may be any shape or material, sacred to the workings of magic and representative of the West and Water. The ritual cup of Coven Carles is named Cottus and was in the keeping of Mrs. Weed, The Water Maiden, and then of a witch called The Cupbearer.

Pentacles: May be a star, star-shaped stone, medicine bag with symbols on it, or a disk, usually also engraved with a magic symbol or star. Sacred to the workings of magic and representative of the North and Earth. The ritual pentacles of Coven Carles is named Enceladus and was in the keeping of the high priestess, "Magda" Harmon.

SPEACIAL NOTE: My use of the word 'pentacles' may differ slightly from that of other practitioners, but to keep terms straight for readers of fiction, I offer the following. The tool referenced herein is always referred to as a plural. The use of 'is' or 'are' is based entirely on what sounds better in the context, but as much as possible, 'pentacles' always refers to the tool, no matter what shape it takes. The singular form, 'pentacle,' is the *design* on the tool. The design is not necessarily star-shaped. Of the forty-four known pentacles of Solomon, only two designs (the second pentacle of Venus and the first pentacle of Mercury) have a five-pointed star. In magical workings, however, a five-pointed star is often drawn on the floor or even in the air. This specific symbol is a 'pentagram.' There are many ways of drawing the pentagram (forward, backward, upright, inverted) and each has its own use. But all are five-pointed stars.

Witches often name each of their tools, but I am only listing above the names of the Four Faces of Carles, the sacred tools of the grand coven.

Names of places and things:

OLD CELTIC WORDS are sometimes used when those intimate with the circle are speaking. Coven Carles might be referred to as *Cobhan Carles* and the children or members of the coven might be referred to as *cildru*.

A *grimoire* is a book of witchcraft with spells, chants, rituals, and various charm-making recipes. It is usually intended to be copied and/or passed on to another witch.

A *Book of Shadows* is a journal kept by a witch, chronicling what he or she has learned, including dreams, rituals, spells, and lore. One witch's *Book of Shadows* may become another witch's *grimoire*.

Pagan holidays fall at the quarters and cross-quarters of the year, in other words, the four celestial holidays and four between them. They are:

Yule, the winter solstice. This is considered by some traditions to be the start of the pagan year. ~December 21.

Imbolc, in the United States it is Groundhog's Day and in the Catholic church is marked as Candlemas. ~February 2.

Oester, the vernal equinox. Originally the feast of Astarte, near Jewish Passover and Christian Easter. ~March 21.

Beltane, or May Day. The first of May has long been celebrated as the great fertility festival. May 1.

Litha, the summer solstice. While westerners largely consider the quarters to be the beginning of the season, old references point to the fact that these were considered mid-season, as in *A Midsummer Night's Dream*. Longest day and shortest night of the year. ~June 21.

Lughnasad, also called Lammas or first harvest. This festival celebrates the death of the corn king. ~August 1.

Mabon, autumnal equinox. End of the harvest season and sometimes celebrated with the burning of a wicker man. Current celebrations in the U.S. that arise from the tradition include Burning Man over Labor Day weekend. ~September 20.

Ritual Reality

Samhain, or All Hallows Eve, Halloween. This celebrates the end of the pagan year as it descends to the darkness of Yule. It is said that on this night, the veil between the worlds (of the living and dead) is thinnest and both humans and spirits may walk between them. October 31.

Indianapolis. As much as possible, the places in and around Indianapolis are real or were real in the '60s, though some names (especially around the college) have been changed. And yes, there really was a tour of *Hamlet* to England, but in 1970, not 1969, and the people who went on the tour would recognize little about this story other than the locations. As it happens, the calendar days and days of the week in 1968-69 align exactly with the calendar days and days of the week in 2013-14.

England. As nearly as I can remember them, the locations in and around Keswick, England are described accurately for the time, and the geography is at least nearly the same, though some landmarks have been moved for convenience.

The Grand Coven Carles Castlerigg (*Cobhan Carles*) comprises four smaller circles, named for the landmarks that surround the stone circle, Skiddaw (in the north), Threlkeld (in the east), High Lodore (in the south), and Braithwaite (in the west).

Theatre. Okay, maybe it was pretentious of us, but when I majored in it, a theater was where you saw movies and the theatre was where live performances were given. Therefore, we majored in theatre and went to movies at the theater. Live with it. Oh. And my sister, bless her little old Hoosier heart, pronounces it with the accent on the second syllable and a long a, as in "rate."

Cast

Wayne R. Hamel, junior Theatre Major at Indianapolis City College. He is the Props Master and Technical Director for the college theatre. Initiated into the Art by his uncle and given the secret name Promethean, to be known as The Unbound.

Judith Harmon, sophomore standing, transfer student from England majoring in English Literature. She's actually a few years older than her classmates. Involved as a consultant in the theatre's production of *Hamlet*. In the Great Coven of Carles Castlerigg, she is known as The Swordmaster.

Dr. **Rebecca** Hart Allen, Professor of Anthropology. In the Coven she was known as The Hart, but after last year's challenge at midsummer she is also known as The Huntress.

Lissa, the doughnut lady. Just a late-night doughnut stop for Wayne until she learns he has been introduced to the Art. Under her coven name The Chameleon, she undertakes some of his training.

Elbert **"Uncle Bert"** Parker, Wayne's great uncle. The former spy living in an underground fortress quickly initiates Wayne into the Art and gives him his first tool. He also gives him a robe and a *Book of Shadows*. His secret name is Prometheus, and is known as The Bound.

Dr. McBride, the High Priest of Coven Carles, also known as The Barber.

"Magda" Harmon, High Priestess of Coven Carles and bearer of the Fourth Face of Carles, the pentacles, Enceladus. Judith's mother.

Serepte Allen, Rebecca's thirteen-year-old daughter. Already savvy about the workings of the coven.

Jim Richards, Theatre Professor at ICU, just trying to get a show on the road.

Glenn Little, Wayne's best friend and fellow theatre person.

Gail Bremen, student costumer at ICU and on-and-off girlfriend of Glenn.

Beth Donaldson, student lighting tech for the theatre.

Joe Hamel, Wayne's cabinet-maker father.

Dean Krannert, Academic Dean

Dr. Crowell, University President
Lena, Chuck, Steve, Phil, Carol and other theatre people.

And people who are present only in their absence:

John Keats, English romantic poet (1795-1821) who once got lost while on a walking tour of Northern England and to our cast is known as 'The Vagabond Poet'.

J. Wesley Allen, Rebecca's husband caught in a rift between the worlds in Greece in 1955. Missing ever since.

Ryan "The Blade" McGuire, former High Priest of Coven Carles, known as The Blade, and bearer of the First Face of Carles, the sacred *Athamé*, Creüs. Judith's father. He was lost at the same time as Wesley, possibly into the same rift between the worlds. The *Athamé* called Creüs was also lost and has not been seen in fourteen years.

Benjamin "Firebrand" Wilton, a scholar and adventurer whose legacy was to bear the staff until he gave it to Doc Heinrich. Wilton was sometimes known as The Firebrand and was the only one this century who was known to actually call fire with Iäpetus.

Mrs. Alice "Hebe" Weed, The Water Maiden of Carles and Rebecca's sponsor for initiation fourteen years ago. She keeps the Third Face of Carles, the Cup, Cottus.

Doc Heinrich, The Flame Keeper, bearer of the Second Face of Carles, the Staff of The Vagabond Poet, Iäpetus.

1
Opportunity Knocks

Friday, 18 October 1968

WAYNE WAS cold, tired, and hungry, wandering through a desolate countryside. Firelight glowed at the top of the steep hill… if only he could make it that far. Warmth and rest—maybe even food.

He crested the hill to see the looming shadows of a great stone circle with a fire at its center. "Toto," he whispered to himself, "I've a feeling we're not in Kansas anymore."

He crawled forward toward the fire, insinuating himself between dark shapes that seemed not to notice him. *What a stupid thing to do.* Finally feeling the warmth of the blaze penetrate his freezing hands, he raised his head. And stared straight into the eyes of Dr. Allen— auburn hair, falling loosely from her normally severe bun; dark brown eyes probing his soul; lips pursed. They knelt stark naked facing each other across the fire.

"My god!" he whispered and stood to run.

THE DREAM ABRUPTLY ended with the class bell jolting Wayne awake to gather his books and join the exodus of students. He hadn't meant to sleep. It was so hard to keep his eyes open through these 7:30 a.m. lectures—especially since he hadn't had more than three hours sleep any night this week. He should have just cut class but the slide presentation on Druidism sounded interesting. As soon as the lights were out, so was Wayne.

As his eyes focused on his surroundings, he saw no student exodus taking place. In fact, the lecture hall was empty.

Empty, that is, except for Dr. Allen, standing behind the podium staring at him.

"I'm still dreaming," he pled with himself struggling to wake up. "Please let me still be dreaming."

Dr. Allen was still staring and Wayne could only assume that he was facing reality.

"Hamel, Wayne R. Correct?" asked Dr. Allen

"Yes, Dr. Allen. I'm sorry…"

"For being who you are?" the professor asked. "I'm beginning to worry about you, Mr. Hamel. Are you well?"

"I think so, Dr. Allen."

"You have slept through every class this week. Is there a reason you come here at all?"

"I try to never cut classes," he answered truthfully enough.

"I ask you again, Mr. Hamel: Are you ill?"

"No, ma'am."

"Are you on drugs?"

"No, ma'am!" Wayne exclaimed. "Never!"

"Is it then that my lectures are simply so intensely boring that they put you to sleep? Please be honest, because I do make every effort to make these classes interesting and if I am failing, I would like to improve."

"Why couldn't I be dreaming?" Wayne muttered to himself.

"I beg your pardon?"

"Nothing, Dr. Allen. I just… I'm sorry."

"You mentioned that." The professor moved around the podium and walked toward Wayne. She carried a sheaf of papers in one hand and her walking stick in the other. Exhausted and humiliated, Wayne was about ready to disgrace himself.

"I've taken the liberty of checking your records, Mr. Hamel. Many professors are quick to judge and all too slow to consider potential problems with promising students. You are a junior?"

"That's right."

"Excellent grades in English literature. Straight As in Theatre. Your major, I believe."

"Both of them."

"You are an intelligent student, Mr. Hamel. There is no reason for you to be failing my course."

"I have to have this class, Dr. Allen," Wayne pled. If he missed this he'd drop below the minimum number of credits for the term and that spelled draft. He had no intention of ending up in Viet Nam.

"If you were not a bright student, or had a reputation as a trouble-maker, or if I had any reason to suspect you were on drugs, I would dismiss you from this class and simply submit an involuntary withdrawal for you," Dr. Allen said. "But after thirteen years at this school, I am inclined to offer redemption rather than punishment. Do you like opportunities, Mr. Hamel?"

"Yes ma'am. Uh…What kind of opportunity?"

"What—during your waking hours—has interested you most in this class?" Her biting sarcasm was not lost on Wayne. Somewhere along the line she'd dumped the sheaf of papers on her desk and approached with her ever-present walking stick. It made him nervous. She seemed to sense his discomfort and leaned the stick against the podium.

Wayne quickly called into focus a few things that he had heard in class before production got into full swing. The past two weeks he'd spent every night until early morning on stage.

"The uh… myth… mythology parts. It's uh… a different perspective than we get in literature. I uh… think the part about, uh…"

"Don't overtax yourself," Dr. Allen broke in. "You've proven that you heard something. Have you read much mythology?"

"A bit," he answered. "They had mythology comics when I was in junior high. It was my favorite reading."

"Comic books?" She actually laughed. She wasn't bad looking when she smiled. "To what is the world coming? You learned more from comic books than from this class?"

"No ma'am," he said. "It just got me started. Mythology plays a very important part in all literature. Take the show—er… *Hamlet*—that opens tonight. In one scene Hamlet confronts his mother because she has married her husband's brother," he rattled on, caught up in his narrative. "He pulls out the locket that he wears with a picture of his father and the locket that she wears with a picture of his uncle. Then he compares them, 'Hyperion to a satyr,' he says. Without studying mythology, who would know that he was referring to his father as the great and glorious sun-god and to his uncle as a goat-legged drunk?"

"Very insightful, Mr. Hamel. There is hope. Now about your opportunity."

"Usually when my dad says he has an opportunity for me it means more chores to do."

"Your father is wise. You have the opportunity to pass this course."

"Thank you, Dr. Allen. What do I need to do?"

"Two things. I am not going to ask you to stay awake during my classes, only that you not sleep in them. That's right. Stay in bed. I don't want you in class if you can't listen to what is being said. As it seems your schedule makes an early morning lecture impractical, I am changing you to independent study, though you may attend class whenever you can stay awake."

"Yes ma'am!" This was too good to be true.

"Don't be too relieved," she continued. "There are two things."

"What else?"

"This class normally requires a fifteen-page term paper at the end of the semester. Your ending term paper—write this down—will be to trace a mythological image, since that interests you most, through a phase of literature—one of your majors. Take the image you just described of Hyperion and a satyr, for example. You might analyze Shakespeare's perspective as reflective of the Elizabethan era and compare and contrast his view and expression of the myths with the anthropological perspective. Are you taking this down? The paper should include both the analysis of the era which you choose and the cultural origin of the myths. Is that clear?"

"Yes ma'am." Wayne scribbled the notes rapidly. "In fifteen pages?"

"No. It would be unfair of me to limit you to fifteen pages for a paper of this scope. To do the subject justice, your paper would be no less than, say, fifty pages, but you are not limited to that, either."

"Fifty pages?" he breathed trying to think if he even had a notebook that big.

"Typed. Double-spaced. One-inch margins. Not including the bibliography and end notes. A wonderful opportunity, right?"

"Right," he sighed. Dr. Allen stood to leave. "You'd love my dad," he said.

"Mr. Hamel," she said, "do you have any friends and neighbors back home you'd like to hear from?"

"Well…" he began then let his mouth hang open as he gathered in her reference. "No, ma'am."

"Believe me; I don't want you to hear from them either. This is…"

"…a wonderful opportunity, Dr. Allen," he finished for her. She smiled at him and then turned to leave.

Not only was this a rotten way to start his morning, but when Wayne glanced up at the clock he realized he was late. And late was much worse than asleep. Dr. Allen might have had a great opportunity for him, but it couldn't compare to the one he was missing right now. With a howl of distress, he grabbed up his books and ran out of the classroom, out of the Lily Science Hall, and across the parking lot with Dr. Rebecca Allen watching in amazement.

WAYNE RAN FULL tilt through the empty lower hall of the Academic Building, which also housed the theatre. Sitting quietly on a box outside the scene shop was Judith Harmon, perhaps the most exquisite woman Wayne had ever laid eyes on. She was going to give him fencing lessons and she had waited!

It was not often that Wayne attracted the attention of a woman. Certainly, he had his share of girlfriends, but Judith was electric. Her short blonde hair framed a lightly freckled face with slightly upturned nose. Very British. She exuded energy and sparkle that was way more than her diminutive frame. Someone had packed a bigger than life woman in the body of a pixie. Of course, there was nothing *serious* between them. Not yet. But she had waited for him, even though he was very late.

"I'm sorry I'm late," he began sputtering before he had come to a stop. "You wouldn't believe what a rotten morning I've had. I'm really sorry I'm late and I'm glad you waited."

"Hi," she said. "Are you all right?"

"You're the second person who has asked me that this morning. I guess I'm better than I deserve. I just got out of my 7:30 class."

"Your professor must have been long-winded," she responded. "It's after nine."

"No, I mean…yes. She sort of kept me after class," he said. "But I got out of it. Not that I'm sure I'm better off than if I was in it. But I'm out of it and I don't have to go back, but I can if I want to and I probably will just to show that I'm not taking unfair advantage of her or anything. I just have to stay awake when I go back."

"You Americans are very confusing sometimes," she said.

"Yeah, I know what you mean," he said. "I'm just glad you waited. How are you today?"

"A little peckish. I'm afraid I skipped breakfast to meet you," she said smiling.

"Oh geez! I'm sorry. Look. We don't have to do the fencing lesson," he kept apologizing. He was always apologizing to someone. "I owe you—just for waiting. Let me buy you breakfast."

"You don't have to do that, Wayne," she smiled. "But I'll join you if you're interested."

"I'm interested," he said, regretting that he had sounded *so* interested. "I know a little doughnut shop, unless you like bacon and eggs and stuff."

"Continental breakfast would be fine."

"What's that?"

"Just tea and rolls."

"Great! That's just what a doughnut shop is," he bubbled. "At least, I think they serve tea. I always drink coffee. If not, I'll buy a teabag and make you a cup." They left their books in the scene shop and Wayne picked up motorcycle helmets from the workbench. "You don't mind a motorcycle, do you?" he asked.

"Sounds like fun!" she answered.

As they rode to Donut World, Wayne luxuriated in the feel of her arms around his waist. Life was just too much!

JUDITH LIKED WAYNE. In fact, as a new student at the college she found him one of the few people who were approachable. She'd had to scramble when she enrolled late this fall. It was all she could do to get a study visa and get to America before it was too late to enroll at all. Then she had to catch up.

She would never have become involved in the theatre this term if it had not been for Wayne. He approached her after hearing her voice in the one class they shared. She was English, right? Would she help with accents in their production of *Hamlet*? When the director found out that she was also a fencing master, she was sucked into the fathomless commitment of the Theatre Department.

Well, she was more at home on stage than faking her way through her academic classes. Even her professors were a little curious about why an English girl would come to Indiana to study English poets. She just couldn't risk getting into courses she hadn't already studied. She had to be just another ordinary student, even though foreign.

Over doughnuts, Wayne explained what had happened to him in his early class. Judith laughed with him over his apparent good fortune; but when Wayne mentioned his professor's name, she became much more interested in his project.

"Dr. Allen?"

"Yes," Wayne said. "Do you have any classes with her?"

"No. I've heard she's very tough, though," Judith probed.

"Hard as nails," Wayne said. "I have to say, she's more than fair, though. She could have just flunked me on the spot."

Judith calculated the possibilities in her mind and decided to push ahead. She'd come to America to protect Dr. Rebecca Allen. It suddenly seemed possible to get a message to her without risking exposure. She was not happy to use her new friend as an unwitting conduit, but if she helped him pass his class, then Wayne would be the beneficiary, she reasoned.

"Did you think about the possibility of combining the project with one for another class?" she asked. "Perhaps you could select a poet for the English Romantic Literature paper that used a mythological image."

"Great idea," he answered. "I couldn't hand in the same paper, but that doesn't mean I couldn't use the same research to write both. All I really need is a good angle on a poet. Got any tips?"

"Well, I'll think about it," she said. It wouldn't be good to give him too much at once. *Let him think he discovered The Vagabond Poet on his own.*

Wayne took her back to the scene shop to collect their books before they went to their 11:00 classes. He was stalling, fumbling with the key, clowning. She could tell that he was trying to say something else, but she was halfway out the door of the shop before he finally got it out.

"Oh, Judith," he said as she was leaving.

"Yes, Wayne," she answered pleasantly. Encouragingly, she hoped.

"It's opening night tonight."

"Wonderfully exciting, isn't it?"

"Yeah, but… We have a tradition here of having an opening night party after the show."

"Really? How delightful!"

"I was wondering if you were planning to go."

"Well, I hadn't thought about it."

"Actually, I was wondering if I could take you." He'd got it out and was blushing under his shaggy beard.

"Wayne, do you mean take me, as in 'give me a lift,' or take me as in 'on a date?' I'm still getting used to American idioms."

"Well… I mean… like… on a date, you know?"

"I was hoping that's what you meant," she smiled. "See you tonight then."

She knew he was watching her back as she left and hoped he understood she meant yes.

Tuesday, 22 October 1968

Scarce images of life, one here, one there,
Lay vast and edgeways; like a dismal cirque

Of Druid stones upon a forlorn moor,
When the chill rain begins at shut of eve,
In dull November, and their chancel vault,
The Heaven itself, is blinded throughout the night.

"Thank you, Judith," Coop said. "It's lovely to have the words of English romantic poets brought to life by a lovely British voice." Professor Cooper had begun each class this semester with Judith reading a short passage and the wistfulness of his voice indicated that he would gladly listen to her for the entire class if he didn't have others around. Wayne had become acutely aware of the professor's apparent fondness for Judith and over the past week had found himself a little jealous. He and Judith had only had one date, but it was really nice. He liked the way she hugged herself to him on the back of the motorcycle and was thinking of ways to get her to do it again—for longer.

"So why do we look at the one piece that Keats didn't finish?" Coop asked. "Surely, we could study a Keats masterpiece like 'Endymion' or his sonnet, 'Bright Star!' and learn more. Let's look at the words he used when abandoning 'Hyperion.' He said it had too many Miltonian inversions. What does that mean?"

Coop went on. Once he started rolling, he was so enthusiastic that the small class couldn't help but pay attention. For the most part. Wayne was still a little distracted and just enough of a romantic to imagine himself a consumptive poet like Keats, pining for the love he knew he could never have. After lines for *Hamlet* were down cold, he'd practiced memorizing poems from the class while he worked on the set. He loved the fierce defiance of Shelley's *Prometheus Unbound* declaring to Jupiter that "One only being shalt thou not subdue…" As Coop continued to describe inversion—"Ten paces huge He back recoil'd"—and doodled on his pad of paper. The words came to him and he jotted them down, scratched them out and wrote again.

Are you my Bright Star, myst'ry of my morn—
Love's light seen afar as new day is born?

"Well it isn't Keats but not a bad couplet," Coop said. *When did he start wandering around the room?* Wayne looked up at the professor in panic. Coop was smiling. "I withdraw the question."

"What question?"

"That's why I'm withdrawing it." The class laughed. "Now here's the difference, class. There are fifteen of you here—make that fourteen as I see Boomer didn't make it again today. How many of you have written

words of poetry? Be honest, now. I'm not going to ask you to read it."
Everyone raised a hand. "Good. You see if you don't write poetry when
you are a teen or in your twenties, you have no heart. Of course, if you
are still writing poetry when you reach my age, you have no brain."
They all laughed. "But that's the difference. Keats, Shelley, Wordsworth,
Blake—they didn't just *write* poetry. They studied it. They criticized the
works of Milton and Spenser and Shakespeare. They learned everything
they could and criticized their own works based on what they learned,
perfecting the craft and allowing themselves to reject their own works if
they didn't measure up to the standard."

"WERE YOU WRITING a poem?" Judith asked as they left class and headed
to lunch. They'd been walking a lot together this week.

"Just doodling with words, really," Wayne dissembled. "Nothing I'd
show anyone. I wrote it as a rhyming couplet but the fifth syllable of
each line rhymed, too. A quatrain in a different meter. I'm embarrassed
Coop saw it."

"Must not have been too racy, at least. I'm sure he would have made
fun of that. Maybe someday you'll write something I can read."

"We'll see."

"Any great inspirations for your big paper? It was an interesting
class this morning."

"Yeah. I was actually thinking of using the Shakespearean image
of Hyperion vs. the mythological version of the ancient Greeks, but I
didn't think I could develop fifty pages around four words from *Hamlet*."

"Keats certainly made more out of it. That fragment of only 880
lines makes it sound like Hyperion was the king of the Titans instead
of Saturn."

"Hey. Maybe if I used the Keats fragment for a good analysis, I
could turn that part of the paper in for Coop and use most of it for
Allen as well."

"Wow! What a great idea. Pay Tom and Tim with the same coin.
Personally, though, I'm sticking with *Prometheus Unbound* for my paper.
There was something about Shelley that just calls to me."

> *To suffer woes which Hope thinks infinite;*
> *To forgive wrongs darker than death or night;*
> *To defy Power, which seems omnipotent;*
> *To love, and bear; to hope till Hope creates*
> *From its own wreck the thing it contemplates;*

Neither to change, nor falter, nor repent;
This, like thy glory, Titan, is to be
Good, great and joyous, beautiful and free;
This is alone Life, Joy, Empire, and Victory.

"Your accent is getting quite good, you know?" Judith said when Wayne finished the quote.

"Why thank you, my lady," Wayne bowed. "I know it's rather late to be asking, but if you don't have a date for Brown County Day tomorrow, I'd love to take you. As in give you a ride on my bike and have a date."

"I love the idea of a date, but what is Brown County Day?"

Wednesday, 23 October 1968

WEDNESDAY DAWNED CRISP and clear, a beautiful day for a ride to the state park in Southern Indiana. "Ha!" Wayne thought. "Southern." For those who bothered with maps, it was obvious that the north and south were divided by U.S. Highway 40 through Indianapolis in the middle of the state. Now it was Interstate 70. But if you grew up in Northern Indiana, you knew that culturally the south lay just across U.S. Highway 30 running from Ft. Wayne to Chicago. It even bore the name "Lincoln Highway" along most of its length. Heck, the Grand Poobah of the KKK lived in some Indianapolis suburb. But the landscape was beautiful south of Indianapolis if you stayed off Interstate 65 and followed the state highway down to Nashville.

"Are you sure you guys don't want to ride with us?" Gail asked after we'd all met up at breakfast.

"On a day like today? This weather was made for a bike," Wayne laughed. No way was he sharing Judith with Glenn and Gail today. Let them figure their own relationship out.

"I'm not sure I want to be trapped in a car alone with Glenn," Gail laughed. "He farts," she whispered to Judith.

"Hark, the cannon roars," Wayne said in response.

"I'll take my chance on the back of the scooter," Judith said. "More ventilation."

"Well, if it starts to rain, you can ride back with us," Glenn said after punching Wayne in the arm. "He can ride the death-mobile on the wet pavement."

"No rain today, my friend. But let's meet in Nashville for a late lunch. How about two o'clock?"

"Great! See you guys there!" With that, Glenn and Gail piled into his Corvair and were off.

"They'll be there half an hour before us," Wayne said. "But you know what Nader says: 'Unsafe at any speed.' Would you believe Glenn volunteered to pick him up at the airport when he came here to speak last year?"

"And your motorbike is safer?" Judith asked, smiling.

"Just hang on tight," Wayne smiled back. She did.

IN THE PARK, the two walked around, greeting the few upper classmen friends they met and watching the freshmen vs. sophomores tug-of-war. Someplace between the contest and the barbecue, Judith's hand slipped into Wayne's. They took only a single hamburger from the grill and split it with some chips since they were meeting Glenn and Gail in Nashville.

"We didn't plan where to meet," Judith said as they shared the burger. Is there someplace special?

"Last time I was in Nashville, there was only one street and it had a burger joint at the east end. We'll just cruise down the main drag and watch for them. Most of the folks there will be students. We're talking Nashville, Indiana, not Nashville, Tennessee."

They held hands as they walked the trail from Hesitation Point to the fire tower and then climbed the tower to look out across the valley. When they were at the top, Wayne slipped his arm around Judith's waist and held her to him. He was intent on being polite and not pushing his luck, so was busy pointing out the sights to the East and missed her upturned face. He led the way down the ladder, looking up at her approaching derriere. By the time they got back to the parking lot, it was already past two.

Wayne gunned the motorcycle out of the lot and headed into Nashville. The little town was rapidly becoming an enclave of hippie-types from Indiana University who had begun to remake the area into a Christmas village. Several shops had opened along the main drag featuring crafts by IU students including Christmas ornaments, candles, leather goods, and art. It had grown since Wayne last saw it a year ago. They met Gail and Glenn at the burger shop and by four they were on the road again. Wayne savored the feeling of Judith cuddling up to his back and didn't push the speed limit heading back to campus.

Sunday, 27 October 1968, early morning

"WHAT HO, FAIR maiden?" Wayne said as he entered Donut World, his helmet tucked under his arm.

"Now aren't you a gallant gentleman," the doughnut lady drawled. "Did you tie your steed at our hitching post? You must want a strong cup of coffee and nourishment before you ride off into the sunset. Or, I guess at this hour it's into the sunrise."

"Lissa, you're a card," Wayne said. "Now that accent was pure Georgia, but Wednesday night you were Mexican. What's a guy to think if he can't get a handle on where you're from?"

"Just keep guessing, dahlin'. That's all I can say."

"Well, coffee and a couple doughnuts sounds like a good idea. I haven't decided whether I'm going to bed or not."

"What's up?" she asked as she put a hot cup of coffee and two of his favorite chocolate coated old fashioneds on the counter for him. Wayne dumped half a cup of cream in his coffee and started to eat.

"We closed the show tonight," he said. "You know, *Hamlet*, over at the college."

"I didn't get to see it. But that had to be hours ago. It's almost three o'clock in the morning, sugah."

"Well, we had to strike the set and get it off stage so the stupid music department can put risers in tomorrow for their fall concert. Sharing a stage sucks. But, I guess it's good experience for when I'm doing rep work. And I get paid for lighting their concerts. The theatre work is all volunteer. I don't think there are any musicians strong enough to lift anything heavier than a checkbook." He felt talkative tonight and realized he'd better slow down. But Lissa was a good listener. He'd found her here on his first midnight doughnut run in September.

"Still, the show had to end hours ago. How big was your set?"

"Well, it was pretty big, but there was a cast party after. I just got tired of the inane conversation and had to get out of there. And my girlfriend… well, I think she might be my girlfriend… wasn't available."

"Why not?"

"Oh. It's the first day of her period and apparently she gets really bad cramps. She went straight back to the dorm and her heating pad after the show."

"Happy First Day to you," Lissa sang.

"Shh. She'd kill me if she knew I said that." Wayne paused. "Actually, she probably could."

Ritual Reality

Wayne finished his doughnut, showing Lissa the copy of the review in the Indianapolis Star. "With Wayne Hamel, quite good as the Player King." It was his first review for a performance. It was past four when he pulled into the dormitory parking lot and locked up his bike. The dorm monitor scarcely looked at him as he went through the lobby and up to his room. *Hamlet* was over. Now it was time to sleep.

2
Midnight Caper

Thursday, 31 October 1968

JUDITH TUCKED her hair up under the short black wig until no blonde strands could be seen. She positioned the black broad-brimmed hat on her head and fastened the cape neatly around her black bodystocking, its red silk lining adding the only color accent to her costume. The cape also served to cover the black shoulder bag that was slung behind her. Finally, she fastened her rapier to the belt.

This was her third date with Wayne in two weeks—a kind of dating speed record in her experience. The first date had been the cast party on opening night. The second was Wednesday for 'Brown County Day,' when the entire school took a day off to go play in the woods at the state park near Bloomington. She'd ridden the sixty miles on the back of his motorcycle with her arms wrapped around him. They'd held hands all day as they walked through the park and on the return trip she'd made sure her hands were kept warm under his leather jacket. Of course, she didn't count the group outings after the show each night when they went to the Waffle House or the TeePee. Nor did she count meeting in the lobby of the dorm to study together or to walk to class in the morning. Perhaps it was odd to have a date on Thursday night, but tonight was Halloween and they were going to a theatre costume party.

She turned toward the door and then turned back. One more thing. She knotted the black mask over her eyes. She had designed it so that a corner could be pulled down to fairly cover her entire face. That would come later.

The knock at her dorm room door was perfectly timed. She opened it to Wayne, who stood gaping at what he saw. She was pleased with his response.

"You are gorgeous!" he exclaimed. "Zorro never looked so good."

"Who is Zorro?" she asked.

14

"The Spanish noble who put on a mask and cape and took on all the Mexican injustices in the California territory. Isn't that what your costume is?"

"No. It's the Highwayman, from the poem by Noyes," she answered.

"I thought the Highwayman was a dandy in scarlet and doeskin!" he said.

"Poetic license. He dresses in what makes him look good and so do I."

"No kidding! That is…" Wayne paused while he looked her over carefully. Very carefully. "That is really sexy."

"Now, let me guess you." She walked around him, giving him just as thorough a once-over. He was resplendent in a gold lamé tunic. He wore gold tights and sandals. He did look good in tights. He had an ivy wreath in his hair and carried a strange stringed instrument beneath his arm.

"You must be an angel with that harp," she said, pointing at it.

"Lyre."

"Am not."

"No, this is. A musical instrument of the ancient Greeks."

"Hah! Gave it away. Apollo," she guessed.

Yes, said the supreme shape,
Thou hast dream'd of me; and awaking up
Didst find a lyre all golden by thy side,
Whose strings touch'd by thy fingers, all the vast
Unwearied ear of the whole universe
Listen'd in pain and pleasure at the birth
Of such new tuneful wonder.

"From the Keats poem I'm doing for this paper. It's great, don't you think?"

"Fantastic. I should have known," she answered. "I think I'll still call you my angel." Actually, she *did* know. Wayne had taken her hint to analyze Keats's use of mythological imagery in his fragment "Hyperion" and thought the idea had come from Dr. Allen when he quoted a line from *Hamlet*. It was a good idea, she justified to herself. She was taking advantage of the situation, not really using him. He would do very well on his paper and never mention to anyone that she had suggested it.

And tonight, she would see to it that he could find the appropriate references. That made her edgy. Judith was more than she appeared to be and had learned her craft from some of Britain's finest teachers. They could never have anticipated how she intended to use it.

The party was all theatre people who had access in one way or another to resources of costumes and make-up. The result featured characters from plays that had been performed over the years at the college. There were also a good number of people who had set their imaginations loose to develop costumes that were out of this world.

It didn't take long before the party was swinging. There was plenty of food and lots of music. In passing a closed door, Judith could smell that there were things more exotic than beer available as well. To each his own. It didn't seem that she had to worry about Wayne. He never made a move toward the room, but was quite the attentive date. For her part, she made a show of getting fresh beers frequently. Each, however, she would take a careful sip from and conveniently lose.

As the evening wore on, the party mellowed out and the group sat around telling ghost stories. Judith tipped her head against Wayne's shoulder and looked up at him.

"I think I've had too much to drink," she said. "I'm feeling rather squiffy."

"Oh god!" he answered, suddenly alert to her needs and remembering how many beers he'd seen her open. "Is there anything I can do?"

"Oooo. I hate to ruin your night," she moaned.

"No, no. Don't worry about that," he said. "Here, lean against me. Okay?"

"Would you take me home?"

"Sure. Can you stand the ride?"

"I'll make it. But I think I'd better go."

"Okay."

"Sure you aren't mad at me?"

"Hell, no. This ghost story stuff always freaks me out anyway," Wayne confessed. "Much rather take you home. The fresh air will do us both good."

It was just after eleven when they reached the dorm. She leaned heavily on him as they walked in. The dorm monitor at the desk carefully turned his head away as they signed in. As long as they weren't disorderly, he wasn't going to turn them in as drunk, even though it was obvious.

Wayne walked Judith to the door of the women's wing and then paused. She tilted her head toward him, and for the first time their lips touched. Talk about electric. Judith almost forgot she was supposed to be sick.

She broke away from him suddenly and looked him straight in the eye.

"Can you hold that thought till later?" she said.

"Sure," he answered.

"Like tomorrow?" she asked.

"Okay."

"Good." She covered her mouth, turned and bolted through the door to the women's wing. Wayne started after her to help, but it was after hours and the dorm monitor was glaring at him now. He turned and went slowly to his own room.

JUDITH DIDN'T EVEN slow down at her room. She continued right on past and out the back doors. She had jimmied the alarm earlier and set the doors so she could get back in. With a quick check to see that it was still set, she hurried out into the cool night air.

Samhain—last spoke of the wheel of the year. She wished she could take even a short step between the worlds tonight, but it simply wasn't possible. Wayne had already started his research in the library. She wouldn't have another chance without being obvious. She wrapped her cape around her and hurried on, keeping to the shadows—just another kid in a Halloween costume.

She had spent Thursday, Friday, and Saturday nights during performances of *Hamlet* prowling the Academic Building, timing security guards, and locating the most vulnerable entry and exit routes. When she reached the building, she pulled down the mask to cover the rest of her face. Tonight, she was a shadow—part of a nether world that to most people did not exist.

No one bothered to check for vulnerabilities on the slightly elevated main level and Judith had discovered a casement window with a broken ratchet. Four feet beneath the window, she paused to center herself. There were lights on this side of the building illuminating the stainless steel letters on its side. Indianapolis City University—ICU. She cringed at the idea. Tonight, she wanted to be seen by no one.

Eventually satisfied that no one could see her, she jumped. Her hands found the window ledge and she hoisted herself up, hooking a small jimmy beneath the casement window and swinging it open. She dove through the opening into the library, pulling the window closed behind her. She stood there catching her breath and reached to straighten her mask and hat. It was gone. Looking out the window, she saw the hat she had forgotten to secure lying in the bushes.

"Blast it!" she whispered. Well, she'd just have to pick it up on the way out. She shut the window and turned toward the interior of the library. She'd done her share of library research in the past week and didn't need to use her flashlight until she reached the card catalogue. Interpreting the Dewey Decimal system and cross-referencing her entry had been the most difficult part of her task. She had taken blank cards from the back of a drawer, carefully dipped them in tea to turn them brown and old-looking, and had typed the information on one of the free manual typewriters in the library. The electrics cost ten cents for ten minutes. Now she quickly placed the entries in the main card catalogue.

That was the easy part. The real task was about to begin. The Rare Books and Manuscripts Collection was on the third floor behind locked doors with a new electronic alarm system. She had been at the library the moment it opened three days in a row. Luckily, she had a good ear for tones and was certain that she had the disarming sequence down pat. If not, her caper—and her study visa—would end quickly.

The key she stole earlier in the week made getting into the room easy, but when she opened the door she saw the red flashing light to her left. Forty-five seconds to touch the right keys in the right order. One error or one second late and the alarms would go off. The panel was shaped like the keys of a touchtone telephone. The tones were the same. She had practiced the four-note sequence over and over on the payphone in the dorm lobby. Now her hand was shaking as she pressed the keys. The red light went out, the green came on. She was clear.

Her plan was simple. Rebecca Allen had been given a task that endangered her life and anyone else's she involved in it. It had been Judith's fault. If she had not challenged Rebecca's nomination as high priestess of Coven Carles, the door would not have been opened for the power-hungry high priest to twist it into this impossible task. Judith had inadvertently led Rebecca into the middle of a power struggle, and after that night four months ago, she would never listen to Judith again. She might, however, be persuaded to heed a different voice. Judith went down the rows of file boxes on the shelves until she found what she was looking for: Benjamin Wilton.

Rebecca's husband had catalogued all the personal papers of Benjamin Wilton fifteen years ago and Rebecca had been obsessed with Wilton's esoteric writings since her husband disappeared shortly afterward. The story of The Vagabond Poet was a little-known treasure of Coven Carles. Judith had copied it once in her own *Book of Shadows*. Carefully worded and with her handwriting as disguised as she could make it, she had recopied it on old scraps of paper, treated much like the catalogue cards had been. She coded them to match the library's catalogue system and dropped them in place behind Wilton's other writings.

Judith was closing the file drawer when she heard a key click in the door. She flicked out her torch just in time to see the red alarm light flash as the door opened. The newcomer was more adept at the security code than Judith. The tones sounded without so much as a flashlight directed at the keypad. The light turned green.

Judith was flattened against the file cabinets at the end of the room, scarcely breathing. There were no windows up here, so she could only hear the steps of the intruder. They moved to the side of the room opposite Judith and she heard another key in a lock. She edged her way around the center row of files to see a figure suddenly silhouetted in the moonlight streaming through a high-placed door to the roof.

The robed figure that Judith saw stopped her heart. Rebecca Allen stepped through the opening and disappeared, not letting the roof door quite close behind her.

Judith allowed herself only enough time to swallow her heart and then moved back to the entry door. She opened it and saw the red flashing light appear. Her hands were shaking as she reached for the keypad. Her finger slipped on the first key she touched. The red light held steady for a second just before the piercing scream of the alarm system filled the room.

Judith glanced behind her to see the roof door open as she bolted down the stairs from the room. Brilliant, she thought. Just what she needed. Caught between The Hart on the roof and security guards already at the front doors of the library.

She ran to the window she came in by, but could see a patrol car parking across the street. She slid down the stair rail to the basement and dove into one of the soundproof typing rooms. Lights came on all over the library. *Well, Hart, I don't suppose everyone knows you're up there either, but that is your problem. Mine is getting out of here.*

Judith climbed onto the desk in the private room and peered into the darkness of an air vent above her. She worked the grate loose and slid it inside, then, using the coin-operated Selectric on the desk as a stepping stone, she hoisted herself up into the darkness. It was a good thing she was small. The air duct gave her just room to edge into and smelt of dust. She wiggled her way down the pipe, nearly choking on her cape until she pulled it loose. She wrapped it around her sword to muffle its clatter against the duct. At least she should be safe here until the search died down, but she'd better start working on a way out. She pushed the grate back into place with her foot and began crawling.

After what seemed like hours in the air duct, she came to a vent that looked out into a darkened room. She was out of the library. She stuck her dusty head through the opening, flashed her light around what proved to be the theatre's prop shop. This was where Wayne spent so much of his time as props master and student technical director. Judith slid head first through the opening, scraping her hand on the shaft as she did. It hurt. She could feel the warm pulse of blood from the scrape. She quickly wrapped it in her loose cape as she headed for the door.

At least the doors to the outside of the building weren't alarmed. The school's minimal budget directed that alarm systems be placed only on their most valuable areas: the rare books room, the vault, the women's dorm, and the cafeteria. Judith took the first available exit and raced for the shadows. She zigzagged her way from bush to tree until the Academic Building was out of sight before running like blazes for the back door of the dormitory.

FROM THE ROOFTOP, Dr. Rebecca Allen, The Hart, watched the unknown figure disappear into the darkness.

It made no difference, really. Her rituals were never what they once were. There was no real power. It was just a beautiful ritual that soothed her. She'd lost so much of the beautiful music of her art, so short-lived that she sometimes had trouble remembering what it was like. Had she really called fire?

She let the door to the stacks close before the police arrived. She had an alternate way off the roof through the theatre fly space. But she didn't need to go yet. No one would come to the roof. She went back to where the pentagram was sketched out on the roof of the academic building—where for fourteen years she had performed rituals eight times a year if she was in town.

"Powers of air, the East, the rising sun, attend me this night. Protect and guard me and take sweet perfume from my gift to you." She knelt, facing east and lit a small incense burner. She paused to inhale the smoke and felt the first wave of peace wash over her. She moved on to the South. "Powers of fire, the South, the burning embers of my soul, attend me tonight. Protect and guard me and take this tiny flame to be your home." She lit a candle, then rose to move again. "Powers of water, the West, the vast oceans, attend me tonight. Protect and guard me and quench your thirst from my cup." Moving to the North she made her final salutation. "Powers of earth, the North, the rock beneath my feet, attend me tonight. Protect and guard me and take this offering of salt to flavor your feast." Rebecca sprinkled salt around the saucer she laid at her northern gate. She turned the full circle again, depositing her *Athamé* at the East, her wand in the South, her cup in the West, and her pentacles in the North. Then she spun. She let her robe fall to her feet, and naked under the Samhain stars she spun in place until dizziness overcame her and she collapsed on top of her robe.

She could feel a shimmer of power around her, subtly glowing on the darkened rooftop. She giggled a little. She still had power. At least a little. She hoped the glow wasn't visible from across campus. The glow dampened, but she could still feel the power.

"World of flesh and world of spirit," she whispered, "part and let me walk between. Bring to me that which my heart desires." If she could summon the sacred tools of the coven in a small ritual, her task would be complete. It would be a relief and she could take the position of high priestess of Coven Carles. She'd been so isolated and alone; she couldn't imagine why the coven wanted to elevate her when she was nearly four thousand miles away. Perhaps it was time to move to England. But then Serepte… Her daughter would be taken away from her friends and the only home she'd known. At thirteen, that didn't seem right.

Rebecca drifted in the midst of her circle, waiting. Perhaps she slept, but she noted that new incense had been lit to keep the Eastern Gate active. When had she done that? And why was she not cold? It was the end of October and even though Indianapolis hadn't become really cold yet, there was the likelihood of frost before dawn. As Rebecca pulled back into herself, she realized there was a difference in air. It was somehow pure. Her eyes focused over the Eastern Gate and she saw a figure approach.

At first it looked like two people, but as they drew nearer, they merged and Rebecca's heart sped up. Her summoning had not been for the tools of Carles, but rather for her heart's desire.

"Wesley? Is it you?" The figure sat opposite the incense from her and smiled, somewhat wistfully. As they sat looking at each other, he gained more substance and finally found a voice.

"My darling Rebecca," came the whisper through the night air.

"Oh, Wesley. Does this mean you are dead and speaking to me through the veil of the worlds?" He looked around, puzzled.

"I don't think so. I don't feel dead. Just trapped. Or transported. I just don't know how to get back. I'm so sorry I abandoned you, my darling."

"But you are back. You are here." She reached out for him as he reached toward her but their hands passed through each other. She could feel the tingling up her arm as his insubstantial form caressed her.

"I think I cannot fully pass through. So sad, though, to see you here, naked in front of me and not be able to touch those beautiful breasts." Her nipples hardened as she felt the tingling pass across her body. It had been so long. Her body was responding even to the insubstantial presence of her husband. And it was apparent that he responded as well.

"I can't stand not having you," she said. "How long will we have to be apart?"

"Apart? There really is no apart, darling. We are here now. We will always be here now."

"I feel so alone, but I try, Wesley. I try to be a good mother. Our daughter is so beautiful. You would be so proud of her."

"I *am* proud of her. Don't worry love. We talk. She knows I am here. She is the key."

"They've set me the task of gathering the tools of the coven," Rebecca said. She didn't know why, but she assumed that Wesley would know what she was talking about, even though her membership in the coven occurred so quickly after her marriage that they'd had little time to talk about it. There was too much going on in Greece. "The *Athamé* was lost at the same time you were."

"Yes. I think this is important. You can't achieve your goal without a partner. I can't be there and would be a poor choice for what you have to do. Choose wisely and do not be afraid to take him to you. I don't know why I know this, but he is important to all of us."

Wesley's shape wavered. Beyond him, Rebecca could see the lightening eastern sky. Rebecca looked down and saw the smoke from the incense dying.

"No! Don't go." She scrambled to get another stick lit from the ember of the dying fragment. Wesley's shape was almost gone.

"We are always here now," he whispered. "Always. Here. Now."

The sun crested the horizon and Rebecca had only the voice in her head. She quietly moved contretemps around her circle, gathering her sacred tools, whispering her thanks to the spirits of the earth, water, fire, and air, releasing them back to their elements.

She was suddenly chilled. She pulled on her robe, gathered the evidence of her circle into her bag, and moved to the fly space of the theatre where she could ease herself through the fire window and down into reality once again.

3

Revelation

Friday, 1 November 1968

WAYNE REMEMBERED the kiss. But to his credit, he didn't dwell on it when he saw Judith Friday morning, much as he wanted to simply crush her to him and passionately devour her. She came down at her usual time, though, and the two walked together to the cafeteria.

"Are you feeling better?" Wayne asked.

"Do you mean am I hung over?" Judith laughed. "Not too bad. Some American coffee should help. I'm not ready for steak and eggs."

"I'm glad to hear that. I suppose we shouldn't make a habit of going out to party on a school night."

"I'm so sorry I spoiled our date. I haven't done that in ages—not since my wild days in London."

"I'm a sheltered Hoosier boy. These *are* my wild days in London. Um… Indianapolis. You'll have to tell me about yours someday so I'll know what I'm missing."

"Still, I'm sorry. Let me make it up to you. Please?"

"Not that it's necessary, but what were you thinking of?" Wayne was thinking of the kiss. He could only hope she was, too.

"Katherine Hepburn."

"You want to give me the incredible Kate as a make-up present? I guess I can't really turn that down," he laughed.

"*The Lion in Winter* just opened. I know it's not usual for girls to ask boys out here, but if you are free tomorrow evening, I thought we might have a date that's my treat. You can still provide the transportation, though. I rather like sitting on your bike." Something about the way she said that sent shivers up Wayne's spine.

"That really sounds wonderful."

Saturday, 2 November 1968

WONDERFUL ONLY BEGAN to cover it. From the moment Judith opened the door for Wayne, they held hands. She greeted him with a soft kiss on the cheek and they went to the motorcycle. It was too bad he didn't have a car as he was sure if he did that she'd have worn a skirt instead of the brown wool slacks. The light blue angora sweater under her jacket, though, was a delight to touch as she kept hold of his hand placed carefully around her shoulders in the theater. Their seats in the balcony caused a little distortion in the Panavision image seen from slightly above. Wayne had a hard enough time focusing on the film, though, with Judith cuddled against him.

After the movie, they walked around Monument Circle at the heart of Indianapolis and even ventured north along the grassy plaza. Rather than simply holding hands, Judith pulled his arm around her waist and held his hand firmly against her side, just touching her stomach above her hipbone. For Wayne it was like walking through a dream. When they reached the steps of the World War Memorial, she turned in his arms and as naturally as long-time lovers pressed her lips against his. He bent his head to meet her and their kiss intensified. When it finally broke, they were both panting. Wayne's arms were wrapped all the way around her small frame and his fingertips were pressed lightly against the sides of her breasts. What a glorious feeling. She pushed away from him.

"We'd better go back now," she whispered.

"I'd rather stay with you," he answered.

"Yes, well every family has their ups and downs," she quoted. For Wayne, it was definitely up at the moment. They held hands as they walked back to the motorcycle and she gripped him tightly as they rode back to campus. She didn't give him a chance to catch her in another clinch in the parking lot, but led him immediately up the steps to the dorm lobby. At the door to the women's wing, where they were in full view of the monitor, she met his lips again.

"Judith," he said as they caught their breath. "Do you have plans for the holiday?"

"Holiday?"

"Thanksgiving. We have Wednesday through Sunday off and I was thinking that if you'd like, you could come home with me and… uh… meet my parents and stuff." *Especially stuff.*

"Oh, that holiday. I forgot. Actually, I already accepted Gail's invitation to her home. I wish I'd known this first."

"Well. That's okay. I mean. Maybe it's a little too early to meet the parents."

"Maybe so. Let's just take it slow. But you could kiss me again."

Wednesday, 27 November 1968, early morning

"Just stopped to wish you a Happy Thanksgiving, Lissa," Wayne said as he entered Donut World. It was nearly one in the morning on Wednesday. Wayne and Judith had been out with friends for a drink and then parted at the dorm. He simply didn't feel like sleeping yet, even though he faced a 140-mile bike ride in the morning.

"Vy tank you, dahlink. You are so… how you say?… thoughtful."

"Are you Russian tonight?"

"You are American ven you come in for coffee; Russian ven you leave. And ven you get home? European." Wayne howled.

"You are so funny, Lissa. I guess I'll have that coffee. And a doughnut. It will be my last one for a while. I'm headed up north in the morning."

"Taking your little girlfriend with you?"

"She had other plans. I'm still not sure she's my girlfriend. I want her to be. I'm not dating anyone else and I don't see how she could be, but the idea of going steady is foreign to her."

"So, you haven't gone all the way?"

"Just barely touched second base. I'm trying not to rush, but damn she makes me hot. I tell you Lissa, even without petting, I could sit and kiss her all night long."

"You need to think ahead."

"What do you mean?"

"When do you get back from your break?"

"Oh. Monday."

"And how long before your holiday? I mean Christmas vacation."

"Just two weeks. We've got the Holiday Musicale the first week and finals the second week. Having Thanksgiving so late in the month this year really plays havoc with the schedule."

"So, from right now you have two weeks to pick the perfect Christmas present, make arrangements for a special date, and charm the pants off her. You shouldn't have too much trouble with that. No?"

"Yes. Oh man! I completely forgot how soon Christmas was and that I need to give her a present before she goes home. What am I going to do?"

"Something she loves and something that is a part of you—so inseparable that she can't abandon your gift and she can't face it without thinking of you."

"What?"

"How vould I know? You haf never brought her to meet me. Are you ashamed of your leetle Russian doll?"

"No! I'll bring her in as soon as I can." He looked around and grabbed a napkin. His pen started sketching. Of course. There was only one thing that Judith loved enough to never give up. "I have to run, Lissa. Thanks for the coffee." He laid three dollars on the counter—easily twice what his late-night snack cost—and headed for the door.

"You see?" Lissa called after him. "Now you're a-rushin'."

"Dad, do you mind if I use your shop for a while this weekend?" Wayne had only been home two hours. They'd just had lunch and his butt was still tingling from the two-and-a-half-hour ride from Indianapolis. Still, he wanted to get right to work on his project.

"Sure. Anything special you need?"

"Do you have any black walnut out there?"

"Black walnut? I'll come with you." His dad followed him to the workshop. For half of Wayne's life, his father had been a cabinetmaker. He'd seen the demise of Studebaker looming on the horizon and knew he needed a skill. From 1959-1961, he'd commuted to Nappanee to study woodworking with an Amish cabinetmaker. Before Studebaker closed up shop in 1963, Dad had left and was established in his wood-working shop. They passed the '56 Golden Hawk under its canvas cover on the way to the shop.

"Is it still running?" Wayne asked.

"I've got the engine torn down. Needed the valves ground. Have it ready to drive this summer."

He unlocked the woodshop and they went in. The shop always made Wayne smile. It smelled like fresh wood and tung oil.

"Now what's your project?" Wayne pulled out the sketches he'd made the night before after talking with Lissa. It was perfect. "You love making boxes. Who is this one for?"

"My… uh… girlfriend."

"It's a little big for a jewelry box."

"Yeah. You know what I worked on all last summer? I need to put a matching handle on it."

Wayne and his dad worked side-by-side in the shop all afternoon. He'd taught Wayne everything he knew about woodworking and was happy to show him some new techniques as well. Wayne planned to use a mortise and tenon corner joint, but his dad had a new machine that would cut a blind secret mitered dovetail. When the pieces slid together, you couldn't see the corner joint at all. Wayne cut the sides out of two matched four-foot black walnut boards. The reversed grain looked like the sides of the box grew together. When the lid hinged closed, it made it look like a solid block. His dad's tips and an occasional extra pair of hands helped move the project along. But Joe, Wayne's dad, was careful to let him manage his own project. He never tried to do something for him. Wayne loved working with him.

Once the box was assembled and drying, Wayne put a six-inch-long block of the dark wood on the lathe and his dad helped him align the pattern jig.

"Dad? How do I know if she's the right girl?"

"Mmm. Well. Didn't we talk about this once? Let me see."

"Don't strain yourself. How'd you know Mom was the right woman for you?"

"Well, I still don't know for sure. Seems okay today, but Monday I was sure I'd made a mistake marrying her." Wayne laughed. They'd been married twenty-five years last August. Popped Wayne's sister out nine months later. He couldn't figure out why it had taken four years to get the second kid on the ground. "I guess, it's a lot like your box there," he finally said. Wayne looked over at it. "All the parts have to fit together perfectly. Of course, you get a lot of marriages where the lid is warped a little or where there's a gap in a joint or two. Most of them still hold together. Some of them are just so sloppily made, though, that there's no chance for them to last. And some look well-made, but are used so roughly that they finally fall apart."

"So, I want to find a woman whose parts all match mine and then keep them well-oiled?"

"Don't tell your mother I said anything like that!"

Friday, 13 December 1968

ALL WAYNE DID the next week was type his paper, work in the props shop, and run lights for the Holiday Musicale. Then it was finals week and he still had to type the bibliography and end-notes. He must have dumped about thirty dollars into those coin-operated typewriters in the library. Ten cents for ten minutes, then deposit another dime. But he got it done and handed to Dr. Allen on Wednesday. He was reasonably sure she'd be pleased. He'd even made it to about half her classes.

He was surprised to find a message waiting at the dorm monitor's desk on Friday morning requesting his presence in Dr. Allen's office at ten o'clock.

"WHILE THERE IS no concrete proof that Keats was the Vagabond Poet referred to in early 19th century mystical writings, Wilton's conjecture explains in part Keats's fascination with the Titans and his glorification of them. If what Wilton says is true, Keats participated in a pagan ritual in which four of the Titans were said to have appeared—Iäpetus drawing so much strength from the poet that Keats was sickly until his early death just two years later."

Dr. Allen looked up from reading the paper aloud and stared at the student standing in front of her. She could feel the heat in her cheeks as her anger swept over her again. Control. He looked so smug—so pleased with himself.

"Who do you think you are?" she growled. "Did you honestly think you could pass off this rubbish as legitimate research?" Wayne's mouth sagged open as her words sank in.

"What? It's all there, just like I said," he stammered. "Wilton said…"

"Wilton said no such thing, nor is there any such paper in his files," Dr. Allen blazed.

"I have copies of them," Wayne said. "Right here." He produced a notebook from his pack and flipped over several pages then turned it around to face her. "Here. In Wilton's own handwriting."

"That is not Wilton's handwriting," Dr. Allen responded immediately. "Nor is this in the catalog of Wilton's papers," she continued producing a handwritten file from her own desk. Wayne looked at the writing on his papers and on the ones in Dr. Allen's hands. They were undeniably different.

"Is this Wilton's handwriting?" he asked pointing at the folder.

"No. This is my husband's handwriting," she answered. "He cataloged all Wilton's writings in 1954. I have read all of them in this library and all his pseudonymous writings in the Edinburgh University Library as well. This is not Wilton's writing. Now where did you get it?"

"I swear, Dr. Allen," he said plaintively. "It was listed in the card catalog in the library and I got it out of his file in rare books. The librarian handed it to me herself and made the copies for me while I was there." The professor was softening as things began to come into focus.

"Rare books," she muttered. "Mr. Hamel, we have been had. If the paper is indeed in rare books, I will fulfill my end of the bargain and pass you for the course. However, as a teacher, it is my responsibility to instruct you. Your paper is based on a cleverly conceived fraud. It has no scholarly value. Unless you found reputable primary sources, like an eyewitness account or Keats's diary, to back up your quotes, the entire academic value of the paper is zero. And I assure you that you will not find primary sources to back up your research. If any of what you quoted regarding the pagan rites that Keats supposedly participated in were true, it would be buried in secrecy and heavily protected against just such academic research."

"Shi... uh... da... uh... darn it!" he swore.

"I understand your feelings," she smiled. "They are very similar to my own. I must know who advised you in your research, subject selection, everything that led you to precisely this study. In the world of academic fraud, this could be very important."

"How?"

"'There are stranger things in heaven and earth than your philosophy has imagined, Horatio.'"

"*Hamlet*, act two, scene three," Wayne responded automatically.

"Very good," she answered. "Now who else knew about your research?"

"Well, gee. Everyone knows what I was doing the paper on. All my friends. And Mr. Cooper. I got clearance from him to use the same research for my Romantic Poets course. When you gave me this opportunity, I quoted the line from *Hamlet* about Hyperion and a satyr. I thought it was cool when that same week we read Keats's 'Hyperion' in class. Miss Wilson in the library told me how to go about researching it. That's it."

"Miss Wilson is definitely out. Cooper? No, I don't think so. Did you use any of the Wilton material in your paper for his class?"

"Just in the bibliography. He was interested in poetic structure and interpretation, not anthropology or social studies. He gave me an A for it."

"I'm sure you deserved it. You'll make a fine teacher someday, if you stay awake."

"Thank you, but I want to stick to theatre if I can. You know what they say: Those who can, do; those who can't, teach." Dr. Allen looked at him and raised one eyebrow. "I mean… no offense, Dr. Allen. Anthropology is different than theatre. I mean there isn't really anything to *do* in anthropology except teach. You know?"

"I know, Mr. Hamel. That will be all," she said.

"I passed?"

"You passed. I would like to keep these copies from Wilton's file, however."

"I sure don't need them anymore," he answered. He left. Rebecca assumed he'd never again take a 7:30 a.m. class.

She quickly read through the papers Wayne swore came from Wilton's files. To her eye, even from the photocopy, it was obviously a fraud. Disguised handwriting, she assumed. It bore some similarities to Wilton's handwriting. Fortunately, Wayne had limited his references to the evidence that Keats had developed his poem based on experiences in pagan rituals. He had not gone so far as to tell the entire story of the Vagabond Poet, one with which Rebecca Allen was casually familiar. It was part of the secret writings of her circle of friends. It told of a wandering vagabond, sucked into the circle during the creation of a new tool, the staff—Iäpetus, the Second Face of Carles. It never mentioned the poet's name, though.

The story was retold in such a way as to make it plausible to be in Wilton's writings, especially if one understood the old man's connection to the coven as a vagabond priest himself. But what caught Rebecca's attention and held it was the final sentence the forger had written in Wilton's supposed hand. "The Hart will see and understand."

Someone knew the paper would find its way to her. A warning to her. The last time a new tool was forged for the coven, both the vagabond priest and the high priestess had died.

She thought back to the night when alarms had gone off in the library as she prepared her Samhain ritual on the roof—the shadowy figure running from the building. Rebecca opened the door of her credenza and pulled out the black hat that she had found when searching for signs around the building. So, this was the work of a Child of Coven Carles. But who? And why?

Saturday, 14 December 1968

Judith sat in front of the mirror in her dormitory room. Her bags were already packed for the return trip to England. Everything she owned.

Her flight was tomorrow morning. She sat staring at herself, not wanting to finish, not wanting to leave.

Technically she had completed everything that she intended to do when she came to America. With Wayne's paper submitted to Rebecca Allen, there was no doubt that she would check the reference in the Wilton file. She would have to understand how dangerous it was to create a new tool for the circle, and that she was being used in a power play.

Judith could leave now—go back to England and wait for Rebecca to quit or to go ahead and make the new *Athamé*, with the power-hungry high priest right there to snatch it from her hand when it was complete. Judith was finished—if it weren't for this one other little problem in her life—Wayne.

It had begun as a simple flirtation and had taken on new focus as a means for her to accomplish her goal of getting a message to The Hart. But it kept developing. She'd tried not to lead him on, but he was so nice. She had every reason to believe that he was in love with her, and her own feelings defied her resistance. She didn't *have* to go back to England, after all. There was no hurry. If she returned to classes in January, Wayne would be there. And that was something to consider. She really, really liked him. She was even picking up colonial idioms. Maybe he'd consider visiting her in England and they could sit in front of the fireplace, just…

A knock interrupted her fantasy. Well, we'll see, she thought. We'll just have to see.

"God, you're beautiful," he said when she opened the door. She lifted her face to receive the soft kiss that he offered. She had chosen a Victorian look tonight—not exactly her usual style. She wore a high collared white blouse that had taken her a quarter of an hour to button up the front. Her blue maxi-skirt had a dozen buttons as well—the last seven of which she had left undone, showing her left leg above the knee.

Wayne had raided the costume shop and came out with tails and a top hat. That he was wearing them with grey corduroys and tennis shoes didn't seem nearly as comical as it should have. She handed him her cape and he laid a gift-wrapped box on her bed before helping her put it on.

"Are those flowers for me?" she asked sweetly.

"Well, uh… you'll just have to wait and see," he said. "Our cab is waiting to take us to dinner."

The *maître d'* at the King Cole looked at his outfit curiously, but he was within their dress code and did have a reservation. With a sniff, he led the two to a private booth out of the line of sight. They sank side-by-side into the deep leather seats and slid to the back. The long red tablecloth was draped nearly to the floor in front so that when Wayne sat behind it he really did look fine. Aside from his shoulder-length hair and ragged beard, he appeared to be just like any other patron of the swank restaurant. Judith's sophisticated form beside him helped.

Even the wine steward did not blink when he ordered sparkling wine. He did cock an eyebrow when Wayne ordered Cold Duck, but quickly went to fill the order. When the wine arrived, Wayne slid the box toward Judith and raised his glass in a toast.

"Here's to you, with all my love." She smiled and touched her glass to his.

"May there be many more toasts between us," she said. They drank, and then Judith began unwrapping her present. "It's too heavy for flowers," she said. "At least for any species that I know." The paper came off a shiny walnut box, over three feet long and six inches across. She breathed a sigh of amazement as her hand slid across the glossy surface. At first it looked like a solid block of wood save for the tiny ridge of a brass hinge on one side and the golden clasp and lock on the other. "Oh Wayne, it's beautiful," she said. She turned to kiss him, but instead found him holding up his hand. Between his fingers was a small key.

"There's more," he said simply. She took the key and opened the lock on the box. When she saw the sword against the red velvet lining she was speechless. Her initials were emblazoned on the walnut hilt that matched the box. On the blade were engraved the closing words of Keats's sonnet 'Bright Star'.

Still, still to hear her tender-taken breath,
And so live ever—or else swoon to death.

There was little Judith loved more than medieval arms but this was more than she could have imagined. She turned to him in amazement, shaking her head to get the words to come out. This time he did not stop her offered kiss. The kiss might have continued much longer had the waiter not arrived, clearing his throat at the tableside. They broke apart, embarrassed.

"Are you really old enough to be ordering alcohol?" the waiter asked snidely as he set down their entrées. Judith lifted the short sword from its case and slowly swung its point toward the waiter.

"Would you like to try to take it away?" she asked. There was a cold hardness in her voice that frightened even Wayne. The waiter backed away at once.

"No, ma'am," he said. He pulled the curtains across the opening of their booth, leaving them isolated from the rest of the room.

"Now that's more like it," Judith said, replacing the sword in its case. "Wayne, this is too wonderful for words. How could you ever afford something like this?"

"I made it," he answered. "I hope you don't mind getting a home-made gift."

"Mind?" she exclaimed. "I can hardly believe it. I *can't* believe it. You *made* this?"

"It's what I do. Did you see the look on that waiter's face?" Wayne laughed. "You scared the pants off him—and me."

"Really?" she said, laying a hand on his leg as if to see. "Well, I doubt we'll see him again until we leave."

"Which is quite all right with me," he answered kissing her again. "I suppose we'd better eat this stuff while it's hot," he said at last.

They chatted through the meal and Wayne asked questions about the holidays in England. Judith asked him how he would celebrate as well. Wayne told her that he would visit a favorite uncle over the holiday, but that he would be thinking about her the entire time.

"It's funny. He's my mom's uncle, but I'm the only one going. He sent me a train ticket. I've only ever met him once, but we each send a letter once a month. I don't know if anything he says is true, but according to him, he was undercover all through World War II and through the '50s up until about ten years ago. Then he sent a ticket and asked me to spend the New Year's holiday with him in West Virginia. Just me. I think my mom's a little pissed about it."

"Sounds thrilling. If you've only met him once, why does he suddenly want to see you now?"

"I have no idea, but we've corresponded with each other for years."

They chatted further and after dessert had come and Wayne had paid the bill, Judith turned to face him.

"I have a gift for you, too," she said.

"Really?" he said. "Where?"

"I'm wearing it," she answered. Wayne thumped himself in the chest as if to restart his heart. She was wearing a blouse, skirt, and shoes. And hose. She was sure he could see that on the leg that was mostly uncovered by the open skirt. He reached for her hand, but she gently pushed his hand back.

"I'll unwrap it for you," she said softly as she unbuttoned the eighth button on her skirt, exposing her thigh up to the garter she wore. "Oh.

Wrong button. Sorry." Wayne watched open-mouthed as her fingers moved to unbutton the top button of her blouse and then the next. There were at least twenty buttons on the front of her blouse. Perhaps she'd just give him the shirt off her back. He'd die, right there at the table. That wouldn't be useful.

Judith hadn't planned this. In fact, she had no gift for Wayne when they came to the table, but her emotions, threatening to burst over her for weeks, were taking over. Holding the sword in her hand—feeling the craftsmanship and the power—had suddenly awakened her. The power. As important as her relationship with Wayne was, what she felt was even more important. She was the Swordmaster and Wayne had just become her charge.

The sixth button opened and then the seventh. She folded back the fabric, exposing her throat to him. Then she went ahead and unbuttoned the eighth and ninth buttons, showing her cleavage.

"Do you like it?" she asked. Wayne took a drink before he could answer.

"Like it?" he croaked.

"The necklace, you goose," she laughed.

"Oh!" he exclaimed. "My God!" They laughed. The necklace was a gold chain with a star-shaped pendant.

"Take it off me," she directed. He reached around her neck to find the clasp and placed a kiss on her lips as he undid it. She dragged his hands down her neck when the clasp came undone and pulled them across the exposed mounds of her breasts. Her eyes closed as she held his hands and then she took the necklace from him. She locked it around his neck. He held it up on the chain to look at the star. It was engraved on one side.

"What is this?" he asked.

"A rune. My name sign," she answered. "I wear it all the time. In fact, I haven't taken it off in thirteen years. Please wear it for me. Wayne, it is important that you know that no matter what happens or doesn't happen between us, this is yours and will be important to you. Not for my sake, but for yours, never take it off. Nonetheless, I think I love you." She moved in to kiss him and didn't move his hands when they cupped her breasts. "I think," she whispered, "this is what you call going steady."

Wayne wasn't breathing. She cupped his face in her hands while he continued to squeeze her breasts.

"Darling, there's more."

"More?"

"Focus on *me*, love, not just my breasts."

"I'm sorry. Oh, Judith…"

"Shh," she stopped him from pulling away, holding his hands to her breasts with both of hers. "I like it. But I need this hand." She pulled his left hand from her breast and placed it palm up on the table. "There is a ritual that goes with this gift. It will only hurt a little."

"Huh?"

She pulled the sword from its box and placed the point against the palm of his hand. He froze. His other hand quit squeezing her breast. She applied just enough pressure to draw blood.

"You… you…"

"Shh. You'll see." She placed the point of the sword against her own left palm and pressed until it drew blood. "Take my hand." They clasped the hands, blending the drop of blood each had in their palms. Judith raised the sword and placed the tip against the pendant she had just given Wayne. He held his breath. "Powers of the East, South, West, and North, seal this covenant," she intoned. "Your blood is my blood. My blood is yours. We may not always be lovers. We may not always be friends. But we will always be bound. May my words be sealed within your heart and arise when your training is complete and your questions have been answered. So mote it be."

WAYNE FELT A jolt go through his entire body. He could feel Judith's blood flowing in his veins. He could see a hundred, no, a thousand different possibilities as if he were dreaming of lives he had never lived. And it was all a dream. He shook his head and saw the sword lying in the box he had made for it. It was a symbol of his love for Judith. She held his left hand as he continued to caress her breast with his right and she leaned in for another exquisite, long, loving kiss.

LATE THAT NIGHT Judith sat in her dorm room with the sword lying in its open box in front of her. Her hand continually stroked her neck where her pentacles had hung.

Things had taken an unexpected turn. She was touched—no, overwhelmed—by the beautiful gift Wayne had given her. But it came with a startling realization.

Wayne is a toolmaker.

If Rebecca Allen or the high priest found out he had the talent to forge a new *Athamé*, he could be in grave danger. It was her fault, and Judith couldn't leave Wayne to face that alone.

At the airport the next day, she cashed in her ticket and took a cab to a hotel. She was no longer in a hurry to return to England.

4
Another Gift

Sunday, 29 December 1968

WAYNE FOUND it difficult to concentrate on his trip until he crossed the state line into West Virginia. He moped during the entire twenty-four-hour train trip from Indiana to Huntington, West Virginia including the nine-hour layover in Chicago. It seemed stupid to have to go west before he could go east, but he wandered around The Loop looking at the animated Christmas displays in the windows of Marshall Field's. He was lovesick. His hand was always touching the necklace Judith had placed around his neck. He had filled a notepad with doodles of her namesign. They were going steady. At least he thought that's what it meant.

Once he was off the train, the excitement of meeting his mysterious Uncle Bert took hold. Wayne had corresponded with his uncle since he was old enough to write, but this Christmas was only the second time they had met. He wasn't what Wayne remembered at all. He looked like an old prospector of the type you'd see pulling a donkey along in a cartoon. Wayne wasn't sure if a donkey might have been more dependable than the rickety old pickup Uncle Bert tossed his bag into. He didn't say much on the drive to his home near Newburg. Idle chitchat about how Wayne's trip had been and whether he was hungry—repeated twice.

The mountains were beautiful, though. The weather was cold, but it hadn't snowed much when they arrived. His uncle had retired to a place as remote as any Wayne had ever visited. The road was a dirt track for three miles across the side of a mountain. His uncle's home was halfway between the main roads at either end of the track. The driveway was another half mile long, leading from the dirt road to a modest little house. In fact, Wayne would almost call it a shanty, but the garage door opened at the push of a button and closed behind them. Wayne started to open his door but his uncle held out a hand.

"Give me just a minute before we get out," he said. Wayne watched as his uncle stripped off the beard and a mop of a wig and tossed them on the seat of the truck. He pulled off his shirt and lost thirty pounds. Bert looked at him and smiled. He was clean shaven with a military haircut. "I feel human now," he said. "Can't be too careful when I'm off my mountain."

They got out of the truck and Bert opened the door to the house.

Wayne walked around in amazement for two days. His uncle gave a guided tour of the apartment comprising eight rooms. He explained that while he was removing his disguise, an elevator had dropped them nearly a hundred feet below ground. The apartment was in an abandoned coal mine, of which there were many in the area. Wayne was told not to step through certain doors which led into unimproved portions of the mine. In his curiosity, Wayne checked the doors and found out that there wasn't any way to step through them. They were locked tight.

By New Year's Eve, Wayne was beginning to believe all the stories his uncle had ever told about being a spy. He was enjoying the stories Bert related about life in the secret service. Greece after the war was in turmoil as the communists tried to take over. Children were being sent to hide in the desolate Meteóra to escape the conscription gangs. His uncle had been under cover for ten years, his only contact with family the letters to and from his great nephew, each smuggled out by a courier and posted from an APO address.

"You don't know how much you contributed to my sanity in those days. I was still sent out to collect data occasionally, but was mostly responsible for digesting information and sending reports while I waited for retirement and my retreat to be built. Waiting is a hard-learned skill. You were already in college when I moved here. I wanted to invite you to visit right away, but the company had to be certain my location and movements were not observed. It's no wonder so many of us retire at the end of a pistol."

"Uncle Bert, I always thought you were writing to entertain me. Did you put secrets in your letters? My junior high and high school life must have bored you to tears."

"No. It was the only normal thing I ever saw. There is some pretty outlandish stuff going on in the world. That super spy in the movies—James Bond?—that's only things that movie producers can dream up. The reality is way beyond that."

Wayne settled in for another of his uncle's wartime stories. His mother's uncle had sent him snippets of stories throughout the fifties and when they finally met in '61, Wayne had a serious case of hero-worship. Then his uncle had to "go back into the field."

"The makings of the Greek Civil War were in operation before the end of World War II," Bert said. "Once the Germans drafted security battalions to combat the resistance, the nation became more polarized than ever. The resistance controlled most of rural Greece where I was embedded, passing messages and delivering arms. When the war ended, I should have been able to come home. But by that time it was obvious that the National Liberation Front and the government soldiers were going to war against each other. I was already embedded in the mountains and kept communications flowing between the two sides."

"I had no idea Greece was in a civil war," Wayne said. "It always seems so civilized."

"You think the battle with communists is limited to Viet Nam," his uncle answered. "Didn't you know that Greece was taken over by a military junta less than two years ago? We call it the cold war, but there are places where it is very hot."

"How did you get out?"

"When Papandreou started to rise in '60, we realized that the battle was going to be fought in parliament and no longer in the fields. I was fifty-six years old and ready to retire. My country brought me back to repatriate me. That's when I came to visit you. Then, we discovered a faction of Greek anti-monarchists active here that had targeted me. I disappeared back to Northern Greece where I spent the next eight years on Mount Athos. That's where your letters were delivered to me. The Pentagon figures they've cleaned house and there is no immediate threat. They supervised building me this mountain retreat but I had to pay for it myself. I moved in last year. With luck, they'll forget I'm here before long and I'll be able to move about a little more freely. Right now, I only travel with my mind."

Wednesday, 1 January 1969

WAYNE WANDERED THE West Virginia hillsides. His uncle showed him the access point and codes for entry to the retreat. He'd been underground for two days listening to stories. Bert finally chased him out of the cavern and told him to get some fresh air but to stay out of the mines.

From what Wayne could tell, there wasn't another house within a mile of his uncle. After half an hour listening to the quiet country air, broken only by his own footsteps, Wayne sat down on a tree stump. As usual, he carried his notebook and opened it to look at the dozens of times he'd doodled the name sign on Judith's necklace. It was so quiet. He jotted down the words that came to mind—his uncle isolated from the world.

Hush. The solitude
slowly, stealthily creeps in
upon the unsuspecting prisoner
of its all-encompassing spirit.
The heart beats;
the body relaxes.
The worried ones wait
to see what passes.

Coop would have a blast criticizing that one. A little morbid. He took out his pocketknife and started whittling. He was lost in a world of dreaming about Judith. As he carved in the stump, he realized what he was doing and pulled the chain and star out of his shirt to compare the carving he had sketched with the name sign on the back of the pendant. Yes. He got it right. Memorized. There was no reason to doubt it. "Acting like a teenager," he muttered to himself.

"Well, boy, you are certainly quieter than I expected," his uncle said from behind him. The old man leaned on a cane and wore an overcoat and scarf. Wayne wondered how much of that was disguise. "What's on your mind?"

"I guess I've been a little preoccupied," Wayne answered glancing down at his carving again. His uncle noticed and looked over his shoulder. He lifted the chain and star from Wayne's hand and turned it over carefully to read the engraving.

"I see," he breathed. "I was right. You're being initiated into the mysteries." Wayne assumed that his uncle meant he was in love and sighed.

"Yeah, I guess you could say so."

"This isn't your namesign, is it?" his uncle asked.

"No. It's Judith's. My girlfriend."

"Mmmhmm. And do you have a sign?"

"No. I don't think so," Wayne answered, trying to think if he had ever been told of such a symbol. "Judith said it was a kind of rune. I saw a bunch of symbols like this when I was doing some research, though."

"Tell me about your research."

Wayne told him the whole disastrous story of sleeping in class, his golden opportunity, and about his research paper and the fraudulent notes.

"Yes. Fraud would be an academic way to put it. And your professor knew all about this file?" said his uncle.

"Yes. Dr. Allen's husband compiled a catalog of the entire file box. I guess he died soon after they were married but she had a copy of the catalog in her office." His uncle seemed taken aback by something Wayne said, but he couldn't tell what caused the old man to step away.

"Secrets."

"Huh?"

"Let me see if I can explain what's really going on. If the story you saw was real, it would be the protected property of a secret society. They would guard against the story ever being discovered by any legitimate research project. Someone planted a secret where it could be found by an uninitiated novice. We used the technique during the war. No courier was as dependable as one who had no idea he was a courier. It's risky, but sometimes unavoidable—the only way a message can be safely passed."

"You mean someone left it there so that someone else would find it, but I accidentally stumbled on it instead?" Wayne asked.

"It could be that," his uncle said hesitantly, "or it could be that you were intended to find it and get the message to someone else."

"The only one who saw it was my professor and she was furious. She had an entire catalog of Wilton's writings and spotted it as a fake right away."

"I wonder what message it contained for her. Understanding Wilton's writings is tough work for the most experienced reader."

"You know Wilton's writings?"

"I knew Wilton," Bert mused. Wayne was speechless. "How did you like your Christmas present?" Uncle Bert changed the subject abruptly before Wayne could inquire any further.

"The bow? It's great. I love archery," Wayne answered.

"I understood that from your letters. I've set up a bale and target behind the house. I'd like to see you shoot. I got the bow years ago when I was on a mission in Britain. It's old, but the yeoman I received it from told me it would be good for the lifetime of my children's children's children. Not that I have any, but you may one day. Such bows are frequently passed from generation to generation among the lower classes as their own sort of arms. Many are carved with a genealogy of sorts made of name signs like that one. I have no children, so I've passed it on to you."

"Judith's from England," Wayne mused.

"I suspected," Uncle Bert answered. Then as if he'd just come to a decision, "I have another gift for you."

"Another?"

"In fact, two. Come with me, son."

Wayne stuffed the necklace into his shirt and stood to follow his uncle. Uncle Bert was not headed back the way Wayne had come, though. Instead he entered a mine shaft just uphill from where Wayne had been carving.

"I thought these were dangerous," Wayne whispered.

"They are if you don't know your way around," his uncle answered. But for me they are extensions of my home. Here. Take my hand so you don't get lost in the dark. Some of these tunnels don't have lights installed yet." Wayne took his uncle's hand and walked into the darkness with the old man. A chill coursed its way up and down his spine. He talked, just to break the silence.

"Why did you build your home in a mine shaft, Uncle Bert?"

"I told you, they're ready-made homes for an old badger like me," Bert laughed. "Really? It was here or some desert island that hasn't been discovered yet. I already owned the property, so they were kind enough to do the work. A few well-placed threats helped."

"That's just so unbelievable."

"It's unbelievable unless you have to live with it," Uncle Bert said. "I have enemies who would rather see me dead than retired, both in the government and out of it. You get involved in a lot of things. Some haunt you for the rest of your life. Here we are." His uncle stopped abruptly in the dark.

A moment later Wayne was squinting in the face of bright flood-lights. He stepped forward with his uncle. There was no furniture in the room and the light seemed to come at him from every direction.

"What is this?" he asked.

"The killing room," his uncle indicated. "An alarm sounded inside and the bright lights illuminated the room preventing my spyholes from being seen. If I was inside, I could look to see what triggered the alarms and if it was an enemy, there are various ways to get rid of them down here. Since I'm not inside, I need to key in my password."

The next chamber was a kind of security room. Wayne looked at the spyhole, a series of optics and mirrors that showed the view of the room from different angles.

"Beam me up, Scotty," he said under his breath. "This is unreal."

"This is garbage," his uncle snorted. "But it's necessary. The real secrets are in the next room. In order to enter it, I have to have your word that you will tell no one what you see inside. On your life and honor, nephew. No one."

"I swear, Uncle Elbert," he whispered. "No one."

"Good."

If Wayne was expecting more sophisticated technology and gadgetry, what he saw was disappointing at best. The room was draped in black and his uncle lit candles to provide light. It took Wayne's eyes several moments to adjust. It took longer for him to comprehend.

Chalked on the black floor was a white star. At one point of the star, a flat black rock held a lit candle. Three other candles were located on stands at the sides of the room. The whole setting in its very austerity had a medieval elegance about it. Uncle Bert stepped through the curtains and returned a moment later wearing a black robe. He tossed another to Wayne.

"Here. Put this on," his uncle directed. "Just pull it on over your head. It will block your body from your sight, blending with the walls. A master can work with a robe, in street clothes, or naked, but novices usually need to have some tangible help to shut themselves away from the presence of their flesh."

The robe was coarsely woven fabric but was soft and comfortable. Wayne was surprised that it fit over his parka with ease. It was bulky, but easy to manage. He said as much.

"I wore them in the monastery for years. All my mail went to the APO in Washington so no one would know where I was. They bundled up what there was of it each month and delivered it to me. Most months, your letter was all that reached me. Want to thank you for that." Wayne was moved by his uncle's quiet speech.

"You were really a spy," Wayne breathed. He still had trouble believing it. "It's all true."

"Spies," his uncle mumbled. "Everyone who wants information is a spy." The old man finished his preparations and turned to face Wayne. He pulled the cowl of the robe up over his head and signaled Wayne to do likewise. In the black, candle-lit room the two men virtually disappeared. Uncle Bert's voice gained a disembodied quality that seemed to come from the room itself rather than from the hooded man.

"Would you care to begin?" the old man asked.

"Begin what?" Wayne responded. He was beginning to get the creeps is what he was beginning. All they needed was some eerie music and they would be smack in the middle of *Dark Shadows*.

"Very good," his uncle chuckled. "Never divulge your secrets. You're an exceptional young man." He was exceptionally confused, Wayne thought, but Uncle Bert went on. "Since you don't recognize my sign, I'll cast the circle and take your oath myself. Stand in the center of the pentagram," whispered his uncle, pointing to the star on the floor.

Bert moved to the candle that was to the right of the stone table. "Powers of the air, nameless ones, attend this sanctuary and be welcome. Blessed be." He moved to his right to the candle opposite the table. Wayne pivoted where he was to watch the ceremony. "Powers of fire, nameless ones, attend this sanctuary and be welcome. Blessed be." He kept moving to the right. "Powers of water, nameless ones, attend this sanctuary and be welcome. Blessed be." Finally, he was at the stone table. "Powers of earth, nameless ones, attend this sanctuary and be welcome. Blessed be." He returned to the first candle and gestured in the air. "Now is the circle complete. Let all that is said and done in this circle be protected and sealed against intrusion. Powers of the four watchtowers, attend this solitary ritual."

Wayne detected a palpable change in the atmosphere. It was like there was more air in the room than it would hold and the four candles lit the space inside the circle with more light than he thought was possible from such a small source.

"We use only our secret name when we are in the circle. We don't tell it to people outside the circle. In our tradition, the names are often a variation from Greek or Celtic myths. Do you know the story of Prometheus, the Greek god? Sit here with me while I tell you." They sat on the black table-rock together.

"Prometheus was a second-generation Titan, son of Iäpetus. Iäpetus was a fire-walker. When I met the man you know as Wilton, I discovered he could call fire with a staff he called Iäpetus, but that's another story. Prometheus, it is said, took pity on the misery of humanity and stole fire from heaven for their benefit. Some say it was also Prometheus who created humans. Regardless, his name still means lifegiving, creative, or courageously original."

"Wasn't Prometheus the god who was chained to a rock for a vulture to eat his liver every day?" Wayne asked remembering Shelley's *Prometheus Unbound*.

"Yes. I knew you were educated in the mystic ways," his uncle chuckled. "But you see, my secret name is Prometheus, and I spent my time shackled to a rock in Greece while the government tried to figure out what to do with me. And now, I'm tied to this underground rock. That's why I can give you the name I have chosen for you: Promethean, which means literally of or out of Prometheus. I'll add this epithet as well. Let those who know you by no other name call you The Unbound, and may you always be so."

"Thank you," Wayne said quietly. He could not begin to unravel the mysteries about his uncle, but something was beginning to feel familiar. *Déjà vu.*

"Stand up, Promethean." Wayne stood. His uncle produced a string from beneath his robe. With it he measured his nephew's height and cut the string with a pocketknife. He measured Wayne's head and chest, knotting the cord at the measurements. When this was finished, he spoke again.

"Are you willing to swear the oath?"

"Yes," Wayne answered hesitantly.

"Are you willing to suffer to learn?" Wayne almost choked on that and tried to find his uncle's eyes behind the shroud. "Come, come," Uncle Bert said. "There is no knowledge gained without suffering the loss of innocence. You know what they say: Ignorance is bliss."

"Oh," Wayne sighed.

"Are you willing to suffer to learn?"

"Yes," he answered. Uncle Bert laid the string in Wayne's hand and brought his pocket knife over the tip of Wayne's ring finger. A small drop of blood appeared, much to Wayne's surprise. This his uncle squeezed onto the cord.

"Repeat after me," Uncle Bert said solemnly. "I, Promethean, do of my own free will most solemnly swear to protect, help, and defend my sisters and brothers of the Art." Wayne repeated the words, wondering all the time what he was doing. "I will keep secret all that must not be revealed. This do I swear on my mother's womb and my hopes of future lives, mindful that my measure has been taken in the presence of the Mighty Ones." Wayne finished the oath.

"Kneel. Place your right hand under your foot and your left hand on your head." This was getting to be like a fraternity initiation. But he said the words as he was directed.

"All between my two hands belongs to the Goddess."

"So mote it be," answered his uncle. A sense of recognition warmed inside Wayne, making him more confused than ever. It was like he was seeing the event from two perspectives: one as a participant and one as an observer. As his uncle pulled back the cowl on Wayne's robe and kissed his cheeks, it suddenly flashed on Wayne.

"I dreamed all this!"

"No, it's real," his uncle said.

"I mean I dreamed it all a couple of weeks ago. It suddenly flashed when you kissed my cheeks. I dreamed every word of what we just did, only I didn't understand any of it. I didn't know who I was in the dream and I couldn't see your face behind the robe, but I remember the room and talking about Prometheus and then the oath."

"Go on," Uncle Bert said with interest. "When was it?"

"The night of my last date with Judith before we left school."

"Did you dream about anything that comes next?"

"No. That was the end of the dream."

"Does it happen to you often that you dream true?" asked Bert.

"You mean dreams that come true?" Wayne asked. "Yeah, I guess it happens every so often. Like, I saw a pottery demo last summer. A bunch of people were sitting on the floor around a guy who was throwing pots on a wheel. Late in the demo he had a huge pot on the wheel and said something about not liking it, so he took a wire and slid it under the pot and then raised it up splitting the pot in two. It was right at the moment that he raised his hands that I remembered dreaming the whole thing a few weeks earlier. In the dream, I didn't know how he had split the pot. It looked like magic. When I was actually there, I could see the wire he used to cut it."

"It's a great talent. Do you write your dreams down?"

"No, I never really remember until I'm actually in the situation," Wayne answered.

"Do it," Uncle Bert commanded. "In the craft, most of us keep a *Book of Shadows* that includes what we've learned, dreamed, experienced."

"A diary?"

"Yes, but exclusively for those things that are out of the ordinary understanding of the world."

"But why, Uncle... Prometheus? Why did you put me through all this ritual?"

"I'm sorry I rushed you into this, but I'm getting old. I may have misread some of the signs, but it is evident to me that you are being exposed to the craft, either with some intent or simply through proximity to those who are involved. I want to instruct you myself, but I can't cloister you down here in the tunnels like I am. So, I'll give you some things that will help you, and that I don't want to fall into the wrong hands when I die. This retreat and this mountain will pass to you when I die, which I hope will not be soon. But my colleagues will descend and search the place for anything the government considers secret. It is better that you have these now. I trust you to keep them safe, and to do whatever is necessary with them when I'm gone."

"You aren't that old. You'll be around a long time."

"I hope so, but in twenty years, I've only seen your face twice. I'm not going to risk waiting around another ten before I see you again. Now, the gifts." Uncle Bert turned back to the stone on which they had been sitting and slid a portion aside. It opened like a stone vault. Wayne couldn't see what was inside.

"You gave me this box when I saw you last," Uncle Bert said, revealing the treasure he had uncovered. Wayne couldn't believe that he still had that old 4-H project. It was one of the first woodworking crafts Wayne had made. And it wasn't very glamorous compared to what he could do now. It was just a pine box—shellacked, of all things. He had hinged it and put a tiny clasp with a padlock on it. His uncle had it hidden in a vault like it was a valuable thing.

"I see you remember it," his uncle said. "Well, I've put it to good use, and now I'd like you to keep it for me. Here's the key. Same padlock you gave me." He handed Wayne the box. It was much heavier than it should be.

"What's in it?" Wayne asked, suddenly alert. His uncle was giving him more than just an old box.

"Shadows," his uncle answered. "My own *Book of Shadows* that starts before World War II when I was first sent to Greece. I'll place one last entry in it before you leave my mountain." Wayne could hardly believe his fortune. His uncle had written him letters telling of adventures for many years, but now Wayne had the entire story. It could contain anything.

"Since I can't be with you to instruct you, and I don't know what kind of instruction you are getting from others, this is my way of showing you how to progress in your craft," Bert said. "I strongly advise that you ward yourself and at least initially wear your robe when you read it. It isn't for reading in the school cafeteria."

"Ward?"

"What I did when I summoned the powers to the four cardinal points. The instructions are the first thing you will find in the book. Just follow them and you will be safe enough."

"O-kay." Wayne drew the syllables out, still trying to reconcile the ritual with reality.

"This next gift," his uncle continued, "is one I think you will like. It will be your second tool. You wear pentacles. I want you to have your *Athamé.*" A second bundle was retrieved from the stone vault. It was wrapped in newspaper and inside the newspaper it was wrapped in burlap.

"On one rare trip five years ago when I was able to sneak away from the monastery for a few days without being followed, I stumbled on a deserted and tumbled-down estate. You could see the foundations, but that was about all. In the middle of what used to be the courtyard, though, there was still the remnant of a well. You'll find the rest of the story in the *Book of Shadows*, but suffice it to say that I found this in the well. I hid it beneath my robe and in my mattress until the day I left Greece. Where it came from, I don't know, but it's a rare piece, I know that."

The burlap fell aside and a piece of black silk lay under it. In the dim candlelight, Wayne watched his uncle lay aside the folds. It was a knife—unlike anything Wayne had ever seen. It was sleek, seven inches long in the blade with another five inches of ebony handle. The entire blade was engraved with symbols, but the edge was keen. Eventually, Wayne remembered to breathe again with a gasp.

"That is really beautiful," he said at last.

"It's rare, all right," his uncle answered. "Probably a treasure of one of the lost circles, now passed in the succession of vagabond priests who have no circle of their own. There were some writings about them in the monasteries. Here."

"You're really giving it to me?"

"I'm putting it in your keeping. If any of the writings are true, no one can ever own the treasures. They seek out their own way in the world as if they were living. They could lie hidden for years until the right person came along and then rise up out of nowhere, like this did. I know I'm not doing well by it—hiding it down here—any more than when it was hidden in Greece. Maybe it will find its way with you."

"Thank you, Prometheus," Wayne said. This would be too good if it weren't for the weird stuff.

"One last thing," his uncle said. "What is in that book must be sealed in your mind, never to be divulged."

His uncle took the knife and made a tiny cut in the palm of his left hand. He did the same to Wayne. They clasped hands. Bert put the point of the *Athamé* against the pentacles at Wayne's throat. "Air, Fire, Water, and Earth, seal this union," he intoned. "Your blood runs in my veins, my blood in yours. We will always be bound. Let all that passes between us, whether in direct commerce or as you read my secrets, be sealed in your heart as a dream until the day that it is needed." The pentacles nearly burned into his skin. A light breeze circled the room making the candles flicker. Wayne felt the room dissolve and his mind become muddy with recollections of things he thought he knew. He should tell his uncle, but they were just beyond his reach. Somehow, he knew them—dreams that were beyond what his uncle had said—but he couldn't express them.

His uncle made a gesture as he walked around the circle extinguishing the candles until only the one behind the stone table was still lit. He pulled off the black robe and stuffed it back behind the curtains. Wayne took his off as well, but his uncle told him to keep it. They left the chamber in silence.

5
A Taste of Power

Saturday, 11 January 1969

JOE HAMEL was happy to drive Wayne down to Indy after the holiday. It gave him an opportunity to relax with his son and not be interfered with by the women. He loved his wife and daughter, but they could really dominate a conversation. He'd finished the valve job on the '56 Golden Hawk over Christmas and they felt the Packard 352 engine rumble as they sailed down US 31. They rode nearly fifty miles before either of them said anything.

"You never said how the young woman liked her Christmas present," Joe said. "In fact, I don't recall you mentioning her name."

"You weren't there for that conversation? Seems like everything at home has to be said three or four times," Wayne laughed. "Judith loved the present. When she picked the sword up out of the box, I thought she was going to challenge all comers. She's tiny, but she can be pretty frightening."

"Nothing wrong with a strong woman. You're acting differently than you did with your last girlfriend. A little more mature, I guess."

"Well, I don't expect to be buying an engagement ring in the next few months if that's what you mean. I did kind of rush things with Barbara." Joe nodded sagely. Thank heavens that hadn't gone anywhere, Joe thought. The girl was a bit of a shrew and he wouldn't put it past her to get knocked up to force Wayne to marry her. The engagement ring had probably short-circuited that as she figured she didn't need to put out to get it. From what Joe understood, there had been quite a flurry of letters between the two with Barbara writing very uncomplimentary things about his son. Wayne had responded in kind with a parody of her letter, turning everything back on her. Joe had waited at the end of the lane when Wayne asked him to drive him over to get back the engagement ring. That was his son. If he wasn't confident about his emotional temperament and ability to stay in control

50

while he was driving, he knew he could depend on his dad. Staying in control was the real issue. They were coming past the turnoff for Noblesville before he spoke again.

"Judith… that's her name? Pretty."

"Yeah. She's pretty, too."

"Hmm. Strong and pretty. Powerful?"

"As fast and sleek as this car." They both laughed.

"Powerful car. Powerful bike. Powerful women. They can all be more powerful than you are. But like your motorcycle, power is a dangerous thing if you don't stay in control."

That was the last that was spoken before they pulled into the parking lot at the college. Wayne unloaded his suitcase, a boxful of Christmas gifts, and the long bow his uncle had given him. He hugged his father goodbye and skipped up the steps to the dorm.

Joe was happy. He'd had a good talk with his son.

WAYNE DROPPED HIS packages off in his room and ran for the women's side of the dorm. It was Friday noon and classes wouldn't start until Monday. He had no idea when Judith was slated to arrive back in town, but he could hope. He raised his hand to knock at her door just as it opened.

"Aaaiiiieee!" Judith screamed. The next thing Wayne knew he was sinking down the wall across the hall gasping for breath as Judith hovered over him panting. "Oh my god! Oh my god! I'm sorry. Did I hurt you? I'm sorry. You startled me."

"I think I'll live, but would you mind putting your knife away?" Judith glanced at the three-inch blade in her right hand. She collapsed it and it disappeared in her belt. Wayne watched, but was distracted by what was beneath the belt. Judith was wearing sneakers with about a mile of bare leg exposed between them and the very short skirt she was wearing. How could such a short girl have such long beautiful legs? She bent over to help him up and his gaze shifted to cleavage exposed by the three open buttons of her oxford shirt. "Are we okay?" he asked.

"Okay? Oh god! I've been waiting for you all week. I didn't know how to reach you. I finally got them to let me into the dorm on Monday. There hasn't been anyone here and I wasn't expecting you when I opened the door and your fist was raised…"

Wayne reached for her and pulled her into a kiss that deepened rapidly until both were panting.

"I came by to see if you'd like to go to lunch," Wayne gasped.

"Lunch. Yeah. That would be good." Then they returned to their kiss.

Eventually they did get to lunch. The cafeteria was still closed since school didn't start until Monday, but the new McDonald's was only a few blocks away. They walked over, guided by the lighted sign that said, "Over a billion sold!"

"Man. Who eats a billion hamburgers?" Wayne asked. "I'll have three double cheeseburgers, fries, and a chocolate shake."

"I'll have the fish filet, fries and a Coke," Judith told the clerk.

"JUDITH. I'M GOING to… Judith. Oh god, Judith!"

Wayne's hands were filled with Judith's awesome soft breasts. They hadn't undressed, but when he went back to her room after lunch they'd started kissing again and then ended up on her bed. School wasn't in session and most students wouldn't arrive until Sunday so there was no monitor in the lobby and no one really knew he was in the girls' wing.

"Oh, Wayne! I feel it. I'm… kiss me."

Her lips mashed against his and her tongue drove into his mouth. She rode on top of him rubbing her clit against his now-wet hard-on. Just his jeans and her panties between their genitals—preventing penetration.

They'd just been making out. They lay down on the bed with each other. She let him slip his hands under her blouse and reached back to unfasten her own bra, giving him free access. And they felt so unbelievably good. They'd started moving together, rubbing their crotches, building the fervor until they both climaxed, spewing their juices into their underwear.

"God, that's going to be sticky," he said.

"Don't leave me tonight, Wayne," she gasped. "Hold me close and sleep with me."

She rolled off him, pushing her rear up against him as he turned toward her. She pulled his right hand back under her oxford as she lay cradled in his left arm. His hand on her breasts. All night.

They slept.

Ritual Reality

Sunday, 19 January 1969, early morning

"Hey. Cuppa joe and a coupla sinkers, babe."

"Whata you? Holden Caulfield, tonight?" she answered in a Bronxy accent. She was so damned good with different dialects. "Where ya been, toots?" she asked as she set coffee, a fresh creamer, and two old fashioned doughnuts in front of him.

"Great holiday vacation. Spent Christmas with my folks and New Year's with my uncle. They didn't open the dorms until this past weekend."

"Well, I'm glad somebody had a happy holiday. I almost quit this joint."

"Why?" Wayne asked, alarmed.

"Stupid hold-up. Here I am on Christmas Eve, keeping the coffee on for people who don't have any family or place to be, and two guys come in, pull a gun and demand all the money. On Christmas Eve! Cops are all over the place—too late, of course—and the boss calls me in the middle of the afternoon on Christmas Day and threatens to fire me. Me! Ah, what a bastard. It's over now. I'm still here and he can go to hell."

"Gees, Lissa. I'm sorry to hear about all that. I don't know what this area's coming to. We were broken into over the holiday, too."

"You and your sweetheart?"

"No, the theatre at school. Nobody can figure out what the heck went on. Nothing seems to be missing, but the security guard was making his rounds and found all the lights in the dressing rooms, costume shop, scene shop, props closet—everything—on. All the doors open. Nobody around."

"Haunted?"

"*Blithe Spirit?* I don't think so. Locks on the dressing rooms and scene shop were broken. Other than that, no real damage done. Great way to start the term, though, seeing Jim's dreaded C-ME note with my name attached on the call board. He was pretty ticked off."

"Sounds malevolent. You be careful over there."

"Thanks for the advice, Lissa."

"Now tell me more about your break. Since I didn't have one, I want to live through yours." Wayne obliged her with the usual family stories and mentioned his trip to see his uncle. She seemed very interested in that, but he was careful not to say too much. Heck, it *was* the best dream of his vacation. Until he got back.

Thursday, 20 February 1969

WAYNE GLANCED AT his watch and sighed. Two a.m. and he was perched at the top of an eighteen-foot stepladder trying to control a thirty-pound Fresnel over his head while he tightened the C-clamp.

Production weeks were the pits. His classes went to hell; he slept little, ate poorly, and felt like something dragged him out of a gutter. But the show would open tomorrow night as shows always opened: on time. This was the last all-nighter he would pull for a few weeks anyway. And at least he didn't have any early morning classes this term.

"Dimmer 23," he yelled back to Beth at the light board backstage. The light came up and he made the final adjustment of focus on Judith, standing primly in the beam beneath him. He couldn't believe how their relationship had developed. A little romance changed his perspective on life. "That's it!" He slid the gel into place and started down the ladder.

"Hooray!" yelled both assistants. The house lights came up and the dimmer faded. Wayne heard the unmistakable clatter of the old light board shutting down. The many handles and levers on the antique resistance board required two people to run lights for a show with an occasional hand from an actor walking by. It was amazing that Beth could even shove the handles into position. Someday they would have an autotransformer panel. Until then…

Wayne hit the last step and tumbled exhaustedly into Judith's waiting arms. "Poor baby," she said, stroking his greasy hair. "All tired out?"

"Wiped," he responded.

"Hey, me too," Beth said coming out on stage to join in a group hug.

"How can either of you stand to be close to me?" Wayne asked. "I stink."

"How could I tell?" asked Beth. "I've been shut up in that hot little hole for eight hours. I'm outa here." She gave Judith and Wayne a little squeeze and headed for the door.

"You sure you don't want to wait for company to walk back to the dorm?" Wayne asked as she opened the door.

"No way," Beth responded. "By the time you two finish kissing good night, I'll be fast asleep."

"What makes you think I want to kiss a stinky old fish like him?" Judith called after Beth.

"Take it with a spoonful of sugar to help the medicine go down,"

Beth sang from the hall.

"Say, that would be supercalifragilisticexpialidocious," Wayne laughed.

"Much more interesting if you got a shower," Judith said mugging a face.

"We couldn't get into the dorm and out again this late at night," Wayne answered. "Do you know what time it is?"

"Bedtime?" she asked innocently.

"I wouldn't even insult my dorm sheets with this body."

"Use the shower in the dressing room then," she offered.

"Mmm, yes?" he said, kissing her again. "Join me?"

"I'm clean," she answered. "Besides which, when I bathe, I like a big tub that I can lie back and relax in. Not standing in a little cubicle with it raining on me."

They locked the stage door and walked down the back stairs to the dressing rooms. Wayne unlocked the door for them. The shower stall was exactly what Judith had described: a metal cubicle that you stood in while it rained on you. He stood under the water letting it drench his body.

"Any soap out there?" he called. Judith's hand momentarily came through the shower curtain with a bar of soap in it. He took the soap from her, but the hand stayed in the shower stall with him. She rubbed his chest with her soapy hand, let it slide down his body to his waist, and then dart out of the shower. "Ah, you devil temptress," he said as she left the room.

Minutes later, Wayne bolted out of the shower stall with a yell that echoed in the tiny dressing room, startling Judith almost off the chair on which she was patiently sitting.

"What in God's name?" she asked, jumping up.

"The water just went to ice," he exclaimed. "You didn't turn on hot water anyplace did you?"

"Well, if you've already had a cold shower," she said, "I'll just go on home." He looked at her as she spoke. She had on a thirties-style dressing gown, left over from *Philadelphia Story*. Combined with a Katherine Hepburn wig and Judith's British accent, Wayne felt like he'd stepped straight into a movie.

The dressing room was full of costumes and make-up for *110 in the Shade* that would open the next night. Racks of clothes lined the walls leading to the door into the costume storage room, a closet of immense proportions which was in a typical state of confusion. Costumes from twenty years of productions hung or lay on the floor of the closet.

Wayne and Judith maneuvered themselves into this nest and closed the door behind them. She pulled away his towel and used it to dry the last drippings of water from him.

Judith spread the towel out on a pile of fluffy animal costumes and pulled Wayne down next to her. He was already hard as a rock, but she didn't seem to mind as she caressed him. When he was lying down, she moved over him to kiss. He was lost—lost in the sensation of her lips and her skin against his.

Skin. They'd been fooling around for a month now, but that still didn't mean they'd had sex. They'd always kept some clothes on, rubbing each other to mutual orgasm. But as Wayne let his hands drift down from her shoulders, he found only bare, sensual skin. *Oh god! This is it.* He restrained himself from grabbing all her naked bits, trying desperately for control—feeling her breasts pressed against his chest and following her lead as his hands found her bare ass. His erection was pressed against her stomach. She kissed him again and humped against his cock, her wet slit moistening it as she moved.

The unmistakable click of a latch and sound of a door opening brought them bolt upright tangled in arms and legs.

"Shit. Night watchman," Wayne whispered. "I didn't lock the door and the lights are on." Footsteps echoed through the dressing room. They heard him moving costumes on the rack—*Odd*, Wayne thought. The hangers slid past one after another as if the guard was examining each one, then pushing on. Judith slid to his side and whipped a cape over their heads. Wayne grabbed nearby costumes and packed layers over them. Judith pecked mischievously at his ear as they listened to the approaching footsteps.

"I might come," she whispered. Wayne kissed her to keep silence. He peaked through a hole in the badly worn garment as the closet door opened. What he saw, silhouetted against the light in the dressing room, however, was not the usual night watchman. He was dressed in a winter coat and gloves with a hat pulled down around eyes that almost seemed to glow. Visions of *Rosemary's Baby*—a movie he'd been too shocked to walk out of—came to mind unbidden. *It's the devil*, Wayne thought. The intruder shone a flashlight down the disordered racks of clothes and shook his head. He closed the door and moved toward the scene shop. Wayne knew it was locked, and couldn't believe he heard the sound of the shop door opening. Moments later another set of footsteps echoed in the hall and once again the dressing room door opened.

"Hello? Anybody in here?" Wayne recognized the voice of the night watchman. He started to answer, but Judith clamped a hand over his mouth long enough for him to remember the state they were in. The light in the dressing room went out and the door was shut and locked. Wayne opened the closet door into the dark dressing room.

"What's going on?" whispered Judith.

"I don't know, but I don't like it," Wayne whispered back.

"Hey! What are you doing in there?" They stiffened at the sound of the watchman's voice from the direction of the scene shop. Something crashed and footsteps ran down the hall and away. A second set of footsteps followed and then silence.

"Key-rist!" Wayne swore.

"You sure know how to show a girl a good time," she joked.

"Let's find out what the hell's going on," Wayne said.

"Better put some clothes on first," she said. "We're not quite dressed for cloak and dagger outings." Wayne stopped in his tracks. He turned toward Judith and, for the first time, truly drank in what he saw. The wig had been lost somewhere in the storage closet. Her short blonde hair framed her pixie-like face above her bare shoulders and the hard pink tips atop beautiful, full round breasts. Her narrow waist and flat tummy accented the slight ridge of the hipbones and the tuft of fine gold hair between her legs.

Judith blushed at his gaze and turned to retrieve her clothes, inadvertently giving Wayne a long look at her luscious ass. She turned as she pulled her sweater on. He was still naked and staring.

"Dress," she commanded. "We have to get out of here."

"Right you are," he grinned, coming out of his reverie. In minutes they were dressed and moving quietly through the theatre. The shop door stood open. "God! What a mess!" Wayne said surveying paint bleeding down the wall onto the floor. "I've got to clean up this paint."

"Not tonight you don't," she said.

"Why?"

"Because we left the theatre at two o'clock, right after Beth did. We've got no reason to be here now. How do you know this happened?"

"Shit."

"Leave everything exactly as it is and let's get home to bed. We'll wait for someone to call you about it," she finished. They hurried out of the shop leaving it as they had found it and headed for the dormitory.

In his room, Wayne sat on the edge of his bed staring blankly at the wall in front of him. The night had been less than satisfactory. Judith had pulled him behind a bush as a police car passed and ground herself against him until they'd both come. Only the cold wet ground had forced them out of the hiding place. They kissed long and passionately at the dorm, but the night-desk monitor stared at them the entire time and they finally went to their separate wings.

As HE SAT, he could feel his heartbeat calming as his eyes crossed with exhaustion. But sleep was playing with him. He suddenly felt wide awake and restless. He could go for a doughnut, but there was still the possibility that someone would call him in the middle of the night about the break-in. If that happened, he had better be in his room.

He reached for his uncle's diary to continue reading. Remembering his instructions, he slipped on the black robe before opening the book. Wayne had found this innovation to be helpful in his other studies as well and was spending a lot of his study time in his room dressed in the black monk's robe. The first thing he had found in the book was an instruction on how to cast a warded circle. Wayne had no idea if this worked, but he dutifully went through the motions and invocations before sitting in the middle of his bed to read.

The *Book of Shadows* had been a real surprise. He'd hidden it until he was sure that he could be alone. It was nearly four weeks between his New Years' meeting and the time when he finally opened the pine box that contained the manuscript. He expected to learn about his uncle's James Bond-like adventures. What he found was closer to *The Hobbit*. It was filled with a medieval sense of magic, written from his uncle's perspective as if it was all actually happening.

Uncle Bert had first met Benjamin Wilton in the 1930s as a comparative religions student studying ancient Greek mythology and then pressed into service as a spy. Wilton had information that was needed by the fledgling army intelligence. Bert couldn't buy the information, but Wilton was willing to trade it for an exchanged vow of silence that he was sure could be trusted. What followed was Bert's initiation into an ancient faerie cult. The initiation closely paralleled Wayne's encounter with his uncle after Christmas. Uncle Bert's initiation was much more involved than Wayne's simple oath-taking, and the journal chronicled each step. From that point on, Wilton was referred to only as "Firebrand."

Tonight, Wayne was caught by something less personal to his uncle but more directly related to Wayne's experience. His uncle had studied different mysteries and cults and documented his findings.

In many traditions, the role of the uninitiated priest holds a rare but profound meaning. The Hebrews had their Melchizedek. The faerie traditions have a similar concept that traces back to Merlin. The most contemporary account is from the 19th century in which the title of Vagabond Priest is ascribed to the poet John Keats.

Keats was on a walking tour with his friend Brown when one night they became separated in the Lakes District. Keats emerged from that adventure having been exposed to a ritual performed in an ancient stone circle. Keats wandered into the ritual unaware of what was going on at first, but seeing the circle of pagans, dancing naked around a fire, he immediately stripped off his own clothing knowing that he had come home to his rightful place.

The goddess/priestess recognized him at once as a Vagabond Priest and ushered him into the inner circle where his own walking stick was consecrated as one of the circle's most powerful tools. While the ritual was powerful, sexual, and charged with heat, it appears that it took its toll on both Keats and the priestess, known to us only as Mari. She died in childbirth nine months later and Keats' consumption advanced to such a stage that within two years he followed her to the grave. But the line of Vagabond Priests, priests after the order of Merlin and Melchizedek, has continued to this day, revealing themselves, it is said, only in the time of absolute need.

It was true. Even if the paper in Wilton's file was a fraud, the story was true. He could hardly wait to show Dr. Allen. He'd no more than thought this and the words slipped into a dream world. He tried to keep track of his dreams, but often they were just out of his reach.

Wayne eventually fell asleep and his uncle's words blended into the images that he saw in his dreams. It was so real that he could see the circle of naked dancers around the fire and himself stumbling into the circle. The face that he saw across the fire was that of Judith and they danced a most erotic dance. Just as Wayne was about to consummate his love, he looked into her face and saw Dr. Allen. A strange sexuality mixed with panic left him bathed in sweat even though he awoke as cold as ice.

Eight o'clock found him staring at the ceiling unable to sleep any longer. The pine box with his uncle's *Book of Shadows* in it was back on the shelf, covered with the black robe. He was still fully dressed. It was all a dream, he thought. My poor crazy uncle is beginning to get to my brain.

He couldn't rush over to the theatre at this hour, as much as he wanted to. He would have to go through his day as normally as possible. Normally, he would sleep until ten-thirty. Well, if nothing else, he could put a little practice time at the archery range in the athletic building. It amazed him that he could get a full course credit in P.E. by putting in thirty hours of target practice and recording his scoring over the term. He reached the range at a quarter till nine and found Judith already stringing her bow.

"Great minds think alike," she said. "Couldn't sleep?"

"I know I slept sometime," Wayne responded. "But I don't feel like I got a wink. Wide awake at eight."

"You out-slept me by an hour," she responded. "I had breakfast at the cafeteria."

"Was it worth it?"

"Is it ever?"

"Shall we match shots?" Wayne asked.

"Kiss a point?" Judith responded with a smile.

When it came to weaponry, archery was the only sport in which Wayne could match Judith. She tried to teach him to fence but he was an easy mark for her well-honed skill. Archery and tennis were co-educational classes since most of the instruction was completed as independent study, so they decided in January to take the class together. At the end of the first flight, they were even.

"Who do you suppose it was?" she asked as they collected their arrows and marked the scores.

"I have no idea," he answered. "Didn't look like a student and seemed to be looking for something specific. I haven't gone over yet. Don't want to get there before Jim does."

"Gail asked what time I got in. I told her that we finished on stage at two and went for a doughnut. Got in at three without being anywhere near the theatre when the guard was there."

"Good thinking. I almost went there. I'll let Lissa know and I'm sure she'll cover for us."

"Lissa?" Judith asked questioningly.

"The doughnut lady on the late-night shift," Wayne answered casually. He'd spent many a late night popping in to Donut World to study.

"Uh-huh, right," Judith laughed.

"Do I love you, or is this just a hormonal imbalance?" Wayne asked, wrapping her in his arms as they collected their arrows and recorded the score. "You pay."

"After every flight?" she asked.

"We could be even at the end of the match," he grinned. "Okay, you owe me two."

"You owe me a lot more than that after last night," she answered, paying the first of the kisses she owed.

"I like this co-ed class," Wayne said.

"Now if they just had co-ed showers," Judith responded, grinning.

"Mmm. I thought you liked baths," Wayne whispered.

"Good idea," Judith said. "So, come home with me for spring break."

"What?"

"I need to go home over Easter," Judith said. "Come with me. I have my own vacant cottage with a big tub waiting for us."

"What would your parents say, bringing an American home for the holiday?" Wayne asked.

"My mother would be delighted to think I was serious over someone," Judith answered. "My father wouldn't know. I haven't seen him in years. I was conceived at the dark of the moon, you know."

"*The Dark of the Moon*," Wayne repeated. "Jim should consider doing that one next year. Witches and magic and great effects. We could enter it in the festival." Judith looked at him, then let her arrow fly.

"I've not read it," she confessed. "Do you have a copy?"

"No. I saw it at a summer stock last year," Wayne responded. "I'm now eighteen kisses ahead of you. What time is it?"

"Almost ten," Judith said. "You're not quitting until I have a fair chance to catch up. Besides you haven't answered my question yet."

"You were serious?" Wayne asked staring at her with a mixture of disbelief and fantasy playing in his eyes.

"Of course," she answered.

"What's a ticket to England cost?"

"In dollars or real money?"

"Our dollars are just as good as your pounds and ounces."

"Shillings," she snapped. "About $300."

"I'll have to see what's left in my student loan account," he said. "What kind of travel money would I need?"

"If you think I'm going to let you out of my little cottage long enough to spend something, you have another think coming," Judith said. Wayne let fly his last arrow and she stepped up to the line. "Besides, you haven't said yet that you want to come."

"I want to come every time I see you," he whispered. Her arrow went way wide of the mark.

"That's not fair! I get that one over." They laughed and walked to the target. Wayne pulled out her last arrow and stuck it by hand in the bullseye.

"You deserve that. Now I pay," he said and pulled her to him to kiss her.

"Hey! There are others of us who have to put in time here, too, you know," said another student stringing a bow at the head of the range. "Can't you find someplace private to screw around?"

"Shit," Wayne whispered backing suddenly away. "Let's go."

"Typical male," Judith growled. "Always coming and going."

"Careful how you talk, there, lady," he said. "Next thing you know I'll come and stay."

"Promises, promises."

"My kind of promises," Wayne sang. "I think I've listened to that album fifty times since Christmas. Let's walk by the office and see if Jim's in yet." The two hung up the practice bows in the equipment room and left the Athletic Building. They walked hand-in-hand across campus to the Academic Building. Someday, Wayne mused to himself, there would be enough famous alumni and benefactors to name all the buildings after someone. It was a weird school that just had functional buildings.

When they reached the hall outside the theatre office they paused to look at the callboard. A note in Jim's writing addressed to Wayne hung on the board.

"It looks like the shit has already hit the fan," Wayne said, reading the note. "It just says, 'C-ME NOW!'" He knocked on the theatre professor's door and Jim's morning growl commanded entrance. "A usual Friday morning, I see," Wayne said looking at Jim's haggard expression.

"I feel like a ghost," Jim said lighting a cigarette. Wayne noted his ashtray was already full and three empty Styrofoam cups sat on his unorganized desk. "I got a security call at four o'clock this morning and I've been over here ever since. We were broken into last night. Have you been to the shop yet?"

"No," Wayne answered truthfully. "Not since last night. Four o'clock? After we finished the lights."

"What time did you leave?" Jim asked. Wayne looked at Judith for confirmation as he answered.

"Must have been about two o'clock. Few minutes after by the time we got cleared out."

"Security says dressing room A was unlocked and the lights were on. They discovered the suspect in the scene shop. Are you sure things were locked up when you left?"

"Sure. Did they get him?" Wayne asked, nearly forgetting the implication of the open dressing room.

"No," Jim sighed. "He got away. I'm afraid there's a mess downstairs for you to clean up."

"Damn. Did he take anything?"

"I don't think so, but you'd better check it out when you clean up." Jim looked hard at Wayne and Judith as he ground out his cigarette. "Wayne, there's one more thing." The young man stopped frozen in place by the edge in his professor's voice. "This is the second break-in this term, plus the library break-in last fall. Over Christmas break, they traced that one into the scene shop, too. Anyone who tries that route again will have a nasty surprise waiting for them. Administration is convinced that the theatre has nothing legitimate to entice a burglar back so many times and apparently take nothing each time."

"It sounds strange to me, too," Wayne responded with a little relief in his voice. "But at least they saw the guy this time."

"Judith," said Jim, "I'm going to let you stay for this, only because it's sometimes good for two people to hear something said and be able to compare notes, just to be sure it all sank in. I will personally hang, draw, and quarter anyone caught in this department with so much as a beer on theatre premises. I will not be so kind if the substance is anything harder. What you two or any of the other majors do off campus and away from the theatre is your own business. But there had bloody well better not be any drugs in that shop or anyplace else around when the administration conducts the search that they have decided is necessary. There's a lot riding on it, believe me. It might be kinder if that word reached the rest of the department through you two instead of through me. I hope you understand."

"Yeah," Wayne said, a little stunned. "Clearly."

"Good. Get that mess downstairs cleaned up."

6
Beware Litha

Thursday, 27 February 1969

AT THREE o'clock Thursday morning Wayne lay in bed wide awake staring at the ceiling again. Production was running smoothly and everyone was catching up on classes. As much as they wanted to get together—and each made a point of telling the other that they *did* want to get together—Judith was unavailable this week as she finished a paper that was giving her more than her share of problems. His schedule was light this term and he had no classes that required lengthy research papers. Instead, Wayne had been reading his uncle's *Book of Shadows*.

He'd read enough—as much as he could stand—but he wasn't tired any longer. Reading the book, even though he had to take time to puzzle out his uncle's sometimes cramped or cryptic writing, often left him energized instead of tired. As long as he stayed in bed, the words were sharp and clear in his mind. As soon as he left his room, they took on a dream-like quality and he was never sure if what he remembered was from his book or from his dreams. He tossed and turned on his bed for an hour, thinking. He couldn't go back to the scene shop and putz around, which he sometimes did late at night. With the current break-in mania, the security guard would shoot first and ask questions later.

Finally, he dressed and slipped out the back door of the dorm without passing the front desk. Technically, he was supposed to sign out, but no one ever paid attention. He kicked his motorcycle to life and headed toward Meridian Street. Even in the city there wasn't much open at this hour. He'd joked with Judith that Indianapolis was just a cornfield with streetlights. It never hurt to show up at Donut World for a late-night pick-me-up. Besides, he needed someone to talk to.

No one else was there when he parked his bike and walked in. As he hoped, Lissa was behind the counter reading a magazine. Her full figure was witness to her job satisfaction, but in spite of a few extra pounds, she was really quite cute.

"You up early or late, sugar?" she asked as she set a cup of coffee down in front of him without his even asking. "Either way, you look like you need a cup of Java."

"Maybe after I finish it, I'll be able to answer your question, Lissa," he answered. "I haven't decided if I'm going to bed or getting up."

"Well, it's lonely here at this hour," she responded. "There won't be much demand for your stool if you just want to sit and talk."

"Couldn't sleep," he said wondering why he was drinking coffee to remedy the situation.

"Old lady got you out on the sofa again?" She was making up wild stories as she went about her business of stocking the shelves. They'd been through the game before. It was fun and he could take any character he wanted to play.

"No, I'm a bachelor," he said.

"Congratulations," she responded. "Avoid that honey-lined trap for as long as you can."

"I just haven't found the right woman," he said cocking an eyebrow at her. "It will take someone with your kind of charm and doughnuts to ever lure me in."

"And someone with less brains than I got to fall for your line," she responded. "Here. Have another cup." She was really cute, he thought absently, and not as old as he thought at first. They chattered randomly for a while, a friendly banter that kept his coffee cup filled and his mind awake. Eventually, Wayne discovered himself talking about his uncle.

Wayne tested himself to see what he could say. He found that he couldn't say his uncle lived in a coal mine, but that he lived in the mountains seemed to be fine. There was so much he needed to talk about.

"I mean, get this. From the time I was a little kid, Mom talked about her uncle the spy. She'd never use that word, but she loved to keep an aura of mystery around what he did. I think she idolized him, and I inherited it from her. When I finally got to meet him, I was about ten. I made a present for him in 4-H Woodworking. It was just a box, made out of pine because I couldn't afford to practice on expensive wood. And when I met him, he was everything I imagined. He was an old man then, you know. Maybe sixty. But he could spin stories about adventures that I ate up like candy. And he'd always leave out just why he was somewhere, or exactly what the secret piece of equipment was that he used to escape from the enemy. You just knew that he was *In Like Flint*."

Wayne had been holding Judith's necklace against his throat as he talked. He discovered it was easier that way. He glanced at his left hand and then opened the palm to look more closely at it. He couldn't see a scar, but his palm tingled. Wayne's voice drifted as he remembered his childhood.

"When I was little, my best friend Paul and I decided we'd become blood brothers. Got the idea from Cochise in *Broken Arrow* or something on TV. We went out in the woods and did an Indian dance in a circle around a leaf fire that we knew we'd get beaten half to death for if anyone ever found out. Then we took a needle, because we'd been taught that you could get an infection from a pin, and each pricked our own ring finger and pushed them together. It was kid stuff. We were blood brothers, sworn to live and protect each other for the rest of our lives. One for all and all for one. That sort of stuff. Until the next year Paul moved to a different town and I never saw or heard from him again. It was hokey. Like I said, kid stuff." He looked at the palm of his hand again. Lissa glanced at it.

"It's like that. We're… It's like that." Wayne paused as he considered what he had just said.

"Well, it could be like that, couldn't it?" Lissa asked. She watched him absently play with the necklace he wore around his neck as he sipped his coffee. She reached out to look at the jewelry. Wayne chuckled.

"I haven't had that off since my girlfriend gave it to me for Christmas," he said. Lissa turned it in her fingers and saw on the back of the star the name sign. She gave a little gasp as she dropped it.

"Swordmaster," she breathed quietly.

"Huh? Her name is Judith," Wayne said.

"That's very pretty," Lissa said. "Kind of an old-fashioned name. Tell me about her."

Wayne needed no further encouragement on that subject. He began telling Lissa all about how they met and what they did together.

LISSA WAS ALL but tuned out to the prattle as she pondered how to approach Wayne. It was obvious that he had had a rudimentary initiation and The Swordmaster had given him her own pentacles. Perhaps his uncle was involved as well. But if he was left to discover his own way, it could be too late for him to be of real use, or worse yet he could be used by the wrong people. There was more going on in Indianapolis these days than met the eye. Wayne was telling her for the third time how beautiful Judith was when Lissa decided to help him her own way.

"Wayne, honey, I want you to look in my eyes," she directed him. The request was so sudden and out of the blue that Wayne automatically looked up and into the intense green eyes of the doughnut lady. She began to speak softly so that Wayne had to lean forward slightly to hear her. Lissa had learned hypnotism from one of the finest stage magicians in the world. Sleight-of-hand was second nature to her, as were accents and disguises. Lissa pulled a necklace similar to Wayne's out of her blouse, holding it before his eyes. It was the perfect trigger. In his sleep deprived state, Wayne was an easy subject to hypnotize, staring at the necklace that Lissa waved before his eyes.

"I'm not going to take you into a circle, sweetheart," Lissa said calmly when she was sure he was under. "But we need to be able to identify each other when we meet on the spiritual plane. I am known as The Chameleon. By what name will I know you?"

"I am The Unbound," Wayne responded with the name his uncle had given him. A chill ran down Lissa's back.

"I'm going to help you learn the craft and prepare you for great things," Lissa said. "You wear pentacles around your neck."

"What are pentacles?" Wayne responded.

"The star you wear on a necklace," Lissa answered. Okay, so Judith was not trying outright to draw him into the circle, but to give him her pentacles? She must be madly in love. "Have you received other tools?"

"Tools? I have a whole shop full of them."

"Tools for your craft. Knife, cup, wand?" Wayne thought for a minute.

"I have a knife."

"That's the *Athamé*. Part of your task over the next few weeks will be to gather your other tools. They will come to you. There are four tools that every practitioner of the craft has," Lissa said. "In addition to the *Athamé* and the pentacles, you will receive a cup and a wand. These will seem as natural to you when you receive them as your own name. When you have all your tools, you will be ready for your full initiation."

"I'm confused," Wayne said.

"That's understandable," Lissa said. "You are going to become a practicing witch. I can see already that you have a lot of power in you. You will study with your mistress and with me. You will memorize spells and I will teach you how to use your power. Anytime you have questions, you will be able to ask me and I will answer them."

"That's a relief," Wayne said. "It was hard not having anyone to talk to."

"Keep a *Book of Shadows* and write down your instructions and your dreams. Make them your own," Lissa said. "Bring your questions to me and I will help you."

"Fair enough," Wayne said.

"We'll become blood brothers, too. Give me your left hand." Wayne held out his left hand. Chameleon pulled a small knife from somewhere that Wayne didn't see and pressed it into the palm of his hand until a red drop appeared.

Here we go again, Wayne thought.

She pierced her own left palm and pressed until it drew blood and grasped his left hand in a handshake. Lissa placed the tip of her knife against Judith's pendant at Wayne's throat. "Air, Fire, Water, and Earth, seal this union," she intoned. "Your blood runs in my veins, my blood in yours. We will always be bound. I swear to teach you without harm and you will learn without barriers. My words are concealed in your heart and will arise when your training is complete."

"So mote it be," Wayne responded. Lissa was surprised, but pleased.

"It's time for you to go back to bed now," Lissa instructed him. "When you reach your motorcycle, you will remember only that we talked about life at school and what is going on in your life. Any time I touch your pentacles, you will return to this place where we can talk freely. You will know that you can always trust me."

"Of course, I trust you, Chameleon," Wayne said standing and stretching. "But I really need to get back and get some sleep before my first class in the morning."

"You drive careful now, sugar," Lissa waved at him as he left the doughnut shop. She shook her head. She'd come here only to observe The Hart and what she would do in her quest. To step in to protect her if needed. The task that had become boring. Rebecca Allen seemed intent on doing nothing.

But now things were looking more interesting. The Swordmaster was here and her boyfriend was in training.

The furthest thing from The Chameleon's mind had been taking on an apprentice. But, the best laid plans…

GOD, HE WAS tired now. He kicked his motorcycle to life and instantly regretted having spent the night more than a step away from his bed. But hell, she was sweet and the hour and a half had been kind of fun.

The cold blast of March air in his face as he took off on the bike brought him wide awake. That was one thing about a motorcycle—it was hard to fall asleep at the wheel.

Saturday, 1 March 1969

"Hammer!"

"Hup!"

"Crowbar!"

"Hup!"

"Screw!"

"Hup, hup, hup, hup, hup!"

"And the flying Wazinskis are high again!" yelled Wayne as he disconnected the last brace from the set and the troupe carted the flats off-stage to the shop. Wayne jumped from the third step of the ladder down to face Glenn who hopped back a step up the small platform they were about to move. "Hup!"

"Ho-oh!" The mock acrobatics were about as corny as any tension breaker could be, but they served the purpose. Striking a set on closing night was a downer but when the whole cast got into the swing of playing traveling circus, it went a lot smoother. The two men horsed the last platform through the doors of the shop and set it down.

"If you can ever be glad to see a show over, it's this one," Wayne said, leaning on the platform.

"Me too," Glenn agreed.

"Hey boss—you don't mind if I call you boss, do you? You are kind of the boss down here—what should I do next? I finished washing out all the paint cans. I'm ready for the next job." Wayne looked at Brian with a pained expression on his face.

"I don't know, Brian," he said. "Did you check with costumes?"

"Aw, that's girl stuff. Don't tell me the men do laundry here. I want some real work." Wayne glanced at Glenn who pretended to be occupied sorting through the flats.

"You're right, Brian," Wayne said slowly. "I guess I haven't been giving you enough responsibility, being the new guy and all. But you're doing a fine job. I tell you what. I do have a delicate job that needs to be done, since you already know where the shop sink is." Wayne reached to the lighting bench where Beth was sorting and hanging cables and grabbed a handful of color media. Most of it was pretty burnt with the heat of the lights, but he always salvaged what he could. This time he'd make an exception.

"I usually do this myself the day after a show," Wayne said to Brian. "These things are fragile, and expensive. We clean them up good after each show so we don't have to buy new ones for the next show." Beth turned to look at him but caught Glenn's eye and stayed quiet. "You've shown that you're dependable, so just take these out to the sink and wash them down good in warm water and soap. But be careful, okay? Can you handle that?"

"Gees, sure boss. I'll do it right." Brian carefully took the stack of gels in both hands and left the room. As soon as he was gone Glenn turned and broke out laughing.

"That was mean as hell," he choked.

"I know," Wayne laughed, "but he's such a little queer. Besides, I had to wash gels my first show here. It's just a sign of equal treatment for all."

"You never had me wash gels," Beth said with her hands on her hips. "What's going on?"

"Be thankful you never pledged Alpha Psi Omega," Wayne said.

"You want to go watch?"

"No, we'll find out soon enough." The two leaned back against the wall and caught their breath for a moment. Beth returned to her bench with a shrug as the two men sorted through the tools and props to store them. The last of the flats came down and Glenn helped organize them as he chatted with Wayne.

"Hey, what's with you and these late-night doughnut runs?" he asked. "Rumor has it you've been sneaking out late and coming home early. You got a hiding place where Judith comes to meet you?"

"No. Just a friendly conversation with the doughnut lady."

"The one that works all night at Donut World?"

"Lady named Lissa. She's a real card."

"You wouldn't throw Judith over, would you?"

"Hell, no," Wayne answered. "There's nothing between Lissa and me, I guarantee you. But if we go off and start a commune somewhere, she comes, too. She makes a mean doughnut."

"I think you're gaining weight."

"While we're on delicate subjects," Wayne said glancing around and turning his back to Beth. He dropped his voice to a whisper. "You haven't been stashing dope in the scene shop, have you?"

"No. Not a bad idea though. Can I borrow your keys?"

"You do and I'll kill you," Wayne said politely. "Admin's been searching the place high and low because of the break-ins."

"Don't worry," Glenn smiled. "My connection's in Chem Lab, not in theatre."

"Oh shit!" They heard the scream from the hall, breaking off their conversation. "Damn! He'll kill me."

"Not very subtle, is he?" Glenn laughed. He and Beth followed Wayne out of the shop into the hall where Brian was coming out of the janitor's closet with his hands dripping with melted gelatin. He ran right into Wayne as he came out of the closet and looked up at him. "Oh God, no!" he yelled and put his hands on his face to cover it from Wayne. The sloppy gel smeared all over him. "Shit!"

"Brian, what did you do?" Wayne asked concealing his laughter as well as he could.

"I did it just the way you said," Brian moaned. "Honest. I just ran a little warm water over them and they melted in my hands."

"Warm water?" Wayne exploded. "Glenn, did I not tell this little twerp to use cold water?"

"Cold water. That's what you said," Glenn affirmed, almost choking on the words. Beth couldn't hold it any longer and ran back into the shop where Glenn could hear her howling with laughter.

"She's *really* upset," Wayne declared. "If I can't trust you, Brian, you'll have to report to costumes. And don't try to duck out now. You've got two more hours of shop work if you want to finish your pledge duties for Alpha Psi."

"Ah, shit," Brian said. He was almost in tears. "I didn't mean it. Honest."

"Go tell Gail," was Wayne's only response. The wounded boy left the presence of Wayne and Glenn and entered the dressing room with his hands still dripping and gelatin in his hair.

"God, I love strike!" Wayne howled when Brian had disappeared.

"That poor kid," Glenn responded. "What are you going to do?"

"Oh, don't worry. Gail's been through this often enough. She'll get him straightened out."

"That was mean," Beth said emerging from the shop. She was grinning from ear to ear and wiping her eyes. "No wonder I never pledged Alpha Psi."

"Aw, it's not that bad," Wayne said. "Just a little gel."

"Not that," said Beth. "I mean sending him in there." She pointed at the dressing room.

"I don't envy Brian walking in there right now," Glenn affirmed.

RIGHT NOW, IN fact, Gail was summoning court to judge the pledge.

"Judith, Carol, Pam!" she called when Brian reported for duty. "Would you look at this?" The other women came to stare at Brian. "I think that Wayne has sent us a pledge that needs to do penance."

"He can't touch costumes with that slime all over him," Judith said.

"But we need the help in storage," Carol chimed in. "There's all those dance belts to be sorted and folded."

"Well, then," said Gail. "Let's clean him up and put him to work." Brian stared helplessly and open-mouthed as the four women surrounded him and proceeded to strip him down to his shorts and shove him into the shower. As soon as the cold water hit him, Brian panicked and ran, out of the dressing room and down the hall screaming. He smacked straight into Jim Richards, the director of theatre and stood staring and sputtering. It took only a moment for the professor to realize what had happened and to collar him.

"Okay, everybody front and center!" Jim yelled in the hall. The dressing room and shop doors opened and a silent troupe of theatre majors filed out. "I know what happened, and I know who did it," Jim said. Gail handed Brian a towel and his trousers. "Now, who is going to explain?"

The job fell to Wayne as perpetrator of the crime. Gail returned the rest of Brian's clothes to him and he accepted the joke as something that all pledges went through, and which he would also conduct next year. Gel melts in water, no matter what the temperature is.

"If we've got this hazing done with now," said Jim, "let's get cleaned up and out of here. There's champagne at my place and I have a very big announcement for you." There were hoots of delight as the cast cleared out of the shops and went to party.

JUDITH STRADDLED THE back of the motorcycle behind Wayne and they headed out.

"Gee, I've missed you," she said hugging herself closely to his back.

"Ditto that," he answered, dropping a hand to touch her leg.

"Any news on our midnight visitor yet," she asked.

"No," Wayne answered over his shoulder. "I don't think it's drug-related. Glenn's clean and he'd know. I can't place any other reasons for it though. They always come and look, but never take anything."

"Say, are you ever going to give a girl an answer to her question? Spring break is only two weeks away, you know." Wayne parked the bike and the two dismounted. He wrapped Judith in his arms.

"I have recently discussed this situation with my checkbook which is the official guardian of my student loan. It has informed me that one economy class trip to England has been approved," he said. Her kiss was affirmation of her pleasure at the news.

They stood outside, letting their hands get reacquainted with each other's body. It was hard to do much groping when they were wearing winter coats, but Judith slid her baggy coveralls down and off her legs. Under, she was wearing a vinyl miniskirt. She was instantly back in the clinch and Wayne's right hand found her bare legs. Two other cast members went into the house, but the couple was hidden in shadows beside the garage. Wayne cupped Judith's mostly bare butt in his hands as he ground against her.

"Third base, Wayne," Judith whispered. "Go to third base. Make me come before we go in. I need you bad." That was all the encouragement Wayne needed to let his hand slide from her ass around to the front where he cupped her hot, wet sex. In a moment, he'd pushed her panties aside and was pushing a finger into her slit. Judith moaned her appreciation into Wayne's mouth, her excitement mounting rapidly to a climax that made her sag against him, his finger still inside her.

"You are so hot," Wayne said. "How'd I ever get a girlfriend like you?"

"In England in two weeks," she whispered. "All of me. All the time."

"Hey, you guys! Quit making out in the shadows and come to the party," Glenn yelled as he and Gail mounted the steps. Wayne and Judith jerked apart.

"Busted," Wayne laughed. *Damn it, Glenn. Just ten more minutes out here and...*

Judith straightened her skirt, tossed her coveralls into the saddlebag on the motorcycle, and the two went to join the cast.

INSIDE JIM RICHARDS's suburban home, the cast found actors from both shows of the season gathered. The party was already in full swing at midnight. Hot food lined the table and hungry students attacked it like locusts. When everyone had arrived and things were pretty settled in, Lena Bowen began distributing plastic champagne glasses around the crowded room. Jim called for everyone's attention and stood with the unopened bottle of Cold Duck at the center of the room.

"It's a rare privilege to work with not just one fine cast in a year, but so far with two. I hope that our spring production of *Antigone* will be every bit as successful," he began. There were responding cheers. "But the reason that I invited you all over tonight has nothing to do with the show we just closed."

"You're pregnant," volunteered one of the students, giving rise to a bit of laughter. Everyone was far too interested in what Jim had to say by now, though, to pay attention to the heckler.

"I received a letter on Wednesday," Jim continued holding up a piece of paper. "I've talked it over with Dean Krannert and President Crowell to get their approval before I presented it to you. Here's what it says: 'Dear Prof. Richards, The Restoration Arts Festival has selected your production of *Hamlet* as a winner in its 1968-1969 Shakespeare contest.' By the way, none of us knew that this festival was judging our production," Jim added as an aside. "We don't know who entered us. 'As a winner, you are invited to join our American Shakespeare in Britain tour this summer. Your production will be one of six which will tour The Lake District of England in two shifts of three weeks each.' The rest of this just gives the details of the tour and how we can participate," Jim finished, folding the letter up. There was a moment of stunned silence as the cast let the message soak in. They would tour England with their production of *Hamlet*. The pop of the champagne cork brought them suddenly and loudly to life.

From there on, the party went wild. There was dancing, more food, and plenty of champagne as the cast members from the production of *Hamlet* gathered around Jim to discuss the details of the trip. According to Jim, the cost per participant would be approximately $750, but that the college president had agreed to go to work to raise funds to support the school's first international tour. If he was successful, the trip would be considerably less expensive. The important part was to get the commitment of the cast to undertake remounting the production and that meant rehearsing two productions simultaneously this spring. The excitement was high enough to carry the party well into the early morning hours.

BY THREE O'CLOCK, the general mood had quieted into mellow exhaustion. Some dancing occasionally still erupted when the Beatles were cranked up, but the casts sat in smaller circles talking and engaging the opposite sex in elaborate mating rituals. In one corner, strangely enough, Brian captured a group with a Ouija Board. The group intently concentrated on the messages that were spelled out in answer to their generally inane questions about the upcoming tour. A rather morbid fascination seemed to keep the small group growing. Wayne and Judith found themselves watching from the side as well. Judith was invited to use the board but declined with some comment about preferring not to leave her destiny in the hands of spirits.

"Ask if it has a special message for anyone here," Glenn suggested from the sidelines. They watched the scribe move to the yes mark. "Who?" he asked again. The group spelled out the letters one at a time. W-A-N-E. "Whoever this spirit is, it can't spell very well," Glenn laughed. "Come over here and get your message, Wayne." Wayne could see the set-up a mile away. With Brian on the board and Glenn asking the question, it was obvious that the pledge was going to get him back for the dirty trick with the gel. Well, Wayne was a sport. Might as well take what was coming to him.

"What message do these mighty and exalted spirits have for me?" he spoke in a mock religious tone. Once again, the group began to spell out the letters as the scribe moved. B-E-W-A-R-E-L-I-T-H-A. "Be warel it ha?" Wayne asked. "What's that supposed to mean?"

"Don't play dense," Glenn laughed "Beware Litha. Our thpirit hath a lithp. I know who Litha ith, and tho do you."

"You peckerhead," Wayne laughed and the two tussled good-naturedly. "You trying to get me into trouble?" He glanced over at Judith, but she was silently staring at the board, not noticing Wayne and Glenn's horseplay.

To JUDITH, LITHA had another meaning—Midsummer Eve, the shortest night of the year, the summer solstice. She looked at the young pledge happily playing with his toy and pleased for all the attention he was getting. No, he had just played along to set up Wayne in return for his trick earlier in the evening. It was nothing. Couldn't be.

"Hey sweetie, you okay?" Wayne asked her.

"Yeah, sure," she responded. "I'm beat, though. Want to take me home now?"

"Do I ever want to take you home," he said wrapping an arm around her. They gave their goodnights around the room and climbed onto the motorcycle in the chill March air. She hugged him closely as they traveled the few miles back to campus. Her hands slipped inside his jacket and stroked his chest. Wayne, however, was silent as they rode. They pulled up in front of the dorm and stood in the shadows outside before going in.

"What's on your mind?" she asked as they held each other in the chill morning air.

"I was just thinking about the tour and all," he said. "I can only afford one trip to England. If I go with you for spring break, I might not be able to go in June." She looked up at him in the darkness. The glint of a tear in her eye reflected the lamplight. He hung his head. "I'm sorry."

"Sure," she said. "I'll show you England in June." In the back of her mind was another image.

In June, at Litha.

7

Innocence Lost

Saturday, 8 March 1969, Indianapolis City University

WAYNE WAS puzzled. More than puzzled. He was a little pissed off. They were supposed to have a date. Judith canceled. She *said* she'd just started her period and felt crappy. Well, she'd certainly been acting crappy all week.

Not that he'd been great company to be around. There was all the excitement surrounding the cast being invited to England to perform, but people were just beginning to realize how much work was going to be involved. Wayne had to draw up plans for the set that the festival promised to replicate for them. They would take the props and costumes with them. Every prop and costume would have to be itemized for customs. Much of the work would be done while they were building and rehearsing *Antigone*. And Jim wanted to do that show with full masks. Carl, their technical consultant and designer, had already brought over a model of raked platforms for the set design. That was going to be a hassle to build, especially if Wayne was focused on mask-making.

Judith had walked with him to breakfast and classes, but had barely kissed him when they parted. In the evenings, he hadn't seen her at all. He missed the gentle camaraderie as well as her enthusiastic loving. Well, loving without actually going all the way, Wayne reminded himself.

Damn it! It wasn't his fault that he couldn't afford to fly to England with her for spring break. There was no way he could come up with that money and the money for the trip in June. Still… Maybe he should just do it anyway. He'd tell her he'd like to come with her and then let summer take care of itself.

WAYNE SHUT DOWN his motorcycle in the Donut World parking lot and headed inside. Lissa's back was to him and he took a moment to appreciate her *ass*ets. Sometimes she didn't look nearly as old as he thought she was. But, dammit, why was Judith being so standoffish after their beautiful time together last week. He'd never understand women.

"Why zee long face on my noble cavalier?" Lissa said without turning around. Wayne realized the back of the doughnut case was a mirror and she was watching him look at her rear. "Does monsieur not like what he sees?" So, this week she was a French courtesan? Unfortunately, Wayne's French accent sounded exactly like his English accent.

"Oh, monsieur likes very much," Wayne laughed. "But he is upset about his… how do you say?… mademoiselle."

"Heere. Have *café et un beignet* and tell Madame Leeza all about it," Lissa said, handing him a cup of coffee and creamers. She put his favorite old fashioned doughnuts next to the steamy drink.

"I don't know, Lissa. I can't seem to figure out what to do. I really love her and all, but we run hot and cold. At the moment, it looks like it's cold."

"Let me see if I can help," she said as she reached across the counter and touched the charm beneath Wayne's t-shirt. He stiffened slightly. "Relax and tell me what is really happening."

WAYNE KICKED THE motorcycle to life and felt its horsepower in his bloodstream. He was wide awake and knew exactly what he needed to do. He was careful driving down Shelby as there had been speed traps all along the way lately. He parked his bike at the dorm and ran in, scarcely acknowledging the monitor at the front desk. He ran to his room and grabbed his guitar. Everyone in the theatre played and sang, even though he was nowhere near as good as Glenn on the guitar. He knew the song he was going to play. He left by way of the back door. It was so weird that the women's side door was alarmed, but the men's wasn't. He ran around the back of the dorm and counted the windows. Third down from the corner.

It was dark.

Wayne scrabbled around on the ground until he found a handful of pea-sized pebbles and started tossing them at the window eight feet overhead. Not too hard. He didn't want to toss too hard and break anything, but he had to get them up there. The first pebble fell a foot short. He tossed the next one higher and it hit. Nothing happened. He kept tossing pebbles at the window, one after another, watching for a sign of life.

The curtain twitched.

Wayne dropped the pebbles and pulled his guitar around in front. The light didn't come on, but the curtain moved again and the window slid open.

"What are you doing?" Judith whispered out the open window. Wayne answered in song.

Yesterday, all my troubles seemed so far away.
Now it looks as though they're here to stay.
Oh, I believe in yesterday.

He strummed. He couldn't really do the riffs yet, but he'd learn them eventually. And he sang. He was no Paul McCartney, but it was such a simple, mournful tune that he didn't need to be a great singer. The window opened wider and Judith leaned out over the edge. Wayne finished the song, "Oh I believe in yesterday," and let the guitar trail of with a couple of hesitant chords. He stood there below her window looking up at Judith. She took a deep breath and he thought she was going to retreat.

"You idiot," she said softly. He realized she was crying.

"I'm sorry, Judith."

"How the hell are you going to get in here so I can fuck you senseless?"

"Stay right there! I'll find a way," he said. He spun back the way he'd come, then looked back. "Don't go away!"

"Where would I go, you beautiful man?"

Wayne ran down to the end of the building and realized he hadn't blocked the door open. It was locked tight.

"I need Glenn," he whispered. "By all the powers that be, I need Glenn here, now!" Glenn's window was on the third floor. There was no way to toss pebbles up that high.

A car careened around the corner into the parking lot and slid to a halt in the only remaining space. The door slammed and Wayne saw Glenn stumbling toward the side door. He ran to meet his friend.

"Wayne! Little buddy. I am so wasted. Can you get me into the dorm?"

"Glenn. Man! You shouldn't be driving in this condition."

"Couldn't help it. I was there and bed was here. Damn! That was some good shit."

"Amigo! I need your help. I need you to give me a boost into Judith's room."

"Sure… but what about me?"

"Jordan is at the front desk. He'll never look twice."

"Okay. But… I think I locked my keys in the car."

"Here. Take mine. Crash in my room. But first come and give me a boost."

"You're a real friend, Wayne. Did I ever tell you that?"

A minute later they were back under Judith's window.

"Are you still there?"

"I can't go anywhere."

"Rapunzel, Rapunzel, let down your hair."

"Idiot. My hair is six inches long."

"My buddy is six-and-a-half feet tall," Wayne said as he stood up on Glenn's shoulders. That got his chest above the window sill and Judith helped pull him into her room. He turned and waved to Glenn, who staggered off with Wayne's guitar toward the dorm's front entrance.

"JUDITH…" WAYNE HESITATED. He could feel his cock touching the moist warmth of her opening. "Honey… I've never actually done this before. Show me how to make love to you."

"Oh, babe. You've got a good start. Just push forward slowly. If you don't last the first time, I'll make sure you have lots more opportunities." Wayne slid into her, doing his best to hold back and worried that he would hurt her.

He didn't disgrace himself, but didn't last long enough to get Judith off the first time. The second was a different story. And the third.

"How did you know?" Judith whispered between kisses. They were naked in her narrow bed and he was sliding into her hot core again. Daylight was seeping through the curtains. "How did you know 'Yesterday' is my favorite Beatles song?"

"I just took a chance. Judith, I've missed you," he panted. "I think I've fallen in love with you. I'm so sorry I can't go with you next week."

"Shh. Hush, baby. Just make me feel how much you love me."

He pushed into her again and before long they were both convinced.

Thursday, 13 March 1969

THE WEEKEND TOGETHER changed them. They weren't swearing eternal faithfulness to each other, but holding hands as they crossed campus to class and stealing kisses in the shadows became second nature. And Judith began to open up to him about her life in England.

"I'm just going to buy a ticket and come with you. Hell with every-thing else," he declared Thursday night. There hadn't been a chance for a repeat of the events of the weekend and both were horny.

"You can't do that. It was a bad idea in the first place. I have to take care of some business that would keep me away all night at least once."

"Sounds like monkey-business. What keeps you out all night?"

"Darling, I belong to a group that meets just once every six or seven weeks. Lately, there have been no meetings and I've been here since September. I got a message that advised me to be present at the equinox. I don't know how many others will be able to make it."

"Do you always meet at celestial events?" Wayne asked. This reminded him of something in his uncle's book. He couldn't figure out why he could never recall things clearly when he talked to Judith. It was as if that part of his mind got shut off.

"You are a quick study, love, and so observant. We meet at a 'cirque of druid stones upon a forlorn moor.'"

"I'd like to meet your friends someday."

"Somehow, I have a premonition that you will."

Friday, 14 March 1969

On Friday afternoon, Wayne borrowed Glenn's car to drive Judith to the airport and see her off for the holiday. They walked into the terminal in near silence. Wayne thought she seemed totally preoc-cupied. Still, there was a sort of sadness in their parting that they couldn't deny. They walked to the gate where Judith checked in and received a boarding pass. Wayne was staring down the hallway when she returned to him.

"Damn!" he said and quickly turned away from the hall and embraced Judith.

"What is this all about?" she asked.

"Dr. Allen's coming down the hall," Wayne said. "You know, the one whose classes I slept through all last term. I don't ever want to meet her again." Judith looked down the hall to confirm that it was the illustrious Dr. Rebecca Allen, chair of the Sociology Department. She was check-ing in for the same flight, carrying her ever-present walking stick.

"Wouldn't you know it," she echoed Wayne in his ear. "We're going to be flying companions." She mashed her lips against Wayne's and kissed him passionately as Dr. Allen passed by.

When the boarding announcement came over the speakers, they finally broke the kiss.

"Well, I'd better go," Judith said. "Goodbye, lover." She kissed him soundly. "Don't get too involved with your doughnut lady late at night. I'm only going to be gone a week." She exited down the ramp and Wayne watched her cross the field to the plane.

He'd wait.

JUDITH SETTLED DOWN in a seat in the back of the plane and watched, unnoticed, as Dr. Allen boarded and sat in the bulkhead. If she was lucky they would not meet on this flight at least. She decided to change her ticket in Boston to avoid a meeting over the Atlantic. In the mean-time, she reached for her bag and pulled out the letter she received three weeks earlier.

Swordmaster
The Hart is moving. I trust you will not miss the hunt.
Blessings light and dark, The Barber.

Beneath the cryptic signature was the sigil of the High Priest of Carles.

Judith shuddered. The information was certainly correct. The Hart sat just twenty rows ahead of her as they flew east from Indiana. Why would The Barber be so interested in having Judith back for the event? If anything, her less than open-armed treatment of him over the past two years had alienated him. But she had, after all, inadvertently started this stupid hunt. Still, he gave her the creeps, inside the circle and out. He had designs, all right; and an idea that every woman in the circle should be part of his private harem. Possibly the men, too. It disturbed her further that he knew where she was and how to reach her. She hadn't even told her mother where she'd be.

She put the letter back in her bag and settled back to sleep as much as possible before she arrived in England.

REBECCA ALLEN WAS, indeed, journeying to the stone circle called Carles Castlerigg, but she had no intentions of calling the *cildru*, or coven members. She would talk to the High Priestess and have herself released from this task. Something malevolent hung in the air about the whole thing. Since Samhain, her rituals were disquieted, and there was the discreet warning to her, concealed as it was in a student's term paper.

She was sure that came from one of her coven sisters or brothers. After that, her Yule ritual had seemed empty, even as she acknowledged the end of the sun's downward journey and its impending return. At Imbolc, when she attempted to truly raise power for the first time in fifteen years, she was answered with cold silence. Now she was only thirteen weeks from the required completion of her task and she was no further than when she began. Rebecca was going to her priestess to confess her impotence and to resign her task.

She fought back tears as the BOAC Boeing 707 jet soared above the Atlantic. Resigning a task of the circle was no simple matter of saying that she quit. For all her reluctance to raise power in her rituals, Rebecca had built a life around the simple pagan festivals into which she had been initiated when a young woman. They fed her with hope and faith. They supported her through a world of trials. And she believed them.

At one time, she had experienced massive surges of power, had called down fire, had healed, and had let that power control her in an unexpected sealing of her husband's fate. She swore to herself that she would not raise that kind of power again. And now when she had need of it, she found that she *could not* raise the power.

On Oester evening, when dark and light were equal, she would walk as a solitary to the great stone circle. There, she would lay down her staff, her knife, her cup, and her pentacles. She would bring the one tool of Cobhan Carles that she did have, the Cup—Cottus, the Third Face of Carles—to the center of the circle and drain its salty water on the ground. She would remove her ritual robe, the robe of her quest, and lay it with the other artifacts. Last, she would lay the string, the measure of her height, heart, and head, marked with a drop of her own blood, in the center of the pile. And naked, as she had first entered the circle, she would leave through the great northern gate, never to return.

Rebecca wept silently, even in her sleep, until the jet landed in London.

Saturday, 15 March 1969, The Lake District, England

JUDITH SLID THE key into the latch of her cottage near Thirlmere Lake in Northern England. She had hoped to be home for Yule, but because of her unexpected attachment to Wayne Hamel, had spent the holiday in a cheap motel room waiting for the dormitories to re-open. She had to admit, it had been worth the wait, but it was still good to be home.

Her hand froze as the door moved unexpectedly, opening a crack. It was unlocked, and as Judith listened, she could hear voices coming from inside.

"This is my daughter's cottage," said the first. "She's away, following her own quest. I'm sure she would not mind that you stayed here."

"Thank you," said the second. "But after I have finished my Oester ritual, I fear that no one in this valley will welcome me again."

"I beg you," said Judith's mother. "Reconsider what you are doing. Go to the circle if you must, but use its power to augment your own. Call the tools from there. It is their home. Daughter of my heart, please don't resign your task."

Judith winced at the endearment and fought her own tears back. Twice her mother had placed Rebecca Allen ahead of their own relationship, and this time had opened Judith's own home to her. She paused, poised between the desire to break in and declare herself, chase them both out of her home, and the desire to run away and never come back. Eventually the remainder of what was being said also sank in.

"I simply don't have the power," Rebecca was saying. "It would be better for the circle to go on without me."

"You don't know what it means to all of us," Judith's mother continued. "Cobhan Carles is slowly disintegrating. There has been an underlying power struggle for five years now, ever since The Barber became high priest. If he consolidates his power, the coven will disintegrate. If you can bring the tools back to the circle, you will break his power and unite us with a spirit of love and commitment. I didn't want this task placed on you. I thought that the time would come when my daughter would take the task on herself and lead the coven. But for all her independence, she is too young. It wasn't a kindness to you to choose you as my successor, but I can't stand the thought of her testing her strength against The Barber's."

"For your sake, I'll try," Rebecca finished.

And so will I, Judith thought, surprising herself at her defense of the mother that had slighted her. *I'll be damned if you'll let my mother down now. And I'll be damned if you stand in that circle alone on Oester night.*

She turned from the door and made her way back toward town. So, what's one more holiday in a hotel room?

Thursday, 20 March 1969

EQUINOX NIGHT WAS crisp and clear in northern England. There would likely be a frost on the ground by morning. Rebecca shivered at the thought as she drove slowly down the narrow lane approaching Castlerigg stone circle. She remembered her first trip here, bouncing along in a bus that was almost too wide for the track fourteen years ago. It had been as if the earth shifted.

Tuesday, 21 June 1955

She was in a trance, the bus fumes, motion sickness, Mrs. Weed's perfume, the power she felt when she entered the stone circle in the company of the tourists, had all combined to leave her disoriented. She followed Mrs. Weed like a lamb to the creek and found herself swimming naked there with the old lady. Rebecca had studied occult societies while working on her thesis. She had been told she would be contacted in Edinburgh, but hadn't expected her sightseeing tour to be interrupted.

Mrs. Weed looped a soft rope around Rebecca's right wrist and left ankle, loose enough to walk, but not so long as to trip her. "Thus are all brought to stand before the mighty ones," Mrs. Weed said.

The bus and their fellow tourists had long since gone. The July night was warm against Rebecca's bare skin. As they walked up the hill she could see the stones silhouetted against firelight and the figures of people dancing. It was her first experience of Litha. She passed between two stones on the north side of the circle and a man with a black hood stepped in front of her pressing a long-bladed knife between her breasts. Her heart stopped in panic and she began to retreat, but Mrs. Weed was behind her.

"Who comes to the gate?" demanded the guardian.

Not an assault, Rebecca reminded herself. It was ritual. Perhaps the hood over his face prevented him from seeing her naked in front of him, but she had no difficulty seeing him as he was naked below the hood.

"It is I, The Hart, a child of earth and starry heaven," Rebecca said. Her voice quaked. The noise of her heart in her ears almost drowned his next words.

"Who speaks for you?"

"It is I, The Water Maiden of Carles, who vouches for her," said Rebecca's companion. The challenge, however, was not yet over and the sword's point nearly forced Rebecca back a step.

"You are about to enter a vortex of power, a place beyond imagining, where birth and death, dark and light, joy and pain, meet and make one. You are about to step between the worlds, beyond time, outside the realm of your human life. You who stand on the threshold of the dread Mighty Ones, have you the courage to make the assay? For know that it is better to fall on my blade and perish than to make the attempt with fear in thy heart!"

In spite of the ritual phrasing, Rebecca felt the guardian was in deadly earnest. But this was what she had been seeking. It was part of the purpose for her visit to England and Scotland. This was who she was meant to be.

"I enter the circle with perfect love and perfect trust," she intoned with her head held high. Her subtle straightening pressed the knife more firmly between her breasts and she could feel a drop of blood trickle down her abdomen.

"Gatekeeper!" a voice beyond the man snapped. He turned to face the woman who wore only a crescent moon-shaped headdress. Rebecca gasped as his hand darted out and the point of the knife pricked the skin between the priestess's breasts before he stepped away. The priestess stepped forward and embraced Rebecca, mingling the blood between them.

"My blood in your veins and your blood in mine make you ever inseparable as you are bound to us. Welcome to Cobhan Carles. Tonight will be your initiation."

Thursday, 20 March 1969

FOURTEEN YEARS LATER, Rebecca dressed in her deep red ritual robe before leaving the cottage, convinced it would be her last visit to the sacred circle. It was all she wore and her bare toes curled around the pedals of the little car. In her satchel were the things she needed—her sacred tools, a small kettle, water, dry wood and leaves gathered that afternoon. On the car seat, there was a change of clothes—just in case she left the circle naked.

She stepped out beneath the quiet starlit sky. A scarce sliver of the new moon hung low in the west. It was so dark out that Rebecca could barely discern the shadows of the great stones as she climbed the fence and made her way in their general direction. She was in the circle before she realized it.

Standing alone in this ancient shrine was unlike joining her brothers and sisters here. It took on a feeling of vastness, like standing on a mountaintop. She could faintly see the shapes of the stones around her and they were more like the living beings of the legends than their monolithic counterparts. Yes, what Keats had said about the circle was true.

Scarce images of life, one here one there,
Lay vast and edgeways; like a dismal cirque
Of Druid stones, upon a forlorn moor...

The Titans surrounded her, waiting for her to awaken them.

Rebecca shuddered, feeling the living presence of ancient powers within the circle. She hurriedly set up a small brazier and lit the kindling in it. On this she placed her kettle and filled it with water. She began a long sweeping invocation to the powers of Carles, beginning by standing facing east, her walking stick outstretched as she summoned her wards.

"Eastern Guardian, Titan Creüs, power of the air, arise. Arise, I bid you come and set your watch on this the eastern quarter of my circle. Let no ill influence pass your gaze, but like the stones of this sanctuary, surround me with your presence."

The hardest part of ritual magic was giving voice to the words. It was like talking to herself loudly—embarrassed to be making statements to the empty air. But the words could not be mumbled and expect any true raising of power. And she was alone, so who was to tell her that she couldn't speak to the empty circle.

She took a deep breath and continued a clockwise rotation, her staff outstretched, her eyes focused inward, summoning the powers of each of the quarters as she passed. Creüs, Iäpetus, Cottus, Enceladus. At last she faced east once more.

"O Goddess, be with me now in your aspect as Maiden of the forest—the fair one who brings joy and new life—to break the winter's stillness and silence." There was an almost imperceptible stirring in the eastern quarter of her circle. A stone that seemed to move slightly in the breeze. Rebecca continued. "O laughing God of the Greenwood with your pipes and cloven hooves—shepherd of creatures free and wild—come nearby, and with your warmth let life be born anew."

Rebecca stared eastward across her cauldron and was more certain than ever that something moved and took shape in the shadows of the great stones. She began to hum, an old habit from her childhood that cropped up from time to time. She swayed before her cauldron, focusing on the shape, willing it to materialize and come forward. It did, with wand outstretched, swaying as she walked—a perfect mirror of Rebecca seen across the fire.

A moment of doubt sent chills down her spine. This was a deserted moor, a mile from help, and Rebecca was alone to face whatever had materialized in her circle. But the thought was suddenly comforting as well. This was her circle, protected from malevolent forces by the very presence of the stones and her invocation. Her breathing calmed. She would accept the visitor as part of her ritual.

Rebecca stretched a closed hand above the fire and opened it to deposit her handful of leaves in the heated kettle. The figure opposite, shrouded in a red robe matching Rebecca's, mimicked the gesture, dropping a handful of leaves in the cauldron. Yes, Rebecca thought. This is a co-celebrant at least, perhaps the goddess herself. All things are possible. She bowed to the apparition and the being returned the gesture.

"May the strength of the old enter into the new and life arise once more. O Great Ones of the forest, make this potion strong and giving of new life," Rebecca chanted over the brewing mixture.

"So mote it be," responded the figure from the opposite side. Yes, a woman, Rebecca thought to herself in confirmation. Not unlike the High Priestess. That must be it. She opened her mouth to call her by name but was motioned to silence by the figure before the syllable had been emitted. Rebecca bowed. Her priestess was to be trusted.

The two began to dance, slowly at first, then faster and faster around the brazier opposite each other. Rebecca kept trying to catch a glimpse of the face of her companion, but darkness ruled and only the shape was visible, carefully beyond the range of firelight. Soon, both were too enrapt in their dancing to strain for any other contact. They laughed and sang wordlessly. As they neared exhaustion, both collapsed to the ground with a shout.

Rebecca, now fully The Huntress of Carles, The Hart, could feel the infinite surges of power returning to her over the vast distance she had placed between it and herself. She was caught in the feeling. She had danced for power before, spun the cone of it over her head and called fire into her wand. She tasted the power as it returned into her once more. Perhaps there was a chance that she could recall the tools after all.

When Rebecca looked up from her reverie, her co-celebrant was removing the pot carefully from the brazier and pouring cups of the tea to share. Then she stepped back to wait patiently as they sipped the heady potion. How would she begin to call together the Four Faces of Carles?

Rebecca removed the silver chalice from her bag and set it near the brazier. She did not fill it with its accustomed salt water. If she was to call together the Four Faces of Carles, she would begin by calling them to life. For the first time since this task had fallen to her, she felt capable. She was being fed energy from her companion, stoking the fires within her. She would begin by requiring that the cup fill itself. Then that the fire wand, Iäpetus, would spark. Then she would call for the pentacles, Enceladus, to shake the earth. Finally, she would stretch out and call Creüs, the *Athamé* of the circle to raise the winds. Wherever it was, even if beneath the sea, he would be blown toward her.

Her partner in the circle seemed to understand what was required and Rebecca did not speak to her as they began raising a cone of power around the cup. For the first time, they touched, and Rebecca knew that whoever had joined her in this circle was skilled and powerful, and that she was lending that power to Rebecca to reinforce her. Soon they would know if that power—even combined—was enough.

8
A Little Wind

Thursday, 20 March 1969, Indianapolis City College

HALF A world away, Wayne Hamel was watching the sunset from the school park in Indianapolis. It had rained most of the day as it usually did in March in Indiana, but the evening sky had cleared and he determined to go through with his experiment in spite of the wet ground.

He'd been to see Lissa last night... well, this morning would be more accurate. Somehow, he never showed up at Donut World before three a.m. She always had advice for him, even though he never actually remembered talking about the things that he remembered later.

HE SAT CHATTING with her—the friendly banter they'd had every night this week. He'd decided to stay on campus instead of going north to visit his family during the break. Last week, Carl had brought over the concept sketches for Antigone to show Jim and Wayne had impulsively volunteered to make the Greek masks. That kept him busy in the shop each day and let him watch daily for intruders. He'd been leaving the shop about two in the morning all week and heading to see Lissa. He kept telling himself he'd get up earlier, but always slept past noon. It seemed he stayed at Donut World for hours.

Lissa set a cup of coffee in front of him with a couple of doughnuts. Then casually reached across the counter and touched the pentacles at his throat. Wayne entered a different world. He could suddenly remember everything he'd been taught—every word he'd read.

"Why is it that I always have this feeling that I should be remembering something but can't figure out what it is?" Wayne asked. "Like my pentacles. Until you touch it, I forget it's there. Then all of a sudden, I remember everything."

"You have it all down inside. Don't worry. You practiced setting wards, right?" Lissa asked.

"Yeah. I'm sure I got the words right and everything, but I can't feel anything. I could just walk right through them."

"Don't. You need to believe in them. If you *believe* you can't walk through them, then no one else can either. Even if you don't have confidence in them yet, you still respect them and practice them. The Zen masters say it takes a thousand repetitions to make something a part of you."

"I've got a few dozen to go," Wayne laughed. "What is next?"

"I think it's time you tried it out," Lissa said. "You need to perform a ritual. And Oester, the spring equinox is a perfect time to do it. I've written you a simple wind ritual."

"Sure," he said. "I just go out under the next full moon and dance naked around a fire and see if I blow up a storm. If it's a tornado, I know it worked."

"Mind if I watch?" she said with a wink.

"I never dance naked in front of strangers," he smiled.

"Might have to sometime. The secret is to focus on the ritual. It isn't about the nudity, it's about *being* The Unbound," Lissa said. "And you shouldn't wait for a full moon. Tonight is the Vernal Equinox. It's the perfect time to engage in some playful ritual. Do you have a place to do it?"

"I suppose I could go out in the school park. The gate is locked at sunset if they remembered to unlock it that day at all. I happen to have a key. I go out there sometimes when I really want to be alone in the city."

"Okay," Lissa instructed him. "You are going to have a day of intense clarity. Memorize this ritual, take your tools out into the park at sunset, and try it out. Don't try for something too big, just make it your own."

"Won't you come with me?" Wayne asked.

"You are a solitary, not part of a circle. You need to work alone before you begin working with others. I'm just a teacher. Now it is time for you to practice what you've learned."

"If you think so."

"Go get some sleep," she said, touching the necklace again. "Tomorrow it will be clear."

He was getting the slightly muzzy-headed feeling of having been sleeping at the counter again. "Well, I better get some sleep," he said turning to leave.

"I'll see you tonight," Lissa said. How did she know he'd be back tonight?

Now Wayne sat overlooking the small outdoor amphitheater that in years past had been used for theatrical performances. That was why he had a key to the gate on the theatre key ring. It had been an incredible day—well, afternoon. He still didn't wake up until almost noon, but when he did, he knew exactly what he had to do. He cast a circle in his dorm room, donned his black robe, and retrieved his uncle's Book of Shadows. The first time he read through the simple ritual in his hand, he remembered a similar ritual in the book. He found the reference and instead of memorizing from the slip of paper, he memorized from the book. He liked this one better. It appealed to his sense of theatre. He memorized the lines and blocked the scene in his room as if he were going on-stage.

He had added some of his own touches and wrote them in the little journal that he now considered his own *Book of Shadows*. It included stripping down to his skivvies and then pulling the black robe over his head. The ground was wet beneath his bare feet and squished with each step, but he didn't find it unpleasant. Almost as an afterthought, he slipped out of his underwear as well and added it to the pile of clothing in his knapsack. Now he was truly 'unbound'. He would feel like a fool if anyone saw him like this and was glad he had locked the gate of the park behind him when he came in.

Dressed in the black robe, he experienced the feeling that Bert had described as having his body disappear in the lengthening shadows of dusk, especially when he pulled the cowl up over his head. Finally, he pulled a small dish with incense in it from his bag and the burlap and silk wrapped shape of the knife his uncle had given him. He lit the incense and held the knife hesitantly in his hand. He was ready to begin. In his mind, he imagined a curtain going up and himself lit on stage. It was just like a private rehearsal. He had done it a hundred times. He shook off his stage fright and proceeded.

First, draw a circle to stand in, he thought. All these rituals were done in a circle, it seemed. As an afterthought, he remembered his uncle's secret cavern with its white star on the floor. He drew a five-pointed star in the center of his circle. He set his wards in the way he'd practiced dozens of times in his room. Even though he couldn't feel them, he'd never been interrupted. The curtain was rising. It was time to begin. He cleared his throat, but the first words of his chant almost choked him anyway. He coughed again, scowled at his own shakiness and started over.

Winds of the east, winds of the west, winds of the north and south:
I summon you to meet me here and dance around about.

Ring my circle. Ring my fire.
Dance a dance as I desire.

An unnatural stillness settled over the clearing. Wayne breathed deeply of the heavy air and then decided to keep going.

Hern, the god of woodland fair;
Ariel, goddess of the air.
Move the currents, make them dance.
Fill the air with sprite romance.

The invocation was almost sung. It was a damned good thing Wayne was trained in theatre. He could never have voiced these words if he weren't used to rehearsing and performing.

At the edge of Wayne's vision, there was movement in the shadows. A shape seemed to emerge to his right that seemed human but had unmistakable horns on its head. Or maybe it was a bush and a tree-limb. Wayne looked the other way and a diaphanous mist crowned by the crescent moon low in the sky shifted and gave Wayne the feeling of a person taking shape. He almost ran, but then centered himself. After all, he called them. They should appear if any of this worked. He just wasn't expecting it to be so literal.

He began circling his little pot of incense and chanting the words over again. Now he could feel palpable movement in the air. He found a rhythm to the words he had memorized and practiced during the day. They moved his feet as he chanted them now and he began to spin as he circled the incense. His right hand, still holding the knife, raised in the air of its own volition as he spun, pointing his left hand down toward the damp grass beneath him. He was as much caught up in the chant and dancing as he was directing it.

The shapes he had summoned were caught up in the dance as well, and though they stayed outside the circle he had drawn, he could see them clearly—two robed figures, red and green. The one dressed in green wore a headdress decked with the horns of a stag. The other, obviously female beneath her crimson robe was crowned with a crescent moon on her head. The two were not, however, focused on Wayne. He could feel a tension building between the two and lances of light seemed to shoot from one to the other, deflected and piercing the night sky. Even when Wayne collapsed on the ground exhausted from his dancing, the two continued to circle him, locked in their own combat.

His head kept spinning as well. The point of the knife that he held in his right hand continued to circle in front of his eyes, and to Wayne's affected sight, it looked like it was glowing. In fact, if it weren't for the witness of his hand holding it, he would swear it was glowing hot. His hand jerked involuntarily as the sense of touch caught up with the sense of sight and he realized he was holding a red-hot brand. It flew from his hand straight up in the air, turned twice at the peak of its flight and came hurtling straight down. Wayne stepped aside just in time. The missile stabbed point first into the ground at his feet.

Thursday, 20 March 1969, The Lake District, England

FOUR THOUSAND MILES away and six hours ahead, Rebecca picked herself up again. Her companion rose slowly. A shake of her head showed Rebecca blonde hair, but she quickly adjusted the hooded mask she wore. It was not the High Priestess. This naked woman was young—possibly younger than Rebecca. But she was giving great power to the ritual. Rebecca had stripped her own robe off after the sudden downpour had drenched her. When she finished the chant summoning Cottus to fill his cup and summon his brothers to the feast, the clouds burst without warning. Both women were knocked to the ground with the suddenness of the drenching rain. The cup had filled and the rain was gone.

The women had extended their wands toward the fire—Rebecca's red walking stick, and the other's short black wand. They moved together around the fire as Rebecca chanted the names of fire-gods and angels, summoning Iäpetus to bring fire and invite his brothers to the feast. The flames began to climb higher and the two moved back from them, keeping their focus until Rebecca shouted, "Iäpetus, come to me!" Lightning struck so suddenly and so near that the women were thrown twenty feet back from the fire that flared high into the night sky connecting heaven and earth. Witch's fire.

Enceladus shook the earth, throwing the women to the ground a third time when Rebecca summoned the powers of the north, the earth, the Fourth Face of Carles, the pentacles.

Both women were panting as they stood for the final summoning. This needed more. This needed all they could give. Rebecca moved to her right around the fire wordlessly chanting. There was only one way to get this degree of power. The other sensed her intent and backed away. After a moment, her red robe dropped to the ground revealing the small blonde woman, The Swordmaster who had challenged The Hart at Litha last year. This was the woman who had stood before the coven and required that The Hart show her power before she inherited the mantle of high priestess. And now she was here.

No. It had not been she who had shaped the challenge into summoning the Four Faces together. That had been the conniving high priest, known as The Barber. But it was this woman's fault. Now she was here in the circle lending The Hart her power. Could she be trusted?

Fully The Huntress, Rebecca closed the distance between them as they completed a full circuit around the fire, eyes locked on each other. The Huntress held out her left hand and pricked it with her *Athamé*, daring The Swordmaster to join it with her own. The Swordmaster grimaced as she pricked her own palm and reached to grasp The Hungress's. Steel flashed in the firelight. The Huntress's knife was met in the air by that of The Swordmaster.

"I am Sadb, the transformation," Rebecca whispered. "Your blood runs in my veins. My blood in yours."

"I am Badb, the cry of battle," her partner whispered. "We are bound to each other. We are one in the fight."

It was a dangerous game—a play for dominance—and Rebecca refused to submit. They moved faster and faster contretemps around the fire, pushing each other away and drawing each other back, their knives sparking against each other as their left hands gripped each other painfully, the blood mixing in their palms. Thrust, parry, counter. Their dance flowed as a mystery, steps advanced and reflected as they moved. An observer, had there been one, would not be able to tell if they were dancing, fighting, or making love. In fact, it was all three. Rebecca's left hand found her partner's sex and dipped within her. She could feel the response in her own womb as The Swordmaster plundered her with her fingers.

"Creüs!" Rebecca screamed. The other echoed her call an instant behind. "Windmaster. Spirit. Air. Archangel Michael. Dhritarashtra. Gandharvas. Awaken Titan! Awaken and let your presence be known. Your power. Your majesty. Master of the spring, of love, of fertility. Come to me, Creüs, the First Face of Carles!" The women were intent on each other, drawing closer and closer as they danced—their hands and knives touching, their breasts pressed together, their mounds with hands trapped between dripping with sexual passion, and finally their lips. Their knife hands stretched skyward together as they fell to the ground.

Soon after her initiation Rebecca had let the passion of ritual sex control her and light the sky on fire. Now she let the passion rule the wind. And both women climaxed.

Thursday, 20 March 1969, Indianapolis City University

THE WET GRASS hissed when the blade struck it a foot in front of Wayne. Steam rose in swirls around the knife widening out from its point in the ground. The swirls connected themselves together around the vortex of the circle in the school park and continued spinning their way upward as Wayne watched in awed wonder at the spectacle. The two figures stopped their combative dance to watch the swirling currents in their midst. They fell back, then turned and ran.

Wayne was laughing. He couldn't help himself. It was working. A wind was rising in circles around him. It worked!

He raised his head to follow the path of the little wind upward and gasped at what he saw. As lightning played across the sky, he saw billowing clouds of two weather fronts colliding above him. He saw a distant reflection on a much grander scale of what was happening on the ground. As the fronts boiled together, the swirl of clouds took on shape and sound. A roar of wind shook the park as an unmistakable funnel dropped out of the sky.

Wayne stood in shock as he watched the tornado rip out of the sky turning everything black around him. A tree cracked not a hundred yards away, drawing Wayne's attention. Bearing down on him out of the insane blackness was another black form, striking him, bearing him backward and down as the wind howled overhead and Wayne lost consciousness.

When he awoke, he was soaking wet. There was still a wind, but it was not nearly so dark. Sirens in the distance still wailed the tornado warning, but they were mixed with another sound, a chant picking up the wailing notes and turning them into words. He opened his eyes and saw the dark figure standing above him. Its hands were raised to the sky and as the chant continued, the wind died down, or moved on. The stillness that Wayne had felt a bit ago was returning, broken only by large drops of rain falling in his face. At last the figure turned and faced Wayne.

"Where is your mistress?" the figure asked. Wayne stared.

"My what?"

"Your girlfriend. The one you told me about on the mountain."

"Uncle…?"

"Names!"

"Bound One?"

"Where is your mistress?"

"In England." What was Uncle Bert doing out here? This was too bizarre.

"Workings of the circle, I suppose," the old man said and pushed back the cowl of his robe. "What in the name of all the powers were you trying to do here? This is hardly an equinox ritual."

"I just wanted to see if it worked. The things in your book, I mean," Wayne answered.

"And?"

"It works."

"More violently in your hands than I've ever seen it work before, in fact," his uncle affirmed. "Couldn't you have started with something simple?"

"I thought this was. Just a little wind."

"Read in the newspapers tomorrow how little the wind was."

"It had to have been a coincidence. I couldn't have done that."

"In other words, you're still not convinced and will come out here and risk your life and many others lives as well by trying it out again. And if there is another coincidence?"

"I guess it works."

"It may not be my place, boy, but let me give you some advice." His uncle reached beneath the robe and pulled out a wallet. From this he extracted three dollars. "Here. Go see a movie."

"What movie?" Wayne asked.

"*Fantasia,*" his uncle answered emphatically.

"I've seen that." Wayne answered.

"This time pay attention," his uncle said. He turned and walked away.

"But, wait. Why are you here? Where are you going?" Wayne was following his uncle into the wooded park, but he had lost sight of him completely. "I don't understand," he said weakly and then returned to his circle, collected his clothes and knife, and left. The incense burner he couldn't find. It must have been blown away.

Slowly he made his way back to the dormitory shaking his head. He couldn't understand why his uncle would suddenly appear and then disappear as quickly. And who else had joined him tonight then run away?

A DARK FIGURE stood quietly amidst the wreckage of the scene shop at ICU. It was to have been a simple and quiet feeding, but sudden chaos had broken out and he barely escaped without injury. This was the strongest crossing of ley lines in the area, but the power outside had drawn his passenger. It was more power than even he could bear.

He had learned how to slip past the campus security guards after his first narrow escape. He could now walk in darkness until he was securely inside the shop. This spot lay directly below the rooftop sanctuary that The Huntress had created for herself. He had fed from her rituals at both Yule and Imbolc drawing the power out of them and into himself. He'd been sure he could draw the Oester power directly from the bedrock that lay four floors below her circle.

The experience had been less than satisfactory. Someone interfered and nearly killed him. He had carefully sketched out his circle on the concrete floor, set his wards, and begun the feeding ritual. It would solidify his power if it were he, and not The Huntress, who brought the tools back to Carles. He knew he would need to re-forge the knife, but he could use her for that as well.

His feeding ritual had been going well until the wind began.

He ignored it at first, but it gradually dawned on him that there should be no wind in the basement where he had set up his ritual. His mind was drawn by a different summoning and soon he found himself outside the circle of a solitary witch summoning wind. He raised his hand to quell the intrusive spell, but was suddenly confronted by another being defending the boy-witch. And she was powerful. They were locked in a contest of wills until the wind rose so strong that it blew them away from each other.

Back in the scene shop, tools, wood scraps, and props blew around him in a vortex, taxing all his strength to avoid injury. Then it all went silent. Spinning scenery dropped suddenly to the floor, leaving wreckage all over the scene shop.

Well, too bad for the ones who would have to clean it up. He couldn't spare thought for the mess. He dismissed his circle and rubbed out the chalk markings on the floor where he could reach them. Who were the other powers he encountered? Could it be The Huntress who came to the defense of a new protégé? The Swordmaster? This complicated matters. The High Priest of Coven Carles would not tolerate complications to his plans. He had paid too dear a price already for the power that rode within him.

Friday, 21 March 1969

"Jim, you are not going to believe this. And I guarantee you won't like it."

"Get to the point, Wayne."

"We were hit again. And it was no innocent poke a head into the shop. We were ransacked."

It was two o'clock Friday afternoon. After his adventure last night, he'd gone back to his room. He was so tired that he passed out on his bed, still wearing his black robe. He hadn't woken up until noon.

By then, the entire adventure had become dreamlike. He couldn't believe he'd tried to go to the park in the middle of a tornado. He'd passed out somewhere along the way. When he came to, he was drenched to the skin. He dragged himself back to the dorm and went to his room. When he woke up, he looked at himself in the mirror to see if he had a visible knot on his head. He must have been hit by something, but there was no mark or sore spot. Then when he'd showered and left the dorm to get food, he found his bike tipped over. There was a gouge in the paint and gas all over the pavement. A tree limb lay across the two cars on either side of the bike. He guessed he was lucky, but it took a while to get the bike cleaned up, drained, and refueled. Then he'd driven to the Dutch Oven for breakfast. He couldn't help himself. He was hungry and there was a waitress at the restaurant whose peasant blouse was fuller than her breasts. When she bent over to serve him, which she always did slowly and deliberately, he had a view of uncharted hills and valleys. She had an innie. He'd had a couple extra cups of coffee and finally made it back to the shop at two.

What a mess. Where there were downed tree limbs and power lines outside, inside the shop looked just as bad. He'd taken one look and went for a pay phone to call his professor.

JIM WASN'T HAPPY.

President Crowell wasn't happy.

Wayne wasn't happy.

After the police and an insurance adjuster left, Jim sat Wayne down.

"I thought you worked at night. You didn't see anything?"

"I've been working on these fucking masks all week. I decided I needed a night off. I went out to dinner and then got caught in the storm. Now they're all ruined." That was pretty near to what happened. He thought there was something else he should remember about the storm, but sitting there with Jim, that was really all he could recall. He was still holding one of the damaged masks in his hands. Maybe he could fix it.

"Let's go have dinner. My treat. It's almost seven and I'm famished."

"Sure."

Jim drove Wayne over to the Ponderosa Steak House and encouraged him to order a big New York Strip. Wayne piled his plate high at the salad bar. He hadn't seen a fresh vegetable all week. It was nice of Jim to take him to dinner, even though so much of his work had been destroyed by the vandal.

"Dean Krannert wants you to have a psychological evaluation," Jim said. Wayne looked at him trying to figure out what he was talking about. "Fuck, Wayne. You're the most talented props master I've ever seen. If the stress is too much, you've got to tell me."

"What? Are you saying I'm a suspect?" Wayne couldn't believe what he was hearing.

"Not until today. Frankly, I don't see any sign that you could be, but Krannert has been trying to close down the theatre program ever since I got here. He says you are the only one with access twenty-four hours a day. He wants to pin the whole thing on the instability of theatre students."

"Shit," Wayne laughed. "That is really rich. You know those people on campus who have drugs get them from the Psychology Department? It's kind of scary to think the mental health of our country is dependent on Psych majors." Jim joined the laughter.

"I'm glad you've still got a sense of humor."

"Don't let it hide the fact that I'm pissed," Wayne said. "But I'll take whatever tests Kranny wants me to. I just wish they'd put some security on that actually guards the building. That dude out in the box keeps his binoculars trained on the women's dorm most of the time."

"You know that for a fact?"

"All you have to do is look. Anybody could get into the building if they have a key."

"Which reminds me…"

"All my keys are for the interior of the building. I have to go get the guard to let me in if it's locked."

"I had to ask."

"Yeah. Do you mind if I wait till tomorrow to start cleaning up down there? I don't think I could handle it right now."

"Wait till Monday when you can draft some help. But let me see that mask you're still carrying." Wayne handed the mask over to Jim. "Don't throw any of these away or try to mend them. Which is this?"

"Tiresias."

"I want to show this to Carl. It's given me an idea. If you don't start clean-up until Monday, what are you going to do?"

"I think I'll take a run home tomorrow. I'd thought of doing that anyway. You know, it isn't good to keep the parents wondering what you're doing on spring break."

"Lissa, what happened to this place? Why is the front window boarded up?"

"Well, sugah, that was the best we could do on the day after the storm." She looked at him strangely. "Are you okay? I've never seen anything quite like that."

"Yeah. I'm fine. I don't know why, but I feel like I should be apologizing to you."

"Come heah and have a cup o' coffee. I don't expect anyone else in tonight. In fact, Gus doesn't even know I opened up." Wayne looked at the shelves of doughnuts. There was only one kind—his favorite chocolate frosted old fashioneds. There was only a dozen of them.

Lissa walked around the counter and locked the door, closing the blinds on the door.

"What's going on?"

"I only opened so I could talk to you." She walked straight up to Wayne and hugged him. "I'm so glad you are all right."

"But…" She touched his pentacles. "Oh." There was a moment of disorientation as memories flooded back in on him. Then he hugged Lissa back. "That was me?"

"Yes," she said. "Now let's see if we can figure out what happened in the woods. I was only there in spirit."

"Well, the spirits that were there sure seemed to be real. Who was the other guy?"

"I'd like to know. He was only there in spirit as well—as if you'd summoned him."

"And then my…"

"Who else showed up?"

"I can't say, but it wasn't me that stopped the storm, or released the spell. Then he just disappeared, too, and I was alone picking things up in the park and walking back to the dorm. Why could I see and interact with all these 'spirits' when I was real?"

"Well, we were 'real', too. But we were all interacting on the spirit plane. It seems that you were in both. That is… strange."

"You're telling me. Then to find out today that the shop was totally wrecked last night by the damned intruder…"

"Wrecked how?"

"Looked like a torna-… Shit!"

"Oh dear."

"Do you think I did that?"

"Mmm. Probably your power, but it wasn't you in the shop. That settles one thing, though. Your intruder is a powerful practitioner."

"Dean Krannert wants me to take some kind of psychological test to see if I'm cracked up and some kind of psycho."

"I think we need to give you some protection so that you don't reveal anything that might make them suspicious."

"You can do that?"

"It's not easy, but if you want to try, I'll work with you."

"I think I need all the help I can get."

9
Special Delivery

Thursday, 3 April 1969

REBECCA HART Allen, PhD, Professor of Sociology. The name was on the door in bold black letters. Wayne could no longer delay the dreaded meeting. He had not been Dr. Allen's favorite student last term and he found that genuinely regrettable. His grade point average showed as much. At least he didn't have to base his chances for graduate school on that single pass/fail class. He was generally a good student and enjoyed school, which was unusual for people in theatre. But it hadn't shown in Dr. Allen's class.

Neither was his poor performance her fault. He slept through her classes. He deserved less than he got. She kept her end of the bargain, even though she said it was fraudulent research. He passed. Never again would he schedule a seven-thirty a.m. class. Sometimes theatre and school just didn't mix.

He wouldn't be in front of her door if it weren't for the added work-study he'd been granted to help him earn money for the summer trip to England. Next fall they would pay him for his work as theatre technical director. This spring, however, he was nothing more than campus delivery boy. He considered leaving the package at Dr. Allen's door, but Miss Peterson in the mail room had distinctly said, "Deliver in person. If she's not there, wait." It must be important. Maps, if he was any judge of what would come from New York in a five-foot tube that weighed this much.

He raised his hand to knock.

The door swung open just as Wayne's fist started down and he narrowly missed punching Dr. Allen in the face. She ducked aside, scattering papers on the floor and flattened herself against the wall behind the door. Wayne dropped his package and then fell to his knees to gather the papers she had spilled, spluttering out his apologies as he scrambled around on the floor.

"I'm sorry, Dr. Allen," he said. "I was just knocking. I'll pick all this stuff up for you. I'm really sorry." He raised his head to see the club in her hand being lowered to the floor. "Jesus," he breathed. "I mean, I'm sorry, Dr. Allen. Really."

She was medium in build and height, but she dominated a room. She was an attractive—Wayne guessed—thirty-five or so. He'd heard she was the youngest department chair ever at the university. Even when he had been awake in her classes he was afraid to ask questions. She was skittish around people and quick-tempered when faced with indolence. Wayne had heard stories more horrific than his own. They said she had been attacked on campus a couple of times. With the recent antiwar demonstrations, he understood a little of why she kept her door locked, even when she was in. He knew a massive demonstration was planned for the weekend. She saw students only in her classroom or by appointment.

As she lowered the stick to the floor, Wayne could only pity anyone who tried to attack her. She always carried that stick or had it leaning against the wall behind the podium in her classroom. No. You'd have to be a fool to tangle with this woman.

"Well, Mr. Hamel?" asked the professor. "To what do I owe the surprise of this visit? Pipe bomb from the student liberation front?" She still didn't set the stick aside, making Wayne more nervous than he had been.

"Delivery, Dr. Allen," he said. He felt very young and foolish in her presence. "Miss Peterson said to deliver this in person." He laid the papers on the desk and picked up the cardboard tube to hand to her. "I figured it must be pretty important."

"Thank you," said Dr. Allen.

"Is there anything I can do for you while I'm here?" Wayne asked cautiously. "I mean, like, something to be delivered to someone else? That's my job, you know."

"Yes, I am aware of your function," said Dr. Allen. "If you can stay a few minutes, I need some exhibits taken to Good Hall. I was afraid it would take me two trips."

"Yes ma'am," he said.

"And do get up off the floor, Mr. Hamel. It's not necessary to kneel to me."

"Yes, ma'am," he said as he scrambled to his feet, cracking his head painfully on the desk in the process. Dr. Allen had the envelope torn from the tube and graciously didn't notice. Wayne glanced around the room at the array of relics on the shelves. One set of shelves was filled with figurines of women—some stone, some china or ivory, some wood. In the midst of these stood two goblets. One was pewter and the other silver in a brass stem. Both were heavily decorated. It was a bizarre collection. He turned to ask Dr. Allen about the collection of old "dolls."

Rebecca Allen sat with a wooden staff in her hands, the cardboard tube discarded. The note lay on the desk in front of her. Her shoulders were shaking in sobs. Wayne stood on the opposite side of the desk, stunned at the sight. He was concerned about Dr. Allen, but he couldn't tear his eyes from the walking stick. It was so familiar—so charged with power. He tore his eyes away and looked at the weeping professor.

"Mrs.… Dr. Allen," he said. "Are you all right? Is there something I can do?"

"No," she answered. "Nothing." She searched around on the desk until she found an empty tissue box then swore beneath her breath as she pitched it into her waste basket. For once in his life, Wayne's timing was impeccable as he offered a clean handkerchief to her. She took it with quiet thanks and wiped her eyes.

WHEN SHE LOOKED up, the boy was gone. She sat still in her chair, gently stroking the length of the worn old walking stick. She read, again, the note in front of her.

> *Dear Rebecca, I'm penning this note at Phillip's request. He's nearly blind and so weak that writing is impossible. I can't tell you how worried I am about him. I'm not even certain he is being coherent in the message he has asked me to write. You will have to be the judge of that. He insists it is imperative that you receive his walking stick.*
>
> *A couple of weeks ago, we sat in his study as a storm raged outside. The lights went out. Phillip was muttering beneath his breath and I leaned closer to hear what he was saying. From his perspective, I could see his staff leaning near the fireplace. I don't know how to say this, but I swear that it began to glow. We were suddenly hit by a massive bolt of lightning that deafened me. The wood in the fireplace leapt into flames. This is true, as certainly as I am writing it. Now Phillip won't rest until I've sent you his walking stick.*
>
> *In all the years that I have known him, he has never parted with it for more than a weekend, and then not without duress.*

I think he believes the fire was a sign of some sort—perhaps that he is dying.

William is waiting to take this to the post. Please come and visit soon. Bring Serepte.

Love, Margaret

"Please Doc, don't die," Rebecca whispered. That would make this whole mess unbearable. She knew what he must be going through. Her own staff was inseparable from her. And this which the famed explorer had carried with him for over three decades would mean so much more. It held so much of the man's personality—perhaps had created so much of him—that she could almost speak to it and expect Doc to answer. Perhaps seeing the fire leap once more from Iäpetus was a sign. She knew he had seen the rod call fire once before, when it was placed in his hands the first time. This was, after all, the Second Face of Carles. She and The Swordmaster had called it to life just two weeks ago at the equinox.

There was a soft knock at the door. Rebecca looked up to see the student messenger once again. He held a glass of water in his hand and offered it to her. Rebecca smiled.

"Mr. Hamel. How very gallant of you," she said. "A glass of water and a clean pressed handkerchief for a lady in distress. Chivalry is not dead. Thank you."

He shifted a little from foot to foot.

"My dad said that the mark of a gentleman was to always carry an extra handkerchief. You never know when it might be needed."

Rebecca looked at him. About twenty, she estimated—perhaps twenty-one. Ragged blue jeans and a shirt that looked like a paint rag. His hair was shoulder length and his beard had never been trimmed. There was a twitch of a smile at the corner of her mouth and finally she burst out laughing. Wayne smiled, too, a little unsure if he had made a joke or was one; and not really caring. She was a pretty woman when she smiled. What he had seen in the past few minutes had shown that she was not totally invulnerable.

"Thank you, Mr. Hamel. You have brightened a gloomy day," she laughed. "I wish I had seen that side of you while you were in my class."

"I'm sorry, Dr. Allen. It wasn't that I don't like cultural anthropology. It's just… well, I got what I deserved," he admitted.

"Oh, you got better than you deserved," she said. "I did enjoy your performance in *Hamlet*, however."

"You saw the show?"

"Oh yes," she answered. "If I am going to get up at the ungodly hour of five o'clock and spend my morning lecturing to a zombie, there had better be a trade-off."

"Did you sleep through the performance?" Wayne asked, almost hopefully.

"No. You were far too loud."

She turned her focus from the boy again and back to the walking stick lying across her lap. Stroking it once gently, she laid it on her credenza. "Hang in there, Doc. We need you," she whispered. She turned back to see Wayne staring at the staff again. She needed to get this moving.

Rebecca picked up her own red walking stick and the armload of papers that Wayne had gathered for her. She pointed at the box next to her desk. "This is the heavy box, if you would be so kind." He lifted the box and went out the door. She paused to lock it and led him down the hall and out of the building.

"We're going to England with it, you know," he said conversationally. She looked at him curiously.

"Antecedent, Mr. Hamel?"

"What?"

"It what?"

"Oh. It, *Hamlet*, the production. We've been invited to tour England," he explained.

"A bit like carrying coals to Newcastle, isn't it?"

"Why argue? We get to go to England this summer and that's what counts."

"Yes, I suppose it makes sense in that light. It appears that I may *get* to go to England this summer, myself."

"You go there a lot, don't you?" She looked at him sternly. *Why would he think that?* "Are you taking one of the slots in the show?"

"No. I didn't know there were any 'slots' available." It was an interesting thought, though. She filed the information away to be considered later. "I simply need to return an item to its makers," she said sadly.

"That staff you just got. Dr. Allen, is that... I mean, it just looks like... That's *it*, isn't it?"

Rebecca was alert and cautious. He'd written about the staff in his term paper in December. Had he made the connection? Did he have any reason to suspect this was it? Could there have been a picture?

"I'd rather not discuss the staff," she said abruptly. "It belongs to my daughter's godfather. He's very ill."

"I'm sorry. If there's anything I can do…" He left the sentence unfinished. "I mean, if you'd like me to help cart all this junk back to your office after your lecture tonight, I'd be happy to." He plopped the box down on the podium in the lecture hall.

"This junk, if you have not just broken it, happens to be artifacts of the Inca Indians," she said. "But I *am* a bit nervous about being out alone lately. Will you stay for the lecture?"

"I, uh…"

"Don't need a nap tonight? I see," she smiled.

"That's not it," he rushed. "I'm supposed to work in the scene shop tonight. I'd love to hear the lecture, really." She laughed again.

"That's considerably more enthusiasm than you showed for it last term," she was saying through her laughter. He laughed with her. "But I really shouldn't tease you like that. You've been a great help and a perfect gentleman this afternoon. I want you to know I appreciate it."

"You want me back then?" he asked.

"Class is out at a quarter after nine. It will take me ten or fifteen minutes to pack it all up and then I could certainly use your help if it is not too inconvenient."

"I'll be here at 9:30," he said quickly. "See you later, Dr. Allen."

"Thank you, Mr. Hamel." The boy was gone in a flash. *Lord, what a charmer. But why the curiosity about the staff?* Rebecca began unloading the box and setting the artifacts out on display, forgetting him with the thought. Tears once again fell from her eyes as she worked.

REBECCA WAS NEARLY finished packing the displays when he came running through the door of the lecture hall with his wet, stringy hair stuck to his face and neck. He'd stopped to shower and change into clean clothes before he came to help the professor.

"Well, Mr. Hamel, tough night in the scene shop?"

"Sorry I'm late, Dr. Allen. It was a real mess. We didn't finish up till after nine."

"Really?"

"We did dutchman tonight."

"What is 'doing dutchman'?" she asked.

"Well," Wayne explained, "when you put up flats—you know, the walls on stage?—there are cracks where they come together. So you take long strips of muslin cloth and dip them in wheat paste, wring them out, and smear them across the joints to cover the cracks. You get in wheat paste up to your elbows, and with our crew, it's all over the place. But it will be dry by tomorrow morning and we'll start painting. We were lucky to have a long weekend to get this set up."

"And you got all cleaned up just to come help me? How thoughtful."

"I couldn't have touched anything in the condition I was in," he said honestly. He shifted a little. "Besides, since tomorrow is Good Friday, it's like we have an early weekend. We can't work on set until it's dry, so a bunch of guys are going down to the Waffle House after rehearsal is over."

"Ah. Guys?" Rebecca asked with a smile.

"And gals," he said. He knew he was blushing and couldn't help it. Dr. Allen was an attractive woman when you weren't sitting in her class. For some reason, talking with her about his date was embarrassing.

"Well, I shan't detain you," she said. "In fact, it is a shorter distance to my house from here than to my office. This is the last use for these items this year. If you wouldn't mind helping me, I'll just store them there for the summer."

"No problem. Rehearsal won't be out till ten."

The two left the administration building which had recently been renamed Good Hall after some famous alumnus or something. Wayne didn't know who, but that sort of information was only good for freshman hazing anyway. Dr. Allen's house was, as she indicated, only a couple of blocks away from this side of campus. She brought him into the house and called out as soon as the door was open.

"Serepte! Are you here, love?"

"Yes, Mom." A skinny girl came out of the kitchen with a peanut butter sandwich in one hand and a glass of milk in the other. She wore blue jeans and a t-shirt and was barefoot. She was as tall as her mother but thin as a rail. Her long red hair hung straight down her back in the best Haight-Ashbury fashion, like that folk singer, Joni Mitchell. Wayne guessed that she must be all of thirteen or fourteen and a copy of what her mother must have looked like at that age.

"Oops, sorry. I didn't know we had company," she said upon seeing Wayne.

"It's okay. This is Mr. Hamel. He's carrying a box for me. Mr. Hamel, this is my daughter, Serepte. Honey, would you show Mr. Hamel where to put that box upstairs?" Serepte popped out of the living room and then back in with empty hands.

"Sure. C'mon." Wayne followed her upstairs and into a room at the top.

"Just put it over there with the other boxes," she said, pointing to one corner. The room was furnished like a study and was very clean. The boxes were the only thing that looked vaguely out of place.

"Is this your mom's study?" he asked as he stacked the box on top.

"No. It's my father's. We never use it except to store boxes in," she said.

"What's your dad do?" he asked as they left the room.

"He's gone," she said.

"Travel?"

"Nope. Gone." Wayne didn't pursue it any further. He'd never heard mention of a Mr. Allen. Serepte didn't really sound hurt or angry, but blunt and definite.

"Serepte," Rebecca said as they returned downstairs, "there was a casserole in the refrigerator for supper. You didn't have to eat peanut butter."

"I ate the casserole after school," the girl responded. "But I was hungry now, too."

"Where do you put it? Well, Mr. Hamel, may I offer you a peanut butter sandwich and a cup of coffee for your pains?" Rebecca asked.

"Thank you. I'll pass on the sandwich, but I'd love a cup of coffee, if it's no trouble."

"One cup of coffee," she answered. "Whenever I empty the pot, I get it ready for the next time so all I have to do is plug it in. It'll be just a minute. Anything in it?"

"A little milk or cream if I may," he said.

"Tell us about your trip to England," Rebecca said. "When and where are you going?"

"We go in June and we'll be in northern England. All I know is that they call it The Lake District and we have two weeks of performances and then a week in London just to sightsee." Wayne couldn't help himself. The closer they got to it, the more excited he got.

"I know the Lakes pretty well. In fact, I was planning to be there in late June, myself."

"Can I go this time?" asked Serepte. "I want to be there for Litha this year."

"Litha?" Wayne asked, his interest suddenly piqued. "What's Litha?"

"It's a… local holiday," Rebecca answered, staring at her daughter with a creased brow. Serepte slumped in her chair. "Honey, let's talk about this later, when our guest is gone."

"Okay. I'm sorry," she pouted.

"There's really a Litha, huh?" said Wayne. "Funny. I should know that. Judith didn't mention it."

"Who's Judith?" asked Rebecca.

"My, uh… Well, there's nothing official. We're friends. And we date. And stuff. She's our fencing master and came over from England last year."

"Student?"

"Yeah. Sophomore, but it's like she was out of school for a while in England and the credits didn't transfer right or something. She's a couple years older than me."

The Swordmaster. Things began to fall into place in Rebecca's mind. She felt her heart beating faster. Oester ritual had been so powerful and… intimate.

"So, I suppose Professor Richards is looking for chaperones for this little jaunt."

"Chaperones?" Wayne frowned. "Come on! We're all adults. Everyone who goes on this trip works. Half a dozen roles are available, though. Some of the original cast can't make the trip."

"Sounds like fun. Any walk-ons?"

"Everyone doubles as courtiers at some point," Wayne answered. "Why don't you come over and talk to Jim. I mean, Professor Richards. We could use someone else along who knows the territory."

"Maybe I'll give him a call tomorrow."

"Holiday. Why don't you come on over tonight?" Wayne's enthusiasm was running over. "He'll be at the Waffle House."

"You're really a promoter, aren't you," she laughed. "What do you think, Serepte?"

"I'm for anything that will get me to England," the girl answered.

"Well, start by heading to bed then. If I go see the professor tonight, will you be okay alone?"

"Aw, can't I come, too?" Serepte pled.

"That is not an answer to the question I asked," Rebecca said sternly. "*Your* school is not closed tomorrow and I don't want you sleeping through class." Wayne hid his face in his hands.

"Good advice, Serepte," he said through his fingers. "If you sleep in class your teachers will never let you forget it."

"Are you the one who slept through Mom's class?" she asked wide-eyed. "Lucky you're alive to remember it!"

"Serepte," chided Rebecca.

"Okay," she said smiling at her mother. "I'll be fine. Good night."

"Good night, honey. I'll lock all the doors when I go out."

"Good night, Mr. Hamel."

"You can call me Wayne," he answered. "Hope I see you in England."

"Me too!" She turned and ran up the stairs. Wayne turned to Rebecca.

"The *one* who slept in class?" he asked. "I'm the only one who ever slept in your class?"

"Not exactly," Rebecca smiled. "Just the only one who passed."

"Holy gees!"

"Shall I drive?" Rebecca asked as she stood from the table and locked the back door.

"Thank you. I think I missed my ride over, but I can get a lift back," he squeaked.

AT THE WAFFLE House, seven people had already squeezed into a booth and were chattering noisily when the two arrived.

"Does everyone here know Dr. Allen?" Wayne announced as they came up to the table. There was sudden silence.

"Dr. Allen, what a pleasant surprise," Jim Richards said a little shakily as he simultaneously stood, snubbed out a cigarette, and extended his hand.

"Thank you, Professor Richards," Rebecca answered. Technically, he was a Mister and not a Professor, but elevating him by title wouldn't hurt once. "I've been hearing some intriguing things about your department and decided to come check them out in person."

"Oh dear," said Jim. "Wayne, what have you done?"

"It's great," Wayne said in his own natural exuberance. "Dr. Allen wants to join the cast for our England tour. She's been there a lot and could help us find our way around."

"Easy, Mr. Hamel," said Rebecca calming him down. "Mr. Richards, I just came over to find out if there might be a way to help you out. The Lake District is a favorite spot of mine and I would love to visit it again this summer."

"That's wonderful," said Jim. "Pull up a chair. Have you met everyone here? This is Lena Bowen, my assistant director. Glenn Little, here. Our own resident English expert, Judith Harmon…" For Rebecca, the other three introductions slid past without acknowledgment. Judith Harmon leaned forward from behind Glenn's bulky frame. She was short with closely cut blonde hair. She was compact and looked tightly wound. Her moment of doubt was erased by the woman's own pugnacious smile. Rebecca was facing a child of Cobhan Carles.

"Miss Harmon, was it?" she asked. "You're from England?"

"Yes, Dr. Allen," the woman responded. "I believe we've met."

"Well," said Jim. "Tell me about your interest in traveling with us. Have you ever been on stage?" The instant of private communication was broken and the group was plunged into conversation over the coming trip to England. By the time they broke up at midnight, Rebecca Allen had been assigned a role in the troupe and was helping plan the details. As they prepared to leave, Rebecca saw Judith step toward the restrooms and excused herself to follow.

Judith was waiting when Rebecca came through the door.

"Merry meet, sister," Rebecca said calmly.

"Why?" Judith demanded, ignoring the common greeting. "Why are you getting involved with the theatre? And with Wayne?"

"Because it would be almost impossible to miss your group when I go back for Litha," answered Rebecca. "It's far better than trying to explain why I'm there."

"Litha. Are you so close already?" the girl asked.

"Iäpetus came to me today."

"I'll bet that surprised the old man," Judith said. "Sorry. I know he's some special person to you. I've only met him once."

"Iäpetus would have come anyway. Doc is dying."

"I'm sorry."

"We know where Enceladus is. As for Creüs... Litha was my limit, thanks to you, Swordmaster. If I can't raise the power to recreate him, I'll have to leave the circle."

"Recreate? Didn't any of the messages soak in?" Judith asked hotly.

"You? All the time it was you!" Rebecca nearly shouted in return. It was beginning to make sense now. "Are you trying to scare me off the challenge? Are you so afraid I might find the power to complete the task?"

"You don't understand," Judith began.

"Oh, I believe I do," Rebecca cut her off. "I have a hat that must belong to you. I can't believe that you'd be so callous as to lead on another person and get him to write fraudulent research to meet your ends."

"There are more important things at risk," Judith started again. "I didn't challenge you to have you throw away your life and others with you."

"You will have to do better than that to scare me away from the challenge now."

"If I wanted to stop you," Judith whispered. "I would do it. I have the power. And I'm not afraid to use it."

Judith stepped close to her and Rebecca's hand went automatically to her knife. But Judith pulled Rebecca's face to hers and kissed her. She brooked no protestation, but pressed her tongue into Rebecca's mouth and brought her left hand to Rebecca's breast. The circle. The celebrant. The one who lent her so much power.

"Merry part, sister," Judith whispered as she slipped out the door.

"Oh shit!" Rebecca murmured as she leaned back against the sink. She hadn't handled that very well. In fact, she hadn't done the handling at all. Her breast still tingled and she could feel the energy coursing through her body, down to her core.

Very well. If Judith was preparing Wayne for a position in the coven, she must have a reason. Rebecca would not hinder her. If the opportunity arose, she'd help. But she hoped Creüs would simply come to her. Deep inside she was frightened.

10
Raising Power

Wednesday, 30 April 1969

THE THIRD arrow struck the target. It was wide of the center, but definitely in the target. Wayne turned to Glenn and smiled. "It works!"

"Yeah. Congratulations. But why?"

"Because I made it right."

"I know why it works. Why did you *want* it to work? It's just a prop," Glenn said shaking his head. He could be so dense.

"Nothing is *just* a prop," Wayne explained to his friend. "How many of us are guards on the battlements?"

"Two."

"And how many bows did we have?"

"One."

"So how can we both carry a bow on the battlements if there is only one bow?"

"So, we need a second bow."

"Give the man a cigar."

"So why should it work?"

"Because the other one works. If this one works, then it's like the other one. Maybe not as accurate—yet—but still a working model."

"What are you going to be when you grow up, kid?"

"Robin Hood. And you can be Little Glenn," answered Wayne.

"What I'm going to be when I grow up is alive," said Glenn. "And that doesn't include running around playing with sharp sticks."

"What we've got here is a failure to communicate," said Wayne. "Now look. What if things really go to shit and they scrap our deferments. Nixon talks about peace in the same breath that he starts carpet bombing Cambodia. What's next? Laos? China? What do we do then?"

"Run."

"Just like Chicago last summer. The real antiwar pacifists were hiding in the basement of Marshall Field's. So, we run, jogga, jogga, jogga," Wayne mimed running in place as they left the archery range. "Hey man! You've got to get in shape. So, we get up to Canada. What then?"

"We start a commune and go into farming."

"That reminds me. I've got to ask Lissa how she feels about farming. God, she could be a hawk, can you believe it?"

"She could be married for all you know," Glenn punctured Wayne's little balloon.

"Well, on to bigger and better things. It's a long way to Canada. We've got to be ready to live off the land. No one out there to cook doughnuts for us. No McDonald's. Neither one of us will pick up a gun. What do we do?"

"Become vegetarians."

"Don't be dense," Wayne chimed back. "We tried being vegetarians. Remember, when we were trying to date the vegetarian twins? But no matter what the FDA says, they still put meat in a double cheeseburger."

"They sure flipped out when they found the hamburger cartons in the back seat."

"Yeah. 'Someone threw them through the window.' Great line, my friend. But if we're going to live off the land we've got to be able to hunt game or we'll starve."

"You really think you could point that thing at a bunny rabbit and pull the trigger? Or string?"

"I don't know," Wayne confessed. "I nearly passed out when we had to dissect a frog in biology. I suppose it would depend on how hungry I was. It's a whole new branch of situation ethics."

"Speaking of which, we just missed lunch."

"What's that got to do with situation ethics?"

"Not ethics. Hunger."

"Hey! That's why they invented McDonald's."

They walked across campus toward the familiar golden arches. It was one of those friendships that had come out of nowhere and which no one, least of all Wayne, would have expected. Glenn was six and a half feet tall. Wayne felt like a dwarf when he stood straight and tall at six feet—well, five-eleven-and-a-half. Glenn easily tipped the scale at two-thirty. Wayne kept his balance at about one-seventy. Both were sharp and intelligent students, but Glenn tended to maintain a slight edge academically.

"What's the story between you and Dr. Allen, Romeo?" Glenn asked.

"No story. I got her into the department so Jim made it clear that I was responsible for babysitting her. Cheap shot to make me act next to her. She could have played Guildenstern. Rosencrantz and Guildenstern are dead anyway. You'd think I had enough to worry about with all the props for this bloody show."

"Methinks the lady doth protest too much," laughed Glenn.

"Well, she's neat, I won't deny that," argued Wayne. "But face it. She's got to be pushing forty. And you know you can't trust anyone over thirty."

"Older. Experienced."

"Bullshit."

"How about Judith? You and the WASP don't seem to be getting along too well lately," Glenn observed.

"No shit, Sherlock. There's another story. She's been PO'd at me ever since Dr. Allen joined the cast. Even before that. I don't think she's ever forgiven me for not going to England with her over spring break."

"It shows."

"Do you know how many foils she's gone through in the last month?" Wayne asked. "I'm doing nothing in the shop lately but repair her weapons. Then she's got this weird thing going with Chuck's dagger and how his sword has to be cross-hilted for the ghost scene."

"I keep telling you, they're only props. You build like the royal army is going to war. You dumb hippie."

"Gimme a head with hair, long, beautiful hair…" Wayne sang. "Anyway, lately it's just been slap a handle on it and polish it up. There's just too much to do."

"Well," Glenn said, "if you decide to make your little dispute permanent and drop her for an older woman—or a doughnut lady—I'd appreciate it if you'd drop her on me."

"Kind of soften her landing?" Wayne chuckled. "Looks to me like she's the one in the driver's seat. She hardly lets me near her lately."

They finished their burgers and shoved the trash into the overfilled basket. Wayne picked up the bow and quiver of arrows.

"I gotta get this stuff back to the shop before class," he said.

"Yeah. I'm just going to get another shake to take along. See you at rehearsal tonight," Glenn finished. Wayne turned around and faced his friend.

"Look, Glenn," he said, "if you think she's interested, go for it. I mean I know your thing with Gail has been going nowhere. Don't worry about, like, our friendship or anything. We're solid." He turned and went on back toward the scene shop.

ONCE BACK AT the shop, Wayne found that he was not much in the mood to attend another lecture by Coop on English poets. Too many projects demanded attention to deal with T.S. Eliot. He sat at the workbench and opened his art box. He carefully unfolded the drawing of the next piece on his project list, Hamlet's dagger. The drawing looked strangely barren when Wayne looked at it. It was the exact size and shape of the knife his uncle had given him at Christmas, but had none of the decorative hieroglyphs on it.

Two identical blade blanks lay in a drawer under the workbench with others for swords and knives. He always bought the blanks in pairs. He pulled one out and felt along the length of it, allowing the touch of the steel to penetrate his senses. This would be a beautiful piece when he was done with it. He had ground both blanks down to the same shape, but of course he would not sharpen it for the show. Pointed would be enough. After the show, though, it would be his to keep. Then he would sharpen it and tool it down to be decorated. His uncle's journal said that making a tool endowed it with the strengths and characteristics of its maker. If that was true, he hoped Judith never used the sword he made her in a duel. She could get hurt.

Thinking about Judith was another pain. Things had been going so well for them before her trip to England. Even then it looked like they'd get it back together until Dr. Allen joined the *Hamlet* cast. Alone, they were okay, but there weren't any alone times lately. They hadn't had a date with just the two of them in three weeks. There was tech weekend, then two weekends of shows, and now finals were coming next week and they'd have to spend the weekend studying. And at rehearsals, she was cold, especially when Dr. Allen was around.

He balanced the blade on his finger and began adding wood chips to the handle end until the balance point was where he wanted it. He wrapped a piece of duct tape around the shank and woodchips. When it was secure he glanced across the empty shop to a stack of polystyrene beadboard used in construction. Taking careful aim, he threw the knife. It hit and stuck—handle end first with the blade sticking out at him. He sighed. He didn't know if it was the blade balance or his lousy throwing.

"Why don't you let a pro handle that part?" Judith asked from the doorway. "You don't throw a knife like a baseball."

"Why don't you teach me the right way?" Wayne said turning to look at her.

"Sure. It would be easier to teach you than Chuck. He's got a beautiful voice, but his hand-eye coordination sucks. I think he's a little cross-eyed." She retrieved the knife from the foam block. "What's all this junk taped to the end?"

"I was trying to determine how much weight it took to balance it."

"Balance is only half the battle," she said, stripping the taped woodchips off the shank. "First find out if it flies right. Then you can adjust your hold to compensate for the balance." She raised her hand and threw the knife at the polystyrene block. It sank in perfectly, blade first. "See? Nothing wrong with its balance," she said walking to get the blade again.

"What about when I put a handle on it?"

"Put one on it. I'll teach him to use it right," she answered. "Black, I think. It should be a black handle so it blends in with the rest of his costume until he draws it. Not too shiny on the handle. The silver blade comes to life against the black backdrop of his chest." She sidled up to Wayne with the blade still in her hand and pressed it flat against his chest as she spoke. "Like that idea?" she asked pressing herself against him as well.

"I think you're dangerous, lady," he answered wrapping his arms around her, but afraid to squeeze too tightly with the knife still held between them. In spite of himself, he was getting hard.

"Oh, I can be much more dangerous than that," she whispered, letting the knife hand slide down his torso until he felt it pressing against his cock. "Want to cross swords?" He smiled faintly.

"You should be locked up."

"Just remember who loves you, boyo," she said. With a quick twist, she slipped the knife out from between them and threw it behind her back. She never looked, but over her shoulder Wayne could see that it stuck in the block perfectly again. "You wouldn't want to lose anything near and dear to you, would you?" She muffled his response, pressing her lips to his in a passionate kiss.

"Class," she said, suddenly breaking away from him. "See you later?"

Wayne watched her swaying hips as she walked down the hall. He went to get the knife and contemplated throwing it one more time, but decided against it. He put it back in the drawer beside its twin and the other blanks he'd ordered at the beginning of the term. T. S. Eliot suddenly sounded a lot better to him and he ran to catch up with Judith.

REHEARSAL WAS ANOTHER disaster for the struggling cast of *Hamlet*. Jim spent most of his time with the new cast members. Carol Nygard had stepped up to the challenge of playing Guildenstern and everyone was wondering exactly how they were going to hide her bodacious tits for the man's role. Wayne ran through the play within the play with Dr. Allen only once. Jim hauled him aside after the choppy run.

"Look, Wayne. It's your scene. You staged it last fall like an independent little troupe of traveling actors. Now you've got a new member of your troupe. You are the player king, not me. Get the scene smoothed out with Dr. Allen and bring me something that's ready to polish and integrate into the show. You're falling over each other like it was slapstick. If you need feedback, take Lena along."

"Okay, I'll work on it. But she's terrible, Jim. Her head's never in the same room with the rest of her."

"You got her into this; you can get her through it," Jim said. "When do I see those drawings for the thrones, by the way?"

"Lena's got them. If you approve them, we can send them off in the morning."

"Did you revise them for Judith's specifications?"

"Do I value my life?" Wayne responded. "We're going to have to re-cover it after every performance."

"Then make sure we've got enough pieces of covering for ten performances." Wayne assented and turned to walk back toward the stage. Jim called after him. "I want to see that scene ready to polish Friday night. We're running out of time."

"No kidding," Wayne muttered as he walked away. He spotted Rebecca in the wings. "Dr. Allen, if you can spare the time, we need to find a place to work on our scene for a while."

"It wasn't very good, was it?" she asked.

"On a scale of one to ten, we didn't move the needle."

"Well, I can stay a while to work," she answered. "Where to?"

"Let's see if anyone's using the dressing rooms," he said. They went down the back stairs from the stage to the two small rooms that served the college theatre as dressing rooms. One was strewn with costumes, actors, and the costumer.

"Wayne! Where the hell have you been? You've been called for fitting three times."

"Sorry, Gail. I've been busy making new props. Jim just sent us out to rehearse the dumbshow."

"For sure. It needs it," Gail said, not looking up from the hem. "Sign up for another slot when you *can* be here, would you?"

"Sure," Wayne answered, looking at the sign-up sheet. "I'll be back at ten."

"If I stay in this dump till ten o'clock, you had sure better show up, mister."

"Have I missed a fitting, too, Miss Bremen?" Dr. Allen asked quietly.

"Oh, Dr. Allen," said the costumer. "I didn't see you there. It's okay. We knew you'd be busy this month with finals and all."

"Can you see me right after Mr. Hamel tonight?"

"Sure. No trouble. I'm always here till eleven or so." Rebecca signed the schedule. Gail bared her teeth at Wayne.

The two left and went to the next dressing room. They found it occupied by Hamlet and Ophelia. The line coach shooed them out of the room before they even got a good glimpse of what was happening.

"They sure have their acts together, don't they?" Rebecca asked as they turned away.

"They should. They're both headed toward the pros. Where are we going to rehearse this damned thing?" His frustration was cut short as they were backed against a wall to allow two students maneuvering a sheet of plywood past them.

"Wayne," one of them said. "Can you check out the crate? I don't think it's strong enough for what we're sending."

"I'll be down after my fitting tonight, Brian. Just keep building," he said. "We can reinforce it if necessary."

"Okay, but I don't think it's strong enough."

"Brian..."

"Come with me," Dr. Allen cut him off and took him by the arm. "We can rehearse in my living room. It doesn't look like there is a quiet space anywhere in this building. It's only a couple of blocks and we'll be back in time for our fittings." Wayne followed her out of the building with a minor protest as he watched the sheet of plywood disappear with a noisy scrape into the scene shop. Her voice had left no room for objection.

FROM THE THEATRE stairway, Judith watched Rebecca take Wayne's arm and propel him toward the door. She moved her mouth as if to say something at their backs, but bit her lip instead. "If *she's* training him, *I'm* damned well training him. He's *my* apprentice!" She went back upstairs.

REBECCA UNLOCKED HER front door and they went into the living room. Wayne was surprised she didn't call out to Serepte.

"Let me plug in the coffee pot," she said. "I think we're going to need it." She finished the preparations while Wayne fidgeted in the living room. "Are you in trouble?" she asked bluntly when she returned.

"No," he said, taken aback. This sounded strangely reminiscent of her interrogation last semester.

"So, tell me what's wrong."

"I guess it's just another lousy term."

"With us, Mr. Hamel. Stop discounting. Why are we not doing well?"

"I don't know," he started. "It's just hard to…" He left the sentence hanging.

"Hard to play a love scene with a woman twice your age?" she volunteered.

"God, no! It's not that much of a love scene."

"But it is that much of an age difference," she filled in. He was embarrassed about the question and then about his response. Like he wouldn't like a love scene with her. If she didn't scare him quite so much.

"You're a professor."

"So?"

"So no one expects you to be a pro. I'm supposed to be a pro. The scene isn't right, it's my fault. I miss a fitting, I get dragged over the coals. I'm supposed to be better than this."

"And if I miss a fitting, 'We understand, Dr. Allen.' I see."

"We all accepted those limitations when you joined the cast," Wayne scrambled to save the situation. "I'm just not performing the way I should. And I don't know how to fix it."

"Mr. Hamel, I believe I have done you a great disservice." He looked up at her questioningly. If she backed out of the show he would be blamed for that, too. "I should have failed you."

"What?" he said standing up in disbelief. *Fuck! Let her quit!*

"Sit down and let me finish." His knees buckled under him and he collapsed back on the sofa. "If I had failed you, I would have had you back in class with the opportunity to teach you what anthropology is really about. As it was, you left my class believing that you understood. Or thinking me a fool. Or both. But in spite of your passing grade, you don't know anthropology."

"What's that got to do…?"

"Don't do me the same disservice," she shot back at him. "I've failed my first test as an actress. I slept through your class. I didn't even audition. Because I'm an influential faculty member, I walked into the Waffle House and was instantly cast. Don't think I don't know that. I have eyes and ears. Now I'm ready to endure the show thinking this is a rinky-dink operation where people yell at each other a lot and get applauded on opening night. I don't have the least idea what goes on in your head as an actor or a props master or a technical director. Don't let me fail, Mr. Hamel. Now what do I need to do?"

He looked at her with his mouth open as he began to comprehend what she was saying. His throat was dry and his voice squeaked in a very un-actor-like manner when he finally forced the words out.

"Call me Wayne." She looked at him and smiled. "Every time you call me Mr. Hamel, I'm afraid I've been asleep and missed something important."

"Very well," she said. "On one condition. As long as we are partners in this, you will call me Rebecca. Now, how about a cup of coffee before we get to work, Wayne? We only have an hour until our fittings."

"Thank you… Rebecca," he answered. "I'd like that."

"I'll trust in your good judgment to know if it's not appropriate," she said. "Why don't you explain to me a little about our scene? How do you see the context?"

"Sure. You know, there are only three female speaking roles in the play. It's Ophelia, Gertrude, and you. The player queen was probably a boy's role too, like they played it in *Rosencrantz and Guildenstern are Dead*. But then, most of Shakespeare's women were boys. The players come to Elsinore and Hamlet sees his opportunity to expose the king's treachery by having the players perform a work called *The Murder of Gonzago*, in which the king's brother murders him. Uh… you weren't here for the staging of the players' meeting with Hamlet. I'll have to get you up to speed on that one. The general staging is set up to reflect the king's and queen's positions as the players play out the scene. The play's the thing…"

Thursday, 1 May 1969, very early morning

"THERE HE IS. I knew you'd be here eventually."

"How'd you know that, Lissa?"

"Haroo, hooray, the first of May. Outdoor fucking starts today."

"Darlin', we haven't even fucked indoors, yet."

"And we never will. Outdoors, though… All rules are suspended when it's outdoors. Come sit at the counter and tell me all about life in the theatre." Wayne sat and when Lissa brought his coffee and cream she casually reached across the counter and touched his pentacles. It was like Wayne suddenly woke up from a good night's sleep.

"Whoa. Man! How do you do that? It's like I suddenly remember all the dreams I've had this spring. I really want to put it all together this summer."

"You will, Unbound. I'll be sure you have everything you need when you are in England. Now tell me about things."

"Things are better. I had a real breakthrough with Rebecca tonight. Uh… that's Dr. Allen."

"Really. Sounds like the Wicked Witch of the West is melting."

"Maybe it's me that's melting. She seems more human now. Maybe even vulnerable."

"You always have to protect her, Unbound. It's your sacred duty."

"I will always protect her, Chameleon. I figured that out tonight. She's as lost in the theatre as I was in anthropology last fall. I have a duty to make her successful and I can do it."

LISSA LISTENED TO Wayne as he talked about his professor and their new understanding. She wasn't sure, but it sounded like The Huntress was teaching him things he'd need to know. He'd recognized Iäpetus. She just wanted to make sure they were all teaching from the same book.

She knew Wayne was going to play an important role this summer. He needed to understand that his duty to The Huntress was greater than making her successful on stage. She didn't want him marching into the circle as a vagabond without understanding. And if she was repeating lessons that the other two had already taught, it would simply reinforce it.

"And how about your girlfriend?" Wayne had never offered even a code name for The Huntress and The Swordmaster. They were both locked away so deeply that he referred to them as if they were just pedestrians.

"I don't know. Chameleon, she confuses me. I really, really like her, you know? I mean, like, maybe I love her. But she runs hot and cold. She's barely had time to talk to me for the past month and then this afternoon she comes in and makes up, all sultry and lovey. And dangerous. Really dangerous. Sometimes she scares the shit out of me."

"Think of it this way, Unbound: Her only friends for the past fifteen years have been sharp pointed objects. I bet she didn't tell you that six years ago she won the British Youth Championship in all three events—Epee, Foil, and Sabre."

"Shit! I knew she was good, but that's unbelievable. How'd you know that?"

"I looked her up in the Public Library after you told me about her. I thought I recognized the name from somewhere. She'd have been an Olympic medalist last year if she'd had a better draw. She went up against one of the world's greatest fencers in her first round in Mexico. I'm sure that by '72 she could take Ildikò, but now she's got that Russian, Novikova-Belova, to contend with. They're the same age, but she hasn't had the experience that the Russian has, in spite of practicing day and night for the past ten years."

"God! I love her."

"You are right, though. She's dangerous. She trained at a gym in London that is known for unconventional training. Not the London Fencing Club. She trains there, of course, but the Kingsgate Knife and Weapons Club. In addition to various circus acts, they turn out the largest percentage of London's street fighters. They actually fight with edged instruments."

"Somebody could get killed."

"Somebody did. In fact, several somebodies. They always keep it covered up, but Judith Harmon is what she is. Ryan McGuire is said to have started her training when she was just a toddler."

"Who is Ryan McGuire?"

"His nickname was The Blade. You might hear about him someday. Some say he was burned in a fight and hasn't been seen or heard from in nearly fifteen years."

"Lissa, what do I need to do?"

"Tonight? Haroo, hooray..."

"Yeah, and here we are sitting in a doughnut shop."

Lissa came out from behind the counter and locked the front door, turning the sign to "closed."

"Did you know there's a greenbelt behind this shopping strip?" she asked. Wayne shook his head. "Come with me, apprentice. I'm going to show you a mystery."

HE DIDN'T HAVE tools with him. She told him never to bring them to the doughnut shop—except his ever-present pentacles. She'd said a greenbelt, but instead, she took him up a ladder to the roof. It was the only way the air conditioner could be serviced. She'd put all she needed on the roof at midnight. By the time Wayne got there at two, everything was set for their training. It was a clear night and the nearly full moon had risen at eight o'clock. It was cold, but they danced naked around a candle flame. In his suggestible state, Wayne had no difficulty stripping and when he saw her naked, his erection made the rest of his inhibitions float away. When they'd danced in a circle, raising a cone of power, she lay back and he entered her. They kept building and when they climaxed, the blue-hued dome above them expanded outward.

"Now, Unbound. Do you see it? Look around. The uninitiated cannot see what you see now."

"There are blue lights all over the city." Well, she thought, not all over, but the first time an initiate saw them, they seemed more plentiful than they were. There were three near the college campus, two due west, and four could be seen farther south.

"They are the lights of the practitioners conducting their Beltane rituals. They don't all have sex, but why not? It makes it so much more fun."

Lissa continued to give him instructions as they lay on the blanket she'd arranged on the roof. When he hardened again, they fucked. That one was for pure lustful satisfaction. It had been such a long time.

She carefully set wards around his memories so he wouldn't become confused when he was back in the 'real' world. It was one thing to have sex when you were connected to the spirit plane, but quite another if you had to deal with all the messy relationship issues on the physical plane. Besides, she didn't want The Huntress or The Swordmaster to know she was here just yet. Or for The Swordmaster to know she'd just fucked her boyfriend.

11
Serve and Protect

Friday, 9 May 1969

THERE WAS nothing wrong with her doing this, Judith told herself. *I love him. Well, I think I do. Even if I didn't, finals are over and I'd do it anyway. Probably.* She wasn't completely convinced, but he certainly wasn't going to argue about it. And she knew The Huntress wasn't above using sex to raise power. Their climax together on Oester was evidence of that. And frankly she'd enjoyed it. That was refreshing.

She applied her lipstick and looked at herself critically. Frosty pink lips. Blue eye shadow. Black liner and lash extensions. A little highlight on her cheeks. She wondered absently what she'd think of this fashion in thirty years. She wore a patent leather miniskirt and platform shoes. They wouldn't bring her completely up to his height, but he wouldn't have to bend over so far to kiss her. And he was going to kiss her. *Oh yes.*

The amount of traffic in and out of the dorm on the last day of school made it easy for Wayne to come to her room and knock on the door. Judith adjusted her tube top to make sure her flat stomach and navel were showing and that it only covered high enough to hide the essentials. She'd embarrassed herself when she went into Block's Department Store and asked for a boob tube. Well, that's what they called them in London. Instead, she'd been directed to televisions. She opened the door and stood back.

"Holy shit! God! You are gorgeous!" Wayne said when he could finally get words out of his mouth. *My God! He's actually salivating.*

"Thank you, lover. You look pretty hot yourself." He was wearing a new pair of khaki shorts and a white tennis shirt with an alligator embroidered over his heart. She glanced at his feet to see that he was wearing sandals. That was a relief. She couldn't have gone out if he was in socks and shoes. His fashion sense wasn't always great.

Wayne crossed the room and pulled her to him, pressing his lips to hers as he hugged her. She let her lips soften and soon welcomed his tongue into her mouth. They parted, panting.

"I don't know who taught you to kiss, but I want to thank her."

"Special tutorial in high school," Wayne smirked. "Best grade I ever got."

"You have to tell me about that sometime," she said. They kissed again. Eventually they had to come up for air. "Are we going out? We could just stay here."

"I did promise you a hot dog basket and a schooner at Lum's. Glenn and Gail are waiting for us in the car, so maybe we should join them. Otherwise I'd have to go out and explain to them that I can't keep my hands off you."

"Are you having trouble with that?" she asked coyly. He let his hands slide down from her bare shoulders across her breasts.

"Oh yeah."

"The sooner we go, the sooner we can get back."

WAYNE'S RIGHT HAND had been trapped between Judith's bare thighs all the way back to the dorm from the restaurant. Really high up between her thighs. It had been trapped there when he turned to kiss her, gliding up her leg from her knee until she clamped her legs closed just as he touched her damp panties. There it stayed as they continued to kiss until Glenn had turned off the car and opened the door.

"There's no desk clerk on duty tonight," Glenn said. "Therefore there is no reason to stay in the car to make out."

"My room, lover," Judith whispered.

Wayne followed her straight to the women's wing. He noticed that Gail had opted to head to the men's wing with Glenn. Well, he'd follow Judith anywhere right now. Anywhere she wanted to go, he was hers.

She barely got her key out of the lock so the door could swing closed behind them when they were back in a clutch. This time she didn't stop his hands, no matter where they roamed. He found out quickly how easily a tube top could be adjusted. They were still standing inside the doorway when he had bare breasts cupped in both hands and Judith was moaning into his mouth. She pulled his tennis shirt off over his head and pressed her bosom to his chest.

"Oh, Judith. You feel so fucking good."

"Baby, I am going to feel so good fucking."

"I don't want to just fuck you. I mean, hell yes, I want to fuck you. But I want to make love to you. I want to hold you in my arms and never let you go," he whispered.

Hold me, hold me
Never let me go until you've told me, told me
What I want to know and then just hold me, hold me
Make me tell you I'm in love with you.

Judith sang to him as they began dancing together in her room. She sang the whole song as they swayed around the room, her beautiful contralto voice softly ruffling the few hairs he had on his chest. When she sang, "Kiss me. Kiss me," he did. Somewhere in the process he found the zipper to her skirt and she stepped out of it when it fell to the floor. "Now you," she whispered. He thought a moment.

I don't remember what day it was
I didn't notice what time it was
All I know is that I fell in love with you
And if all my dreams come true
I'll be spending time with you.

He sang. His voice was pitched lower than the singer from Spiral Starecase, but it still fit the song. "I love you more today than yesterday..." That was as far as he got. His shorts fell to the floor and he stepped out of them, still holding Judith. She looked at him and picked up the next song.

Children behave
That's what they say when we're together
And watch how you play
They don't understand.

It was campy, but they were spinning in a circle in each other's arms and Judith's platform shoes came off just as she sang, "I think we're alone now..." Wayne kicked his sandals off and they had only the layer of his jockeys and her black hip-hugger panties between them. They'd begun to sweat, but there was something about letting the music take them wherever they wanted that kept them spinning in each other's arms. Judith pulled the tube top the rest of the way off so they were skin-to-skin. Her breasts slid against his sweaty chest.

When you hold me
In your arms so tight,
You let me know,
Everything's alright...

Wayne sang. They touched Judith's bed and sank down on it. Sometimes singing, sometimes kissing, whispering lyrics as they lay down together. When Wayne sang "I'm hooked on a feeling…" he hooked his thumbs into Judith's waistband and dragged her panties down off her feet. He knelt before her.

"Make love to me, baby. Everything is ready."

"I've always wanted to do this," he said as he lowered his mouth to her pussy. He didn't know exactly what to expect, though he had learned the rudiments of where her clit was. The taste was sweet and he knew he'd crave this all his life. When he found her bud, he teased it, licked it, pressed it, sucked it until she was writhing on the bed.

"Oh God! Wayne, I wanted to wait for you, but I can't. You're doing such wonderful things to me. Oh baby!" Judith climaxed and pulled Wayne up by his ears before he could bring her off again. "In me. In me, baby. Oh Wayne, make love to me."

Wayne found the slippery channel and sank into her depths. So warm, so smooth, so right.

"Goddess, be with me. Powers of the East, come to me. Powers of the South, come to me. Powers of the West, come to me. Powers of the North, come to me. Blessed be. The circle is complete," Judith chanted softly as Wayne plowed into her again and again. It didn't disturb him that she was chanting these things. Somehow, they seemed right—natural.

"So mote it be," he answered her chant.

As they neared the peak their attention was drawn away momentarily.

"Look, Judith. Look at what we've done. It's beautiful!" Lights bounced around the room, ricocheting off the walls and ceiling. Multiple colors. "We're doing this, darling. You and me. It's so beautiful."

"Yes!" Judith called as she exploded into the lights. Wayne was with her this time and the glow stabilized around them as they settled.

"You see it. You know," he said softly.

"Yes. I am The Swordmaster."

"I am The Unbound." Judith shivered beneath him and he embraced her more fully as she came again. Judith put her hand against his chest and touched the pentacles—her pentacles, but now completely his—with her index finger.

"How did you know what to do? Has she done it with you?"

"I don't know who 'she' is. I think I dreamed it. I get confused sometimes and then there's a moment when the dream comes true and I see it all clearly."

"It's okay. I'm not going to share you with anyone as a lover, but ritual and the raising of power is different."

"Is that what this is? Just raising power? I don't even know what that means. Or maybe I do, but I can't think of it."

"This was so much more than raising power, love. So much more than a dream. But the power is there, too. You can feel it, can't you?"

"Yes, but all I want to feel is you."

"I want you to be safe and protected. This is just for us. Then we can just make love all night long."

Judith closed her eyes and touched the pentacles again. Wayne felt a warmth wash over him. His eyes drifted closed as he was enclosed in the celestial feeling. When he opened them, Judith spoke again. "Whenever I touch your pentacles, you will remember all we have done to prepare you. But when you leave my presence, that part will be like a dream. It will become clear whenever you have need of it. You are more than my apprentice. You are my lover." She touched the medallion and Wayne felt her flow into him. He hardened in her again and they began a dance that would last all night.

Wednesday, 21 May 1969

REBECCA ALLEN SAT in her office watching the academic building across the parking lot from her window. It was late. Rehearsal had been cancelled because of yet another break-in. She watched the police leave at last and the lights in the building go out. On the steps of the building, she could see two figures pause to talk as a security guard locked the doors behind them. It was an animated discussion. Though she could not see clearly in the lamplight, she knew the participants would be Wayne Hamel and Jim Richards.

She reached into the credenza behind her and pulled out the hat she had kept there since finding it last fall. It didn't make sense. She could at least understand The Swordmaster's motive for breaking into the library in October. But why the rash of theatre break-ins?

The subject had been discussed at faculty meetings twice. The prevailing opinion was that theatre students were long-haired hippy freaks. Hippies used drugs, so the break-ins must be drug related since no theatre equipment was stolen. It was no secret that Rebecca's participation in the theatre's England tour was about the only thing that kept cancellation of the trip from coming to a vote.

The problem she faced now was the distinct possibility that The Swordmaster might be sabotaging the tour to keep Rebecca from completing her task in England. It seemed so ridiculous; so petty. But the thought kept nagging at Rebecca.

From her talks with Wayne over the past couple of weeks, she knew that he was still very much attached to Judith. In fact, enthralled might be a good word. But Judith seemed to pay little if any attention to Wayne whenever Rebecca was around. And she was developing enough concern for the boy that she was irritated to find him being toyed with by Judith. It just didn't make sense.

Rebecca moved decisively from the chair in her office, stuffed the hat in her satchel, picked up her walking stick and left. She hated to do this, but she had to be certain. Her power was adequate to do a reading on the building, of that she was certain. She would use the hat as a talisman to determine if Judith was the culprit. If she was, it was not a matter for the police.

Her master key led her swiftly through the academic building and into the library proper. She was thankful for influential friends as high as the president emeritus of the college who saw to it that her key was always current and that no one asked why she needed it. She opened the door of the rare books room and keyed in the numerical sequence that aborted the alarm. The light blinked green.

She did not like this room—never had. It had been refurbished four years previously and an elaborate alarm system had been installed. The shelves and boxes that once stood here were changed to air-tight vaults for the preservation of rare texts and manuscripts. But this was the room in which The Blade first attacked her husband and the encounter still reverberated in Rebecca's ears as she opened the high door to the roof.

Over the years, this had become her private sanctuary. No one came up here. She had discovered, soon after her initiation into Coven Carles, that there was an intersection of ley lines beneath the building. The junction, while not as powerful as those found in many of the holy shrines, was still strong enough to give a sense of stability and balance to her rituals. She had a better view of the sky and stars than she could get amid the city lights below. Here she celebrated each of the sabbats when she was unable to join her brothers and sisters in England. Just three weeks ago, she'd lain on the roof, delighted to see her lights joining others celebrating Beltane and had wondered if one of the lights had been the joining of Wayne and Judith. She was surprised to find herself aroused by the thought.

In the center of her circle she placed the hat. She invoked the guardians of the watchtowers as she had been taught years before, naming each cardinal quarter and inviting it to attend her ritual. She felt a charge of electricity as she visualized the white light that would surround her workings as it flared into existence. This was how power was meant to feel—pure, fresh, cleansing. Perhaps she had been wrong to deny its use for so long. Half-remembered words attributed to Aleister Crowley crept into her consciousness. "The difference between white magic and black magic is that white magic is poetry and black magic works." Was that what she was so afraid of?

She stood on the north side of the hat and stretched her walking stick out over it. In ritual use, it was her wand, Pele, that Doc Heinrich had helped her cut fifteen years ago—the first step toward her eventual initiation. She began humming as she so often did when she worked, letting breaths become notes and notes become words as she put together a chant of divination to determine whether it was Judith who kept breaking into the theatre beneath her. Rebecca was convinced that it was someone with power that kept them from being discovered.

She had barely begun her chant when she sensed a presence nearby. With the half-aware reflex of a person who had lived much of her life ready for attack, Rebecca spun away from the center of the circle as a knife materialized in the air. It hit and stuck straight up through the crown of the hat. Instinctively, Rebecca willed her wards to greater strength and crouched, her own knife coming readily to hand. She listened, straining her ears for the least sound breaking the silence.

The circle flared white all around her, but there was no other movement.

Rebecca dropped her wards and slipped into shadow. Her knife stayed ready in her right hand and her staff was clutched firmly in her left. She was quite able to defend herself, but needed to find the assailant first. If it was The Swordmaster, perhaps she was not quite so able to defend herself. The young woman had earned her title. But Rebecca had once defeated The Blade. She would take her chances against this new opponent. She moved carefully around the walls of the library stacks that jutted above the roof level at which she worked, keeping her ears cocked for a sound from above. A full circle of the area brought her back to her sanctuary and she faced the only other structure that jutted above the roof at this height—the fly space and fire windows of the stage. She could see no shadows moving; could hear no sounds.

Determined to flush out her attacker, Rebecca sprang out and rushed across the thirty feet from the wall at her back to the theatre windows and then spun to look back. She saw only the slight movement of the door to the rare books room closing. She ran to it and pulled at the handle. It was locked tightly. The doorstop she had used to prop it open lay nearby. Her way off the roof was blocked.

"Damn!" she hurled at the closed door. She spun to face the knife in the crown of the hat. She was furious. It had no handle and was dull, scarcely the shape of a knife, not the finished product. Yet that shape was familiar. She had seen Creüs before—done battle with its caretaker—had seen the knife descending toward her breast.

This replica was perfectly placed in the crown. It had not been meant to hit her. It had landed exactly where the thrower intended. In fact, as she remembered, it materialized directly over the hat inside her wards. *Was it a sign?* Rebecca's power was not that of the wind. When her power first rose in her those years ago, it had been the power of fire.

She stretched out her wand toward the blade, flexing her right hand with remembered pain and remembered power as she did. The end of her wand touched the knife.

Burn.

The word was on the tip of her tongue but unspoken as she remembered ritual fire that had burned out of control. The charred handle of the knife she now carried and the red color of her staff were constant reminders of that night. *Burn.*

Saturday, 8 August 1955

IT WAS ONLY a few days after Lughnasad when she came into her room in Edinburgh to find the sacrificial tableau. There was no question in her mind regarding who was responsible. The Blade, keeper of the First Face of Coven Carles, had his own agenda and had violated her private space. But in his act, he had provided two new tools. Her walking stick, given to her by Doc, would become her wand. The knife that The Blade had left impaling it would be her *Athamé.*

"May you find pleasure in my act, oh most high ones. May you see a tool of good sanctify and purify a tool of evil and turn it to your service. I name this wand Pele! Firerod, flaming beauty, angel of fire, purifier of the unclean. Brigit, goddess of fire, to you be this rod sanctified."

Rebecca, now fully the witch Sadb, raised her hands to the East and began slowly turning clockwise, gathering into her more power as she commanded the blessings of the powers of all the elements on her wand. She stumbled a little as she came back to the East and saw the sacrificial tableau again. She could feel a crackling surge of power all around her and faltered beneath the influence of the assault on her senses. She was filled with strength and power that she was not sure she could control. Her eyes focused on the mock sacrifice, the stiletto still protruding from her sanctified wand. Rage overcame her doubt as she glared at the scene.

"How dare you!" she screamed. "I will not be intimidated by you. You will be pure. You will be free!"

Sadb raised a hand to point at the dagger without touching it. She could feel the force gathering behind her for what she intended. She spun, gathering the powers of the elementals together again and felt another surge in her hands.

So, this is power, she thought as she drifted once again around the circle with arms outstretched, collecting more strength as she passed each point. This is what Phaethon felt when Helios handed him the reins of the Sun Chariot and told him to drive the horses of dawn. No wonder Zeus struck him down. Such power could destroy the earth. And I am the focus of the cone of power. It lives in me. I can do whatever I will.

She focused her eyes on the stiletto and on her wand. She stretched out her hands and began to chant.

"I name thee Elhin. Wind master, air spirit, *Athamé*. May the fires of Brigit purify you. May Pele rise in the volcanic forge to burn away the dross of your making. May you be lifted ever and only in the service of the goddess. May that hand which wielded you feel and know the force of this power."

I bind this spell by three times three;
As I do speak, so mote it be.

"Burn!" Smoke rose from the staff as it darkened and flamed. All around the knife, the fire danced from her wand, licking up the blade of the knife.

The four winds whipped a cyclone around her. It fanned the flames rising from her wand. The fire had a life of its own, running the length of the wand and licking up the blade. The red candle melted to a mere puddle, the flames hanging like some overripe fruit about to fall. And fall it did, dripping flames back onto the dresser, burning some invisible fuel on the surface. Then they reached deeper into the finish and into the charring wood.

Sadb realized with a sudden fright that she was no longer in control of the fire. She burst into tears at the knowledge of what she must do even before the searing physical pain of the hot knife penetrated the nerves of her hands. She jerked it out of the burning wood and raised it above her head, screaming in agony. Then she drove downward with all her might, burying the knife again, this time into the floorboards. With that act, all her barriers dropped and she released the warding powers that had ensured her privacy.

Wednesday, 21 May 1969

BURN. The word did not pass her lips. She placed her staff back on the gravel roof and felt the flood of energy drain from her as she was grounded. That was the power she had sworn never to use again. The power that destroyed, that had destroyed everything she loved. She might die in an attack, but she would not attack herself.

What she needed now was a way off the roof. She packed her belongings and headed toward the fire windows.

It was midnight and Wayne was pissed as hell. Rehearsal had been cancelled. Instead he spent four hours leading administration officials, police, a private detective, and two dogs through the scene shop, props closet, and costume wardrobes on a drug hunt. They were convinced now that drugs were hidden on the premises somewhere. Four break-ins in a year. *Unbelievable.*

And Jim was turning on him. After the hunt, he had made it perfectly clear that Wayne's future as technical supervisor for the theatre was also in jeopardy, as was the trip to England. It was a real mess. Wayne couldn't see past his nose for the fury that burned in him.

Back in his room, after seething and swearing for a good hour, he turned at last to the little shrine on his top shelf. A pine box with his uncle's journals in it. A knife wrapped in black silk and burlap. A black robe. The incense burner that had been there was missing, an acute reminder of the last time he experimented with what was written in the book. Well, this time would be no experiment, he determined, as he reached for the box and robe. His uncle had written of a means of protecting a building from break-in that he had used during the war. It was a complex spell and when his uncle had done it, he was inside the building. Wayne would have to try to do it from outside. It should work, he thought. He'd just have to think it through inside out. Somehow, that made sense to him in his angered state.

He'd never thought that a bulky black robe might be good for sneaking across campus without being seen, but when he donned it, he felt absorbed into the midnight shadows. They were easy to find and he slipped from one to another without a chance of being seen. Had he found any other way to spend his anger, he would have thought what he was doing was terribly funny.

"Berserk student dons black sheet and does hocus pocus dance around school building," Wayne mentally read the newspaper headlines. "Boy burned at stake for practicing witchcraft," the next one read. *What in the name of all the powers are you trying to do? Go to a movie.*

The thoughts were kept just below the surface as Wayne traced a circle around the entire building with the point of the knife just touching the ground as he walked backward. It took nearly five minutes to completely circle the building the first time. He kept going when he passed his starting point, chanting the words he had learned from his uncle's *Book of Shadows.* A breeze caught up with him as he went. By the third circuit he could feel a regular wind following him.

His third circuit was nearly complete when a figure dropped out of a window above him, hit him in the shoulder and sent him sprawling. It knocked the wind out of Wayne and he was slow getting up. He could just see the figure disappear across the parking lot when he got to his feet.

"Damn you!" he said beneath his breath, not daring to shout into the silent night air. "I'll get you. I will get you for this." His anger renewed, he finished the last ten feet of the circle, jabbed the knife angrily into the ground and said, "I'll blow you to hell when I get you."

The sudden wind nearly knocked Wayne off his feet. He thought first of the tornado just a few weeks before and then of his uncle's words afterward. "Oh shit," he whispered. But the wind did not increase and away from the building it scarcely seemed to move at all. But when he reached for the knife where it stuck from the ground, he could feel the constant wind, blowing the same direction that he had traced the circle. He knew that something was working right.

REBECCA WAS FIGHTING a wind as she struggled to get down from the roof of the building. The fire windows over the theatre had recently been inspected, locked, and the loose window she had once used replaced. Well it was only three stories, she reminded herself as she tested the guy-wire of the school's radio station sending tower. On one side of the building, the wire was anchored into the ground some sixty feet away from the building. The angle should break her fall enough to not get seriously injured if she could brake her descent. But this was *not* her idea of fun.

She folded the hat in half, placed it across the wire and then placed her staff across the hat. Taking hold of both ends, she launched herself out and away from the edge of the building, sliding at peak speed down the cable. As her feet touched the ground she crumpled and rolled, continuing the forward motion from her descent. She lay there gasping for air, inventorying her body to see that everything was intact. It was, much to her relief. She gathered her belongings from the ground and struggled home. She had not learned what she wanted to learn, but she had certainly found more questions.

"You wouldn't have believed it, Chameleon," he said. "I cast the spell and it worked. I pushed toward the door of the building and I couldn't make it. The farther in I pushed, the hard the wind was to push against. Three feet away you can barely feel the air move. A foot away and you are being blown back and away."

"And how long is this spell supposed to last, Unbound?"

"It will last until I lift it, I suppose. Is there a magic half-life? Does it get weaker in the daylight? Shit! People have to get into the building in the morning. They won't understand. I thought I did it all right. I'd better get over there and dismiss it."

"Don't panic, sweetheart. You did good. You just need to be there before the first person arrives in the morning. Let's see, sunrise is at six-thirty. If you are there to release the spell at six o'clock, you should be fine. What shall we do till then?" she teased.

"Uh… are we going to have sex again?"

"I'm not your lover, apprentice. For me, sex was simply a way to open you up to the fullness of your power. We might do that again, but not tonight," she said.

"I feel powerful, but I don't feel complete, yet. I don't know what to do."

"Well, one thing is the gathering of your tools. You've been given a knife and pentacles. They are powerful and you are working way advanced spells with nothing else. But I have a little gift for you, too."

"You've been very generous to me already, Chameleon. I don't need a gift from you."

"That's why it is such fun to give you something. Finish your coffee. I mean drain it completely this time."

Wayne drank the coffee, bracing himself for grounds in the bottom of the cup. There were none and when he looked into the cup he saw a star painted on the bottom. He looked more closely and discovered a pattern of stars and astrological symbols all around the bottom of the cup.

"This isn't a Donut World cup," he mused.

"No. This is *your* cup. It's the same shape as a Donut World cup, but it is customized for you. I think the cup is a special symbol for you. It's usually filled with either very fresh water, like from a running stream, or salt water from the ocean. For you, though, you will always have power flowing through you when you drink coffee from your cup."

"That seems so silly, Chameleon."

"So does speaking the words of a spell aloud when you are alone. But that's the only way it works. Magic isn't about the unusual, but rather about the common being recognized as magical. We use magic every day and never think a thing about it. We utter spells, prayers, oaths. It's when we are reminded about it that it becomes special. Now when you drink your coffee, you will be reminded of the power in your cup. And now that you have three tools, your power will grow again."

"It would if I could ever remember it. I didn't think about it at all tonight until I was in my room, swearing and taking out my frustrations beating my pillow. Then, all of a sudden, I saw my robe and *Athamé*, and I knew what I had to do. Until they became my focus, it was all like a dream."

"Relish the dreams, Unbound. In them you will learn the secrets."

12
A Walk in the Park

Friday, 30 May 1969

"OKAY," JIM said as the cast stood to leave after Friday night notes. "We've got it pulled back together. Good rehearsal." The cast cheered. "Don't forget the reception Sunday afternoon. Dr. Crowell has gone to a lot of work to get us funding for the tour. It's only right that we show our best side to the patrons on Sunday. Be there at 12:30 for lunch in the Lilly Room. Anything else?"

"Party tomorrow!" yelled Steve. "Spring tour of Brown County. Meet in Nashville at the town pump at two o'clock."

"And drive carefully," added Jim. "We don't need any accidents at this stage of the game. Stay sober."

The cast filed out of the auditorium with various hoots of freedom. Rebecca stopped Wayne with a hand on his shoulder.

"Well, coach?" she said. "How'd we do?"

"You heard him," Wayne answered. "Right on!"

"Yes, but how did you feel?"

"It's going to be better than it was in the fall," he smiled. "And it was all pros then."

"Good! I finally feel like it will be fun."

"Are you going to the party tomorrow?" he asked.

"I hadn't really thought about it."

"I'd…uh…pick you up if you want to go," he stumbled. She thought for just a moment before she responded.

"Well, I am part of the cast. I suppose I should act like it. What time?"

"How about nine. Take a spin through the park and poke through the shops in Nashville before we meet the group," he bubbled.

"You're on," she said. She walked out the door toward home. He looked after her as she disappeared down the street.

"Wow!"

"Judith's going to kill you." He turned around to see Lena, the assistant director standing behind him making notes on her clipboard. Down the hall he heard Judith's voice and looked up to see her talking animatedly with the actor playing Hamlet. They left together. He smiled sheepishly at Lena and backed toward the door at the opposite end of the hall.

"What a way to go," he said.

Saturday, 31 May 1969, early morning

"No, SERIOUSLY. IT's supposed to fill itself with water?" Wayne asked Lissa late that night. "How am I supposed to believe that?"

"Did you call wind with your blade?" she asked.

"Well, a wind blew each time I did a ritual. The last one was more controlled than the first. I guess I must have been responsible. But that's just moving air currents. This is actually drawing water from someplace it is to someplace it isn't."

"What is so different?"

"It's… I don't know."

"Each tool has its own element that you tune it to. Your *Athamé* is attuned to air. Your cup to water. Your pentacles to earth. And your wand to fire. In order to work the spell, you have to work with the tool, practice with it the same way you do with the woodworking tools in your shop."

"May I have another cup of coffee, please?" he asked. She reached for the pot and refilled his cup. "It worked!"

"Smartass. Still… in a way you got it right. You fully expected the cup to be filled. Not only do the tools represent an element, they represent a power… a personage that has power. There are different traditions. Some practitioners use angels—Michael, Uriel, Raphael, and Gabriel. I always name them clockwise from East to North. Some practitioners use demons, Native American spirits—Raven, Coyote, Beaver, and Badger—fairies, Celtic gods, Norse gods, Greek gods. It really doesn't make a difference whom you choose. In fact, I suspect they might all be one. So, when you cast a spell, especially an elemental, you invoke the name of the power for that element and ask him or her to serve you. Respect them because they are powerful, but be firm. You have to be in control."

"That's what Dad says. Like a motorcycle, it's only dangerous when it's out of control," Wayne mused. He neglected to add that his dad was talking about women.

"Smart man."

WAYNE PULLED UP in front of Rebecca's house promptly at nine o'clock Saturday morning. She was sitting on the front porch with a cup of coffee and a newspaper, but scarcely glanced when he pulled up.

"Rebecca?" he said, stepping up to the porch.

"Hi!" she said in surprise. "Oh! My God! That was you?"

"Were you expecting someone else?" he asked.

"I wasn't expecting…" she stared at the street, "…a motorcycle." Wayne burst out laughing.

"I thought you knew."

"I knew you *rode* one, but I didn't know that was how you intended… Oh, my God!"

"Well, would you like to try it out?" he asked. "If you're really uncomfortable, we could still catch Glenn and hitch a ride with him."

"It's… I…" Rebecca stammered. "Do you know how old I am?" she said finally.

"A gentleman would never ask, but I have to assume you are over eighteen. I hope."

"I don't believe I'm doing this," she said, walking to the motorcycle with him. "I'm a mature, stable, responsible adult and I think I have just lost all my marbles. What do I do with Pele?"

"Who's Pele?"

"My walking stick."

"You can put it here," he said, showing her how to strap the stick into place.

"Her," corrected Rebecca.

"Okay," responded Wayne. "Put her here, but don't try to swing your leg over the back of the bike or you're likely to get a good sharp poke." He mounted the cycle and kicked it to life, then assisted Rebecca with her helmet. "Climb aboard," he called to her. She slid easily into place behind him and he felt her arms lock firmly around his waist. He accelerated away from the curb.

"This is crazy," she said and he felt her bury her head against his back. Fifteen minutes later they were cruising south on Highway 31.

"How's it going?" he called over his shoulder.

"I love it!" she yelled into the wind.

By 10:30, they were in Nashville and entered the gates of the state park a few minutes later. He parked the motorcycle and they got off to stretch.

"Well?" he asked. "Like it?"

"Other than being passed by semis," she answered. "It was wonderful. But parts of my body may not stop tingling for a while. Is it always like that?"

Wayne laid down his helmet and reached both hands behind him to rub his seat. "Every time I've ever ridden it has been. But it's worth it!"

"A girl could get to like that too much," Rebecca muttered as she unstrapped her staff. They walked along the trail through the woods and fresh greenery a while in silence. Finally, it was Wayne who spoke.

"So, are you glad you joined the cast?" he asked.

"It's had its little trials and tribulations, but yes. I'm having fun."

"I wanted you to know," he said quietly, "that I'm really glad that I've been able to work with you. I mean, getting to know you as a person instead of a professor has really... I mean you're a neat person."

"Thank you, Wayne. May I say that getting to know you as a person instead of a somnambulist has been a treat, too." They laughed and walked on in silence for a long way.

"Say, what's Serepte doing today?" he finally asked. "I haven't seen her in a while."

"She's been around, but since school is out now, she's visiting her godparents. I told you he was ill. There's been some trouble around campus this spring and I don't want her here when we go to England."

"I didn't hear about trouble, except the damned theatre break-ins. One of the frats getting high?"

"No. No. It was a personal problem."

"Gosh, I'm sorry," Wayne said. "It must be really difficult being a single parent."

"It's not between Serepte and me, Wayne. I really can't get into this..." They were cut off by a voice not far away.

"Bloody, bawdy villain! Remorseless, treacherous, lecherous, kindless villain!"

"Someone's rehearsing," Wayne said. They shared a surprised glance at each other and proceeded forward into a clearing. They stopped just at the edge beneath a large tree to watch. There, Judith stood with her back about three-quarters to them. Beside her stood Chuck, the actor playing Hamlet.

"No!" Judith said. "You've got to know precisely where that throne is. You can't turn around and hunt for it. Mark the spot. Now watch." They all watched as she raised the knife in both hands in a self-sacrificial pose. She drew her first syllable out over a full range of emotions from self-pity to a roaring inferno of rage. "Oh, Vengeance!" she shouted. She spun toward Rebecca and Wayne. He saw a flash in the air and shoved Rebecca to the ground.

The knife hit and stuck in the tree under which the two had been standing. Wayne scrambled to his feet swearing at Judith. He could hear her equally uncouth reply. He helped Rebecca to her feet and apologized for the roughness. Rebecca, however, seemed totally absorbed in the knife that protruded from the tree. Wayne laid his hand on the hilt and worked the blade free.

"Damn it, Judith!" he shouted. "Who checked this out to you?" These props are all supposed to be crated and ready to ship now."

"T-take it easy, Wayne," Chuck said. "We looked for you last night, but you were gone already. I n-need the practice and talked her into bringing it down."

"It wasn't made to be stuck into trees," Wayne lectured the two. "You'll split the handle off, throwing it around like that."

"I'm supposed to throw it on stage."

"Into a beadboard-backed throne, not into a chunk of wood."

"Wayne," said Judith next to him. Her voice was low but edged more sharply than the knife itself. "Give me the fucking knife. Take your lady friend and get lost. Or did you forget that this was supposed to be our date today?"

"It looked like you already had an alternate plan," Wayne said, matching the edge in her voice. "If you'd spoken to me anytime in the last week it still would have been our date."

"Give me the knife!"

"Hell no! This is going into my bag and straight to the props chest."

"What are we supposed to rehearse with?" she demanded.

"Here," said Rebecca. "I'm sure you can use this one. And I don't think I'll be needing it anymore." She produced the flat steel blade from her bag that had landed in her circle a few days before. She laid it flat in her hand and held it out to Judith. The younger woman looked startled for a moment.

"You're going to replace it," Judith said in disbelief. "After all the warnings, you're still going to do it." The two locked eyes. "Don't do it, Huntress," Judith whispered, her back to Chuck. "Please, don't do it. I love him."

"The task has to be completed, Swordmaster."

The words hardly reached Wayne's ears. His attention was captured by the blade being passed between the two women. In his mind, he saw the drawer in which he kept steel blanks for swords and knives. Of the two matched blades he ordered, was one still in the drawer with the other blanks? He wasn't going to fight them for that one right now. His stomach was churning so hard he felt like throwing up. Huntress. Swordmaster. It should mean something to him, but it was as if it were behind a veil. Another of his elusive dreams.

"Just be careful, would you?" he shot across to the two. "That scene's too damned dangerous on stage anyway. Get in lots of practice, okay, Chuck?"

"Sure. Look, would you just let us get on with it?"

"Yeah," said Wayne. He looked into Judith's eyes. They dropped slightly and he shook his head. Why was it so difficult with them? "Enjoy yourselves," he said shortly. He led Rebecca out of sight. They stopped at a picnic area where Wayne worked vigorously at a pump and took a long drink. He kept pumping long enough for Rebecca to drink before they sat at a table.

"I'm sorry," he said at last. "Things have been up and down between Judith and me lately."

"Dating can be like that. I'm sorry I've come between you."

"It's not like that, exactly. I mean… I hope I didn't hurt you when I pushed you down."

"I learned how to fall a long time ago," Rebecca said. "You have good reflexes and reaction time. You just need to learn economy of action."

"What do you mean?" he asked.

"I've had some pretty good teachers—almost as good as Judith's, though I'm not as skilled with a blade as she is. If a simple move of your head will save your life, you don't need to roll on the ground. If you react as little as possible, you will be upright, positioned to defend yourself. You will be the calm in the midst of the storm."

"With the winds whistling around me," Wayne said. It meant something, he was sure. Rebecca looked at him intently. "You always expect to be attacked, don't you? Why?" he asked.

"It's a paradox. I was attacked several years ago and found myself defenseless. I swore I'd never be unprepared again. The more prepared you are, it seems, the more likely you are to attract attacks. It's a hopeless circle."

"Nixon should take lessons from you," Wayne cracked. "How many times have you been assaulted?"

"Three, on campus. Four if you count the most recent. But I never saw the attacker that time." A sudden moment of enlightenment struck Wayne.

"That knife you just gave Judith?" he asked.

"Arrived at an unexpected moment in the middle of the night," she answered.

"It wasn't Judith." The idea was too diabolical to put into words.

"I don't know."

"I know where that knife came from," Wayne said into emptiness. "It's a perfect match for this one." He held out the prop knife. "I buy them in pairs. I'm sure I'll find the mate to this missing when I get back to the shop. That must have been what was taken in the last break-in. Only I know that it's not Judith. I was… with her then."

"Regardless, it wasn't meant to hurt me… this time. Maybe it was a message. Maybe it was meant to scare me." Wayne listened to the words, still thinking of Judith even after vindicating her.

"Away from me?"

"Or toward someone else. Say," Rebecca broke the train of thought. "May I see the other knife?"

"Sure," Wayne said, handing her the hilt of the knife. The weapon was smooth, shiny and very plain, like a key blank that was waiting to be cut. The handle was of ebony and reminded Rebecca of what her own *Athamé* had once looked like.

"Where did you locate this?" she asked.

"I made it," he answered. "I like crafting things out of wood mostly, but some metal. Especially jewelry and that sort of thing."

"Really? Where did you get the pattern?"

"My…" Wayne was suddenly confused. He felt like he should be able to talk to Rebecca about this, but something prevented him. When he tried to get to that part of his brain, it was all muzzy. "I found a picture that I liked. I have a favorite uncle who sends me stuff like that."

"You must be very close," Rebecca said.

"One of those weird things, you know," Wayne said. "We write to each other a lot. I have all his letters. But we've only ever met twice. Or three times," he added, thinking of that night in March. "Isn't that weird?"

"Stranger things have been known," she said, handing the knife back to him. Their hands touched briefly as he took the knife from her. Neither made any effort to hurry as they slid slowly apart. He tucked the knife away in his travel bag and coughed slightly.

"That sure is a beautiful cane you've got, by the way," he said pointing at her walking stick.

"Cane?" laughed Rebecca. "No woman who rides a motorcycle behind a man for an hour and a half to take a walk in the woods and have a knife thrown at her is old enough to use a cane."

"I didn't mean that! I mean… walking stick, then," he spluttered. "I mean, I was just thinking that the first time I ever really looked at it, it was raised over my head like a club."

"She's very protective," said Rebecca.

"You said 'she' once before."

"Sure. Every walking stick has an individual personality," she answered. "It retains a part of the character of the person who shaped it, held it and used it. I suppose there are 'its' in the world, but I've never met one. In my experience, they've all been 'he' or 'she'." This sounded familiar to Wayne. *Something about the tool retaining the spirit of the maker. What was it?*

"That's neat," he said at last, grasping a simile he could understand. "It's sort of like building a set. You feel like there's a part of you in every paint splash. Only then you strike it and it's gone. That's why I take so much time making some of the props, like the swords for *Hamlet* or the masks for *Antigone*. I buy the materials for special items myself and keep them when it's over. I'll have a little bit of each show reserved for old age."

"What a wonderful sentiment," she said. "I had no idea what it really meant to you." They sat silently for a few minutes listening to the birds and the wind. When Rebecca spoke again, her voice was far away. "Pele was cut not far from here. Doc Heinrich and Margaret Jacobsen brought Wesley and me down here before my first trip to the British Isles, fifteen years ago. Doc told me all about wood and trees and staffs. Then he helped me cut her out of the forest."

"Is Wesley your husband?" asked Wayne quietly.

"Mmmhmm."

"Serepte told me he was gone. I'm sorry."

"Gone but not forgotten," she said. "He used to teach at the college. He was lost on an archaeological expedition with Doc and Margaret in Greece. He's still alive though, I'm sure. I'd know if he was dead. He's either wandering around not knowing who he is, or imprisoned somewhere, unable to get out."

"God, I'm sorry. It must be awful. My uncle told me about the unrest in Greece. He used to live there." They were quiet. Listening.

"Look, young man," Rebecca turned the subject aside abruptly. "Margaret once told me that you could wander the world in any condition you wanted to, but you couldn't tour Great Britain without a walking stick. Come on. Looking at you, I'd guess that hickory would be your wood. Let me tell you about it."

IN THREE-QUARTERS OF an hour they had located a stand of young hickory trees and Rebecca helped select a piece of standing deadwood for his walking stick. It was a sturdy two inches across at the base, tapering to a little over an inch about six feet up.

"Just one problem," Wayne said. "We don't have a saw." He involuntarily jumped as Rebecca's knife materialized in her hand. His eyes never left the straight thin blade of her *Athamé*. "Gees!" he exclaimed as she opened her hand to show the entire knife to him. Attached to the four-inch blade was the charred remnant of a wooden handle. "That was a slick maneuver. Where do you keep that thing?"

"Hidden but at hand," she said. "I prefer my staff for protection, but sometimes the blade is necessary."

"It's not a weapon, though."

"Look at the stone over there," she said, pointing to a fist-sized rock. "It is neutral. It could be used as a weapon. It could be used as a building block. It could be ground up and used as cement. It could be carved into an idol and worshiped. You could simply fall over it if you weren't looking where you walked. Stones are defined by their use, not by their nature. The same is true of any tool. I use this knife for… ritual. But it is quick at hand if needed for something else. Like cutting your walking stick." She wasn't sure Wayne got the message, but she saw a glimmer of recognition in his eyes. She assumed Judith had placed a block against him talking about his instruction, a sensible precaution. She would have to do the same thing if she taught him more. Like the importance of his staff.

"Ach! Hickory is hard wood," she complained as she cut at the dead sapling.

"Here, let me work at it a bit," he volunteered. She stopped cutting and stood up, ready to simply decline. The intense look of excitement on his face changed her mind. She remembered when she cut her own stick, impatiently waiting for Doc to let her help. And that was before…

"Let me see your hand." He held out both hands, palms upward. "Elhin is very cautious about who touches him," she said.

"You named your knife, too?"

"Is that so unusual? I heard you calling your motorcycle 'Troilus' this morning. Regardless, he is very dear to me and to place him in another's hand is a sign of perfect trust." His eyes didn't waver from the knife as she lightly traced a star in the palm of his left hand, the point of the blade scarcely touching his skin. "I do trust you, Wayne, as you obviously trust me." In the center of the star she pricked his skin. Then she did the same to her own left palm. They clasped their hands together. "Your blood now courses through my veins and mine through yours. Our tools unite to our common good for all time."

"So mote it be," Wayne whispered. Rebecca smiled. She laid the blade across his open palms. The grove went silent with her whispered invocation and Wayne stood as if he were simply absorbing the power from Elhin. He bent to finish cutting his staff. When he had finished, he straightened with the stick held firmly in his left hand, the knife held out in his open right hand.

"What are you called?" Rebecca asked softly.

"The Unbound."

"A vagabond," Rebecca gasped.

"Like Keats," Wayne answered. Finally, he could let her know he understood.

"Exactly like Keats," Rebecca answered. "I am called The Hart, or more commonly now, The Huntress." She took the knife from him.

"Two sides of the same coin."

"Indeed."

"What happened to the handle?" he asked softly.

"It was in a fire," she answered. "A long time ago."

"I'll make a new one for him if you'd like," he said.

"Would you? I'd be very pleased and proud." Their eyes locked together for a moment. She could see him leaning toward her, her upturned face a magnet for his lips. She was a woman and unmistakably responded to him as a man. She turned away and the moment was gone. "Let me tell you how to care for your companion there," she said as she led him from the thicket.

Saturday, 20 August 1955, Kastraki, Greece

His lips irresistibly pressed against hers and she was locked in the embrace before she was fully awake. She opened her lips to accept the invitation of his tongue and their kiss rose in passion. How odd for

Wesley to make such an open demonstration in the courtyard. He took her so much by surprise while she was still in her half-waking state that she could not help responding to the intimacy.

He lifted her, dancing around the courtyard… dancing like they had on the mountain, still lost in that intimate kiss. Flickering images behind her tightly closed eyelids reminded her first of the dance on the mountain and then of the dances around the fire at Carles. Naked dancing bodies circling the fire. The intimacy of the spiral dance, of feather caresses against each of the coven dancers. Her lover was even more passionate than he had been in the City of the Gods, in their bed, on the bridge.

She felt her body lifted in the air as if she weighed nothing—perhaps supported only by the passionate kiss. She was raised and lowered horizontally to their bed, yet so much higher than the bed in their cottage. Still, the breeze began to play beneath the buttons of her blouse and she felt the fabric fall away. She felt his soft caress of her breasts and moaned into his mouth.

When a sharp point began caressing her flesh, dreaming fled from her head. She'd felt the bite of this knife at the stone circle when she was initiated. It traced a familiar pattern between her breasts and then slid beneath the front of her bra, slicing through the fabric and letting it spring away from her tender breasts. A sickening sensuality mixed liberally with fear and revulsion as she pushed away from her lover. He held fast to her lips with a hand clenched in her hair and the knife continuing to trace patterns on her bare torso. It generated a pain in her stomach—a sickness that made her revolt from the continued passion. She drew into the sickness and exploded outward, thrust her sadistic would-be lover away from her, and opened her eyes to see Ryan McGuire grinning above her.

She lay stretched out on the platform that had been built to hold the old man's funeral pallet, her breasts bare to the sky. Surrounding herself and the entire well was the shimmering light of a warded circle through which she could scarcely define the shapes of the surrounding cottages. Beside her, stood The Blade, a black leather-gloved hand still stretched out to touch her with the ritual *Athamé* of Cobhan Carles.

"What is this?" she demanded, taking control and pushing his gloved hand away from her. "Are you afraid to leave fingerprints in your criminal activity?" The arousal and passion had fled from her as soon as she opened her eyes. She could stand naked before this man and have no response.

He grabbed her healed hand and looked at it, then held his gloved hand up next to it.

"I am not as quick to heal as you, Hart. Or were you faking an injury at the hospital?"

"There is no faking the power of the goddess," intoned Rebecca. "Let me help you—heal you."

"Oh, you will help me. You will help me raise the power that I need to open the veil. Your friends failed to bring down the goddess. I will not."

"There was no failure. You seek something that is not there."

"I have already searched and have found nothing, but your husband's notes. They will be helpful in opening the gates."

"It doesn't help to know *how* to search if you have no idea what you are looking for. You will find nothing on the mountain either. There is nothing there. And I've no interest in helping you raise power."

"You are past choosing," Ryan answered, pushing Rebecca back down on the pallet. "I want the goddess and you have the power. There may be more pleasant ways to raise it than under a sacrificial blade."

"Forget it, Blade. You are not who I thought you were. Not who I ever thought you were. You are far too late for a virgin sacrifice." Her hands darted out and clasped his gloved fist. She squeezed the injured hand with all her might, remembering the pain in her hand that she had suffered. The tender burned flesh beneath the glove tightened around the hilt of the *Athamé* and he yelled in anger and pain. The back of his good hand connected with her face, knocking her back down on the bier. The knife changed hands and Ryan's anger turned to laughter. There was a manic glow in his eyes.

"So, you like pain, do you? I'm very good at that." He moved toward her again with the knife poised, confident in his superior size and strength. This time the steel was met with her own blade and she rose upon the platform again, swinging her feet over the edge.

"A blade between us, as you told me," she said. "I'll leave now. I think you should, too."

He laughed. "Leave? You have missed the point. This is *my* warded circle. You cannot walk through someone else's wards. You can't leave me. We are locked here until love or death sets us free." Rebecca looked critically at the wards as she circled the well, staying on the opposite side from Ryan.

"Where are your pentacles, Blade?" Rebecca asked. She flicked her knife back and forth. A worn engraving caught her eye. "Did you give me something more than your Athamé when you attacked me? You did, didn't you? You combined your *Athamé* and your pentacles into a single tool and now they are in my possession."

"What difference does it make? Don't believe all that rubbish about witch's tools. They are merely symbols of the power held within. Magic is all in your head. The more powerful your mind the more powerful your magic."

"I see. And is the power of your mind supposed to make me fear your wards?" He lunged at her but she slipped beneath his guard in a feinted lunge. He spun on her and tripped her. Rebecca rolled away and placed herself between Ryan and the shimmering wall of light that surrounded the well.

"You are a pretty fighter, Hart. Circle now. The power is rising. Power is neutral. It is as strong in anger as it is in sex. You can feel it swirling around you in a vortex—yours to raise, mine to command."

"It's about to end," Whispered Rebecca. "You don't understand the powers you have been playing with. I can see from here that the lust for power has consumed you and controls you." Rebecca lifted the star stone from her pocket and held it between her fingers. "Have you looked deeply into your heart? Look at my pentacles, Blade. A hungry star-shaped void in space." The jewel sparkled in an odd way, as if the rays of light that missed it were more pronounced because of those that hit it and disappeared. She placed her stone against the engraving on the knife and could hear it his as the image on the blade disappeared. "It likes you, Blade. I like you, too. If we had met under other circumstances… Well, never mind about that."

She reached toward the warded wall of light with the black shimmering jewel in her fingers. Where it touched, the light ceased to be. The empty space in the ward grew until the entire shimmering wall of light was absorbed—sucked into the jewel—and was gone.

Ryan sank to his knees and dropped the *Athamé*. Both hands came to the sides of his head. "Stop it, Hart! For the Goddess's sake, please stop it!"

Rebecca placed the black void stone in her pocket. Ryan still knelt with his hands clutched against his forehead.

"My head. It tried… Battering my head."

THREE DAYS LATER, The Blade, the *Athamé*, her husband, and the teen who guided them were gone. The Hart was left with her daughter growing inside her. Rebecca Hart Allen swore she would never again tap the destructive power that she now knew lay dormant within her. And that was enough.

Until the High Priestess announced her intent to step down and her choice that Rebecca would take her place.

Friday, 21 June 1968, Northern England

"No!" THE ANGUISHED voice cried out. Rebecca watched the young blonde step into the circle. "You can't, mother! She hasn't the power to lead the children. You can't make her the high priestess. I challenge her!"

Rebecca was prepared to lay down her tools and leave the circle rather than face the challenge of the High Priestess's daughter. She simply wouldn't do it. But the High Priest stepped between them.

"The words of the High Priestess have been challenged. But it is not to you to determine the nature of the challenge, Swordmaster." The Barber—his name a satirical nod to his profession of doctor—had been chosen High Priest five years ago, a decision many in the coven regretted. "You challenge the power of The Hart, Swordmaster. Therefore, our decree is thus: The Hart shall have one year to use her power to gather the Four Faces of Carles. At Litha next year, she will present those tools to the gathered children. As she is the last person known to have seen Creüs, it will fall to her to call him to her or to consecrate a new blade for the coven. This will be done on the shortest night of the year, thirteen moons from now."

"That's not what I meant," The Swordmaster objected. The Barber smiled. The blonde marched to the northern gate, swept her sword in an arc and left the circle.

The priestess collapsed as Rebecca rushed to her.

"It is not what any of us wanted," she said. "From this moment forward, The Hart has become The Huntress. May you dream true. Blessed be."

"Blessed be," the circle chanted before it dissolved.

Sunday, 1 June 1969, Indianapolis, Indiana

THE WAY HAD been shown to Rebecca. There was never a doubt that the other tools would come to her. The Water Maiden placed the cup

Cottus in her hand that night, defying the High Priest. The staff had already been sent to her. The pentacles of the circle were known and would come when bidden. The proof of her power would be to either draw Creüs to her or to consecrate a new blade.

The blade that had found its way into her circle was an exact match for the lost tool, albeit without a handle or engravings. A blank waiting to be formed. Then she had seen the blade at its second stage, shining if not sharp, with an ebony handle polished to a dark sheen.

And she had discovered that Wayne Hamel, her one-time student, was a toolmaker.

13
Just Between Friends

Monday, 2 June 1969

WAYNE STARED at the contents of the crate with the declarations slip in hand. It would double as inventory when they packed and unpacked. He was ready to close the lid.

"Gail, is that everything from your end?" he called.

"Just a minute," she called back from the dressing room. She entered with a plastic box of assorted thread, needles and buttons. "Don't know why the last thing anyone ever thinks to pack is a sewing kit," she said. Wayne noted the addition on his list.

"Well, there shouldn't be anything else left in there for you to bring. We've packed everything the theatre owns."

"You didn't do too badly yourself," she said looking around at the clean and stripped-down shop. "You coming down for the party tonight?"

"Naw. I haven't even begun to put my own things together yet," he answered. "I've got two days of laundering to do before I can pack."

"Well, I'm off and out of your hair then," she answered. "You'll lock up?"

"Yeah, I'll check everything." She left and Wayne shifted the lid of the crate into place. He carefully hammered down the nails and secured the metal straps. It would travel just fine if anyone could lift it. Finished, he sat at the workbench where he had done so much props work in the past year. His art box sat in front of him on the bench. He had finished a couple of other projects in the last three days as well. His hickory stick lay across the bench, glistening with a fresh coat of tung oil. In his hands lay two polished pieces of rosewood. He carefully wrapped them in a piece of tissue and laid them in the box, then closed the lid.

"This place sure looks empty," said Judith from behind him. He jumped.

"Judith. My god, I didn't hear you come in," he said turning toward her.

"I'm a silent walker," she said. "Like a cat on the prowl. Meow." She did remind him of a cat the way she sidled up to him.

155

"The fog creeps in on little cat feet," Wayne quoted. There was a moment of silence as they looked at each other. "I… uh…" he started. "I'm sorry about Saturday."

"I came over to apologize, so don't take the words out of my mouth," she said. "Unless you intend to do it lip to lip." She kissed him. "I'm sorry. I haven't been much of a girlfriend lately. Too many things happening. Too much to regret."

"I haven't exactly been the King of Hearts," he answered. "I don't know what to say or do to make it better."

"Let's not muddy the water with anything but our apologies tonight," she said. "That way when we meet next time it can be fresh and new. You can find some clever way to introduce yourself."

"Hello. I love you. Won't you tell me your name?" he sang.

"Not bad, but I'm sure you can be more original than that." She leaned down and kissed him again lightly on the lips before she turned and left the room. Somehow, Wayne thought, there was a note of sadness in the way she had kissed him. He couldn't quite place it. Maybe he should go after her now.

No. He'd made a promise.

He picked up his walking stick and art box and checked to see that all the doors were locked. He took a quick glance at his watch then shut out the last of the lights. He was late already. He'd told Rebecca he'd be over at eight o'clock.

REBECCA MET HIM at the door and assured him that his late arrival had only allowed her enough time to finish getting ready. She led him to the kitchen. The table was arrayed with artifacts, among which were her walking stick and knife. When they entered the room, Wayne stared at the array. He felt a sudden shiver down his spine. Rebecca turned toward him from the kitchen door. In some way, he felt as though he had just been locked in. It didn't strike him as sinister or threatening. He felt secure, accompanied by a sure feeling that they would not be interrupted. He returned his attention to the table as they sat.

In addition to her walking stick and knife, the other staff that Wayne had brought to her was on the table and Wayne laid his own next to it. Two goblets were also on the table. One was pewter. The other was silver, set in a bronze stem and base. Both were heavily inscribed with some foreign letters. Wayne detached himself from the scene in his mind and tried to get a better view of the layout on the table. There was something special about it. Rebecca's staff, Wayne's staff, and the one that had been delivered lay side-by-side-by-side. Opposite them at the far end of the table lay a small ring, set with a black star-stone. Wayne's hand went automatically to his throat. Rebecca's knife lay on the table opposite the two cups. She had lit a candle in the center of the table.

"What are these things? I should know. I should put this over there," he said with his hand pulling the chain from his shirt.

"It's not necessary. You should keep it on. This is my circle and your tools are welcome guests."

Wayne's head had that cottony feeling that he got when something important was just beyond his reach. He knew something, but he couldn't bring it together. And the dreams this weekend confused him. Sometimes he couldn't separate them from reality. He really needed to get more sleep.

"Let me help," Rebecca said. She placed her hands on his temples gently rubbing to relax him. He smelled something that opened his senses.

"What is that?"

"Tiger balm. It will help to clear your head. You'll be able to focus. Now what you are seeing is a set of items that are said to work together as a focus for psychic power. You are working on one of the items—the knife you know as Elhin—so it was only fitting that the other items in the set be present for the restoration."

"Are you some kind of psychic?"

"Some kind. Most people have psychic power of one sort or another. If you are ready, you can begin with Elhin. Can I pour you coffee?"

His cup was missing. And his knife. That's what was needed. He should have brought them with him, but he'd already sealed them in the crate.

"Yes, thanks," he said sitting down at the table. His eyes came back once more to the array of objects as he opened his art box. There was a kind of sense to the way they were laid out on the table. He set to work on the small knife with carving tools and pliers.

"This arrangement reminds me of something. I should know it. Did I sleep through that class?"

"Yes, you should—and probably do—know it. But it wasn't covered in class. She's told you. It's just locked inside until you need it. I'll tell you, too, and put my own seal on your memories so you will dream true. They represent the four cardinal directions." A light came on in Wayne's mind.

"East for air," he said. "South for fire. West for water. North for earth."

"Right," Rebecca answered. "And the tools represent those elements. The *Athamé* or knife for the East, the staff or wand for the South, the cup for the West, and the disk or pentacles for the North."

"What is the language inscribed on the cup and staff? Is it Greek?"

"No. Not exactly," Rebecca said. "Why?"

"The letters are on my cup and knife and pentacles, but I don't know what they mean. I know the knife came from Greece, so I thought the letters might be Greek."

"Well, if you don't know Greek, it would be easy to confuse. I don't know the actual origin of the symbols. The alphabet is called Theban. It's a mystic rune alphabet. Each letter stands for a certain story, in addition to the letter itself."

Wayne carefully pried off the last of the charred handle from Rebecca's knife. He worked with the practiced ease of a skilled craftsman. He smoothed the shank with fine sandpaper and steel wool until it glistened.

"Now," he said to Rebecca. She sat across the corner of the table next to the ring watching every move. "I think you will like this." From his art box he produced a small, tissue-wrapped bundle. "Would you like to open it?"

"This is exciting," she said, accepting the bundle. She had not let him take the knife out of her sight to work on it, but she was far less reticent about letting him touch it. If he had the choice he would have done all the work in his shop and brought her the finished product. But she had insisted that the actual repair work be done in her kitchen. He watched as she unwrapped the little package and exclaimed in delight.

"It's beautiful!"

"I'm glad you like it. I know it means a lot to you," he said with obvious relief.

"Oh, I knew I'd like it," Rebecca answered. "But it is so much more wonderful than I imagined." She unwrapped the other half of the rosewood handle. In her hand, it was like a fine piece of red silk. With the limitation of only three days to complete the project, he had gone for simplicity and elegance. They were two smooth perfectly shaped and polished pieces of wood with one, almost overlooked, surprise.

"Wayne, what is this?" she asked. He was blushing. His cheeks felt like they were on fire.

"In all the best romantic literature, it's always a jeweled dagger. It's the only jewel I had. I hope it's okay."

"Okay? It's wonderful! But how did you ever...? You didn't buy this, did you?"

"I had an aborted engagement a couple of years ago, just out of high school," he explained. "I had the ring and... well, I wanted to do something special with it, but I couldn't exactly give it to another girl if I ever decided to get married, and..."

He was cut off by the woman's arms wrapping around him, pulling him up from his chair so she could kiss him as she hugged him tightly. "Thank you, oh, thank you, my friend."

Wayne was confused. She was a professor. She'd nearly flunked him out of school. Now they'd just kissed, and it wasn't just a friendly peck on the cheek or stage kiss. He'd become aroused and now—*shit!*—she was crying. He fumbled for a moment and pressed a clean handkerchief into her hand. She took it, but reached out to wipe a drop of moisture from his own cheek before using it.

"I'm sorry, Dr. Allen," he said. "I didn't mean to overstep..."

"Oh hush. And don't ever call me Dr. Allen when we are in a protected circle. No one has ever given me a diamond before."

They both started laughing, giggling as she pushed him down in his chair again. Wayne checked the fit of the handle on the shank of her knife, mixed epoxy, and spread it on the surfaces. He pressed the pieces together. Rebecca poured fresh coffee while he held them. He handed her the freshly hilted knife, its rosewood handle lying in her palm, the single diamond eye winking out at them.

"I guess we're ready to go to England now, Hart. Or are you now The Huntress?"

"I am known by both names. But let me tell you about consecrating a tool," she said. "In the process, I'm going to set up a sign between us so that what we say will be kept where you can process it but not talk about it until it is released. Look into my eyes."

Somewhere in the back of his mind, he remembered being hypnotized by Chameleon. There was nothing to worry about. The Swordmaster had placed a spell around certain memories so they would only come to him in dreams. There was nothing to worry about. Even his uncle had forbidden him to talk about the book and set a seal on his memories. There was nothing to worry about. The Hart entered his mind through his eyes. As he looked into their green depths, he could feel the locks being put in place that would let him access memories but not talk about them. Rebecca touched the pentacles at his throat to seal the covenant and Wayne knew that when she touched it, he would have full access to all he had learned. There was nothing to worry about.

He realized that Rebecca had his hickory staff in her hands and the point of her knife against it. He nodded.

"And what name has been given to this wand?" she asked formally.

"Er ist der Zauberlerling," Wayne answered. "I took a German reading class with Frau Doktor Mueller last year and we read Goethe's Sorcerer's Apprentice—*Der Zauberlerling.* With my record, it seemed like a good reminder."

"I don't know your record, but I wish I'd had that reminder when I was starting." She began to scratch into the wood with the point of her blade. Wayne cringed at first, but trusted her. He saw the shape as she inscribed it. "This first sigil is a name sign. It is the name of the staff. This second symbol is a gift sign." He watched her carve, carefully removing slivers of wood, as he drank his coffee. "Trust," she said almost to herself, "is the basis of friendship. It is why I let you work on my knife. It is why you let me share in your staff. It is why we must mend bridges between our brothers and sisters. Remember this. You are always welcome to enter the circle of my friendship if you come with perfect love and perfect trust."

"I come with perfect love and perfect trust," Wayne recited. The words were familiar. He knew he had said them before and would say them again.

"You wrote a paper last fall that I criticized harshly. In spite of the paper on which you based your research being a fake, the story it told was true."

"I know," Wayne said. "I dream things sometimes—well, a lot of the time. I was dreaming in your class the day you kept me to give me an opportunity. I'd dreamt the entire story before I found the paper in the library."

"A true dreamer? I should have let you sleep."

"I met someone who… knew…" Wayne was struggling against something, but if he didn't say his uncle's name or talk about his gifts he should be okay. "…who knew Wilton. I found out the story was true."

"I would like to know more about him sometime."

"I can't now, but when we can."

"They say The Vagabond left his spirit near Keswick as price for passage across the Derwentwater and it still walks the moors with its stick in hand."

"This stick," Wayne reached out and touched the walking stick still lying on the table next to Rebecca's. "This is Iäpetus, the staff of The Vagabond Poet."

"Your recognition is good. Do you recognize the cup as well?"

"No."

"It is Cottus, the cup of power. Now as to the dedication of your own staff, some of the older folk of the area are inclined to ask strangers on walking tour of the district if theirs is not the staff of The Vagabond Poet. If you are ever asked that question, you must show them this inscription and say simply, 'The Hart is in the Circle.' It will be a sign of recognition and any service they can render you, they will."

She handed the walking stick back to Wayne and he stared at the simple but elegant carving. Two tongues of fire crowned a heart. The whole was enclosed in a circle.

"You are The Hart," he said.

"I'll share my secret name with you, Unbound. In the circle I am Sadb, The Hart, now called The Huntress. Will I know your name?"

"I am Promethean, The Unbound."

Rebecca pondered that a moment and reached for a pad of paper from the kitchen counter. She carefully drew a sigil in the ancient rune alphabet.

"Here. I am giving you this name sign. You should carve your own sigil in your staff to bind it to you."

Wayne pulled a carving tool from his art box and traced the sigil onto his staff below the heart. In a few minutes, he admired the finished work.

"Merry meet and merry part and merry meet again," Rebecca said.

"Blessed be," Wayne responded automatically.

"Hold my secrets here in your heart," she said, touching the pentacles. He felt the release in the air almost as if he had been holding his breath. Rebecca moved to the right around the table, touching each of the objects as she went and placing the ring on her finger.

"Now, my friend," Rebecca said, "I've a favor to ask. I have a packing problem."

"All this?"

"Yes. It's one thing to carry a walking stick on board a plane. It's another thing for two people to carry them. But when one person has two staves, it becomes awkward at best. I can't travel without mine, and I must get this one back to England. Can we pack a couple of pieces in with the props?"

Wayne thought about the crate he had just sealed shut. But for Rebecca...

"Sure. We could take them over now if you'd like."

"Thank you."

Wayne pointed them away from the auditorium and down the street.

"We have to check in with the security guard," he explained. "I don't want to be caught down there after the building has been checked. We've had too many problems lately." The guard recognized Wayne and offered to unlock the building. Rebecca indicated that she could handle the doors with her passkey. The guard made a note in his book and told them to go on; he'd be by in half an hour to double-check the doors.

They walked to the auditorium building feeling the security guard's eyes on them the whole way. Rebecca's passkey got them into the building and Wayne used his keys to unlock the shop door. Inside, the crate waited on its dolly, banded and sealed as Wayne had left it.

"Oh no! I didn't know you had already closed it up."

"It's okay," he answered. "It'll only take a minute to open. Stand back." He cut the bands and pried the lid open with a crowbar. "The straps and nails are just for transit," he explained. "We know they'll cut them in customs for inspection. After that we just snap on the padlock and go from there."

Rebecca laid the staff and cup among the costumes. Then Wayne laid his own staff in the crate.

"You aren't carrying *Der Zauberlerling*?" she asked.

"Well, I was just thinking of what you said about carrying a staff on the plane and luggage and all. I don't particularly *need* to have him in hand until I'm in England."

"You're right," Rebecca said. "That's smart. If I could stand to be parted from Pele for that long, I would do the same thing."

"I guess I'll toss this in, too." He pushed his art box into a corner of the crate. "Never know when I might have to make a repair on something small." He made the necessary notations on the disclosure statement. As he moved items around to make room for the box, Rebecca saw the cloth wrapped shape of a dagger.

"Is that Hamlet's poignard?"

"Yes." Wayne didn't mention that he'd packed his own ritual knife in the bottom of the box as well as an extra blank blade.

"Wayne?" Rebecca gently touched his shoulder as he fastened the straps again. He stood almost stumbling into the crate. "If I asked you sometime, would you make me a knife like that one? *Could* you do it?"

"Sure," he answered. "But if you really want it, you can have that one when the show's over. I bought the materials for it myself, so it belongs to me."

"Really?"

"Yeah. I'll sharpen it up for you," he said. "I don't think one that size would fit in your pocket, though."

"I promise not to try to put it in a pocket," she laughed. He finished fastening the new bands around the crate.

"Well, I guess that's it," he said. They turned toward the door. He snapped out the lights and closed the door behind them as they stepped into the darkened hallway.

He wasn't exactly sure how it happened, but his hand found Rebecca's waist and the gentle squeeze that he gave her turned to an embrace. Their lips met and parted. The passionate kiss robbed Wayne of his breath. His heart was pounding so loudly in his ears that he could hardly hear what she was saying as she gently disengaged his arms but kept tight hold of his hand. He was not insistent. In fact, if anything, he was dumbfounded at his own brashness. She leaned back into the encircling arm and Wayne saw in the diffuse light of an exit sign that her eyes were glistening.

"I'm sorry, Wayne," she said softly. "Not now. There is such power in your kiss, I know that one day… Just not now."

"It was my fault," he said. "Please don't be angry."

"Don't be so chauvinistic. It takes two to kiss like that. And what's the fault when something is shared as deeply as that?"

She kissed him again. He swore he hadn't moved. It was not the lingering kiss of passion that had just passed between them. Instead it seemed to Wayne, it was more like a promise—or at least a hope—of something to come.

"Will you walk me home now?" she asked quietly. They carefully avoided exiting where the night watchman could see them.

"It's so cool," Wayne jabbered on. "It's carved and named and has my own sigil on it."

"But you can't remember any of the ritual?"

"No. Not exactly. I remember doing the ritual, but I don't remember the ritual. Does that make sense?"

"Like you would not believe. So, it was The Hart."

"The Hart is in the Circle."

"What?"

"It's part of my staff. A carving of a flaming heart in a circle."

"Okay, Unbound, we have a lesson here. You need to know circle protocol for Litha."

"How will I know this?"

"You'll dream."

14

Demon-Man

Tuesday, 3 June 1969

"I'M IN love, I'm in love, I'm in love with a wonderful gal!" sang Wayne as he and Glenn finished packing their suitcases.

"You're insane. You're insane. You're insane," Glenn mimicked back at his friend. "Who, prithee, dost thou love?"

"Aye, there's the rub," Wayne quoted then improvised. "Whether it is nobler in the mind to suffer the slings and arrows of young love or take up arms with age and experience for new. Who would bear the whips and scorns of passion's roller coaster, the pangs of despised love, when he might fly to others with love unrequited? Or shall he take up his cup, fill it with coffee and have a doughnut?"

"You'd part with the passionate princess to worship the ice-cold queen?" Glenn mocked.

"No. It's the underlying enchantment, hidden glances, secret touches, but forbidden love. Like Lancelot and Guinevere."

"You and your King Arthur," Glenn grumbled. "Look where their secret love led them. You can't survive on unrequited love for the rest of your life."

"Not unrequited," Wayne sighed, "just unconsummated."

"Like I'll die soon enough that I can see you live a life of chastity. You can't put a woman on a pedestal and worship her these days."

"Watch me!"

"Chip, chip, crumble, crumble. Shovel, shovel, out the rubble," Glenn quipped. "Love from afar if you must, but I'll take a goddess in the flesh any day." A knock at the dorm room door cut Glenn off. "Who's there?" he asked in his best falsetto.

"It's Judith. Is Wayne there?" Glenn looked at Wayne questioningly.

"A goddess in the flesh," Wayne said, stepping to the door. He swung it open and fell to the floor at Judith's feet. She was wearing a short-sleeved sweater, a skirt that stopped where her legs began and sandals. "Oh, fair goddess! Is there a temple where men come to worship you?

Or may I lay my life in adoration at your feet here beneath this humble roof?" Judith burst out laughing.

"God, Wayne. You're so… What do you call this, Glenn?" she asked.

"Cornball," he responded. "Certifiably insane. Cuckoo!"

"Melodramatic," she added. "You're so Midwestern."

"Moonstruck!" exclaimed Wayne. "I can't help myself. I slept beneath the full moon and it addled my wits. Let me introduce myself. Let me kiss your feet. Let me nibble your toes. Let me…"

"I'll let you, already. Glenn, call off your dog."

"Down, Fido!" Glenn yelled. "Stop sniffing."

"Hey! What's all the noise?" called a fourth voice from behind Judith. "Wow! Wayne's in his proper place at last," Gail continued as she stepped up beside Judith. She was similarly attired and did not appear to be there by accident. Wayne sat back on the floor looking up at the two of them.

"Can you believe this?" Wayne asked Glenn. "Venus and Aphrodite come knocking at our door."

"Venus and Aphrodite are the same person, you dope," said Judith.

"Split personality, I see. Well, it's okay. Glenn and I are the same person, too. Apollo and… uh… Apollo 11."

"Hey, Judith," Gail cut in. "Sun gods, right? They ought to be able to get us something big, round, golden…" It was Glenn's turn to cut in, singing.

> I got spurs that jingle jangle jingle
> as I go riding merrily along.
> And they sing, 'Oh, ain't you glad you're single?'
> And that song ain't so very far from wrong.

"The one and only Gene Autry, ladies!" Wayne announced.

"Pizza!" said Judith and Gail together. "How about pizza?"

"I think we were just invited out," Wayne said to Glenn.

"How convenient. I just hate it when I have to make up my mind who to call. I bet I still have to drive, though."

They left the dorm and piled into Glenn's car. Judith slipped her hand into Wayne's in the back seat and leaned over to kiss him.

"Not a bad intro," she whispered. "What's the second act like?"

"All improv," Wayne smiled as he kissed her back.

AFTER THREE HOURS of pizza and beer, the four parked in front of the dorm again. Glenn pulled Gail to him in the front seat and they kissed.

Wayne and Judith broke from a kiss that had lasted most of the way home. They looked at the scene in the front seat and laughed. Wayne leaned over the passenger side and opened the door.

"'Scuse us, kids," he said. "After all, it's your car." He and Judith climbed out of the back seat.

"Don't go away mad," Glenn said, reaching out a hand toward them. Wayne could see the joint extended to them and gently pushed it back to Glenn.

"Just go away," he finished. "Enjoy yourselves." He and Judith walked up the sidewalk a few steps before he stopped to kiss her again. "Want to go for a walk before we call it a night?" he asked.

"Mmm. Yes," she answered through yet another kiss. Wayne's hand wrapped happily around her left ass cheek as he pulled her tightly to him. "What time are you getting up?"

"Truck leaves at five, I'll be up at four," he answered. "Have to get that crate loaded before we all head to the airport."

"Who ever invented the six-thirty flight?" she asked. "I've got an idea. Let's stay up all night."

"Together?"

"Of course, silly. This is my last night in America."

"Well, now that you mention it, mine too," he said. "We're on the same flight."

"That's true." Judith turned in his arms. "But you have a return ticket."

"You mean you're not coming back?"

"You're quick on the uptake."

"But why?" It sounded whiny, even to Wayne.

"Because England is my home. I don't fit here," she said. "I didn't want to come in the first place, but I had to."

"You'll have to tell me more about that. Every time I think I understand, my head gets all muzzy. It's the weirdest thing. Is there anything I could do to make you change your mind?"

"You did once, but not this time. I didn't mean to fall for you, Wayne."

"I hit bottom right beside you, if it's any comfort. What can I do, Judith?"

"Spend the night with me. God knows what may happen once we get to Kendall. Somehow I think we'll walk between the worlds."

"Where to?"

"Use your imagination."

Wayne thought for a moment. The theatre was out. Either of their rooms was a possibility with relaxed summer security, but this should be special.

"I've got it," he said with a flash of inspiration. "Stay here in the shadows so no one can see you. I'll be back in a flash."

He ran to the front entrance of the dorm and straight to his room. Two minutes later he came out the back with a blanket and a pillow under his arm. "Turf!" he said as they joined hands and skipped away from the dorm. They arrived at the locked gate of the school park a few minutes later. It was always locked at sundown. The school simply couldn't afford enough security forces to keep it properly patrolled.

"Maintenance would shit if they knew I had this," he said, inserting the key into the lock. It popped open.

"Where did you get that?"

"It was in a batch of old theatre keys I inherited," he said as they walked into the park and shut the gate behind them. "Safe, secure, and private."

"And a little spooky," Judith whispered as they walked deeper into the park. "Is a girl safe with you out here?"

"I'm not sure. I've never had a girl out here. How safe do you want to be?"

Judith wrapped her arms around Wayne's neck and pulled herself up on him, wrapping her legs around him.

"As long as you don't do damage, I don't think there are any limits to what I'd do for you, baby. God, Wayne! I want you so much. I want so much more than we can have. Just for tonight, make me yours. Be the reason I came to America."

"I want to be what you remember, Judith, because I'll always remember you. I'll always miss you. I want this to be the best night of your life." Wayne's hands supported her butt and he squeezed gently, eliciting a soft moan.

"Then make love to me. Show me. Show me."

There was a note of desperation in her voice that Wayne barely registered. He spread the blanket where they stood and they lay down on it. Lips were on lips as Wayne found the clasp for her bra and slipped it open. He pulled her sweater and bra together over her head and she tugged at his t-shirt until he lifted so she could pull it off. They pressed their chests together and held each other.

"I love to feel your skin against my skin," he whispered. "I can't believe it. I haven't had that much experience, but nothing I've done comes close to having your breasts pressed against my chest."

"Show me you appreciate them."

He let his hand drift up her side and pulled back far enough to cup her breast and lightly graze her nipple. He kissed down her cheek and neck, nestling into the crook of her neck and kissing as she pushed her head against him and her breast into his hand. He continued kissing his way down across her shoulder and onto the mound of her breast until his lips brushed her nipple.

"Oh! God, Wayne. You do so much for me."

"I can do more," he said with sudden confidence. He didn't know where the words came from, but he placed kisses on her as he softly chanted. "Your lips breathe with the air of desire. Your breasts fire my passion. Your golden sex is liquid with lust for me. Your feet ground me in this earth. Your hands lift me to other realms."

"The five-fold kiss? Oh goddess! Wayne, how did you know?"

"I think I dreamed it. Look!" As Wayne rose over her, they looked at the glowing dome arching over them.

"You have so much!" Thinking Judith was referring to the rod Wayne was pushing into her pussy, he couldn't help but swell a little with pride. "I felt that!"

"Judith, I think I've fallen in love with you again."

"Hush. Please don't say that. I don't know how to respond."

"It seems you respond pretty dramatically," he said. The walls of their glowing dome pulsed with every thrust into her hot core.

"I've never done this with any other man."

"You've never made love?"

"Oh. I've had sex. I've never raised power with a man. It's so… filling. More than you filling my cunny. It's like I'm a vessel for your power."

"I don't understand it, Swordmaster." Wayne's voice became more distant as he rose toward his orgasm. He knew, though, that they were not just Wayne and Judith in this moment. "I feel like a god when I'm with you."

"Make me your goddess, Unbound," she whispered. The dome above them expanded and glowed white, containing their orgasm. "Make a wish, my love."

"I wish for fun and adventure in England with a healthy dose of great sex," he whispered without thinking. The glowing dome exploded.

"I'D HAVE BEEN a little happier if you'd have qualified that and said great sex with me," Judith giggled as the two lay together watching the stars overhead. They'd pulled the blanket up around them and were holding each other tightly. As wonderful as the idea had been to lie under the stars all night, it was getting chilly and it was obvious they needed to dress and go inside.

"Who else would it be? I'm not going to be picking up any other British birds while we're there."

"Well, you've become awfully chummy with Dr. Allen. I'm a little jealous."

"Judith, I won't lie to you. I find Rebecca very attractive and we've become close friends. I even fantasize about her sometimes. But she nailed it when she reminded me that she's nearly twice our age and she has a thirteen-year-old daughter. And she's a professor. And she's married and still believes her husband will return one day. All that means there's an impregnable wall erected between us. I'm thankful for that. It means I can focus on you."

"With this very pregnable erection between us?" Judith laughed, grasping his cock before he had it tucked into his pants. Even with her shirt and skirt on, it was cold and they hurried to finish dressing. "Still, she's dangerous, Wayne. I wish I knew what she had planned."

"Look," Wayne said, pointing across the park. "I locked the gate when we came in, didn't I?" There was a soft, flickering glow coming through the trees deeper in the isolated park. "Maybe someone else is turfing. I don't like the idea of a fire out here, though." He started pushing through the brush toward the glow.

"This give me a bad feeling, babe. I don't think we should…"

They came into an opening and saw a dark figure huddled over a small fire. The glow did not entirely come from the fire—in fact, it seemed contained in a circle. The robed figure slowly circled the fire, casting handfuls of leaves and powder onto the flame, each one making it flare brighter.

"We really need to leave," Judith said. "Let's get out of here." She turned to head to the gate. Wayne stood from where he crouched.

"But…"

As if suddenly aware of their presence, the figure spun toward him. In one smooth motion it flicked a hand out. Wayne saw the shining metal disk flash through the air like a Frisbee.

"Shit!" he yelled as he swung the pillow like a bat at the flying object. He felt the force as it ripped into the pillow, scattering feathers. Wayne didn't wait to find out if the figure had anything else to throw at him. He ran toward Judith and the gate, fumbling with the keys in the lock.

"Hurry!" Judith screamed. "It's coming!"

Over his shoulder, Wayne saw the dark figure on the path behind them. He jerked the gate open and slammed it shut as they ran from the park. They were out in the dark of night. The last glance Wayne took showed the figure standing silent at the gate watching. The eyes seemed visible even in the darkness as if they glowed. Wayne's mind scrambled to make sense of what he saw.

"Shade of Memory!" cried I, with act adorant at her feet.
"By all the gloom hung round thy fallen house,
and by thyself, forlorn divinity.
Let me behold, according as thou saidst.
What in thy brain so ferments to and fro!"

He knew those eyes. He knew them.

THEY REACHED THE dorm, breathless. Judith flung her arms around him, too exhausted to sob.

"That thing was evil," she breathed into his chest. She reached up and touched the pentacles at his chest.

"What is it Swordmaster?" he asked. He pulled her into the shadows next to the dorm.

"Unbound, there is truly more in heaven and earth than your philosophies have dreamed. I'm frightened for you. I want you to be ready. You were so wonderful tonight raising a shield without even trying. Kissing me with the five-fold kiss. And by the way, I could stand to have the fifth fold kissed a few more times, lover. But there is still so much you don't know."

"Teach me, Swordmaster. When I looked into its eyes they looked familiar. But my head is so full of cotton most of the time that I can't sort out what I should know. I almost knew how to fight it."

"There are stories of dark grimoires—books of magic. I've never seen one. Please understand that in our circle we practice ritual magic and pray for the betterment of the world. We're not evil beings. But some people just want more power. The Blade was one of those. He was certain that he'd found where there was an ancient goddess idol that would give him unlimited power. His search failed, we're pretty sure. But he hasn't been seen in fifteen years. I'm worried that he's come back. This is where he started his search."

"You think this thing might be The Blade returned? Swordmaster, I know that whoever it was, it was the same person we saw in the costume shop a few months ago," Wayne said. "I need to go check on our crate. If he sabotages it, our trip could be ruined." Wayne dropped his pillow and blanket to the ground to embrace Judith more fully. They heard the muffled metallic clink as it hit the concrete. Wayne kicked the pillow aside and a small metal disk rolled out on the walk. It was a saw blade from the shop. Drawn on it in ragged paint marks was a star with characters written on each point. Judith picked the object up.

"I have to go." Wayne ran from the dorm leaving Judith to examine the saw blade.

WAYNE'S STOMACH TURNED inside out and he wanted to vomit. He took the long way around the campus to approach the theatre from the side opposite the security guard's shack. His rage and fear were in control. All he could think about was the crate, ready to ship to England. Even in light of the break-ins, it seemed he'd never got around to telling security about the doors on this side of the building. Saying something could only give rise to questions about how he knew. He looked through the glass doors to be sure they hadn't been chained. Grasping the handles, he began to gently rock them back and forth, working up a rhythm as he watched the crash bars through the glass. They swung with the motion, a little further with each move. Finally, they swung back far enough to trip the latch and Wayne opened the door and slipped into the building.

He found his way down the dark corridors and into the basement where his workshop and tools would await him. And the crate. He'd come in early this morning and padlocked it just to be sure it couldn't be broken into. He wished he'd thought of that when he'd put Rebecca's things in it. He pushed his key in the door of the shop and it swung open. Unlocked.

Wayne's stomach leapt into his throat and the nausea threatened to overwhelm him. What was it Judith was trying to tell him back at the dorm? Everything about the evening except the sensational sex and the mysterious ghoul in the park had receded in his memory. It seemed like it was important. He flattened himself against the wall willing his breathing to slow so he could hear. Not a sound broke the air. After some minutes of silence, Wayne crept back to the open door. Perhaps the thief had been and gone. It made no difference to Wayne. He had run from danger once tonight and he'd be damned if he'd run again. The crate was in there.

His eyes adjusted to the darkness, lit only by the glow of the ever-present exit sign in the hall. The shop was as clear in his mind as if he saw it in full daylight. The rack of flats was undisturbed. Two rehearsal thrones stood near the door. Table saw, bandsaw, lathe. Wayne ticked off the inventory in his mind. In the center of the room, the crate awaiting the pickup at five o'clock in the morning. Behind the crate, a man.

He was kneeling, hiding behind the crate, but Wayne could see the hat above the box. It was not his imagination. It was the hat. Wayne put out a hand to the tool rack on his right and felt the crowbar in its accustomed place. Once it was firmly in hand, he leapt.

"Got you!" he screamed as the crowbar came down on the hat. The jolt shook his arm with the impact. Wayne realized too late that the hat lay on the crate, not on a person's head. He rolled frantically, flailing with his arms to get upright on the crate again. He could see the man now, towering over him. The crowbar wouldn't come up from where he had struck. It weighed too much for him to lift. The eyes of the demon-man bore into him as he reached out a hand.

Demon-man. Everything flashed with crystal clarity in Wayne's mind. Judith's warning about dark magicians. But more than that. Everything he'd been taught by Rebecca, Lissa, Judith, and his uncle was sharp and at his instant recall, including all the spells he'd memorized from his uncle's *Book of Shadows*. His sacred tools, cup, knife, and wand were in the crate a foot from him. His pentacles around his neck. As the demon's hand reached for him, Wayne willed wards around himself. They flared and brightly lit the room throwing the man backward. He came again and again was thrown back. Wayne recited the banishing spell moving his fingers in the pattern prescribed by the book. The man moved toward him again and then turned to flee.

Wayne collapsed on the trunk. He was exhausted and emotionally drained. The wards dimmed around him and his eyelids grew heavy. Maybe he'd just sleep here tonight.

Wednesday, June 4 1969

HE'D PROBABLY DONE stupider things in his life than spend the night—or what was left of it—sleeping on a wooden crate, but when Jim woke him up in the morning to load the truck, Wayne couldn't think of what it was.

"I just was worried about it sitting here with all the break-ins," he explained. "Geez! I hurt all over."

"Well, these guys have a hydraulic hand lift and if they can maneuver it out of here you'll have half an hour to get showered, dressed and on the bus."

"Oh crap." It was a tight fit. When Wayne figured the turning radius from the shop into the hall, he hadn't figured the extra length of the cart. It fit, but just barely. They rolled the cart up onto the tailgate of the air-freight truck and then lifted it to the bed. The stupid thing was no longer Wayne's responsibility. He ran for the dorm and got ready to go.

"What the fuck is this?" Glenn exclaimed as Wayne got on the bus. He'd managed to get showered, dressed, and his suitcase closed in time to make it to the airport bus. And he was proud of how he looked. It was hip.

"It's a leisure suit," Wayne answered. "Everybody's wearing them."

"What is this fabric?" Gail asked.

"It's seersucker."

"As in he got it at Sears and he was a sucker for buying it," Glenn laughed.

"Hey. My big sister wanted to do something for my trip and made this."

"But what is this fabric," Gail insisted. "It's not cotton."

"Hundred percent polyester," Wayne said. "Resistant to all kinds of stains and almost wrinkle-proof."

"Bell-bottoms?" Judith said. "And a headband?"

"I figured with the long hair and beard, this stuff would look just right. Mom said I should dress up to fly. Why are you guys looking at me so funny?"

15

Customs

Thursday, 5 June 1969, England

THE DREAMS on the plane made it difficult for Wayne to sleep during the time he wasn't staring out the plane at the clouds and taking pictures of them. Beside him Judith laughed and pointed out the window.

"Oh look! A cloud. We're on top of it. Quick. Take a picture." Wayne had his camera pressed to the window before he realized she was teasing him.

"Hey, I'm not a world traveler like you," he complained. "I've never seen this before."

"You are now, babycakes," she said. "Just wait till later."

But later, Wayne was thrashing in his seat with nightmares.

FIFTY NAKED BODIES dancing around the fire, hurtling through the spheres. He held his goddess queen tightly in his arms as their own fire leapt higher than the flames in and around the cauldron. From the cauldron's depths rose a spirit, eyes glimmering as it took shape, beckoning them toward it. Calling them to their doom. Wayne raised his wards, but the demon slashed at them, reaching through to grasp him. Them. He had to protect her.

"WAKE UP! WAKE up!" Judith was whisper-shouting in his ear. He had to protect her and extended his wards to enclose her. No sooner was she within than she reached to touch the pentacles on his chest and he awoke.

"Swordmaster," he began.

"Shh. Not here. Come with me."

They stood from their seat and made their way to the back of the plane. Most of their cast was asleep. A couple of them were playing cards and glanced at them, smiling. When they reached the back of the plane Judith pushed Wayne into the head and locked the door behind them.

"What's going on?"

"Anybody who saw us thinks we're joining the mile-high club," Judith answered quietly. "But in our current state that might be dangerous. We could blow a hole in the airplane with the energy you were generating. Just let me hold you, Unbound. Come down and tell me what was going on in your dream."

"It was the demon-man," Wayne whispered. Details were already fuzzing, but he knew he had to protect them from the demon-man.

"I'm so sorry," she whispered. "I don't know what's drawn him to us."

"I fought him last night," Wayne said.

"In your dream?"

"Maybe. It seemed so real. I had power and pushed him away. He wanted the crate. I slept on it last night."

"Poor baby. It was all a dream," Judith said, touching the pentacles. Wayne reeled slightly and caught himself on the edge of the sink. Judith sat on the stool in front of him.

"What are we doing in here?" he asked.

"There's too much pressure in the airplane," Judith laughed as she unzipped his pants. "We're going to relieve a little of it." She pulled his cock out of his pants and sucked it into her mouth.

"Oh god, baby! You found the release valve."

"Come for me, darling. I've never tasted you yet."

It wasn't a command, but before he let that sink in, he was obeying.

"THERE'S GOOD NEWS and there's bad news," Jim said. Forty pairs of eyes stared at him from the crowded little bus. They had been crammed into the vehicle with all their luggage in Mansfield. For the last twenty hours, nothing seemed to go right. There was an unexpected six-hour layover at JFK Airport in New York resulting in a missed connection and another four hours at Heathrow. They'd been crammed virtually on top of each other into this bus. Now there was more bad news.

"There are no more buses available," Jim continued. "That's the first news. The other two casts are much smaller than ours and were supposed to share a bus. They cleared customs and took a bus each before we even got here. So, it's going to be cozy for the next couple of hours. Get as comfortable as you can. We should open every other window about an inch to keep fresh air circulating. I can already detect unpleasant odors."

A general movement among the cast marked the effort. Windows were slid back. No one could find a more comfortable position, though Wayne wasn't complaining about Judith sitting on his lap. They finally gave up and returned their attention to Jim.

"Second, customs still won't release our costumes and props. They say there are too many weapons in the box." Wayne grimaced but tried not to telegraph his disapproval to Judith. Her fingernails dug into his arm anyway. "Mr. Brown, the tour director, has promised they will make it in time for the show tomorrow, but who believes *The Great God Brown* at this point." Jim's skepticism was shared by all the cast by now. "We'll rehearse without costumes and props. I want everyone to check your luggage tonight for possible substitute costumes if we have to go on without."

"No!" moaned Carol Nygard. "It's one thing to play a boy's role in boy's clothes. I can't play Guildenstern in a dress."

"Dress?" answered Glenn. "This is our opportunity to make an artistic statement. *Hamlet* in the nude."

"At least we won't need the rapiers then," laughed Chuck.

"And you the judges ware a beary eye," misquoted Steve.

"Damn you all," cried Carol. Chuck put a comforting arm around her.

"We're not going to stay in Kendall as we were told. We're headed to Keswick. It's about thirty miles farther north, but is supposed to be a delightfully charming little town. That means, though, that we won't be getting in until about nine tonight. For those of you who haven't set your watches yet, it's now six-o-five local." Several people reset their watches according to the announcement.

"One more thing…"

"He's really full of this stuff, isn't he?" Glenn whispered over the seat to Wayne.

"The group is too big for any single hotel in Keswick. We will be split up in three different locations. We'll work out the room assignments on the way up," Jim finished. "Now the good news."

"Thank god," Wayne said. "I thought he was going to say that was the good news."

"Dr. Allen has been on the phone," Jim said. "One of the innkeepers has agreed to make us a late dinner. There'll be a good meal waiting for us when we get there."

"Hooray," chorused a half-dozen weary voices.

"And by the way," finished Jim, "we *are* in England. That ought to be worth something." And, in fact it did spark a bit more enthusiasm as the bus lurched to a start.

"I don't care about a meal," Wayne said. "As long as there's a good bed in my room."

"Always looking for a place to sleep, aren't you?" said Judith. "Thought all you needed was a blanket, a pillow, and the stars."

"Hey, it held great potential. I didn't exactly go out and hire a clansman to throw darts at us."

"Well, maybe we can pony up to go halvsies on a room. That would ease the shortage."

"Save water, shower with my girlfriend."

"Am I your girlfriend?"

"I hope so."

"Lover?"

"One and only."

"Wayne," Jim said, fighting his way over the luggage in the aisles. "I need to talk to you a minute."

"Trouble," Judith said under her breath.

"Sure. What's up?"

"Do you have a copy of the declarations slip?"

"Yeah. Right here in my camera bag."

"Along with twenty-eight color glossy photos of clouds on the way to England," Gail laughed from in front.

"…with circles and arrows and a paragraph on the back," Glenn chimed in.

"You can get anything you want," they sang in unison until Gail shut him up the easy way.

"Is there a musical accompaniment to everything? I'm going to have to send you back to London," Jim said. For a moment Wayne thought he was referring to Glenn and Gail, then realized Jim had returned to talking to him. "Apparently, we need a representative at customs in the morning. You packed the box, you know what's in it, you're the technical director, you're it."

"Tag," Wayne said.

"Shit," Judith responded.

"How am I getting to London and why am I going three hours in the wrong direction first?" Wayne grumbled.

"We'll get settled in Keswick first, then head back to London so you can be there at eight o'clock when the office opens," Jim answered.

"Maybe I should go, too, since I'm English," Judith volunteered.

"Dr. Allen has agreed to go with him so he doesn't get lost or have legal problems. She represents the school." Wayne felt Judith stiffen and then slump against him. "We'll change drivers in Keswick and send you back by bus so you've got a place to put the crate."

"Terrific. One more night sleeping sitting up for that damned crate."

"I'm depending on you, Wayne. I know it's rough, but we've got to get the goods."

"Yeah. I'll bring it back, dead or alive."

Jim moved back toward the front of the bus. Wayne looked up at Judith. She glared back.

"So," she said acidly, "spend your first night in England with Rebecca. See what I care."

"I didn't choose this," he complained.

"You certainly didn't object."

"What was I supposed to do? Sorry, Jim, I've got other plans for tonight?"

"At least make a show of being disappointed. It doesn't take a medical examiner to see your eyes go out of focus every time you get the chance to spend time with her."

"If my eyes went out of focus, it's because I went to sleep."

"Then stop poking me in the ass with that thing. You've had yours."

The silence turned stony as Wayne closed his eyes to attempt to sleep the remainder of the way to Keswick. Eventually, Judith relaxed on his lap and cuddled as they tried to get sleep that didn't come. Wayne held her close and they kissed, holding their lips close to each other all the way to Keswick.

Disappointed not to spend the night with Judith? Yes. Disappointed in the prospect of traveling back to London with Rebecca? Maybe not.

AFTER DINNER, WAYNE lay down on the bed in his room. It would be midnight before they left again and he was determined to get as much sleep as possible before they left. In keeping with school policy, the women had been assigned to the Skiddaw Hotel and the men to the Walpole. Except Rebecca. Because she was working with Wayne to go back to London, she'd been assigned to the Walpole as well. Judith glared at Wayne when she left for her hotel and he couldn't catch up with her to give her a goodnight kiss. Glenn was just a room down from Wayne on one side and Rebecca on the other. He dozed on top of the covers. He didn't hear the knock on the door. He came up out of sleep when Rebecca shook him gently by the shoulder.

Friday, 6 June 1969

"Wake up, sleepyhead," she said. "We've got a bus to catch."

"Oh, gees. Is it midnight already?" he yawned.

"No. It's a quarter after one. We had trouble getting another driver."

"Must be jet lag," he quipped. "Here I thought it was the middle of the night."

"Very clever. Need anything?"

"No. Just a pillow."

"John and Joyce already put pillows and blankets on board for us. Make sure you've got your declaration."

"Got it."

"And passport."

"Oh. Yeah. Anything else?"

"Let's go." They went out the front of the inn and Jim met them at the bus.

"It looks like you're set. Here's the itinerary of where we're playing so you can direct the bus right to the theatre on the way back."

"This is the whole week's itinerary," Wayne said glancing at it. "Is that in case it's Wednesday before we catch up with you?"

"Get back in time for tonight's performance, okay?" Jim laughed. "You've got the first line."

"Who's there?"

"Long live the king." Jim shot back and pushed Wayne into the bus.

"Gees, it's cold in here," Wayne said as he boarded the bus.

"It still gets pretty chilly at night," Rebecca said.

"Waste of fuel to heat the whole bus," the driver added. Wayne noted that he had a heater by his seat.

"Go on and find a comfortable place. Here's a thermos of hot tea and there are the pillows. I'm going to talk to our driver a few minutes."

Wayne picked up a pillow and blanket and settled into a seat about halfway back as the bus jumped forward and ground its way out of town. If the trip in had been cramped and uncomfortable, the trip to London in the empty bus would be rough and bouncy. A few minutes out of town, Rebecca came back and sat beside Wayne.

"Comfy?"

"Not really," he answered. "How long a trip is it back to London?"

"About six hours plus."

"Get there just in time for breakfast."

"Want to share a little of that?" she said, tugging at the blanket.

"Sure." He pulled the blanket around her and laid her pillow against his shoulder. She settled back against him and he let his hand touch her arm. He squeezed her gently closer.

"That's nice," she purred.

He pressed his lips gently against her hair. She raised her head and looked up at him. The rumbling and bouncing of the bus seemed to jar his thoughts uncontrollably between reality and fantasy. Their lips met and didn't part. He felt her hand caressing his head and neck and almost wanted to cry. At last she turned her lips away and laid a hand on his shoulder, snuggling deeper into the pillow.

"You, my friend, have had four more hours sleep than I have."

She drifted rapidly off to sleep, wrapped in the blanket and in his arms. *Protect!* The command in his head had Wayne alert. His eyes were wide open, staring at her awestruck. By the time they reached London, they were even.

They were in the customs office when it opened with their claim ticket and declaration in hand. The mysterious Mr. Brown never showed up. After arguing half the morning, the customs officials agreed that the box would go, provided that every item could be identified for actor and purpose. Rebecca got sandwiches as Wayne sat in the big room for the next two hours identifying each costume, weapon, and prop. By twelve-thirty, they were back aboard the bus with everything repacked in the crate and headed north.

"This is great!" Wayne griped. "At this rate, we'll arrive at curtain time. They'll all be in a panic."

"Take it easy," Rebecca soothed. "The important thing is that we'll make it. You'll be a hero."

"Dead or alive."

"It's not that bad."

"Easy for you to say. You don't have the first line."

"Who's there?" she quoted for him.

"Want to go on in my place?"

"You did a terrific job this morning. If they made me name all those props and costumes, we would still be there. In prison. How do you do it?"

"When in doubt, make something up. The biggest problem was staying awake. My staff is now being carried by Reynaldo. Yours is the staff of office for Polonius. They didn't care about any of that. They thought they'd catch us transporting drugs. Bunch of hippie actors."

"You're kidding!"

"I've been through two rather thorough drug searches in the last eight weeks. I can tell the difference. They went through my art box, the sewing kit, the make-up—handled every article of clothing. No way were they worried about too many weapons," he said.

"It's a good thing we have a clean cast and crew."

"It's a good thing I packed and sealed the crate myself. I wouldn't trust any of them," he grumbled. "Am I getting bitchy?"

"A little."

"Sorry. I haven't slept yet. Would you like your staff and cup now?"

"Sure. I'll drop them off at The Walpole on the way in. I don't go on first," she laughed. They went to the back of the bus and unlocked the box. He had removed all the nails and straps at customs.

"Nothing ever repacks as well as it packed the first time." He pulled out the staff and cup and handed them to Rebecca. He took out his own staff, cup, and *Athamé*, wrapped in its layers of cloth. He had a satchel into which he packed the smaller pieces. Rebecca reached out and touched his pentacles. Wayne had a moment of disorientation before the clarity set in. If only he wasn't so tired. "Hart," he said softly.

"You brought your tools, Unbound."

"Yes. I didn't want to be parted from them. I'm glad they were in the crate last night. Or the night before. Whenever it was."

"Why is that?"

Wayne hesitated. His head was clear, but he didn't want to just plunge into the story.

"These markings on the staff and cup. What language did you say it was?"

"I didn't. The characters are Theban alphabet. Mystic runes."

"And what are they used for?"

"Without getting into too much detail, they assist in focusing psychic energy."

"I remember the psychic part. And sometimes for spells, right? But never on weapons, are they?"

"They could be used to direct negative energy against someone, but the ancients would have considered that to be very dangerous. There is always the risk that negative energy will flow back into the person who sends it. Kind of a backlash. There are some dark grimoires that talk about that use."

"Yes, dark grimoires," Wayne repeated. "Would those cover decorating a weapon and throwing it at someone?"

"What kind of weapon? You're being too obtuse in your questions."

"I think I made a connection between the shop break-ins and things that were missing. First there was the knife blade that you gave to Judith at the park last week." Wayne went on to describe how the blade must have been stolen from the shop. Then he told Rebecca about the saw blade that had been thrown at him.

"When was this?"

"The night before we left."

"Where?"

"In the college park."

"Those gates are locked at sunset. Most of the time they never get unlocked during the day. How did you happen to be in there at night?"

"Not always securely locked," he hedged.

"I'm not sure I believe you. But let it lie. What was the object and who threw it? You are really making this much too difficult."

"Then suffice it to say that I was walking in the park and came upon a person in a clearing dressed in a kind of hooded robe. That person threw a circular saw blade at me that had been sharpened down like a razor. It was decorated with a six-pointed star and a lot of these Theban runes."

"Do you have it?"

"No. Judith has it. I assume she left it in Indianapolis."

"Judith. You gave it back to her?"

"She took it when we got back."

"Wait a minute. Who threw it?"

"I don't know."

"Judith was with you?"

"Yes."

"Ah. Now I'm getting a clearer picture. It might interest you to know that alumni know every possible make-out spot on campus. Why do you think the gates are locked at night?" Wayne felt terribly hot and knew his cheeks were red. How could he explain this to Rebecca?

"I… Don't think… I mean… we…"

"…were chased out of the park by someone throwing saw blades at you," she teased. "It's all right. It doesn't matter that you've received instruction from The Swordmaster. What does matter is that someone doesn't want it completed."

"Doesn't matter?" *Wait, she said 'Swordmaster.' I should know that name.* Wayne was almost more abashed by the lack of concern that Rebecca was showing than he would have been if she had flown into a jealous rage. How strange to talk about fooling around as receiving instruction. She looked up at him and lightly touched his cheek with her lips, assuaging his concern.

"Of course it matters," said Rebecca, "but not how you think. Jealousy and I don't mix well. I've had my share of that. There is no pleasure in it. Tell me the rest." She kissed him again and he could feel the tingling of power building up in his fingers. He went on to tell her about his dream of fighting a demon-man and waking up on the crate.

"You simply called your wards and they were there?" she asked.

"Yeah. That's how I know it had to be a dream. I don't even know a way to fight a demon-man if such a thing even exists."

"They exist, Unbound. How much do you remember from your cultural anthropology course?" He just hung his head. She smiled. "I'm not chiding. Cultural anthropology is very closely related to archaeology. Because of the potential wealth that could be obtained by making a significant discovery, there was once a time when that science bred some pretty powerful enemies."

"I do remember you talking about a famous archaeologist who had a lot of professional enemies. It was an exciting lecture."

"I'm sorry to have kept you awake. When Wesley was lost, so was one of those enemies—as much or more an enemy of mine than of Doc Heinrich's. I looked into his eyes and saw the demon riding him. It was nothing I want to repeat. But if he has come back, it could mean Wesley is near as well."

"The Blade," Wayne whispered. Rebecca looked at him sharply. Before she could respond, he continued. "But why would he throw things at me?"

"Lots of possibilities. Just surprised and reacting in his own defense? Not likely. He wouldn't waste such a powerful weapon. Wasn't after you, but rather The Swordmaster? Possible, but I don't know why." *There it was again. Who was The Swordmaster?* Wayne couldn't ask the question aloud. "Or he sees you as dangerous. I hate to say it, but if he's been hanging around the props room, that's a likelihood."

"You mean, because I am supposed to protect you?" Wayne was grasping at straws. He couldn't make sense out of what Rebecca was saying. She seemed to think he was tuned into her wavelength. The lack of sleep, though was making everything wonky.

"Protect me? I didn't…" She looked at Wayne, nodding off to sleep. "If you are going to sleep through another of my lectures, make yourself comfortable." She put an arm around him and raised his face to her lips. "You look beat. Better get some sleep before you have to go on tonight."

"I just don't understand. Things are fuzzy around the edges. I can't tell if I'm awake or dreaming." It was important to make sense of what she said. It just didn't *make* sense. He listened as she talked. But he wasn't sure he was awake.

Wednesday, 10 August 1955, Edinburgh, Scotland

HIDING. WAITING BEHIND one of the great columns that supported the rotunda of the library—Rebecca could feel his sinister presence. Her footsteps echoed in the hollow chamber beneath the great domed ceiling. Some elderly librarian would surely come running up to shush her for disturbing the peace. She didn't mean to be so loud, but the library was so quiet—so empty. And waiting for her in the quiet empty room ahead was the gatekeeper of Carles. Perhaps he was only there to watch her make her discovery—a manuscript by an unknown author. Perhaps he had some other motive. Perhaps it was only her imagination.

The worst was that it didn't make a difference. He was there, even if he wasn't there. His presence filled Rebecca with a mad desire to run and never look back—run until she knew he was no longer behind her. Run to Wesley's arms.

But he would always be behind her—maybe one step, maybe five, maybe a mile or a year. He might precede her and still his presence would haunt her. He seemed always to know where she would be before she did. So, he arrived ahead of her—following nonetheless.

Her hand ached and she paused to hold it close to her breast, biting back a tear that forced its way through the fear and pain. What kind of bond had she forged between the The Hart and The Blade with her ritual? She forced him to feel the pain of purging his own knife. Had his hand spontaneously blistered like hers? Or had he, indeed, coincidentally reached for a hot skillet at the same moment she chanted her curse? How long would their bond last? If the knife between them was pure, what were they?

He had been here to leave her a message. She unfolded the brief note and caught a piece of black silk in her hand.

I will see you in Greece if you dare. And never carry a naked blade.

The black silk was a fine cover cloth, the exact size of Rebecca's stiletto. Black and unadorned. It was the type of gift one would expect only from an intimate friend and Rebecca wavered between feeling the warmth such a gift should bring and anger at his repeated violations of her person.

What kind of bond had she forged?

16
Ghosts of the Fells

Friday, 6 June 1969

WAYNE AND Rebecca arrived at the theatre an hour before curtain. Theatre, if you could call it that. It was the general assembly room of a school—a large empty room with a linoleum floor and carts of folding chairs waiting to be set up. The stage was slightly elevated at one end of the room with no curtains. Nor were there curtains on the twelve-foot tall windows that lined both sides of the room. Wayne surveyed the setting and stage as the rest of the cast and crew unloaded and unpacked the crate. What a train wreck.

The promised set consisted of a couple of unpainted platforms. The specially designed thrones were two backless wooden cubes. Chuck and Judith were heatedly discussing the re-blocking of his monologue with Lena unsuccessfully attempting to referee.

"Th-thank G-god you're back," Chuck said. He was stressed and needed to shrink into his role. "This is a disaster."

"Jim told me I wasn't going to be a happy camper. What a mess."

"Well, technical director, what are you going to do?" Wayne chose not to acknowledge Judith's snippy tone.

"What can we do in the next forty-five minutes? Lights! Show me what you've got, Beth."

"They're on!" came a voice from back stage. Wayne looked up. Two fluorescent tubes hung over the stage and four spotlights shone from the ceiling in front.

"Dimmers?"

"Switches."

"So much for mood lighting," Wayne cracked. He looked at the row of tall open windows that lined the auditorium. "What time does it get dark here?"

"Next weekend has the longest day of the year," Judith responded. "It will still be light at nine-thirty."

"Kill all the lights—stage and house," Wayne called to Beth. The difference was almost imperceptible. "I think we've got a problem. Judith, could I talk to you for a minute?" They stepped out the back door where the empty bus was pulling away.

"So, what are you going to do, Mr. Hotshot Technical Director?"

"Blow the bugle and call in the cavalry," Wayne answered.

"What?"

"It's in all the movies. The good guys are surrounded by Indians and it looks like they'll all be killed. Then the cavalry comes charging in and saves the day."

"So, who are you calling?"

"You. Look, I don't know why you haven't volunteered to help the show. You're in it, too. You made a big deal out of the fact that you were coming home. You've probably performed right here on this stage, haven't you?"

"Well, yeah. But it was a long time ago."

"Judith, I need your help. I walk on stage with the first line in exactly forty minutes. Whatever has you mad at me, please put it aside for now and help me."

"That's the first time you've asked me anything about England since Rebecca Allen joined the tour." Wayne hung his head. He'd really screwed up. He looked up to her eyes and started to apologize but she cut him off. "Don't worry. What's fixable tonight can be fixed in ten minutes. You will have discovered it and be a savior."

"Saviors always end up getting crucified."

"Well, you won't get that. But it's going to cost you, and I'm going to start collecting tonight." She pulled his head down to her level and kissed him with such fervor that he forgot about the set, the show, and the time. "Now come with me," she said, leading him inside.

In ten minutes, black drapery panels had been retrieved from a basement storeroom and the windows were darkened. Two more lights and a follow spot were located and attached to the circuits. The entire cast and crew were on stage at five minutes till curtain in various stages of dress and make-up. There wasn't an audience yet, but fifty chairs had been set up facing the stage. Wayne was trying to get his bow untangled. Jim gave a last few words of encouragement to the cast.

"It's going to be a little different than we've ever done it before," he said. "I don't know what to tell you other than that. The way you've all worked today is proof that you're all pros. I can't promise you that tomorrow will be any easier, but I can promise you that I'll be very proud of you. Now break a leg."

The cast wished each other luck and the show was on.

THE FIRST PERFORMANCE was not the unmitigated disaster everyone expected. The thirty or forty people in the English audience were more interested in American interpretation than in elaborate staging. The lack of lights and effects didn't lessen their enjoyment. As soon as he was free to immerse himself in his character, Chuck delivered another stellar performance as the Danish Prince.

A reception hosted by the mayor of Keswick followed the performance. Finally, a weary cast and crew struggled out of make-up and costumes. Wayne saw Rebecca only briefly as she left with a group of people from the audience. Judith stood with a friend who eventually left. Glenn finished stripping off his make-up and flopped back on a chair in the stairwell dressing area as Wayne finished his. Gail carefully went down the rack of costumes checking each of them off a list. Shortly, they were the only ones left in the building.

"All right!" Glenn shouted when Jim had finally gone.

"What're you so happy about? Do you have any idea how much work we have to do tomorrow?" Gail quit her pretended inventory and wrapped her arms around Glenn. Judith planted a kiss on the back of Wayne's neck. The three were all laughing.

"That's tomorrow!" Glenn laughed. "Tonight is tonight." His fingers moved in a mock magician's gesture and the unmistakable shape of a rolled joint materialized. Wayne joined the laughter.

"I thought you were all hard at work while I was hassling with customs. Instead you're out making a score."

"Oh, it was in the crate," Gail said. "I sewed half a dozen into the hems of different costumes." Her bright cheerfulness was lost on Wayne. His temper was lost on his friends.

"You what? God damn you idiots. Do you have any idea what they put me through at customs looking for shit like that? You stupid morons!" Wayne stood and lunged at Glenn. Judith and Gail pulled him back.

"Easy, babycakes. We were just having fun on you. It wasn't in the crate. That guy I was talking to at the end of the show passed them to me." Wayne turned to look at her. Tears were running down his cheeks. The day—the whole week—had been too much. Just too much. "Oh, baby, I'm sorry," Judith said, wiping away the tears and kissing him. "I thought the joke would lighten things up. I'm sorry, baby."

"I had visions all day of ending up in some goddamned British dungeon for the rest of my life. You don't know what they put me through there."

"I'm sorry, lover. All the dungeons in England are privately owned. Customs has a nice clean, modern prison." Wayne laughed at her in spite of himself. He was so foolish. "Come on, now. Let's go find a nice quiet place to relax and make love. There's the matter of repaying a certain debt, remember?"

Wayne couldn't argue with that. His reluctance and anger faded away as Judith took his hand and led him through the village toward Friar's Crag. Once out on the Crag they sat and Glenn lit the first joint. The acrid smoke filled their lungs as they passed it around. Wayne was stretched out on the ground with his head in Judith's lap, sharing the smoke back and forth in a kiss.

He wasn't really used to this. Of course, he'd tried it. Glenn took him to a private party where this and harder options were available. He was far more interested in Judith's kiss than the smoke—so soft and sensuous—but it was taking its toll on him regardless. Coupled with his recent travel and lack of sleep, the drug was hitting hard. He knew Glenn and Gail had slipped away farther down the lake shore. He was potently aware of Judith's insistent caresses. She pulled his hand to her breast and he softly squeezed and rubbed it. His vision was going double and he tried to focus.

"Darling, I haven't slept in a week. I can't even tell if this is real," he mumbled. He was on the verge of sleep when she touched his pentacles. His eyes opened, still not quite focusing. "Swordmaster?"

"Unbound, I'm just going to give you a little boost of energy." He felt as if he were just waking up now rather than just going to sleep.

"Are we protected?" he asked.

"No one is here," she said. Wayne was coming wider awake. Even with the rush of energy, he knew he was going to pay for this later.

"I don't want us to be disturbed," he said. Closing his eyes, he reached into the back of his mind and willed his wards to appear. When he opened them again Judith was looking around.

"How did you do that?"

"I just wanted it."

"I'm afraid of you, Unbound. I've never seen that."

"Please, Swordmaster, just lie with me here. Just hold me. I love you." And then he was asleep.

IT WASN'T REALLY sleep. He could have told her that. He was going to answer the sweet seductive voice above him. He really wanted to respond to the intimate caresses. They needed protection. Didn't she know this place was haunted?

So many people were there. Their eyes were staring at him from every direction. He could feel those that he couldn't see. He had to make them understand that he was only there by accident. He stumbled in thinking it was a campfire. He hugged his walking stick closer for comfort. Its smoothly worn shape leant some stability to this bizarre nightmare. Strange, that even having stripped him of his clothes, they left him his staff as comfort.

And what was he to do with the other objects arrayed around him? They were all so foreign, yet so completely familiar to him. If he sat right here with a pen, he could write a verse description of each object. No. He could draw a picture of them. He had never written anything more serious than a term paper. What was that? He was two people. One wrote poetry. One made props. He had to keep them straight.

Everything was somehow warped out of time. This extra, unfamiliar voice echoed in his mind. Or was his voice the echo? He wasn't where he thought he should be. He panicked and clung tighter to the young woman who welcomed his naked body pressed closer to hers. Ah, Judith, his love. He looked into her eyes.

Lissa? The word was in his mind, but the name that was spoken was Mari. Of course, it was only the eyes that were the same. Some relative perhaps.

Around the circle the other naked bodies danced, enclosing the two of them closer and closer to the fire. A wall of fire towered around them and a core of fire stood between them now. Around this they spun like the earth in orbit about its sun. The eyes and other faces disappeared behind the wall of fire and he was alone, making love with Mari.

The energy crackled in the air and when the two touched again, he could see sparks—miniature bolts of lightning cast between the two lovers that snapped and thundered as they closed to kiss. She danced him round and round within this fiery temple. They dropped the metal disk behind them. The knife fell from his hand. The cup tumbled to the ground. At last, all that was left between them was his stout walking stick, oiled by the sweat of their bodies, moving against them as they moved against each other.

Energy, power, sparks flowed through him as Mari chanted some unknown and unknowable language. He held her in his arms willing the world to go away. He could feel himself flowing, not only into her body, but his very life essence flowing with hers into the charmed walking stick. And suddenly he was aware of it as more than a staff cut to aid his walking tour of The Lakes, but as a living, breathing entity that took its name, its energy, and its life directly from the hearts of the two ecstatic lovers. She was the earth mother and he was the sky god, giving life to all things. Iäpetus the Titan was conceived, carried, and born between them and emerged from their midst as a staff charged with the power to command fire.

It was too much to bear. Panic was kindled by the same emotions that fed his ecstatic union with the savage woman. He jerked himself away. The staff stood upright in the midst of the flames. He charged it to take it away with him. The fire was hard and solid. He wrenched at the burning staff and when it loosened he felt the release like an arrow from the bow. He exploded in the flames that surrounded him. They threatened to dissolve him into particles randomly scattered across time. Ever plunging into an outer depth, he fell.

And then someone was holding him, picking up the pieces and pulling them back together like glass shattered and then reassembled. Quietly, the pieces assembled, solidifying him in their embrace, lulling him to peaceful, gentle, sleep.

JUDITH WAS FRIGHTENED. She just wanted time with her boyfriend and she had discovered a powerful mage. He called up a warded circle around them with a thought—something it would take her at least the summoning of each watchtower to achieve. But this was real and glowed around them, protecting them. Somehow, she knew they were protected, as Wayne had said. Not only would the wards be invisible to anyone passing by, but they would be as well.

He loved her. She'd been petty and jealous, but in the last analysis, she had to admit her love as well. It still scared her. And then, he'd sucked her into his vision. She'd seen her own circle, yet not her circle. The passion as he made love to her was unlike anything she'd ever felt. He consumed her, body and soul. She knew it was not just Wayne and Judith, not even just The Unbound and The Swordmaster. They were the high priest and priestess. They were the god and goddess. Where had all this power come from?

In the passion, she'd lost the vision that he held and was simply caught up in his love. Everything else faded away. Just his love and his constant protection. Just his fire and his passion.

As the morning dawned, Judith gathered her clothes and pulled Wayne's pants and shirt back on him. Then she set about the long process of releasing the wards Wayne had placed around them. What had taken him an instant to put in place, took her half an hour to release. She offered prayers and her own blood from a cut on her palm at each quadrant to finally assuage the watchers who protected them.

She finished just as she heard Glenn and Gail giggling up the trail toward them.

REBECCA AWOKE FROM her sleep startled and disoriented. The first rays of morning sun were streaming in through her window at the Walpole. Gradually, she began to pull herself back into focus and forced herself to remember the dream that had awakened her.

She'd dreamt about The Vagabond Poet before, but never so vividly as this past night. Yet the faces that appeared in the familiar roles were no longer the faces that she knew as the poet and high priestess. They had unaccountably morphed into herself and the young man who occupied the next room.

Wayne. How…? Why had she allowed herself to be caught up with the simple romance of this boy? Was it only that she knew that Judith was interested and she naturally felt rivalry toward the younger woman? She dismissed that possibility, but certain images of the dream were disturbing. The definite and more frightening truth was that she was unmistakably attracted to him. That made for a dangerous and explosive situation. If she were kind, she would cut him off from her completely and save him the hurt of later, inevitable rejection. But he was so vulnerable—so charming. The very positions they held as professor and student made it suicidal to extend that bond any deeper than it had already unwittingly become.

So, her dream had been filled with frustratingly erotic images of the boy played against the very field that she had come to England to create. The recent attacks and break-ins at ICU could only have been the work of someone within the coven, of that she was now sure. She sensed within the eroticism a danger to the boy.

And that was what woke her. That sudden panic of being plunged too deeply into a fantasy that she could no longer separate from reality. The flinging away of the dream with such force that her orgasm itself left her with a headache. Oh God! A wet dream at her age. And then the scream of terror from the next room.

She sat straight up in bed and swung her feet over the edge. This was what woke her up. The scream had cut through her dreams before it was ever given voice. She jerked her robe on as her bare feet hit the cold floor and brought her fully and sharply awake. She was through Wayne's unlocked door before the echo had died from the room. Everything else was so still. Was it possible that no one else had heard the voice?

Wayne lay on top of the covers with his walking stick clutched to him like a life preserver in the ocean. The sense of panic in the room was so profound that it almost made Rebecca want to run for safety. She shook Wayne lightly but he was delirious, sweating, and cold. She reached out to him with her arms, with her heart, and held him close, rocking and whispering encouragement. At last the rigidity in his body began to relax and his head leaned more comfortably against her breast. She stroked his hair and kissed his forehead, humming to him as she did.

A scuff on the floor brought her eyes up to see Glenn in the doorway. He stood there with his mouth open taking in the scene of Wayne wrapped in the arms of the barely-dressed professor who kissed him.

"I'm sorry," Glenn stammered. "I thought…"

"Apparently, a severe nightmare," Rebecca said, recovering to a tone of official business. "He still isn't awake, but seems to have calmed down." She lay Wayne back on the bed and smoothed his hair slightly with a touch. She gently removed his walking stick and stood it beside his bed, then spread a coverlet over the sleeping form. Returning her attention to Glenn, she noticed that he was fully dressed. "You're up early. I thought you just heard Wayne's nightmare."

"I was in the can," the big youth replied. "Actually, I was just changing my mind and going back to bed." Rebecca added up the likelihood quickly. Neither Wayne nor Glenn were dressed for bed. Glenn was…

"Going *back* to bed? Where have you two been?"

"Um… well… we just had a little opening night party," Glenn coughed. "No big deal."

"Is he drunk?"

"Well, maybe he did have a little too much."

"That's hardly the way to start our tour, Glenn." She was every inch a faculty advisor now.

"We didn't mean any harm, Dr. Allen," he pled. "Please don't tell Jim."

"Did it not occur to you that he hasn't slept for a week? And you take him out drinking? Where was Judith? Never mind. Your task is to see to it that he is clean, dressed, sober, and downstairs in time for lunch at one o'clock. I'll cover for both of you until then." She moved out of the door past Glenn and sniffed. "Drunk my foot," she said beneath her breath as she stalked back to her room.

WAYNE AWOKE TO sunlight streaming through his window and the insistent prodding of Glenn. By the time he was fully awake, memories of the previous night were fading into glimpses of a strange dream. It seemed vaguely out of place for him to be in bed. He should say 'on a bed'. It was obvious that he had not been under the covers as he was still fully dressed.

"Oh. What time is it?" he groaned.

"Time for lunch," Glenn snapped. "I didn't think you were ever going to wake up."

"What a great idea. I'll just go back to sleep and not wake up."

"The hell," Glenn said, giving Wayne another kick. "You've got work to organize today. I don't care how many nights you went without sleep. I've never seen Judith so freaked out."

"What happened?"

"Well, from the looks of her clothes and your clothes when we found you this morning, hot monkey sex. But she couldn't wake you up. We had a hell of a time sneaking through the streets of the town with you propped between us. We dumped you onto the bed about five o'clock and I let Judith and Gail out the back door."

"God. Will I ever spend a night in bed? What did Jim say?"

"Jim is the least of your worries. It's what Dr. Allen said that counts."

"Rebecca saw me like this?" *How could life get any worse?*

"I get back upstairs from letting Judith and Gail out the door and she has you cradled in her arms kissing your dirty head. What is between you?"

"I wish I knew. Every time I think I got it figured out, it changes. What now?" he asked, standing beside the bed.

"First, you get a bath. You stink. I promised Dr. Allen you'd be down for lunch, clean, dressed and sober."

"Sober? She thinks I was drunk?"

"I couldn't exactly tell her you were stoned out of your mind. At least liquor's legal."

"All right. Bath, lunch, and bed."

"Wrong again. You've got to build a throne for Chuck's precious knife-throwing scene."

"Ah, shit. Bath. It will all make sense after a bath."

17
Watchful Friend

Thursday, 12 June 1969

"**WHAT** A pit," Wayne moaned as he looked around at what would pass for a theatre for the next four nights. The cast had moved to Ambleside on Thursday after a second and third performance in Keswick played to nine people—total. They'd had a day off, during which Wayne slept, and then a day-trip to Gretna Green and Hadrian's Wall. That had inspired an entire first scene re-enactment on the remnants of the great wall. While Judith was friendly with Wayne, something had changed. She seemed almost afraid around him—guarded. Wayne had spent Wednesday hiking around the west side of the Derwentwater alone and was a little down.

"Hey kids!" yelled Carol in mock Judy Garland tones. "Let's do a play. My grandpa has a barn we can use."

"They call us babes in arms," sang out a half-dozen others, "but we'll be babes in armor."

"My god," Jim whispered as he came through the door to see the theater. The stage was a platform raised a foot above the wooden barn floor. The seats were straight wooden benches, some with backs. The stage area itself was hung in royal blue cotton panels with no front curtain at all. When he walked backstage he discovered a tangle of ropes and pipes that was almost impenetrable. Everything was connected, but nothing seemed to support anything else. When he fought his way back on stage through the panels, most of the cast were linked arm-in-arm across the stage singing "Babes in Arms" in their best Busby Berkeley imitation.

"They call us babes in arms, but we'll be like an army!"

Jim whistled for attention and gradually they collapsed on the floor to listen.

"It's a good thing you all still have a sense of humor," he began. "I hate to tell you this, but the dressing room is worse yet."

"Another stairwell?" groaned Gail.

"I heard a definite singular when he said dressing room," joined Carol.

"This time it's the Trust Superintendent's office," Jim answered. "You'll have to make do with the one room. Work out shifts or whatever. The temperature will be about fifty at curtain time and it's the only heated room in the building."

"Terrific," Chuck muttered. "Judith, d-did you really perform on these s-stages before you came to America?"

"This was one of the best," she laughed. "Just look at all the lights." Wayne looked up at the hanging lamps and the rat's nest of cables that connected them.

"Does this beast have a control panel?" he asked.

"Found it!" called Beth from backstage. "Real dimmers." She crossfaded several lights.

"Well, if the audience can stand to sit through it on these benches, at least we'll have a show with a little atmosphere. Wayne, it's all yours," Jim said.

Wayne organized the crews and they loaded in the limited scenery. When the thrones were on stage it looked much better than it had in Keswick. They carefully taped out positions on the stage. Hamlet and Laertes rehearsed their swordplay under Judith's watchful eye. Wayne worked on improvising a grave scene in a theater that had no levels to work with. Backstage, they cleared as much space as possible and tied all the ropes off in one direction.

"Clothesline," Wayne muttered. On stage, he called Hamlet. "Chuck! Look, I'm sorry about the throne last night."

"Only a little embarrassment out of a long night," said Chuck. "Who would ever expect an empty throne to throw the knife back at me?"

"They didn't have beadboard," Wayne explained. "I told you that knife wasn't meant to be stuck in wood. Apparently, you can't get standard polystyrene here. I took the softest wood I could find."

"I'll just cut the bit. Who'll miss it?"

"Judith will, for one," Wayne said. "I've got an alternative, but you've got to be really careful."

"What's the alternative?"

"I'll sharpen the blade. I've got a file and a whetstone. If I can stay out of sight for an hour, I can put enough of an edge on just the end that it should stick. Just don't miss."

"Never fear, it's s-safe with me."

"If anyone comes looking for me, point them someplace else, would you? I saw a wooden table out back of the theater and I'm going out there to freeze my ass off and sharpen a knife."

WAYNE SANK INTO his work on the bench behind the barn theater in the National Trust. He was happy for the few minutes of work on a prop. When he worked on the throne there were half a dozen other people around, all wanting instructions on what to paint and where things should go. He'd managed to attach a back to the throne, but it wasn't functioning the way anyone wanted. He'd tried a dozen different materials in the absence of bead board. Fabric and newspaper were both too dense for the knife to penetrate. He'd tried cotton batting, but it didn't have enough substance to hold the knife in place. The only thing he could think of to do was to sharpen the knife and hope Chuck could stick it into the wooden backing.

He clamped the blade to the table and began filing the edge. It would only need to be sharpened an inch or so from the point. The blades were already shaped, but they were dull. This edge he could hone each night and keep it razor sharp. He put aside the file and began with a whetstone.

"Hi baby," Judith said slipping up beside him. Wayne jumped.

"Oh! Hi. How'd you find me?"

"What a thing to ask. I asked Chuck if he'd seen you and he told me you were out here."

"Great friend. He was supposed to tell anyone who asked that I'd gone somewhere else."

"He might have been a little distracted. He was helping Carol wrap her boobs in elastic bandage. God, that must hurt." Judith shuddered. Wayne chuckled.

"I think she just does it so she can get Chuck to massage them after the show."

"They are getting along well, aren't they? What are you doing?"

"It's a secret, but I'm sharpening the end of Hamlet's knife so it will stick in the wood."

"I thought we were going to cut that bit."

"I know how much you want it in."

"You'd do that for me?" Judith's voice brought Wayne's attention up to her face. Tears glistened in her eyes.

"Sweetheart, I'd do anything for you. Why have you been, well… sort of avoiding me? Did I do something to hurt you?" he asked.

"Fuck. You really don't remember anything about Friday night, do you?"

"I remember going with you and getting high and waking up with all my clothes on at noon. Other than that, it's all weird dreams. Did we make love?"

"Oh baby. I'm so sorry you missed it. It was so intense that it scared me a little. I've never felt anything like it," she said.

"All right. You don't have to tease me. I'm sorry I screwed up again. I'm caught up on sleep now, I think."

"Wayne, honey. Look in my eyes. I'm serious. I've never been overwhelmed like that. You were…" Judith sobbed. "I've been frightened to be near you ever since. Every time I see you, I have to change my knickers. I don't know what's come over me." Wayne pushed the blade out of the way and pulled Judith down on his lap at the wooden table. He kissed her soundly.

"Darling, I don't want you to be frightened of me. I'm so sorry I scared you. It had to be the drugs. I'm not smoking again. The dreams were too weird."

"Did you dream of making love to me?"

"Yes, but there was the other one, too."

"Rebecca?"

"No. She looked familiar, but I would have recognized Rebecca, I'm sure. It was like I was in an old movie. Too ridiculous to believe. I don't know. It was a dream."

"Mari."

"Wait! That was her name. How did you know? Did I call you Mari?"

"Maybe. It was okay. I felt like I was her, too. That's what scared me. It was so powerful. You are so powerful." They kissed again and Wayne slid a hand under Judith's shirt to cup her breast as she ground herself on his lap.

"Thirty minutes!" Lena called from the back door of the theater.

"Thank you, thirty!" Wayne and Judith automatically responded. They broke down giggling.

"I love you, baby," Wayne said. "I'd better get this blade in Hamlet's sheath."

"Later, I want you to get your blade in my sheath," Judith whispered as they walked to the theatre.

THE PERFORMANCE STARTED well. As Bernardo, Wayne was spot on with the first line. There had been enough atmosphere to make the ghost scenes very spooky. After that scene, he changed costumes in the crowded dressing room where everyone huddled for warmth and prepared for his entrance as the player king. He met Rebecca in the wings and they made their entrance with the rest of the rag-tag bunch of players.

Wayne was wound up as he finished his monologue. There was even a good spattering of applause as "The instant burst of clamor that she made would have made milch the burning eyes of heaven and passion in the gods." It was shaping up to be a great performance. The players were given their instructions by Hamlet and exited. Judith met them as they came off stage.

"Hey, you were really turned on out there tonight," she whispered.

"I'll show you turned on. I've got a woody in my tights."

"So that's what Dr. Allen was staring at all through the scene," Judith giggled.

"Shh," he whispered glancing back at Rebecca.

"If you want me quiet, you'll have to shut me up." With that, she wrapped her arms around him and pressed her lips into his. He felt her hips grind against his own. In a moment, the joked-about woody was present and accounted for between the two lovers.

"Bloody, bawdy villain," Chuck expounded from the stage.

REBECCA SMILED AT the couple as they pushed each other farther off stage. That settled it. She was not going to lead Wayne on when her coven sister had such a firm hold on him. Not that she would get involved with Wayne anyway, but just watching them she had to admit she was getting a little mushy between the legs.

She was almost too late to act when she saw Hamlet's blade come flashing through the cloth panel and lodge in the cluster of ropes behind the set. There was a split-second pause as the rope severed completely and the batten fell from above the stage with its weight of unused lights. She dove after Wayne and Judith and nailed them to the wall feeling, even as she did, the scrape of the pipe as it was deflected off her shoulders and bounced down her back. She crumpled to the floor. The last she heard was Hamlet's insane laughter—"This is most brave!"—as he struggled on stage to remember his next line.

WAYNE HEAVED THE batten off Rebecca's back and Judith pulled her from beneath. He swept her up and made it through the stage door a step behind Judith holding it open. *Protect The Huntress!* echoed in his head. Other than the crash of the pipe on the floor, none of the rest of the troupe realized anything was amiss. Behind him, Wayne caught a glimpse of Beth looking from the other side of the stage behind the drapery panels to see what had happened. The door swung shut behind them. Wayne carefully laid Rebecca down on the table where he'd worked on the culprit knife. They coaxed her back to consciousness. Rebecca's eyes filled with tears as she opened them.

"Ahh," she whimpered. "Are you all right?"

"We're fine, thanks to you," Wayne said. "God! Rebecca, you could have been killed. I…"

"Is anyone hurt back here?" a voice cut Wayne off. Rounding the corner of the theatre was a short stocky man. "I'm a physician," he said approaching the three people.

"Dr. McBride!" Judith exclaimed.

"Judith Harmon, is it?" he answered. "Fancy meeting you here. I saw your name in the program. I'll bet that knife work was your doing." He bent over Rebecca and looked into her eyes. "Who have we here?"

"That's Dr. Allen," Wayne said. "How did you know she was hurt?"

"Instinct, boy," the doctor shot back. He looked up at Wayne and there was a glint of hatred in his eye that made Wayne stumble. "I saw the knife and I heard the crash. Was she hit?"

"By a falling batten," Wayne said. He was not about to relinquish his post at Rebecca's head.

"There seems to be nothing broken, but I've no doubt you're in pain. I've something in my bag that will help you," he said. "I'll be back directly. It's in my auto."

Rebecca looked up at Wayne and then at Judith. Then she closed her eyes.

"Wayne," Judith said, "you have a cue coming up. Better get inside." Her voice held such an aura of command that he was on his feet before his mind had mastered his body.

"I can't do that. Not with Rebecca…"

"There's nothing you can do here," Judith said again. "We have a doctor."

"Wayne," Rebecca whispered hoarsely. "Go ahead. I'll be fine. I know Dr. McBride."

"But you're in that scene, too," Wayne said feebly.

"Use your understudy," Judith said curtly. "That's what he's there for."

"Brian? Okay, okay," he moaned. *No kiss tonight.* He squeezed Rebecca's hand and turned to go. He saw McBride returning with a bag. "I don't trust him," he whispered to Judith. She nodded. Wayne whispered a soft prayer for protection of Rebecca and went to the stage door. Judith saw a soft glow settle around the professor and sink into her, but had no time to question Wayne.

WAYNE LEANED BACK against the door trying to catch his breath. Glenn was backstage ready to enter for the court scene. He saw Wayne's pale face in the backlight.

"You okay?" Glenn whispered. "You look like Hamlet's ghost."

"I need Brian, can you believe it?" Wayne whispered back. "Rebecca's hurt and Judith is outside with her. He's got to fake the dumbshow with me."

"Shit. I'll get him. You calm down."

Wayne was much calmer now, in fact. The first thing he thought of was the dangerous knife. He slipped behind the panels of cloth and stepped over the fallen light bar. He dislodged the knife, careful not to cut any more of the fragile lines. The cast was gathering stage left, already buzzing with the news. Wayne ducked out the stage right door and downstairs with the knife. He grabbed a towel and wrapped the blade, then buried it beneath his clothes. That was the end of that bit of stage business. Chuck would just have to go back to the way he did it last fall.

He returned to the stage just in time to grab Brian and enter. On stage, he didn't have to think of the chaos his own risk-taking had caused.

ONCE WAYNE DISAPPEARED through the stage door, Judith whispered to Rebecca, "I don't trust him either." Rebecca nodded.

"Help me."

McBride approached the table where Rebecca lay, but the items he pulled from his bag were not medical. Four ritual tools were positioned at the four cardinal points and in a few moments wards flared to life around them. Within that circle the three *cildru* of Cobhan Carles shifted to their coven names.

"Huntress, you are going to have a nasty bruise there. You should have it x-rayed tomorrow. I could call an ambulance, but by the time it got here, you could be back in your hotel and asleep. Are you staying at your cottage, Swordmaster?"

"No, Barber." Judith's reply was curt. She watched carefully as he probed Rebecca, not hesitating to put his palm on her breast as he checked her heartbeat.

"Barber!" Rebecca gasped out. "Tend to your work." Judith cushioned her and pushed the high priest of Carles away.

"You've examined enough. Do you have anything for her pain or not? And why are you here?"

"I heard you were both in the district and made it my business to find you," he said. He found the package of pills that he wanted. "Can you swallow this without water?"

"Yes," Rebecca answered. He put the capsule on her tongue and she gulped it down.

"Now before that knocks you out completely, suppose one or both of you tell me what Creüs is doing being used as a stage prop," he commanded.

"Not Creüs," Rebecca answered. "Just a stage prop."

"A good one," Judith said. "He sharpened the point to compensate for the wooden throne back. Stupid Chuck missed it."

"When I saw Hamlet draw it, I nearly fell off my chair. I was on my way out before he ever threw it."

"The knife has already been promised to me if we need to re-forge," Rebecca said through a yawn.

"Huntress, you mustn't forge a new blade, do you hear me?" Judith demanded. Rebecca was falling quickly under the influence of the drug and into a painless sleep.

"Swordmaster, thank you for being so kind to me," Rebecca said through lips that would barely open.

"I owe you one. You saved Wayne's life."

"Yours. Wayne's too." She slipped deeper into sleep.

"Christ! What did you give her?"

"Propoxyphene. I have some samples. Give her one for pain when she needs it, but not more than one every six hours. It's a powerful pain reliever."

"Did you have to knock her out?" Judith asked.

"It affects people differently, but now we can talk, Swordmaster. Look at me."

Judith looked into the eyes of the high priest and was mesmerized. Why had she even bothered to look at him? She despised the man and was more concerned about Rebecca. But once she looked, her other questions seemed to fade away. The eyes seemed to glow and she couldn't tear herself away from them.

"You have no pentacles!" laughed The Barber. "You are helpless to resist me."

"What do you want?" There was a note of fear in Judith's voice, but she was helpless to turn away.

"I want you to allow The Huntress and The Toolmaker to develop their *close* relationship. Don't interfere. Encourage it. They will forge a new blade on Litha, but you and I will rule with it. You'd like to be high priestess, wouldn't you? Together we will control all the power of the four combined circles. We will rule the Four Faces of Carles."

"She might not even call the circle."

"There are two ways the great circle can be called, by authority and by power. She has the authority, but we, my plaything, have the power. We will call the circle."

"I don't... want..." Judith struggled to get the words out.

"Don't bother to resist, Swordmaster. Do as I command."

NIGHTMARES. REBECCA HADN'T had such nightmares in years.

She wasn't out completely when The Barber had begun commanding The Swordmaster. How had he done that? She wanted to tell her friend—yes, Judith was a friend—not to pay attention to the high priest. There was something evil about him. He acted possessed.

Rebecca slipped under the influence of the drug and the nightmares rushed to accompany her. The knife came slicing through the curtains. Again and again she saw it flashing in the air; saw it slicing the rope; saw the pipe falling. In her dreams, it fell not on Wayne, but on her husband Wesley, and there was nothing she could do to stop it.

Again, the flash of the blade in the air. Not just the pipe falling, but all the lights dropping and exploding around her. All the curtains falling, draping the cast in ghostly shapes as they struggled to free themselves. The ceiling was falling. The sky was falling. Rebecca was falling. Her whole world was crumbling around her and all she had to hold was one shivering, naked boy as the fires of the coven exploded around them.

Her Vagabond Poet. Just when she needed him most, he stumbled in on the workings of the circle. He seemed immune to the wards placed around them, simply seeking the warmth of the fire. He was ordained by the gods. He carried into the circle the thing they needed most—his staff. The innocent

Vagabond was an instrument of the gods and he came directly to her, the High Priestess. Now he was caught up with her in consecrating the new tool to the magic workings of the coven—the fire-breathing staff, Iäpetus.

The staff rose proudly from the midst of the fire, immune to its destruction and the Vagabond's staff—his sex—rose between her legs, raising power that flowed from their joining into the wand in the midst of the fire.

Some small part of her that was still Rebecca Hart Allen warned her that this was dangerous. She had raised power once. She had called fire. She had seen the flames reaching into the heart of the wood leaving their seed there where she could call upon it to germinate and bloom again into flame.

The power drawn into the staff of The Vagabond Poet made it glow and when they climaxed together, it burst into flame, shooting a shower of sparks into the night air. Then the staff was truly burning. As she watched, horrified, The Vagabond stepped into the flames to retrieve the staff, quenching the fire against his chest.

She screamed.

The knife cut through Rebecca's dream again. It was no longer in a theatre or a coven circle. The knife cut through a blue Mediterranean sky, flashing through the air into the deep rushing waters below. And Wayne, a Vagabond centuries removed from the creation of Iäpetus—foolish boy—followed the blade into the depths and vanished.

"No!" Rebecca arched her back as she rose up off the bed and stiffened. Wayne jumped from the chair nearby where he had nodded off. He pulled her into his arms and softly crooned to her as she surfaced from the drugged depths of her sleep.

"It's okay, Becc. It's all right. Easy. It will all pass. Just a nightmare," he said as he stroked her hair, careful not to let his supporting arm touch the bruises on her shoulders.

"Wes… Wayne," she whispered. "No. Not you, too. Please don't…"

"There was an accident on stage," Wayne said. Maybe she was too disoriented to remember what had happened. "Everything is okay now. You are deeply bruised, but nothing more. You saved our lives, Becc." She looked at him curiously and relaxed into him a little.

"When did you start calling me 'Becc?'" she asked.

"Oh. Um. I'll… If you…"

"Don't be silly. I like it. No one has called me that in many years. It makes me feel safe. I had such awful nightmares. What am I on?"

"Dr. McBride gave you a pill and some samples to take. When we got back to the Inn, Joyce called another doctor and he examined you then prescribed something different. You were still in pain and the chemist wasn't open yet, so he said it was okay for you to take another of these. You won't need any more, though. Joyce picked up the prescription while you were asleep." Wayne handed her the packet of Darvon samples. The second doctor didn't know much about them but said he supposed it was okay.

"Don't give me any more of these. I need my head back. What are you doing here?"

"I looked in after the show and fell asleep in the chair." Rebecca looked at the chair and saw the pillow and blanket still crumpled up there. She grinned at Wayne. "I couldn't leave you, Becc. I had to make sure you were all right. You saved my life and Judith's, too. I couldn't just leave you alone. I'm so glad you woke up before I have to leave to catch the bus for tonight's performance. But Joyce said she'd sit with you while we're gone. Protect you while I'm gone."

"Knowing Joyce as well as I do, it's a wonder she wasn't sleeping in the chair on top of you," Rebecca chuckled. "Take these and get rid of them. Do *not* give them to Glenn. They're wicked. I'm going back to sleep now, dear. Thank you for being here."

Rebecca settled back into her pillow and was soon out of it again. Wayne looked at the packet of pills she'd given him. "Darvon sample pack. Product of Eli Lilly and Company, Indianapolis, Indiana."

What the hell?

18
Reunion

Monday, 16 June 1969

THEY HAD scarcely spoken offstage since Thursday night. Judith wasn't avoiding him and kissed him warmly when she saw him, but each time he suggested they get together, she gave him a gentle shove and suggested that "Rebecca needed him." He couldn't figure it out. Judith had been… well, a little jealous of his relationship with Rebecca, but now she was pushing him toward her. It didn't make sense.

Rebecca rejoined the cast for their last performance at Ambleside on Sunday night, which proved to be their largest audience since coming to England. There were over fifty in the audience. She was still tender and didn't move as freely as she had before, but she was back onstage and part of the cast. Jim reluctantly cut the knife-throwing bit at Judith's insistence.

"Can we spend some time together tomorrow?" Wayne asked as he caught Judith in the dressing room.

"Of course, love," she answered. She kissed him and for a few moments let the kiss deepen into something Wayne remembered of their connection. Then she pushed away.

"We're going to Blackpool tomorrow. Isn't it exciting? I know how you love the Beatles."

"I seem to remember something about how you love the Beatles," Wayne whispered, then sang, "Yesterday, love was such an easy game to play." Judith silenced him with another passionate kiss. "Wait. The Beatles are from Liverpool."

"That's just south of Blackpool. They played there a lot. It's a big entertainment center. Don't you know that John Lennon's father attempted to kidnap him and immigrate to New Zealand from Blackpool when he was just five years old? Imagine. No Beatles!" Wayne looked at her askance. "It's true. I'll show you the very spot," Judith continued. "Tonight, you'd better check on your patient and be sure she hasn't overdone it in the performance. I got you this jar of cream. It's called arnica and has been used here in the country for centuries. I'm told it removes bruising. You should put it on her shoulders."

"Judith…"

"I promise I will be all yours tomorrow, darling," she said as she left with Gail to head to their hotel.

"Uh oh. Trouble in paradise?" Rebecca asked when she opened the door to Wayne's knock. He stood there looking confused. "Do come in, Wayne. You've sat by my bed faithfully for three nights. I don't suppose I can stop you tonight. I thought you would be out with Judith tonight, though. I'm definitely on the mend now."

"I… I don't understand it. I have some ointment she gave me for you. She said I should rub it on your shoulders to lessen the bruising. I just don't understand what's going on."

"Dear sister," Rebecca whispered. "What *is* going on?"

"Why do you call Judith 'sister?' I've heard you say it before."

"Oh. We discovered we are members of the same… society."

"You mean like a sorority?"

"Yes. Very similar. In some ways."

Wayne stood there awkwardly holding the bottle in his hand. *Why is Judith doing this?* Rebecca wondered. Still, the thought of something relieving the bruising on her shoulders was enticing. *She's overcompensating for our disagreement.*

"Well since she was so kind as to send this remedy, it would be a shame to waste the opportunity," Rebecca said. "To relieve the bruising," she added hurriedly.

"I guess I'm supposed to put it on your shoulders. I could call Joyce. I'm sure she'd do it."

"I'm sure she would, but it's late. Let's not disturb anyone else. Just touch gently. It's still pretty sore." Rebecca lay on her stomach and pulled her robe down off her shoulders. She still had her nightgown on. No harm done.

"Um… I think it has to go on the bruises. I can't even see them. I'll just ask Joyce in the morning," Wayne stumbled.

"Oh. I guess they are somewhat covered up," laughed Rebecca. "The bruises." She looked hard at Wayne. The boy had an expression of such confusion and longing that Rebecca was lost. "Turn around." He obeyed. Rebecca removed her robe and nightgown and then pulled the robe back on. She shuddered at the thought of what she'd just done. With Wayne's back turned, she'd stripped to her panties and then hurriedly pulled her robe on. She lay back down on the bed and called to him. "You should be able to reach them now."

Wayne turned to her and she shifted her weight to pull the robe down away from her shoulders and upper arms. She kept it bunched up around her breasts as she lay on her stomach, arms clamped to her sides.

"Okay. It says to just apply liberally to the bruised area and rub in gently."

"The key word there is 'gently.' I'm still very sore," Rebecca replied. She heard him remove the lid from the jar and braced herself for the cold ointment. Instead, she heard Wayne rubbing his hands together.

"This stuff's cold. Let me warm it up a minute," he said. *What a sweet boy.*

When Wayne considered the cream to be warm enough, he gently drew his hands across Rebecca's shoulders. She shivered at his touch.

"Still too cold?" he asked, pulling back.

"No. No, it's fine. I just… I haven't been touched like that in a long time. Go ahead, doctor." Wayne inhaled deeply and began to gently rub the emollient into her shoulders. Rebecca sighed. Wayne started to pull away when he'd covered the area he could see. "Please don't stop," she whispered. She pulled with her fingers and the robe came down to her mid-back. *He can't really see anything.*

"God, Rebecca! How far down does this go? You're bruised all the way to the middle of your back."

"As long as you see a bruise, just keep pushing it down. I trust you."

"Perfect love and perfect trust," Wayne whispered uncertainly. Rebecca relaxed. She let go of the robe.

"It looks like the bar bounced off your shoulders and hit you two or three more times on the way down. I'm so sorry, Rebecca. It was all because of my stupidity."

"Shh. Just put the cream on. It does make it feel better." He rubbed the lotion in softly and she just wanted to purr. It felt so good. He started to pull his hands away. "There's one more, dear," she said. She hadn't intended to tell him about the last bruise, but, 'in for a pence, in for a pound,' she thought.

"Um… really?"

"Yes really. Do you think I'm Mrs. Robinson? I'm not trying to seduce you." *I don't think I am, anyway. Oh goddess, his hands feel so good.*

Wayne pushed the robe down farther and she straightened her arms to pull her hands out of the sleeves. She heard him gasp. She quickly pulled her arms back alongside her breasts.

"What is it?"

"I just… God, Rebecca. It's like someone beat you across your… um… I know you're not trying to seduce me… but… um…"

She felt his hands caress the soft globes of her buttocks. She couldn't help herself. She moaned. She knew the stripe was across the top of her butt, but when his hands pushed farther down to cup her cheeks she didn't complain. If anything, she moaned a little and pushed back against his hands.

He withdrew his hands and pulled her robe up to cover her back.

"I… um… think… I got it… all. I'll leave the jar here in case you need some more. Goodnight!" He fled from the room. Rebecca lay on her bed panting.

"Oh goddess! What have I done?" she whispered. It was not, however, what she had done, but what she was about to do that scared her. Her hand slipped beneath her and her fingers sought the warm, wet folds of her sex.

MONDAY WAS A good if frustrating day. Judith spent the day cuddled next to him in the seat of the overcrowded bus, volunteering to ride on his lap so another actor could have her seat. She kept burying her face in his neck, covering it with kisses. Then she would tell him about what he was seeing in the countryside. He never tried to see beyond what was sitting in his lap. They walked around Blackpool, toured the castle, and rode the nearly fifty-year-old roller coaster at Pleasure Beach called The Big Dipper. They also rode the wooden-track Wild Mouse and Wayne was feeling peaked when he got off.

Judith stood on a pier and declared that this was where John Lennon was made to choose between his mother and his father at age five. It had now been four years since the Beatles last played a concert at Pleasure Beach.

"I've got to tell Glenn this," Wayne said. "He knows so much. It will be nice to have something on him. Let me see. If he was five years old, that would have been in…"

"1946," Judith said.

"Hey, Glenn! Did you know that John Lennon was nearly kidnapped on this very spot?" Wayne asked his friend.

"Yeah. By his dad. His mom found out and came to get him. It's sad, really. He didn't see his dad again until like three years ago. There was a big write-up about it in *Billboard*."

"Shit," Wayne said.

It was dark when the bus headed back for Keswick and Wayne managed to position himself so Judith on his lap was between him and the window. Their seat-mate was turned toward the aisle and Wayne began some serious make-out time. Judith melted against him and encouraged his hand when it slid up under her shirt against her skin.

"I miss you baby," he whispered. "Why don't you stay with me tonight."

"I can't. Haven't you noticed them checking rooms? If we aren't in by curfew, we're toast."

"I didn't know," Wayne said.

"Just keep doing what you're doing now. Jesus, Wayne, you make me feel so good."

"Tomorrow."

"Jim's got us scheduled for another bus tour tomorrow. I don't even know where he's taking us."

"Shit. Kendall. We're supposed to see some production of *The World of Carl Sandburg* that he's thinking of doing next year."

"Who is Carl Sandburg?"

"An American poet. He's all about folk songs and pig slaughtering. Urban industrial art against a rural American backdrop."

"You are the only poet I need," she whimpered as he strummed her nipples with his thumb.

"WHAT IS SHE doing?" Wayne whispered to Judith. He wasn't sure why he was whispering. They were in a huge open field surrounded by monolithic stones.

The show in Kendall had been good. After busting all budgets to get the cast to England, Jim was going to need a low budget show to open in the fall and with just four actors sitting on stools, you couldn't get much lower budget than *The World of Carl Sandburg*. And it was timely. Everybody wanted to sit around singing folk songs and protest songs. If they added a little Bob Dylan into the mix it would be a great show.

But instead of returning directly to Keswick, the bus had taken a short detour to visit this stone circle. Wayne had been almost asleep after they stopped for half an hour to let sheep finish crossing the road in front of them. He never did figure out how many there were. Then he'd stepped off the bus and followed the cast across a low fence—what was that poem about a crooked stile?—and into a scene from one of his dreams. Stones surrounded him. Judith led him between two and made a long circuit with him around the circle. When they were approaching the two tall stones again, he saw Rebecca moving from stone to stone, touching it as if it were an old friend.

"She's saying hello and calling each one by name. The one on the left at the northern gate is Enceladus. The one on the right is Asia."

"These should mean something to me," Wayne whispered. He shook his head. If it would only come clear. Judith was pulling him to the edge of the circle away from the rest of their group. Steve, Chuck, and Phil were leaning against a stone opposite them looking like a scene from the crucifixion with their hands held out and other cast members taking their pictures.

"Look at me, lover." Wayne fixed his gaze on Judith. She reached out and touched the pentacles that hung from his neck.

"Swordmaster," he whispered.

"Yes, Unbound. This is the circle where we meet. The clowns don't have any idea that they are leaning against one of the Titans."

"Scarce images of life, one here, one there…"

"Yes. And she is greeting each of them."

"Reb…"

"Shh. You know who she is." Wayne thought a moment and it came to him.

"The Hart."

"Yes. The Huntress of Carles Castlerigg. This is her circle as well."

"Why is it all so foggy? I can hardly even see the other side of the circle." Wayne said, looking around.

"Foggy?"

The word seemed to echo in Wayne's mind. The fog was disappearing. He'd stepped through a barrier and could see the people clearly. Mari, The Vagabond, the celebrants. He was thankful to no longer be sharing the body of The Vagabond. This time he could simply watch and see how the scene would play out. Vaguely he could see shadows around them and he recognized them as cast members from the play. But they weren't real where he was. Where he was there was only The High Priestess Mari, The Vagabond, The Swordmaster, and The Hart.

"Unbound?" There was a note of panic in the voice of The Swordmaster. "You mustn't. Not now. Not with everyone around." The

Hart looked at him from across the circle, alarm in her eyes. Apparently, he wasn't supposed to be here now. He felt The Swordmaster pull him toward her, felt the point of her *Athamé* at his chest, and he suddenly snapped back into the present.

"Let's go everyone!" Jim called. "John and Joyce are putting together a feast for the entire cast tonight. Let's honor our hosts with the best we can give them!" Everyone headed for the bus again. At the edge of the circle, Wayne turned and looked back. A crowd of naked witches turned toward him, calling him back to their circle. He felt a pull on his arm and a few moments later he was on the bus.

"You saw it," Judith whispered. "What is he?"

She had cornered Rebecca outside the dining room after dinner. The cast was pleased that for once they had not had lamb sandwiches. Judith declined to tell them that the meatloaf was at least half mutton. Wait till they had a Wimpy. But it was the first moment that she'd been able to get to Rebecca when Wayne went into the lounge to have a Baby Cham and sing more folk songs with other members of the cast. Glenn had located a guitar. When Judith saw Rebecca leave the room, she excused herself to use the loo.

"Goddess, Swordmaster. He's a Vagabond. Can't you see it? He took us across a time dimension without even having a ritual. We were there. I saw Iäpetus in the hands of the High Priestess. You saw it, too."

"I've believed in our ancient ways all my life, Huntress, but I've never seen power manifest itself like this. I don't know what to do. You have to help him."

"It may take both of us."

"I feel… something is wrong. I've been weakened," Judith said. "But whatever you want, you may have. If it is to be our own Unbound, please… love him… like I love him." Tears were pouring from Judith's eyes as she left Rebecca in more wonder of what had just occurred than of what happened in the stone circle.

Wednesday morning Wayne awoke to rapping on his door. *Oh. I must have overslept. What the hell?* He struggled out of bed and went to the door. Rebecca stood there. Wayne was suddenly conscious of the fact he was standing at the door in a t-shirt and briefs.

"Um… Hi. Am I late?"

"Kind of overdid it last night, didn't you?" Rebecca asked. Now Wayne remembered.

THEY'D SAT IN the lounge singing and drinking Baby Cham. It was good, but a little pricey, so Wayne switched to beer as he and Glenn teamed up to sing "Walk Right Back" in a pretty good rendition of the Everly Brothers. Judith and Gail were attempting to leave for the night and eventually extracted themselves to head back to the Skiddaw. They sang a couple more numbers in the lounge until there were only Glenn, Wayne, and Chuck left with John, the innkeeper.

"Now lads, you've a treat coming," John said. "How about a little whisky?"

"A shot on the rocks would be a nice nightcap," Glenn said.

"Rocks?"

"He means with ice," Chuck laughed.

"Why would you want a lump of water in your scotch?"

"I think he's Irish," Wayne laughed.

"Irish? That's a Scotsman with his brain removed. This is a Macallan ten. Just standard bar whiskey here." John set up four short glasses and poured a generous shot. Glenn reached to throw the shot back and John placed a strong hand on his arm. "You sip it, lad." The three boys raised the glasses in salute to John and sipped the strong liquor.

"I think I could get to like this," Wayne said after rolling the liquid over his tongue and swallowing. John regaled the three with stories of service in the war, finding Joyce when he was on furlough in Scotland, having his first sip of fine whisky, and ending up married in the morning.

"And that's why I waited until your young ladies were gone before I served you whisky," he laughed.

"Not that I don't appreciate the effort, but without a brain, I think I'll go back to warm beer. I'm getting used to that," Glenn said. Chuck picked up the guitar and began playing something vaguely Spanish. He had tuned out everything around him. John poured Glenn another beer and then turned to Wayne.

"Yeah. I could really get to like this," Wayne nodded as he slowly finished his whisky. John handed him a glass of water.

"Drink this to cleanse your mouth. The next one is better yet." John reached for a clean glass and poured from an unlabeled bottle with sloping sides. "Oban. It's a West Highland. Fallin' short this year. I hear they're building a new distillery, but there won't be any more of this for a few years."

By the time Wayne had finished his second whisky, Glenn was passed out in the lounge and Chuck had disappeared. John sampled a third Scotch so smoky and peaty that Wayne compared it to gasoline.

"In a good way," he said, embarrassed.

"Nah. The island whisky isn't for everyone. You're a Highland man, though I think you might like the Speyside."

"Not tonight, my friend. One more and I'd be asleep with Glenn over there."

"Aye. We'd better get him up to his room so yer professors don't find him in the morning. Ye won't say anything, now will you?"

"Of course not. Thank you."

Now WAYNE WAS wondering what he'd missed and why Dr. Allen was at his door. Somehow, she looked like Dr. Allen this morning and not like Rebecca.

"Um… I guess maybe we got a little carried away."

"You don't look too much the worse for it."

"Did I miss something?"

"Breakfast. But there is a remedy."

"Another opportunity, Dr. Allen?"

"Mr. Hamel, don't act so dour. I expect you up, bathed, and presentable in fifteen minutes. Then you are to march directly to the Skiddaw Hotel and take your girlfriend out to breakfast. You've spent entirely too much time in the company of professors. Go have some fun."

She grinned at him and he couldn't help but grin back.

"Yes, Dr. Allen. I sure hope I ace this class."

"Some days you must make a pass to get a pass," she replied and marched away.

A BRIGHT SPOT began to show on Wayne's horizon and it took the shape of Judith Harmon coming down the hotel stairs. When she saw him, her face lit up and she ran into his arms. They kissed, long and slow.

"What are you doing here at this hour?" she asked when they broke apart to breathe. "The way you guys were going last night, I didn't expect you up before noon."

"Breakfast. I understand you know where the best bakery in town is and would be the one to show me all that I've missed since coming to England."

"That could be arranged," she said. "We'd probably just walk around a lot and get to know each other before we spent the afternoon on the lake in very tiny bathing suits."

"My lady, I am yours to command."

"Oh, don't I wish," she sighed.

THEIR ROMANCE WAS tumultuous at the best of times. In the worst times, it bordered on coming to blows. Now it looked like it would end when Wayne left England and Judith stayed. As a result, both found their moods swinging at the smallest stimulus. Neither one seemed to know precisely what they found so attractive in the other, but the attraction was there. The coolness of the past few days thawed as they finished their cream scones and tea. Wayne did manage a cup of weak coffee. Judith looked at him in his flannel shirt and jeans, carrying his walking stick.

"Well, you are dressed for a walking tour," she said. "Time for you to find out what walkers are really like. We'll need a lunch and water. We'll get you a little knapsack to carry things. It's a ten mile walk and the first half is uphill. Are you ready?"

"Ten miles! It will take us hours."

"That's only if we don't stop to fool around. I can't guarantee that we won't. Let's go!"

In a matter of half an hour, they'd collected a knapsack, lunch, a bottle of wine, and water. Judith stayed on Wayne's left so he could hold his stick in his right hand.

"Where are we going?"

"Up. We're hiking up Skiddaw Little Man."

"Don't call me Little Man. Where'd that come from?"

"It's the name of the peak. If we feel good when we get there, it's only another mile to the peak of Skiddaw, but we're going to climb over 2,000 feet." They set off together and headed for the peak. It took half an hour to get to the trailhead but the walking was pleasant and even though they were climbing steadily, it didn't seem to be a problem. They held hands and talked. And talked. Judith had spent her childhood near here and the trails were familiar to her. She talked about visiting each of the four circles in her youth, but staying with Threlkeld as her home.

Most of what she said, Wayne didn't really understand, but assumed it was just cultural differences. He was too occupied by the sensations of holding her hand, pausing to catch their breath and then lose it again in a kiss.

"Look, we didn't need to bring water with us," he said as they came to a stream rushing down the mountain. "Pure English countryside water."

"Don't drink that."

"Why not?"

"Wait till we get around the next bend and you'll see." They continued to walk and half a kilometer later were surrounded by sheep, also making use of the stream, in various ways.

"Ew, yuck."

"No, ewe uck." They laughed and drank from their canteen, then walked farther.

"Don't you have friends here that you want to see?"

"My best friend is away someplace. Lord knows where." Judith had complained of a lonely childhood. "You saw me with a friend opening night in Keswick. He was passing me the joints that we shared with disastrous results. I just wish you could remember everything that happened that night. You made me feel so good."

"I'm so ashamed that I passed out on you."

"On me and in me. Wayne, I'm worried about the way you sometimes black out. It's like you go somewhere and even if you take me with you, I can't really touch you."

"I'm sorry I got so pre-occupied with Rebecca. But she saved our lives."

"Hey. I know when not to compete with a beautiful professor injured in an act of valor. I…" Judith shook her head as if something was interfering with her thoughts. "I want you to be with her," she whispered.

"What?"

"Just… do whatever she asks. Oh shit!" A tear was on Judith's cheek as they crested the summit of Skiddaw Little Man. Wayne kissed it and she clung to him.

"I love you, Judith," he said. "I don't understand everything that is going on, but the thing that keeps me held together is that I love you."

They sat with their lunch and drank water, deciding wine would be an unwise decision as they still needed to walk back to town. They also decided not to cross the ridge to the summit of Skiddaw. Wayne looked at the mountain and squinted. There was something about it that drew him, but repulsed him at the same time. The path looped back on itself just on the north edge of the mountain and returned near a secluded gully. Wayne began to hurry, but Judith tripped and dragged him to the ground with her.

IT WAS A good idea to go for a hike, Judith thought. She was able to talk to him and he to her, but the silences were just part of hiking uphill, not awkward pauses that either rushed to fill. She felt guilty taking him away from Rebecca, but last night Rebecca had insisted that Judith should spend time with Wayne. She'd refused outright to discuss the possibility of using him in the ritual. That should have comforted Judith, but she felt disturbed. She could not shake the feeling that what she said to Rebecca—or even to Wayne at times—was not what she really wanted to say.

They'd made the top of Skiddaw Little Man, the false summit, and headed toward the ridge to cross to the summit when Wayne turned suddenly and wanted to go back without continuing up the mountain. Judith showed him the loop path from between the two peaks and Wayne seemed in a rush to return. They were in the gully, following the stream when she fell, dragged forward by Wayne's grip on her hand. He stumbled and fell beside her.

There was a wild look in his eyes that terrified Judith. He turned to gather her into his arms and as their eyes met he seemed to melt.

"I think these hills are haunted," he said.

"No doubt," she answered, glad that he was back with her. "I knew a fellow in school who catalogued over a hundred different ghost stories from this region. Most of them are benign, though."

They heard voices and both held their breath as they hugged in the shelter of a small grove. The voices were above them as two other hikers passed on a footpath above the gully.

"Maybe I missed the right path," Wayne speculated.

"Not to worry. It's an easy climb out of this little stream bed," Judith answered. "They all come out the same. And this is a rather nice, secluded spot, don't you think?"

Wayne looked around and grinned. The two sank to the ground and into each other's arms. The kiss was accompanied by touches as they refreshed their memories of their partner's body.

"You know why I always let you lead uphill?" he asked. Judith blushed.

"You've been watching my ass, haven't you?"

"It is such a perfect ass to watch. How did you come to be so beautiful?"

"I'm not that beautiful. My tits are too small, my ass is too big, and I have a soft belly."

"Where on earth did you get that information? Someone has been lying to you. Judith, you are the most perfect woman I have ever met."

"I'm only five foot one. If I had a little more height and a longer reach I'd be a better fencer."

"Perfect! I'm certain that's what makes your shoulders fit just under my arm. And your legs are at least that long. When I look at you in your shorts or one of your short skirts, I can't take my eyes off your legs. And your butt is so perfectly round at the top of your legs, I just want…"

Judith kissed him as his hands did what they wanted to her butt.

"Make love to me, Wayne. Tell me I'm perfect for you. Please?"

"That's no problem at all." He began unbuttoning her shirt, exposing more and more of her flesh. "You're not wearing a bra?"

"I hoped you'd notice eventually," she whispered. He continued removing her shirt and began tickling her with his beard.

"I never understood what was meant when guys used to talk about breasts that would fit in a champagne glass. My parents have champagne glasses and they are all these tall skinny things."

"Those are flutes."

"No one ever tried to play them."

"That's… oh… ah." His tongue a reached out to flick her left nipple and she couldn't continue speaking. He kissed her breast softly.

"John served our Baby Chams in these wide… like pudding cups."

"Coupes," Judith sighed as he bent to flick her nipple with his tongue again.

"Okay. I just kept thinking as I held my champagne coupe in the palm of my hand that it was just the size and shape of your breast—so perfect—so elegant—so sensual."

"Oh, Wayne. Not too hard. It's too sensitive, baby."

"You know, I noticed that the first time you let me touch them. That day after New Year's when you nearly knocked me out in the hall. And then we lay down together and you showed me how sensitive your skin is. I had such a lot to learn. The only thing I knew was what I read in *Playboy*."

"You read the articles?"

"How else is a guy supposed to find out what turns Miss October on? But the stories were all wrong. They talk about a girl's nipples getting stiff and hard. You'd think their diamond tips would bore holes in your chest. But your beautiful, dainty little nipples are puffy and erect, but they're still soft and pliable. I don't want to squeeze them too hard because they're so tender. You are so perfect."

Judith was luxuriating in Wayne's touch and his words. In so few encounters, he'd learned her body so well. She pushed his hand lower to her stomach.

"You don't have a belly. You are flat and athletic. You are strong."

"But it's soft and poochy."

"What makes a woman a woman instead of a man with boobs? I wouldn't want you to look like a body-builder. I love the softness of your tummy. And as soon as you stretch and my hand floats down your front, I can feel every muscle ripple beneath my touch. Especially when I reach your belt and you suck your tummy in like you are now so there's room between your shorts and your skin for me to slide my hand down lower."

Judith mewed as Wayne's hand slipped into her panties and stroked down to the top of her slit. She reached a hand down and opened the buttons to let them fall open. Wayne pulled his shirt off and she lifted her hips so he could put it under her before he pulled her shorts and panties down her legs. *Please touch me.*

"Do you remember the first time you undressed with me? And we were so rudely interrupted in the costume closet. It was the first time I saw your... your uh..."

"My fanny? My pussy? My little cunny?"

"Okay. I like your little cunny. It tastes like honey."

"I don't think that's funny."

"You could be a playboy bunny."

"Just touch it, would you?"

"Yeah." But he didn't touch it. He blew through her hairs and down across her legs. It made her shiver and tense and squirm. "The first time I saw your little cunny I stopped breathing. Like the hair on your head, your pubic hair is so fine and light that any little breeze makes it move." He blew again and she whimpered. *Please get to it?*

Wayne moved down between her legs and blew softly from the other side. She could feel her hair moving in his light breeze.

"When you let me between your beautiful, shapely legs the first time, I didn't know what to expect. Guys have such weird stories. But the smell was so light and sweet—even now after you've been walking for three hours, you smell fresh. I know you've been sweating, but you don't taste salty like I do." He licked up the inside of her left thigh then started up the right thigh. He came close to her bush but never quite touched the sensitive parts. "And the thing I wanted more than anything in the world was a taste of your precious fluids. Not too thick and not too thin, but you were so turned on, you'd kind of dripped down the inside of your leg. You'd be doing that now, but you are lying back and it's all running down your bottom." With that he licked up between her cheeks, gathering what was dripping down between them.

Judith loved the tantalizing way he'd teased her, but she was more than ready. The next time his tongue rose between her cheeks, she grabbed his head and pressed his mouth against her vulva.

"Lick me. Please, lick me, baby." Wayne complied. He thoroughly bathed her hair, her vulva, her clit, and her opening with his tongue. Then he got down to business and focused on getting her off. Judith came in seconds and then came again when he continued his assault. As she was rising toward her third climax she pulled at him. "In me. Baby, put your cock in my fanny and fuck me. I have to feel you in me now."

Wayne pushed his pants low enough that he could comply with her wishes and in moments Judith began to see the sparkling lights that emanated from her lover and encased them in a protective shield. She knew she could cry out—scream out her orgasm and no one would hear. No one would infringe on their privacy. The sensation rose from deep inside her and as Wayne stroked into her again she released in a climax that he joined until they both passed out.

19
Lady's Rake

Friday, 20 June 1969

THURSDAY HAD been a load-in day as the troupe moved into a tent in the park in Keswick. There was no time for anything else before their opening performance in the tent. There was an annual religious gathering in July and the village rolled out the red carpets and half a dozen tents for meetings. They were equipped much better than the local theatre.

Wayne and Judith got back to their hotels late—much, much too late for more than a kiss goodnight. They'd had no time for any loving, but Wayne had great hopes for Friday afternoon.

"Boating? That sounds like fun."

"I'll make a picnic. You bring the wine we didn't drink on the mountain. I have a new two-piece bathing costume. Do you have something to swim in?" she asked.

"I'll come up with something. A two-piece?"

"An itsy-bitsy, teeny-weeny…" Judith sang.

Wayne answered with a kiss.

HE'D SLEPT UNTIL nearly noon, but no one complained since he'd worked all day the previous day and then reset lights after the show. He rummaged around in his suitcase for something to wear swimming and came across a pair of gym shorts. He couldn't figure out why he'd brought them, but it had seemed like the right thing to do at the time. He put them on and then pulled his khaki shorts on over them and a black *Measure for Measure* t-shirt. He looked at his walking stick and shrugged. Hiking was a time for the walking stick. Boating wasn't. He grabbed his knapsack with the bottle of wine in it and headed for Judith's hotel.

The pale blue sundress she wore came to about mid-thigh. It had a small white collar, but no sleeves. She looked delicious.

221

"I brought a couple of towels in case we want to find a secluded spot to lie out," Judith said.

"Are you wearing it?"

"Yes, but I lied."

"Not so itsy-bitsy?"

"Oh, yes, it is. But the polka-dots are blue."

"Mmm. Let's find that secluded spot."

Judith led him to the docks. They paid six shillings to release the lock on one of the rowboats and as soon as they had their bags loaded, they shoved off. Judith sat in the stern and Wayne faced her as he set to rowing.

"I can't see where I'm going."

"You don't need to. I'll direct you. We'll go out past the island."

"Which island?"

"Oh, this one and that one. Pull over a little to your left." Wayne followed the instructions, guiding the little boat gently across the water. They circled Friar's Crag and as soon as they were out of sight of the boat dock, Judith pulled her sundress over her head. Wayne dropped the oars.

"Oh, my Goddess!" he exclaimed. "You are so beautiful."

"It's so tiny. I feel more naked in it than without it."

"Be my guest."

"Thou foul fiend. When do I get to see what you've got on under there?"

"When we get someplace stable so I can move around. Where to now, m'lady?"

Judith continued to guide him by placing her bare feet on his thighs and stroking the direction she wanted him to turn. All the while she spoke of the legends of the area. As they rounded the next island, Judith told him to just drift a while and to get his clothes off. He started to comply and she pulled his knapsack to her.

"This is a better time for that wine," she said. "Where's the screw?"

"Huh?" Wayne had his shirt over his head.

"Corkscrew. To take the cork out."

"Cork? Shit! I've never had a bottle of wine with a cork." Judith started laughing at him.

"What? Do you expect me to chew it out with my long pointy teeth?" She laid the bottle down and crawled toward Wayne. Laughing at the little mistake, she reached for the snap on Wayne's shorts. "Oh, look. There's an interesting ghost story. This is Lord's Island where the Earl of Derwentwater once lived. Unfortunately, in 1719 the Earl threw his lot in with the Jacobeans and was executed for his pains. The army came to get his wife as well and she fled the island, throwing her jewels into the water rather than let them capture them. She swam to shore and climbed that sharp gully up Walla Crag. It's now known as the Lady's Rake. She's seen climbing the cliffs on moonlit nights, some say. Now lift up so I can get these off you."

Wayne stood precariously, in the rocking boat as Judith pulled his shorts down. She grabbed both the khakis and his gym shorts. Wayne was startled and grabbed to catch the gym shorts, overbalancing and stepping back into the rowing bench. He fell back, unable to catch himself before he hit his head on the prow of the boat and lost consciousness.

THERE WERE SHOUTS and screams as soldiers gathered on the shore with torches. One brave man swam the distance to the island and loosed the Earl's boat and towed it back to his fellows on the shore. Four at a time, the dozen soldiers were ferried across the water, ready to assault the manor.

Inside, Lady Derwentwater finished gathering her jewels. There was calm purpose in her actions. She took the bag and left the manor through the kitchen even as the soldiers reached the front of the manor. It did not take long for the servants to give her away. The soldiers rushed through the kitchen to see the Lady at the edge of the lake below.

"You'll never have my jewels!" she screamed as she threw a handful of the gems toward the water. Then she tripped and the rest of the bag spilled out along the shore. The soldiers rushed but fell over themselves when she stripped off her gown and threw it after the jewels. Turning, she clutched a small bag in her hand and dove into the water.

The soldiers scrambled along the shore, gathering up the Lady's gown and searching for jewels. Other than a few baubles, they found only stones.

"Look!" shouted one of the soldiers, pointing toward the land across the narrow channel. The eyes of the other men followed and they saw glimpses of the woman's pale skin against the darkness of the cliff's face as she climbed away from her would-be captors.

The jewels had been a ruse, meant to delay the soldiers while she escaped with something much more valuable. She had to make it to the circle. There she would find peace and Enceladus would be home. She was, after all...

JUDITH PANICKED. SHE crawled over the bench, nearly tipping the rowboat over as she reached Wayne and attempted to wake him. When she touched him, she was drawn into his dream, seeing the Lady climb the rake. Still, she forced herself to function. She grabbed the wine. She had no choice. With a muttered prayer, she willed the cork out of the bottle and poured the wine into Wayne's mouth.

…A WITCH! WAYNE gasped back to awareness. He bolted upright, a sharp sting as the necklace he wore caught on the edge of the boat, cut into his neck, and then snapped. He saw the woman in front of him, so familiar. Behind her, soldiers on the shore. But the woman wasn't the Lady and the soldiers faded. Wayne shook his head, flashes of the dream still playing in his head, superimposing them over what he knew should be reality. He focused on Judith and then on the bottle of wine.

"How…?" Judith quickly bit the cork between her teeth.

"I said I'd use my teeth," she said. "Are you okay?"

"You… I… No." Wayne pulled his shorts up and fastened them. "You're one of them." Behind her he could see shapes of the others he'd dreamed about. They were everywhere. Wayne pushed himself to his feet, standing in the rocking boat, his head still swimming.

Swimming. He looked at the water and dove. Judith screamed.

Wayne surfaced a few feet away.

"What are you doing," Judith shouted at him. "Baby, come back to the boat. Please."

"I'll just leave now," he said, striking out for the shore.

"But what about me?" she called. He rolled over onto his back and looked at her, but not at her. There were so many of them.

"You're a witch. Fly."

"No," JUDITH CRIED as she watched him swim to shore. Every few strokes he would change direction slightly as if trying to avoid something in the water. She watched in tears as he made the shore and ran toward town.

Judith looked at the bottle of wine, still in her hand. She pushed herself up to move to the rowing seat. As she did, she caught a glint of gold hanging from the gunwale. A chain. She followed it and on the bottom of the boat found her pentacles.

"Oh no!" she gasped. Wayne was unprotected. Memories must be flooding his mind with no context. She reached for the charm and an electrical jolt purged her mind of its controls. She'd been pushing him toward Rebecca to make a new tool. *She'd* been unprotected and under The Barber's spell. What else had she done?

WAYNE'S EQUILIBRIUM WAS off. He stumbled as if he were two people going different directions. *What happened to me? I have to get my head together.* He jumped to his left as he saw a ragged man with a walking stick come out of the shadows and then simply disappear in the sunlight. He made it to the Walpole and to his room without drawing attention to himself. His shorts were nearly dry by the time he got to his room, and all the way back he'd simply willed people not to notice the shirtless boy running through the street. He pulled his wallet out and rolled the contents up in his towel then laid them out on the dresser to finish drying. He was exhausted. At least in his room, no visions seemed to be interfering with his eyesight.

He rubbed his head and found a knot on the back of it where he'd hit the prow of the boat. That was going to hurt when he put his helmet on tonight for the first act. He really needed a rest. He locked the door and closed the blinds and was asleep in seconds.

"WAKEY-WAKEY," JIM CALLED as he knocked on the door. "Call in thirty minutes."

"Thank you, thirty," Wayne acknowledged the time he'd have to get awake and down to the tent for tonight's performance. He felt okay now. Just a little groggy from an afternoon nap, but the surreal events of the afternoon were no longer haunting his mind. He just needed time to think, that was all. He'd have to stay away from Judith as much as possible.

And not talk about her being a witch.

Of course, that was easier said than done. She headed straight toward him the minute he entered the tent.

"Wayne, you need this," she started, holding a gold chain out to him. He was mesmerized by it. Every fiber of his being wanted to reach out and grab what was in her hand, but he resisted, backing away from her.

"No. Stay away. I'm sorry, Judith, but I'm breaking up with you. Keep your necklace. I won't wear it."

"Wayne, don't do this. Please," she begged. "We can work it out. I can explain everything."

"I'm sure you can, but I'm not sure I want to hear the explanation. Everything's gone weird on me and I need to get my head back together. I promise we'll talk… later. Not tonight. I have to go sleep after the show." He turned abruptly away from her and went to get his costume on.

"WHAT WAS THAT about?" Rebecca asked, coming up to Judith. "Are you okay, sister?"

"No," Judith sobbed. "Something terrible has happened. He's not thinking straight. No. It's worse. He's hallucinating."

"What are you talking about?" Neither woman was on in the first act so Judith dragged Rebecca outside and began telling her the story. First she told Rebecca that The Barber had managed to cast a spell over her because she was without her pentacles.

"Why were you without pentacles," Rebecca asked, twisting the star-stone ring on her finger.

"I gave them to Wayne. It was spur of the moment when he gave me my Christmas present and I realized he was a toolmaker. I gave him a blood promise and my pentacles to start him on his way."

"The pendant that he wore around his neck?"

"Yes."

"I assumed you'd initiated him, but I didn't know the pentacles were yours. How did you break the spell The Barber put on you?"

"That's the problem. We were rowing this afternoon when Wayne fell and hit his head. While he was unconscious and I was… um… removing a wine cork without a cork screw, he fell into another time-shifting vision and dragged me with him. I'd told him the legend of the Lady's Rake, but the sanitized version. The vision he was seeing was the real version with her naked taking the Fourth Face of Carles up the cliff. When he woke up, the chain got caught on the gunwale and snapped. Suddenly, he was disoriented. He looked at the wine bottle and then at me and dove into the lake. He swam to shore and told me to fly because I was a witch. Rebecca, I used the pentacles with a spell to lock what little training I gave him so he could access it with full memories when needed. Without the pentacles, he's got access to the knowledge, but no understanding of what's going on."

"Oh, dear. This is bad. I used the same trigger, but not a spell to lock the stories and training in the same way. I didn't do much training, but I told him a lot of stories and history, especially of The Vagabond Poet.

Now he'll have those floating in his head without the trigger to understand them. Fuck! Excuse me."

"Wait. You didn't train him? Or initiate him?"

"No."

"You didn't raise power with him… um… with sex?"

"Goddess, no! I knew you were training him. I would never cut in,
especially with your boyfriend. I just wanted to contribute the lore."

"But I didn't initiate him. He already knew what little I taught him.
I just assumed you were teaching him," Judith said.

"And now he has both of our instruction and his own powerful
visions running rampant in his head with no protections."

"Not only that," Judith said. "If you and I both used the pentacles
charm, what if whoever initiated him also used it?"

"We've got to help him."

Performance was going well for Wayne. In fact, it might have been
the best he'd ever done. His Bernardo was good, but when he delivered
Aeneas' tale to Dido, he came alive.

> *But, as we often see, against some storm,*
> *A silence in the heavens, the rack stand still,*
> *The bold winds speechless and the orb below*
> *As hush as death, anon the dreadful thunder*
> *Doth rend the region, so, after Pyrrhus' pause,*
> *Aroused vengeance sets him new a-work;*
> *And never did the Cyclops' hammers fall*
> *On Mars's armour forged for proof eterne*
> *With less remorse than Pyrrhus' bleeding sword*
> *Now falls on Priam.*

It was in Act Three, Scene Two that everything fell apart for Wayne.
The dumbshow had gone well and the play within the play—"The
Murder of Gonzago"—was going well. Rebecca was spot on. She delivered her last lines, "Both here and hence pursue me lasting strife, If once
a widow ever I be wife."

And then she kissed him.

For a moment Wayne blanked. The lips aroused him. The kiss sent
him into another dimension. The words were the same, but the setting
had changed. Wayne spoke his last line of the play, not on a stage, but
on a windy moor. "My spirits grow dull, and fain I would beguile the
tedious day with sleep." He passed out on the stage.

HE STOOD INSIDE the flaring circle of light again. How had he survived the fire? It was as if he had an invisible shield held up in front of him.

She knelt before a great black kettle. His precious priestess, Mari, wanted only the staff and to gaze into the kettle. It held her rapt attention. Even as he watched, she seemed to be breaking up—becoming one with the cauldron. He had to save her. He had to break them out of this prison.

He seized the black disk from its place by the cauldron and hurled it at the wall of light surrounding them. A hole appeared in the psychic fortress. The knife followed and another hole appeared. Mari clutched the cup to her breast, a look of fear in her eyes, but he had the staff. Holding it like a lance, he charged the remaining wall of light.

It exploded in a thousand colors around him, shattering like a great glass dome. From the midst of the flare, he ran.

"Give o'er the play."

"Give me some light: away!"

"Lights, lights, lights!"

Wayne rushed off the stage with the general exeunt. In the confusion, he grabbed his clothes and walking stick from the dressing tent and ran from the theatre. No one would miss him for curtain call.

THEY WERE CHASING him out of the stone circle but he was far ahead. He took them by surprise. He saved Mari from the awful thing that was happening. Too many voices were in his head—shouting, clamoring for attention.

He tripped and fell, rolling a few feet before scrambling back as he realized he was facing the edge of a precipice. There was nothing but clear sky and stars in front of him. Below him was the dark crystal of Derwentwater. Behind him, the shouting coveners drawing nearer and nearer.

May god or goddess or all the powers that ever were take his soul and divide it among them if he must leave it here. That would be as it would be. He stretched the rod across the water like Moses and dove.

"HE DISAPPEARED AFTER the play-within-the-play and never came back for curtain call," Judith said. Jim and Rebecca were standing in front of her and she hadn't lied yet.

"He wasn't feeling well earlier," Rebecca said. "I think he spent the afternoon in bed."

"Do you think we need to call that doctor?" Jim asked. "I don't like the idea of a sick cast member."

"We'll go check on him. If it looks like he needs anything more than a good night's sleep, I'll let you know."

"Dr. Allen, you've been worth your weight in gold on this trip. Let me say again how glad I am you joined our tour."

"Save it for the faculty meeting, Jim. And for heaven's sake call me Rebecca. Even the youngest member of the cast calls me by my first name."

"If they are being disrespectful, be sure to tell me," Jim said.

"Hush. Come on, Judith. Let's go check on our player king."

"DO YOU REALLY think he's in his room?" Judith asked.

"Not a chance, but we should check there and tell Jim he is, regardless."

"Then where?"

"He's had two weeks to get familiar with the area. Where do you think he'd go?"

"I'll go out toward Friar's Crag. That's where we went the first night," Judith said. "Rebecca, I'm worried. I'm sorry I ever made the challenge I did last summer. I'm almost sorry I ever came to America and… and fell in love."

"Sister, don't be sad about that. He's a very lovable boy."

"You?"

"If I weren't married, I'd be head over heels."

"Hart. I've changed my mind and will rescind my challenge of your appointment as High Priestess. I think I know of a way to avoid the outcome."

"What is it, Swordmaster?"

"Don't call the circle tomorrow night. The danger is in The Barber. He's power-hungry and will do anything to control us all. How he got to me, I don't know. I was helpless to do anything but push Wayne at you. I suspect he may be the demon-man Wayne claims to have battled. But he can't call the circle. Only you and mother and the combined priestesses of the four lesser circles have the authority to do so. I'll talk to mother tomorrow, but I'm sure she'll agree."

"It would give us time to sort things out, dispose of the threat, and protect Wayne. I agree," Rebecca said. She hugged Judith.

"Mmm. Uh… I never said 'thank you' for Oester. It was… uh…" Judith said as she pressed herself closer to Rebecca and raised her lips.

"Sensual, delightful, powerful, loving, electrifying. I could go on, but not without thanking you as well, sister." Rebecca kissed Judith deeply until both were gasping for breath. "Now let's go find our Vagabond."

WAYNE WAS SOAKED to the skin, but it made no difference. He'd managed to keep his change of clothes mostly dry as he swam the narrow channel to Lord's Island. He made his way into the woods and stripped, drying his various clothes over a small fire.

How did I get a fire? Wayne could not remember building the fire and had no matches that he could think of. He was really spaced out. He must have rubbed two sticks together. Or maybe the fire was here waiting for him. He looked warily into the shadows around him, expecting someone to approach.

Or some thing.

20
Sacred Trust

Saturday, 21 June 1969: Summer Solstice—Litha

IT HAD been a fitful night sleeping in the middle of an island with no blankets and only his tiny fire for warmth. He'd been visited by ghosts all night long, but one hovered nearby, never leaving. He knew her from the dreams. She'd been the High Priestess at that night exactly a hundred fifty years ago.

"Are you here to torment me?" he whispered.

"No, my Vagabond. I am here to protect you."

"But you are one of them."

"We are all one of them, including you."

"It's wrong—not natural—confusing."

"There is nothing more natural, my Vagabond. I will protect you. I will not let ill befall you. You have seen what happened the last time the tools were called together. You know not to let it happen again."

"I am sworn to protect the brothers and sisters of the Art."

"And to protect The Huntress." Mari's form was nearly hidden in the shadows nearby.

"Mari?"

"I am here. Sleep now. I will watch." In spite of himself, Wayne fell into a fitful sleep.

In the morning light, she was gone.

WHEN HE AWOKE, he realized that he'd need to get back across the narrow channel to the mainland. That meant that he'd be wet through again and no fire to dry beside. The sun rose early. In the distance, Wayne could hear traffic in the town.

Who would be up at this hour on Saturday?

He made his way to the shore where he had crossed the night before. To his surprise, a small boat was tied to a branch. At least Wayne

231

assumed it was a boat. It looked almost like a wicker basket with a paddle on the seat. He wondered if it was safe to cross the hundred or two hundred feet of water. Well, if he fell in, he wouldn't get any wetter than if he swam. He needed to get to shore.

The tiny boat was difficult to control until Wayne got the hang of it. By that time, he'd already struggled most of the way across the channel. It seemed that each time he dipped his paddle in the water, the coracle—yes, that was the name—wanted to spin in a circle. Ultimately, he managed to get across the water and only got a little wet when he splashed to shore, pulling the boat the last few feet. He anchored it and headed toward town, looking up at the cliff called the Lady's Rake. In his mind's eye, he could still see her naked form near the top of the cliff. He shook the feeling off and headed toward the village.

As he turned onto the main street near his hotel, he could see what the noise and commotion were about. It was market day. He was pretty sure his peers would still be asleep and missing this excitement. There were so many people there. It was more than he imagined possible in a modern, even if small, village. Colorful stalls decorated the entirety of Main Street on both sides of Moot Hall. The single hand on the clock above the old building was nearing seven when Wayne began eating his way from booth to booth. Fresh baked goods, fruits, berries, and dairy products were represented as well as dried and fresh meats and cheeses.

There were crafts as well and Wayne found a jewelry maker with a variety of charms on leather thongs. As Wayne perused the wares, a lorry rumbled into town and set its brakes on the hill above the hall. The driver opened the back of the truck and began dealing in chickens off the bumper. An overall aura of excitement dominated the marketplace.

"May I interest you in a love charm?" the woman in the jewelry booth asked him. She was an older woman—well, not ancient, but older like his mother—and had a pleasant voice.

"Um… I don't think I need one of those," Wayne answered. "That one over there. What is it?" He pointed at a gray metal disk hung on a leather thong. The disk was decorated with a six-pointed star and writing around the edge.

The woman looked at him strangely. Wayne wasn't sure why, but there was really no other item in her display that interested him in the slightest.

"Is that not the staff of The Vagabond Poet?" she asked softly.

"The Hart is in the Circle," Wayne responded automatically, not even realizing he'd spoken aloud.

"This is an earth pentacle," the woman said, handing him the disk. "What metal is this? Pewter?"

"Ah, no. This is a rare alloy of seven metals, forged under specific conditions and at the conjunction of specific planets. It is called *electrum magicum*."

"These symbols are not like others I have seen. They aren't Theban runes."

"Very good. They are Hebrew. This is a pentacle of Solomon. These are the Hebrew names of the elementals. You read from the top counter-clockwise. *Adonai ha-Aretz* is the Lord of Earth. *Auriel* is the archangel whose name means Light of God. *Phorlakh* is the name of the earth elemental angel, *Phrat* is one of four mythical rivers of Eden, the Euphrates which ran north of the garden. *Tzaphon* means simply North and *Aretz* means Earth."

"What's with the iron cross between the names?"

"That is a Rose Cross method of sigilisation. The symbol next to it represents the name."

"It doesn't look like it was planned well. There's room for another."

"That is where you would put your own motto and sigil."

"Would it have to be in Hebrew?"

"No. English would suffice." Wayne could see the shape in his mind's eye. He just had to have this.

"How much?"

"Thruppence."

"Huh? Did you say three pennies? This must be worth…"

"…far more than any of us could pay," she finished. Wayne fished the coins out of his pocket and the woman handed him the pentacles.

Wayne was so fascinated looking at the piece of jewelry that he hardly noticed the woman folding up her table and tent. He moved slowly uphill. A donkey squealed and he heard chickens cackling. What a day!

Someone up the hill ahead of him screamed. Angry shouts followed. They rolled into a panicked fervor at the Moot Hall and crested beyond the next street. He looked up to see a lorry bouncing down the street backward. Somehow, he knew there was no driver and he turned to run. The jewelry woman was just behind him. They stood in the path of the runaway vehicle.

He caught her frozen look of panic and in the moment that he locked with her eyes, he ran the risk of spacing out again. He'd been so caught up in the pentacles that he'd never looked into her eyes. It was like seeing Judith in front of him.

He felt his body react without his own volition. He caught her arm and dove to the side of the narrow street. Clean. It would have been such a perfect rescue had not the truck bounced on the uneven pavement and dived right after them.

Economy of movement, Rebecca had said. Don't dive and roll if simply turning your head will do as well; but here he lay, half under the old woman whose legs were still under the truck which lodged against the building. Around them he could barely see a glowing bubble. He looked at her legs as the truck hovered a fraction over them. His staff, extended toward the truck, seemed to hold it motionless. Pulling her toward him, away from the threat, he let the truck drop and bounce on its springs after her legs were free.

She had hit her head in the fall and was only now regaining consciousness. He cradled her in his arms, careful lest he hurt her. The woman's eyes turned to him again. It was so like looking at Judith. The crowds that were closing in the wake of the runaway seemed to recede out of his line of sight. He shivered convulsively and wondered vaguely if he was going into shock.

"Listen to me Vagabond," she said as they locked eyes. He heard the eerie wailing of an English siren. *Why is it taking so long for someone to come and help?* "Tell the Huntress that she must call the circle herself. No one else. Give her this." The woman fumbled with a cord that hung around her neck. "Here. Quickly. Take it." Wayne had the cord in hand and pulled a small leather pouch with it out of the woman's blouse. It lay in his hand and she squeezed her hand over it. "That which you have purchased is powerful. This, many times more so. Give it to her. Tell her."

So fast. It was all too fast to have been real. A policeman was crowding behind the lorry where it had wedged them against the building. Above him a woman screamed.

"Mother!" Wayne looked up to see Judith's head poking from the hotel window above him. "Wayne, don't move. Just stay there. I'll help you. You've saved my mother."

He thought a moment and as the lorry began to shift away from them, Wayne willed himself to disappear.

Then it was all over as quickly as it had begun. The lorry was pulled away from the scene to allow the medics access. Wayne felt a distance closing in around him so that he was far away from the scene. The woman was quickly gone, Judith riding in the ambulance beside her. The crowd was busy at the market again. He stood against the wall of the building with his staff in one hand and the leather pouch in the other. Aside from

Judith's initial outburst, no one had spoken a word to him or had even appeared to notice him beside the woman. It was as if he were invisible.

He ran.

"WHERE IS HE?" Judith gasped as she crashed through Rebecca's hotel room door.

"I… what?" Rebecca sputtered. She laid her book down on the bed.

"Oh! Rebecca! He saved my mother's life and now I can't find him. He's in danger."

"What are you talking about?"

"Wayne." Judith paused. Tears were flooding her eyes again. She'd been near hysteria as she rode in the ambulance with her mother. Having the doctors pronounce her condition as not being critical had left her gasping for breath. It gave her an opportunity to wonder what had happened to Wayne. She'd not been thirty seconds getting from the window to the door of her hotel. But as they moved the lorry off her mother, there'd been no sign of Wayne—no indication he had ever been there. She needed to pull herself together.

"Huntress," she began formally and bowed slightly to Rebecca. Rebecca acknowledged the formal salute.

"Swordmaster. Merry meet, sister."

"We are all in danger. Do you have your pentacles?"

"Of course," Rebecca answered the strange question.

"This morning an attempt was made on the High Priestess' life. I'm sure of it. The Unbound saved her."

"Magda? Is she…?"

"She is recovering in Kendall at the hospital. I only just got back. But, Huntress, she was saved by The Unbound. I don't know how. I could feel his presence but I couldn't find him before the ambulance was ready to leave. Has he been here?"

"No. As much as I can tell, he didn't come back last night. I've been sitting here waiting and listening all morning. Hoping."

"We have to find him."

"I think if we stay still, he may come to us. He wouldn't miss call for the show."

"There is something I haven't told you, Huntress."

"Why does that not surprise me," Rebecca sighed. "We are on the same side, Swordmaster. If you know something that will help, please tell me now."

"It's about the pentacles. The High Priestess didn't have hers."

"Enceladus?"

"Exactly. She hasn't been without it since I was born. I nursed looking at it. If the High Priest got to her or managed to get it away from her, he could be very dangerous. Our hope has been that he had no access to any of the tools."

"We need to find The Unbound," Rebecca repeated Judith's words. "Unprotected, he could be in extreme danger."

HE HAD RUN from her. Again. Well, he just couldn't face her. She was… something he couldn't fathom. Maybe he was, too. He just didn't know. But he knew he had to hide.

"Now ye look like a fine respectable young lad," said the barber as he flicked the apron sending hair in little flurries around the floor. "That will be a pound six." Wayne looked at himself in the mirror as he handed the barber the money. He'd not been clean shaven in three years—since high school graduation. With the short haircut and little wisp of a mustache, he looked positively ready for the army. Jim would have a kitten. He'd have to take care of that next. "I'm always happy to usher a young man into adulthood with a real shave and a good haircut. Now ye can go conquer the world," the barber finished.

Wayne fastened a pair of small wire-rimmed glasses over his ears. He wore a pair of black corduroys and a black turtleneck shirt now. He pulled on the gray-plaid cape and wide-brimmed hat. The cape covered his walking stick completely as he tucked his hands inside. The person who stepped onto the street was not recognizable as the person who had nearly been run over by a truck this morning—least of all, he thought, to Rebecca, Judith, or that damned doctor he saw up the hill earlier. They had never seen him beardless or with glasses. His change of clothes was in a canvas pouch slung from one shoulder.

He made his way by side streets and alleyways across town to the field where the show tent was. This village was so innocent in some ways. A tent like this in Indianapolis would have to be guarded twenty-four hours a day. He slipped in through the tie-down backstage.

This tent in the middle of a field was the best facility they worked in during their entire run. In a few weeks, it would be used for some kind of religious tent meeting. The village was very proud of it. All the electricals were rented. There were adequate lights for both the stage and the house and a portable dimmer pack that was easy to connect and use.

Ritual Reality

The darkness surrounding him was evidence of the good light control afforded by the canvas tent itself.

The stage platform was solid and well-draped. Even though it had no front curtain, the lighting control was so good they could go to complete blackout between acts. The backstage had been furnished and partitioned for dressing rooms in attached tents. It was a shame to deprive the cast of its last performance there, but Wayne couldn't show up for the show tonight. Everywhere he looked there were ghosts and witches. If he met one during the performance it would ruin everything and they'd cart him away to a funny farm.

He felt his way carefully across the backstage area to where the enormous props crate was located. He fumbled for a moment with the padlock but finally got his key into it and felt it snap open. He raised the lid. His art kit would be on the left end of the box. Carefully he lifted it out, opened it and pulled out his penlight. With the aid of the light he selected a screwdriver from his tools and made his way to the dimmer box.

The rental system was fully equipped. Wayne opened the back panel and found the three spare fuses lying taped to the bottom of the box. He pocketed the fifty amp replacement for the main line. Then he pulled the master fuse and replaced it with a fifteen amp fuse. These fuses for the 220 volt system were enormous. He pocketed the remaining spares and carefully reassembled the dimmer panel. The lights would still come on. If only one dimmer were brought up, they would keep working. But Beth would run a light check at 7:15 p.m. With the backstage lights on, the first dimmer would blow the master fuse. There were no replacements and by that time it would be too late to get any before curtain. The show would be canceled.

He repacked the tools and returned them to the crate, keeping the penlight and his hand graver. He searched through the crate and pulled out the long bow after which he had patterned his prop. With a bit of prying, he managed to dislodge three arrows. One more thing. The knife Rebecca and Judith seemed to want so badly. He would just remove it from temptation.

It did not take long to realize the prop was not there. They could not even wait for the production to end. He felt betrayed. They were using him. They all wanted to use him. Or not him, just the tools he could make. The scenes flashed before his eyes one after another—more than a dream, but less than reality.

If they already had the knife, there was nothing he could do about it. His own knife, though, was in the bottom of his suitcase where it had been since he arrived in England. He would have to get it. Besides, the rest of his travelers' checks and his passport were in the suitcase. He snapped the lock closed on the box, turned to leave and ran straight into a strong and stocky man. Wayne fell back a step, but the other man did not move.

"I belong here," Wayne said. "I'm part of the cast."

"Really? Going hunting?"

"Just a little target practice," Wayne answered, thinking fast. "I begged a couple bales of straw from a farmer at market this morning."

"I see." Very slowly, as if he were trying not to alarm a frightened animal, the man reached out and pulled Wayne's cape aside to reveal the walking stick. Wayne pulled back a step and shone his penlight directly in the man's face, but he seemed not to notice. His eyes shined through the beam. He knew that face. The devil-eyes just kept staring at him through the light's beam. It made Wayne's flesh crawl.

"So, you're the Hart's vagabond," the man said thoughtfully. "Very clever disguise."

"I'm no one's anything. But I know you. You are that doctor. You're also the one who kept breaking into the theatre. What are you people?"

"Come now, you know the answer to that. We're part of the legends and folklore of the hills you see around the Derwentwater. Part of your own kindred, I'd guess, though you're no Vagabond Poet. Still, not a bad ally to have." The man gestured minutely and Wayne felt a heightened crawling in his flesh as he saw a dim light increase around him. He thought at first his eyes had adjusted to the dark and pocketed his flashlight. Realizing he no longer needed it heightened the eerie sensations. There was a curious burning sensation on his chest. He dug at it automatically and realized that the heat emanated from the leather pouch he had slung around his own neck after the accident this morning.

"Ah yes. There it is. Be a good lad now and hand it here to me. You have no use for it. You don't even want it. The old lady had no business giving it to you. Hand it here." It was as if Wayne no longer controlled his own body. He was still trying to fight the shifts in time and space and stay focused on the evil man in front of him. Evil. That was how Wayne defined him. And thus defined, Wayne could defy him. His hand was already pulling the leather thong over his head, the pouch in his hand. The struggle was becoming impossible.

"What's happening to me?"

"I'm just helping you do what you want to do. You want to give it to me. Now hand it here."

Wayne looked down at the leather pouch. *More powerful than that which you bought,* he remembered her saying. It was wrong to give power to the demon-man. His perspective shifted again and he was in split places.

He saw the dark disk lying on the ground in front of Mari; saw it flying into the wall of light; saw the wall crashing down.

Wayne dropped the pouch to the end of its thong and started whirling it in front of him, then over his head. For the first time, the other man showed a sign of doubt.

"Easy now. You could be playing with a fist full of diamonds, you know. Something very precious."

Wayne saw the diamonds scattering on the floor of the tent. They were the shattering bits of light as he charged through the illuminated wall, spinning the pouch ahead of him like a lariat. He heard the yelp of pain behind him and turned to see the man fall to his knees with both hands grasping his head in the splintering light. Then it was all dark again and Wayne was fighting with the tie-down to get out of the tent. The man's voice followed him as he ducked out.

"I don't need it, you bastard apprentice. I can call the circle without it and you will be nothing to them."

Wayne was out of the tent and running.

21
Summons

Saturday, 21 June 1969

NO ONE had been to the island. The little coracle was still tied up where Wayne had left it and in a few minutes, he had pulled it into the shelter of a downed tree and made his way to the center of the island.

This, he was certain, was where the manor house had stood once 300 years ago. There were no derelict walls or foundations that he could find other than this one flat slab of stone. It would make a good workbench. When he'd settled in the middle of the stone, he whispered, "Protection," and with a wave of his hand he felt a sudden peace and quiet surround him.

He wasn't startled to see the young woman sitting in his circle with him. The ghosts had been following him all over. He'd started just ignoring them, watching them jump out of his way when he started to walk through them. He even recognized some of them from dreams he'd had long ago. This one was quiet and simply sat across from him to watch. He was pretty sure it was the Lady of the Rake he had seen climbing naked up the cliff on the shore—or perhaps it was Mari, the Vagabond's high priestess. Or someone else he should know. He wondered if they were related. She wore a simple shift and stayed silent. He'd seen her several times since the old woman gave him the strange pouch this morning after the accident. It was like she traveled with it.

But Wayne left the pouch hanging around his neck and instead withdrew the leather thong and medallion he had purchased from the old lady. If he was going to make up with Judith, he needed an appropriate gift. And he did want to make up with her—make out with her—make love to her. If he could just get his head straight. All this mystic mumbo-jumbo was so stupid. They had him half convinced they were witches. *How stupid is that?* It was more like they were playing at a game. He knew someone else—Jacqueline—at school who was a member of the Society for Creative Anachronism. She was so weird in so many ways, but he had a feeling she had just a bit of a crush on him last year. But that was all the group was. They just liked to dress up and play games. He couldn't believe his Uncle was part of that stuff, too.

Wayne laid his tools out around him. Not just the ritual tools, but the engraving tools he'd grabbed from the props chest. He'd planned to spend time after the last show polishing and engraving Hamlet's poniard to give to Rebecca, so he'd brought his hand tools with him. That was before he knew how much of a bone of contention it was with Judith and with that doctor. Well, he could make her one when they were back in Indiana if she still wanted one. But he could still use the tools now to make a gift for Judith. The medallion needed to have a few more symbols and letters inscribed on it.

He laid a soft cloth on the stone and placed the disk on it. Then he removed a small graver. He hadn't done too much engraving on metal. He'd last used the tools to engrave Judith's initials on the hilt of her sword, and a verse from Shelley on the blade. The important thing was to not put a graver through his hand.

He pulled out his notebook and traced out the size and shape of the disk so he could position the characters. Then he wrote the word "Swordmaster" and Judith's name sigil. If she liked to play this game, that was okay with him. He just needed to stay anchored in reality.

He wasn't helped with that by the ghost sitting in the circle with him. Especially when she reached over and took his pencil and paper. Wayne scooted back a bit. No. She wasn't—couldn't be—real. He could see the trees on the other side of the circle right through her. But still she held the pencil and wrote on the pad. She looked at what she'd written, scratched it out and wrote again. This time she nodded and placed the pad and pencil down next to his work. He watched her cautiously and she scooted back away and bowed her head.

Wayne moved up to look at the pad. The symbols she had written were like the characters around the edge of the disk. ראטסאמדרווס. "Hebrew?" he asked. "For 'Swordmaster'?" The ghost nodded. As he looked at her she seemed to waver. Then she was gone. "Thank you," he whispered. He bent to his task.

THERE WAS NO telling how long he'd been sitting there, hunched over the metal disk—*electrum magicum*—but it had been a long time. His stomach was growling. He looked at the finished work. The Hebrew name followed by a rose cross and Judith's sigil. On the back, Wayne had engraved his own name sign, copied carefully from his staff.

This would be his peace offering.

But not tonight. That doctor was planning something tonight and Wayne needed his suitcase from his room. And it looked like it was going to rain. How late was it? He'd been in a trance, engraving the small disk all afternoon. He intended to be at the hotel when the rest of the cast went to the tent. He'd better get over there right away.

He gathered his gear and stood to leave when there was a crack of thunder that sounded like a sonic boom. He ran to the edge of the island and looked up in the sky to see the column of light that extended from the top of Skiddaw into the clouds. Wayne pushed off in the coracle and headed for town.

"Any sign of him?" It was seven o'clock and Rebecca met Judith at the show tent for call. The two had scoured the area looking for any clue to Wayne's whereabouts. They had asked everywhere, describing Wayne and what he was wearing when Judith saw him last. The distinctive walking stick at least should have been recognized. But no one could help. They took turns waiting in his room, but he did not come back.

"Surely, he'll show up for call, won't he?" Rebecca asked as Judith shook her head.

"I certainly hope so," she said. "He's got the first line." They joined the rest of the cast in entering the tent when Beth switched on the work lights. Gail unlocked the props box in Wayne's absence. Judith went sullenly to work organizing the weaponry.

"Dr. Allen!" she called suddenly. Rebecca rushed to the props box where Judith was laying out the various rapiers and weapons. "He's been here. Hamlet's poniard and one bow is missing."

"Light check," called Beth to Lena in the house. "Dimmer one." The lights came up and a bang filled the tent with an accompanying shower of sparks. "Damn! Fuck!" Beth shouted from the light board. The entire tent was plunged into darkness. Jim came stumbling in from one of the dressing rooms where he had been helping with make-up.

"What in God's name…?" he began.

"The damned board just blew," screamed Beth.

"Are you all right?" Jim, Rebecca, and Judith all reached Beth's side where she was stomping around in a circle with her hands waving people away.

"I'm fine," she said angrily. "Probably just a fuse. Flashlight."

"Can't find it!" Gail yelled from the direction of the props box.

"Wayne!" Jim yelled.

"He hasn't signed in yet," Lena called from somewhere in front of the stage.

"He might still not be feeling well," Rebecca lied.

"Great. Hoist the tent flaps over there so we can see what's going on. Can you tell anything, Beth?"

"Yeah. Looks like the fuse in the master circuit by the amount of black charring around it."

"Can it be fixed?"

"Sure, if you can give me a new fuse. There were supposed to be spares taped to the inside of the panel. Nothing here."

"Another testimony to Mr. Brown's great organizational talents," Jim moaned. Judith leaned close to Rebecca.

"I don't think Wayne is coming in for call."

"You think this was meant…?"

"…to cancel the show," Judith finished for Rebecca. Outside there was a crack of thunder. The clouds had been building all afternoon. It appeared rain was imminent.

"Judith," Jim approached the two women. "Can we get replacements for this before showtime?"

Judith contemplated for a moment then decided to back Wayne's ploy. If he was not going to show up, she and Rebecca had better step up the search. "There'd be no place I know of closer than Kendall to get them and nothing there would be open on a Saturday night. A local electrician might happen to have one, but they're notoriously slow even if we found one."

"Bloody electrics!" snapped Jim in his best English. "With this storm brewing we can't even move outside. I think we just lost our last show."

"I don't see that we have much choice, Jim," Rebecca reinforced. "Maybe if you can get hold of that tour organizer, Brown, we can get a repair and do one last show tomorrow night. Even a matinee."

"Well, maybe so," he said. "If I ever get my hands on that bastard…" He left the threat hanging. "Cast, clean-up," he yelled. "Performance is cancelled. Check at the Walpole by noon tomorrow for posting of the alternative scheduling. Enjoy a night on the town tonight."

When they finally got outside the tent, Lena was posting a sign at the main entrance. Rebecca and Judith looked around at the gathering storm clouds.

"Looks like it would have been a lousy night for a gathering anyway," Judith said. Images flashed in Rebecca's mind of the circle dancing naked around the sputtering remains of a fire in a drenching downpour. She had to laugh a little.

"Miserable. Some Litha."

As if to punctuate her words and the thoughts that had occupied both women for the day, there was a powerful crack of thunder that brought all their heads up. As they looked at the northern sky, they saw a brilliant blue flame burst at the top of Skiddaw, some four miles away. It must have been a hundred feet tall to be visible at this range, connecting the mountain peak with the descending clouds above it. But both Rebecca and Judith knew that it would be seen much farther away than where they were. In an instant, the flame was gone. It would only show one time.

Witch's fire.

"It appears the circle has been called whether we would or not," Rebecca said to Judith as they walked on toward town.

"By whom, though?" Judith asked. "I hope Wayne hasn't run into real trouble."

The two women looked at each other and Judith's words sank in. Someone else could easily have followed Wayne this morning, or even led him away. No wonder they had been unable to find him.

"We'd better get ready and go. Be careful, Huntress."

"And you, Swordmaster. Merry meet and merry part and merry meet again, sister." The two women embraced and then trudged back to their respective hotels.

DAMN IT! HE was too late. He saw Chuck and Carol walk in the front door of the Walpole. Wayne ducked out of sight and moved to the back of the hotel. If Chuck and Carol were sneaking back to fool around, the rest of the cast would be back shortly and he didn't want to be caught inside—not now. He could see his window from where he stood in the shelter of a small tree. Glenn's room was one to the left. There was only one thing to do.

He wrote a note on his pad and tied it to an arrow. His clean handkerchief was wrapped and tied around the blunt end. Then he waited. Everyone left their windows open. That was good. Now if only he was as good.

It took half an hour before he saw a light come on in Glenn's room. Wayne stilled himself and drew the bow. He needed to be sure Glenn wasn't coming straight to the window. From Wayne's angle, the arrow would go up through the open window and hit the ceiling—so long as no one was looking out.

He steadied himself against the tree. All the discipline he had learned in years past came to play. It was twilight under the heavily overcast sky and in a moment of concentration, everything around him went black except the one shining lighted window. He inhaled deeply and held it. *Shoot between the heartbeats.* He released his breath half-way and then loosed the arrow. It sailed through the window and clattered off the ceiling. Wayne didn't stop to see what would happen next. He took off at a dead run through the alley and back out to the Lady's Rake.

REBECCA FINISHED PUSHING the ceremonial robe into her bag. She placed the two cups in the bag as well. It would be tricky having to carry two staves tonight, but she would manage. She turned on the light to face herself in the mirror. "This is it," she whispered.

She hit the floor, pulling her knife as an arrow came sailing through her window, struck the ceiling and the sitting chair and bounced, clattering noisily to the floor. She was frozen, fearing another arrow would follow, but from where she stood she could see that the tip of the arrow was padded and wrapped in a handkerchief. A note was tied to the shaft.

She moved quickly to retrieve the message and had not stopped shaking by the time she held the note in her hand.

"Glenn," the note read. "I need my suitcase. Can't come to the hotel: it's watched. Don't tell anyone. I'll explain when I see you. Just shove all my stuff in the suitcase and bring it to the foot of Walla Crag. See you in half an hour. Wayne."

"You're a hell of a shot," she whispered to herself. "I just hope you don't realize you got the wrong window." She flicked out her light and stepped around the door to Wayne's room. If he wanted his suitcase, she would bet he had no intention of coming back. She scooped up his things from the dresser and laid them in his bag. If she showed good faith by taking all his things with her, perhaps he'd wait long enough to let her explain. She latched the bag, tossed her satchel over her shoulder, and left the hotel through the kitchen so as not to attract the attention of the cast partying in the bar.

Wayne had timed it well. The meeting spot was over a mile south of Keswick by footpath, first along the Derwentwater, then through a wood lot. It was a half hour before Rebecca entered the grove. She looked around her and up the cliff that was called Wall Crag. Now, as long as Wayne was close before he recognized her…

"Who's there?" Rebecca strained her eyes in the direction of the voice but could see nothing but the trees. If she answered truthfully, he would be gone and she wouldn't even see him. How would Glenn answer? She pitched her voice as low as possible and responded with the next line from the play.

"Long live the king."

"Bernardo?"

"He."

Wayne stepped into the path directly in front of Rebecca and took a step forward before he recognized her. He froze for a second and spun on his heel.

"Wayne, don't go. Please! I have your suitcase. No one else is around." He turned back to face her. In a way, he wanted to talk to her. He wanted her to tell him it wasn't true; that there were no witches waiting to make a sacrifice of him in the hills; or at least that she was not one of them. He wanted her to help him get rid of the ghosts that were milling about.

"How did you find out?"

"You're a good shot but you got the wrong window."

"Shit."

"It's okay, though," she said. "I did exactly what you asked." She held out the suitcase and Wayne came a step closer. She could see his face in the dim light. *It couldn't be!* "Wesley?" Rebecca sank to her knees as darkness surrounded her.

She wasn't out for more than a few seconds when she was roused by a light patting of her cheek. She looked up into the eyes of the frightened young man. He looked so much like Wesley at first.

"Wayne? My God! What did you do to yourself?" She reached out a hand to touch the smooth-shaven face.

"I needed a disguise."

"You certainly did a good job. I was looking for you all day."

"You among others."

"Yes. Judith told me what happened. She didn't mean any harm. She didn't understand."

"That doctor, too. They want me, Rebecca. Are you… Are you really a witch?"

"What do you think?"

"I think someone's been mucking in me gulliver."

"At least you still have a sense of humor."

"It wasn't a funny book."

"So, think. What does it mean? Witches."

"Devil worshipers, I guess. Human sacrifice. I don't know. My head is so confused. And all these people…" He looked around. Rebecca reached up and placed her hand against his chest, willing him to let go. She was nearly overwhelmed by the images that raced through her mind, seeing the legends of the Lakes surrounding them.

"By your own definition, we are not. I gave you my word. You are always welcome with perfect love and perfect trust."

"Why did you lie to me?"

"I didn't lie to you. I lied to myself. I should have told you more when I first realized you were getting involved. I told myself that wasn't necessary. That you weren't necessary. That I could do it alone."

"Do what?"

"Forge a new *Athamé* for our circle."

"You were using me. You just wanted the knife. Just like Judith. Just like the Doctor and… and… the others. Well, your doctor friend has the knife now. You don't need me anymore. I thought I meant something to you. But you just use sex to raise power. That's all you wanted."

THE RESOUNDING CRACK of Rebecca's hand against his newly shaven face left his ears ringing, his face smarting, and an enormous tear welling up in his eye. The impact knocked his hat off onto the ground. Through a break in the clouds, beginning to scatter overhead, the moon peeked. It would be full in a few days and it shed enough light for him to see clearly the tears in Rebecca's eyes as she struggled to stand up.

But something in his mind had snapped with the impact. He was no longer focused on Rebecca, but on a different time/place.

Soldiers. They were already on the island. He had to escape. He had to find the way.

REBECCA WAS TOO shaken to move. Slowly her thoughts regathered. She couldn't just let him rush off. It wasn't his fault. *Damn the circle. Damn them all.* She hurried up the path after Wayne.

She rounded a curve where the path came suddenly out of the woods onto a rocky promontory overlooking the lake on one side and rising in a sharp crag on the left. She nearly tripped over Wayne's open suitcase lying in the path. Most of the contents were scattered around it.

"Wayne, where are you?" she called. "This path just loops back on itself. Please come back."

"This path doesn't loop back." She looked up for the voice and saw Wayne fifty feet up in a fissure in the rocks.

"Wayne! Don't!" she screamed. "You can't climb up that!"

"It's been done before."

"That's a legend!"

"So is the Vagabond Poet."

SHE WAS RIGHT there beside him. He knew he'd be all right. The naked lady of the manor was climbing up the cliff ahead of him. He looked away. That view was too distracting. He was struggling with his gear. She climbed unencumbered by pack or clothing. He grabbed hold of the white rock protruding from the fissure and wedged himself behind it.

"You've got too much gear on you." In fact, he was caught and couldn't move. He wrenched one arm free and his bow came loose, clattering down the rocky face behind him. The quiver followed. He inhaled deeply. Maybe it was true. His walking stick was stuck through the back of his poncho into the seat of his pants making it almost impossible for him to bend at the waist. His canvas bag almost went with the bow. But he could make it. Glancing back, one thing was certain: He couldn't climb down. He looked up and the Lady's ghost was motioning him forward.

"You're right!" he yelled. "Here. I won't need this. And you are The Huntress, aren't you?" He jerked the leather thong from his neck and dropped the pouch at her feet. "There. That's much better," he called and continued to climb. Ahead, the ghost scampered upward. Another rock came loose and clattered down behind the leather pouch.

"Wayne, be careful!"

SHE CLOSED HER eyes and sank to the ground. With all the power she could thrust into it, she visualized him safe at the top of the cliff. Pebbles rained down on her and she raised her head to see his feet disappear over the top. She didn't know why she was crying. He was safe. Even if he wasn't with her, he was safe.

"I love you," she called weakly into the darkness. "You vagabond maniac."

There was only silence in response.

22
Come to Litha!

Saturday, 21 June 1969

"**B**Y WHAT authority did you call the assembly of the separate circles?" demanded the elderly woman who stood in front of the High Priest. The great circle celebrants were robed in full ceremonial robes for the summer solstice celebration, but having arrived at the ancient stone circle a dispute immediately broke out over The Barber's authority to call the circles together. They had come expecting that either the High Priestess or The Huntress had called the circle. Now the test had come. The woman, whom Rebecca recognized as Counselor, the Priestess of the lesser circle of Braithwaite, brought the formal challenge forward.

"I called the circles by authority of the High Priest as it is written that he may do in the absence of a High Priestess."

"Is it true then? Is Magda no longer with us?"

"She was in an accident this morning in the market. She was hit by a runaway lorry," he declared. The circles broke into murmurs as celebrants turned to comfort each other.

"Hit but not killed," said Judith, stepping up to take her place as Priestess of Threlkeld. "I saw this so-called accident and saw the man who saved her life. She was in intensive care at the hospital when I left her this afternoon, but expected to make a full recovery."

"Then by law of the circles, we are not without a High Priestess. Braithwaite does not recognize your right to convene the great circle."

"Nor does Threlkeld," said Judith. The Priestess of High Lodore was silent. The High Priest belonged to her circle and it was hard for her to oppose her own coven brother in the full gathering. Skiddaw had its own confusion, for without Magda, they were also without a Priestess. It appeared that there might be a stalemate. Rebecca almost wished the circle would dissolve and celebrate Litha independently in their local gatherings.

"You saw the flame from the mountain," the High Priest declared. "And to that flame you gathered. Be it known therefore that I called the great circle because I *can* call the great circle. He or she who would challenge my right to convene this circle must do so by equal power."

So that was his game, Rebecca thought. Trial by power and no one would stand up to that test. Even Magda had refused to defend her office when challenged to this type of duel years before. She moved in the shadow and took hold of Judith's hand, pulling her aside.

"I told you that I would not call the circle without you," she whispered. "And in fact, I cannot call it without you. But together we have authority over all four circles and we can elect a priestess. Much better that than to let The Barber choose one to his liking."

"You found him then?"

"He found me. By accident," Rebecca responded.

"Is he safe?" The question held more anxiety in it than Judith's hardened façade was likely to let out. She really did care about him, Rebecca thought.

"I hope so," she said looking down. "He's out there, somewhere."

"Then you can call the circle by mother's proxy."

"I wish so. But not under the challenge that The Barber issued. And not with the symbol that Magda left. It's not what you thought. She must have assumed I had recovered the *Athamé*. You will have to call Threlkeld."

"So that's it," Judith said. She silently considered Rebecca's statement. "You're good with fire, if I recall."

"You did help."

"Let's do it."

"We challenge the power of The Barber to convene the coven Carles, not by equal power, but by greater," Rebecca called out. The two women stepped forward next to the other two priestesses.

"What? It takes two of you?" he laughed. "I need not match myself against two or against an entire coven if such were your wish. The power divided is already halved. I turn aside your challenge unanswered."

"The arrogant son of a bitch," Judith muttered under her breath.

"What now?" Rebecca asked. Judith looked at her very hard.

"I hope you're up to this," she whispered to Rebecca, then turned to face her own wicca gathered on the east side of the circle. "Hear me, Threlkeld!" she called in a voice loud enough to be heard throughout the gathering. "You have given me sacred trust in selecting me as your priestess. I would not betray that trust. But we are subjects if we are without a champion. Therefore, I adopt The Hart, The Huntress of

Carles, as daughter of Threlkeld Wicca." Rebecca was stunned. She took hold of Judith's arm and spun her toward her with a question on her lips. Judith erased it with a kiss. There was an immediate affirmation by the Threlkeld cildru.

"So mote it be!"

Judith continued looking at Rebecca after their kiss. "Necessity outweighs our differences, Hart. I release you from the promise not to call the circle alone."

"Swordmaster, I don't know what to say."

"Better think of something quick." Turning to her circle she continued. "As Priestess of Threlkeld, I take The Hart, Huntress of Carles, my daughter, as champion and lay in her hand my sword as symbol. Where she leads and where she calls, I and mine shall gather."

"So mote it be!" responded the cildru of Threlkeld. Judith knelt on one knee and lifted the sword that Wayne had created for her at Christmas. Rebecca took it from her, still overcome by the vote of confidence from the other woman.

"Now go to it. We're behind you."

Rebecca swallowed her doubts and raised her voice. There was no longer a choice in her course of action.

"Therefore, I, The Hart, the Huntress of Carles, challenge the right of The High Priest to call the great circle of Carles as he would have it—by equal power, unassisted but for the perfect love and perfect trust of my brothers and sisters." Rebecca stepped to the center of the circle where the fire had been laid but not yet kindled. In the center of the stacked wood sat the cold black cauldron Ops, as old as any of the tools of the coven. The High Priest moved opposite her and as Rebecca moved around the circle, he moved across from her, reflecting and countering each gesture and word. If at the end of her ritual the fire had started, she upheld her challenge. If it still lay cold, The Barber's blue flame would hold as his right to convene the circle. Rebecca began in the East with The Barber facing her in the West. Her own tools she lay on the ground at this point, taking up the implements of her quest.

"As champion of Threlkeld and bearer of the Gatekeeper's Sword, I summon from the East the cildru to this fire. Here at the Eastern Gate I place the Gatekeeper's Sword, the trust of Threlkeld."

She lay the sword on the ground near the wood, pointing directly at the cauldron in the center. Her breathing eased somewhat as she relaxed into her impromptu ritual. She moved on to the south side of the circle, once again facing The Barber in the North.

"As bearer of Iäpetus, the Second Face of Carles and the sacred trust of High Lodore, I summon the the cildru of High Lodore. Here at the southern gate, I place Iäpetus, fire rod, ruler of the dragon, the Second Face of Carles." She lay Doc's old walking stick, the staff of the Vagabond Poet, on the ground with its head toward the cauldron and moved on to the West where the High Priest had first stood. There was an uncomfortable feeling here. It was as if the ground was uneasy.

"As bearer of Cottus, the Third Face of Carles and the sacred trust of my own circle of Braithwaite, placed in my hand by The Cupbearer on the night of my challenge, I summon the cildru of Braithwaite. Here at the Western Gate I place Cottus, purifier of salted water, ruler of the serpent, the Third Face of Carles." She attempted to set the cup on the ground, but could find no place level. It seemed that the cup would fall, no matter where she set it. It was like trying to balance it on a wave.

She smiled across at the High Priest, realizing the spell that he had placed there. Then she calmly spoke again. "May there be floods of blessing poured out upon the fires of Carles," she said and laid the cup on its side with the opening toward the cauldron. It stayed and did not shift. She moved on to the North. As she stood there facing The High Priest with her hands uplifted, a coldness crept into her bare feet. They were numb on the ground before she could speak. Her teeth chattered.

"As bearer of Enceladus, the Fourth Face of Carles and the sacred trust of Skiddaw and our High Priestess, I summon the cildru of Skiddaw. Here at the Northern Gate, I place the sacred pentacles, earth mother, cycle of life and death, Enceladus, the Fourth Face of Carles." The cold was so intense that Rebecca fell to her knees and did not even register the gasp of awe that emanated from the assembled coven as she revealed the shining black disk that bore the pentacles of Carles Castlerigg. As she held it in her hands she felt it begin to warm, to glow and generate heat that filled her body and sent the numbness receding from her feet.

Rebecca stood and continued to the East again. Her circle was complete, but still there was no fire. The cauldron remained black and cold on the unkindled wood. The Barber stood opposite her, arms folded across his arrogant chest, waiting, his eyes aglow with savored victory. Without flame her summons was still invalid. Just a spark. That was all that was necessary.

Rebecca governed her emotions to keep from striking out at the High Priest directly. Instead she began to hum to herself, going inside away from the circle and into its center. Finally, words came pouring out of her mouth that she could not suppress, nor had she ever realized the knowledge that they held. She swept up her own sacred tools from the spot where she had laid them.

"And now, furthermore, on my *own* authority, as High Priestess of Cobhan Carles, I summon the circle. For I received my *Athamé*, Elhin, from the hand of The Blade, bearer in his time of the First Face. I received my wand, Pele, from the hand of The Flame Keeper, bearer in his time of the Second Face. I received my cup, Lear, from The Water Maiden, bearer in her time of the Third Face. And I received my pentacles, Tamar, from the hand of The Goddess, ruler of all the Faces. So now as regent of all the powers of Carles, I command: Gather to Litha! The Sun King lives and from this point forth advances to harvest. Hyperion, show thyself!"

There was a moment of total silence as Rebecca's voice died away. In that moment, she reached out her staff toward the cauldron. She had never felt so alone and exposed in all her life. She supposed that what seemed an eternity to her was less than a second in real time. She suddenly felt power and energy pouring into her from every direction. She had to laugh because the inrushing torrents tickled her from the center of her being. In the midst of her laughter she spun round, collecting the power pouring into her and when she finally returned again to face the firewood, she dropped her hands and said, "Burn, damn it!"

She had the fleeting thought that it was going to be difficult for some government technician to explain a nuclear explosion in the middle of northern England. She never heard the sound. A brilliant shaft of light connected her to the cauldron and to some unimagined third point far above, forming a triangle. The blast that followed the three sides connecting sent her sailing backward with such force that she blacked out, regained her consciousness and lost it again upon impact with the ground some yards behind her. The entire summoned circle fell backward with the shock and she knew before the blackness closed that The Barber had been thrown to the perimeter opposite her.

It seemed like an eternity had passed when her eyelids finally came unglued and she was once again conscious. But as they opened she could see the blaze of fire rising, not only from the burning wood around the cauldron, but from its vast interior—up like a laser beam and fountaining above their heads and spreading like an umbrella to reach the ground again at the perimeter of the circle. Soon all that was left of the shower of light was a wavering dome that surrounded the circle and the completely natural crackling of the fire beneath the cauldron.

Rebecca struggled to her feet using her own staff as a crutch to support herself. She staggered back toward the fire at the center of the circle. She raised her staff shakily in both hands and called out with all the strength that she could muster, "Let the great circle Carles Castlerigg come to Litha!" The shout of the assembled coveners echoed from the walls of the dome.

"So mote it be!"

"Burn, damn it?" Judith laughed as she hugged Rebecca at the center of the circle. "You get nuclear explosions from 'Burn, damn it'?" They were laughing and being swept up in the dance around the fire. It was a time for madness and merriment—Midsummer Night. This night had had enough tensions. As they danced more and more wildly around the fire, the ceremonial robes fell from them and the glistening naked bodies sparkled in the firelight. As they danced, the men of the circle brought forward an image made of woven sticks and danced with the god figure around and around the circle. The women decked the woven figure with flowers and wreaths as it spun among them and they danced with it.

The excitement and charge in the air following Rebecca's demonstration grew now as the entire circle raised its cone of solstice power for the celebration. At last the men were on one side of the circle and all the women on the other. Rebecca stepped up next to the fire seeing only the sun king opposite her. She was equally decked with flowers, a circlet in her hair and leis around her neck. At the very peak of the power she called out to him with arms outstretched, "Come to me!" and the men threw the stick figure into the flames.

The flames from the dry tinder leaped up and the flowers that had decorated it withered and were consumed. The celebrants fell back to sit around the fire and meditate in silence. Only Rebecca maintained her poise at the center with her arms outstretched in that ecstatic union with the sun king who was consumed by his own glory.

The flashfire slowly subsided. Rebecca looked through the flames into the eyes of her priest, his arms outstretched to match hers, the great stag-horned crown riding his head like the moon rode on her own. She had summoned him into the fire and now he seemed to step through it to catch her in his arms. Time was suspended as they stood, locked in each other's gaze, the rest of her circle of friends unable to move or react to what they saw. Rebecca felt herself frozen in the moment.

"Why are you doing this?" she whispered, almost inaudibly. She knew he heard and understood as well as she heard his equally inaudible reply.

"For the same reason that I summoned the circle. Because I can. I can do anything. Like a god. I can summon fire. I can make it rain. I can change the daylight into darkness. They'll all know this High Priest as one of the gods; a substitute no longer."

"But why?"

"Because I can. And I have paid too dear a price for this power not to use it." He crushed her against him in his burly arms, his mouth seeking the cold revulsion of her response. "You'll be queen to me in spite of yourself," he said pressing himself even more firmly against her. She could feel his hardness against her mound and her belly. "In consummating our reign, we will forge the new *Athamé* and I will rule it."

"No one rules the *Athamé* of Carles. It is hopeless."

She saw the flash of the ritual blade held high in his hand. At the sight of it, however, the spell was broken. She knew at once that she could not forge the new blade. Least of all could she submit to the beast that rode within her priest. He was less than a common criminal. She tapped a power deep within her and fed the image she saw of him out around her, letting it touch the minds of the spellbound coveners. The spell snapped. They rose at once in a sudden flurry of action and rushed to Rebecca's aid, the demon no longer holding them in thrall.

The Barber swung her around in front of him, the knife now lowered to her throat, the altar stone of Carles at his back.

"Stay back!" he commanded. "The forging of a new blade for Carles is about to commence. The blood of our sacred priestess be on you if you interfere or refuse to cooperate." Rebecca could feel the movement in the coven on all sides, but with the knife at her throat they would not risk moving on the possessed man. Rebecca first tried logic. If that failed she would be forced to something more desperate.

"You can't give me that blade to forge the new *Athamé*," she choked. "I know that knife and you did not make it. To be consecrated as a tool of the coven, it must come to my hand from its maker."

"Very clever," he said, "but that, too, I've taken care of. The knife you knew was dull except a sharpened point. When it came into my hands, I took the liberty of grinding and sharpening it myself. Now not only is it razor-keen, but I have participated in its making."

"They'll stop you."

"Your brothers and sisters fear too much for your life to interfere with me. As long as they stay back, you are in no danger. And soon we will have our own protective wards and they will do nothing."

"They may fear for my life, but I do not," Rebecca growled.

She grabbed his knife hand in both her own. As she anticipated, it loosened the knife at her throat slightly. She felt him pull back on her to tighten the grip and instead of trying to duck out from under the blade, she threw her weight back against him in the same direction as he was pulling. With the unexpected added force, The Barber fell back a step, hit the low-lying altar stone that he had maneuvered them to, and fell backwards over it, carrying Rebecca with him as he went. With the jolt of that impact his hand loosened and she flung the arm away from her with all the force she could manage.

The knife went sailing from his hand and Rebecca was free.

23

Promethean, The Unbound

Saturday, 21 June 1969

AS SOON as Wayne dropped the pouch, his ghostly companion nearly dove off the cliff trying to catch it. She looked at him strangely, then back at Rebecca kneeling on the ground below. Wayne pushed himself out of his resting place and scrambled upward. He felt a nudge as if impatient hands were pushing him upward and then he rolled away from the cliff. The Lady rolled beside him and glancing back at him in disbelief, she turned and dove off the cliff.

"So that was it. You weren't interested in me at all, were you? Just like everyone else. You just wanted your trinket," Wayne muttered. He'd grown quite fond of the ghost.

The voice caught up with him as he stumbled away from the edge of the cliff. It was no more than a whisper in the back of his mind. He was on his feet and running before it finally sank in. He pulled himself to a stop about a hundred yards from the crag and stood there panting, trying to catch his breath and comprehend what his ears had heard. It echoed, coming back at him from every direction. Rebecca's voice, echoed by the voice of the Lady. She loved him.

She loved him! He hugged his walking stick to him in her place—their place??—and spun round and round, dancing them along with him. She loved him.

"Waltzing Matilda; she loves me; she loves me," he sang as he danced in circles getting dizzier and dizzier as he spun. A stone dislodged under his foot and he came down on his butt with a crack, narrowly missing knocking his teeth out with the staff. The moon above spun in a lazy arc around the sky overhead. He couldn't stand that. Fighting motion sickness, he rolled over on his stomach and scrambled to his hands and knees when he realized he was looking over the edge of a sheer precipice at rocks several hundred feet below him.

He collapsed back away from the cliff. He couldn't believe he'd climbed it. He had to be crazy. Mustering his courage and mastering the dizziness and vertigo, he crawled back toward the edge and looked down. He'd nearly taken a dive off that and it was a long way out to the water from here. There was that other voice in his head. Why did he expect someone to be looking up at him where there were only rocks staring back?

GATHER YOUR SENSES together! Mari. You left her someplace behind. Why did she turn suddenly so cold and strange and then yell as you broke from the circle that she loved you? What did you do? You broke the spell, that was it. She'd been spellbound by the black kettle. If only someone had taught you what to do. What horrendous sight had she seen in its black depths? You must find her. She can't go on thinking that you deserted her. No. You just broke the spell. You must find her now. No hordes are chasing you. There is only the brisk chill of the evening.

WAYNE SHOULDN'T HAVE tried to find his way out here alone. Spooks cropped up at every turning and each tree came alive. Each great standing boulder became a Titan fleeing from Olympian gods into the western world. He should have waited for Glenn.

More spirits occupied these Isles than any other place in the world. You didn't notice them so much in the South where civilization had forced them into the sea with the arrival of the Saxons. The pagans were driven into seclusion. With the pagans had gone the dryads, the nyads, the faerie folk, and gnomes. And the Titans. But the Northern Lakes were a Tolkienesque environment. Spirits were far more likely to be restless around their haunted sidhes.

Scarce images of life, one here, one there,
Lay vast and edgeways.

He stumbled again and spun around, striking out with his walking stick at imagined armies of faerie spirits rising to attack him. Nothing. Just loose gravel and a path. If he wasn't careful he would imagine himself in a dragon's lair or on a stairway to the stars or some such other superstitious nonsense.

I know better. Some voice in my head keeps telling me… showing me… glimpses of a future… or past… so far separate, yet not so distant, not so foreign. But the knowledge that is gained is of such great proportion. Knowledge enormous makes a god of me. Pour me a golden goblet of it like some bright elixir that when I had drunk of it, I would become immortal.

The images that filled Wayne's double mind were too much to be borne. Life becomes ever more beautiful. Later beauty overpowers the first. It was simply a cycle of life.

This must have been what the Titans felt when younger, more beautiful gods than they captured the savor of sacrifices sent heavenward. Such beautiful pain that he would, like Hyperion, fall to an Apollo who not only looked as bright as the sun, but sang as well.

And here, in his primitive body, he was trapped like Saturn without his scythe, with all the voices of his age, petrified.

Like a dismal cirque
Of Druid stones upon a forlorn moor.

WAYNE WAS so lost, so completely caught up in the fantasy of another age playing behind his eyes that the sudden blast that rocked the earth like a giant treading on the ground beside him caught him unawares. He tripped and slid down a short embankment beside the path, then rolled with a splash into the river.

Damn! Must he always wake up with such an unexpected dousing? If he didn't have pneumonia by the time he got back home it would be a miracle.

A laugh bubbled up from beside him as if it arose from the water itself. It was deep and rich and full and female. He struggled up onto the embankment and sat facing the river trying to see who had witnessed his ridiculous pratfall. There she was, out away from shore, her white shoulders glistening above the surface of the water in the pale moonlight.

"Rebecca?" he whispered, straining his eyes to see features in the wan half-light.

"Were you here to meet someone? Should I hide?" said the laughter filled voice. No. Not someone he knew. He had stumbled on a stranger out for a midnight swim in the middle of nowhere. How embarrassing. He'd pick up his gear and slip away.

"Come on in for a swim," she said to him. "You're all wet anyway." That was true enough but he was also basically shy when it came to bathing with a complete stranger in the middle of nowhere. This was a discovery that he had just made. "Come on. Don't be bashful," she coaxed. "Lay your wet things on the rocks to dry and come enjoy the water like it was meant to be enjoyed." The voice had taken on a different tone completely and he had his plaid cape and boots off before he had reminded himself that this was not Judith, either.

"Who are you? Do I know you?" He strained to see her face.

"Who would you like me to be?" she said with a certain provocative uplift to her voice and her body in the water. "I'm flexible."

"You remind me so much of someone I should know." Wayne was standing shirtless with his feet in the water. It felt like something else was motivating his body again and he stepped back deliberately away from the water.

"That's it. You'll want your pants to dry so you can wear them later. You know what they say. Swim naked, go home in your pants. Swim in your pants and you go home naked." Suddenly there was another voice in his head and other eyes looking through his, just long enough to whisper a name. His pants were off and he was in the water before the word had passed his lips.

"Mari?" he whispered as he swam out to meet her. She laughed again and rolled to swim away under water. She came up again behind him. How could a ghost from two hundred years ago take this form? She seemed not to have stopped laughing the whole time. "It can't be. Mari's part of a dream I had about The Vagabond Poet." He kept turning around in the chest-deep water trying to keep the woman in front of him as she swam circles.

"And if I were Mari, I'd be a hundred and eighty years old. Who would you like me to be? Judith? Rebecca? Or are you still thinking of Lissa?" He watched as each of the women she named seemed to come across her face. Then she was the young woman he had first seen in the water who looked so much like Mari of his dreams. "They are all illusions, you see? Like making an elephant disappear on stage. But this one's the easiest and I can tell you like it."

"Why is that one easiest?"

"Because it is me."

"But you can't be Mari. You said so yourself."

"I could be a descendent of hers, though, couldn't I?"

"Yes, but... You're such a chameleon. I can't believe I'm..." Wayne paused. He'd just said something that rang a bell. "Chameleon? I had a dream about Chameleon."

"I'm the stuff dreams are made of. You've been dragging me through your dreams. Now let me take you through one of mine."

"What?"

"Isn't it easier to imagine that you are asleep in bed and I was just a dream playing in your head? That's what you've been doing. Believing it's all a dream and you are safe in bed—no witches, no ghosts, no dreams-come-true."

"It could be that," he sighed. She was close to him in the water now. Their bodies slid sleekly past each other, brushing in the slow current.

"I know what kind of dream you're having," she laughed.

"What kind of dream is that?"

"A wet dream, obviously!" She splashed water squarely in his face, laughed and disappeared under the current. Wayne laughed, too, as he searched for her in the water around him. When she surfaced, she was behind him, her hands clamping around his chest, her dripping body pressed against his back and her head leaning on his shoulder. "You're such a nice dream," she said. He reached behind him and stroked her hips with his hands, turning his head toward hers as she nuzzled deep into his neck.

"I almost wish it wasn't a dream. Does it have a meaning?"

"How about a purpose? Will that work?" she asked.

"What's the purpose?"

"You've lost something and it has left you confused. I want to fix that. I want you to believe in magic, my young vagabond." Her voice was so serious—so mournful.

"That's a little primitive, isn't it? I can only believe in what is natural."

"But magic *is* natural. In fact, all of nature is magic. Magic, like turning a plain piece of wood into a beautiful art object. You understand that kind of magic, don't you?"

"That's just a craft, or an art," Wayne argued half-heartedly. He knew how he felt about making things. She was right. It was like magic.

"Magic, too, is just a craft or art. Do you know what night tonight is?"

"It must still be Saturday. Or Sunday morning."

"It's Litha."

"Beware Litha," he whispered, remembering a warning that he had interpreted as a joke. "It's midsummer, isn't it?"

"Yes. The shortest night of the year. The night when the faeries come out to play and almost anything is likely to happen."

"Like Shakespeare."

"I am your Titania and you are my Bottom," she said, pressing against him and stroking his buttocks under water.

"Am I such an ass as that?"

"You've tried pretty hard lately, but no. It's not all your fault. We all tried to help and ended up confusing you. We need to remove the blinders from your eyes so you can see."

"Can you do that? I've been so confused. Just when I think I have things figured out, my head gets muzzy and it's like the curtain has fallen before the final line."

"Look. Look into my eyes," she said turning him toward her. He gazed into the depths of her eyes and was captured there. "Look into my eyes and become The Unbound." He knew those eyes. A peaceful calm swept over him and he moved to kiss her.

"Lissa. Chameleon," he whispered. She kissed him back and as they kissed, a flood of memories came back upon him. A tornado. A wall of light as they made love on the rooftop. The cup that he carried in his shoulder bag.

"Believe in magic," she said softly.

"To what end?"

"The end, my faerie king, awaits you there, at the top of that hill." He looked up and saw the glow of firelight at the top of the hill, a few hundred yards away. His calm changed to foreboding. No matter where or how he ran away, he would end up under the geas of the same fate. And at the same time, through other eyes that had played so casually with his mind, he knew what awaited him there.

"I'm sacrifice?"

"I think not. You're Vagabond. In these hills, the vagabond is a priest and messenger of the gods. You need only take that message to the ones who need it. They need it, Unbound. They need you."

"I always forget what you've told me and think it is just a dream."

"Tonight, I promise, you will remember. I will be your Mnemosyne." She laid her lips softly but not insistently against his, waiting for his response. And if he did respond? What difference would it make to his fate? There was still so much that was locked up inside him. But in his dreams, she had been Mari and he had been The Vagabond Poet. They had raised powerful magic.

They rolled over again and again in the water, embraced together in their lovemaking, not two people, but four—the dream couple urging them on. Their lips and hands sought each other's secret places as he carried her to the shore and they lay down on his plaid. She was faerie-like. He explored her back with his fingers, seeking a sign of wings. When her mouth enveloped his hard cock, the air around them began to glow. As he buried his face in her sex, seeking to bring her pleasure, he prayed to all the powers there were that they would enlighten him and protect him. Their mutual explosion solidified the walls of a dome of light around them.

He rolled Lissa, The Chameleon, over and she pulled his body up to guide his still-hard cock into her vagina. She placed her hands on either side of his face and he could hear her repeating the same prayers he had just invoked—praying to the powers of the East, South, West, and North, asking the goddess to help her purge his mind of the blocks that restrained him.

"Is it only about the power, Chameleon? Please tell me. I won't hate you, but I need to know. Is it all only about the power? Do you love me?"

"Oh, Unbound. Please don't think that of me. Or of any of us. We cannot enter into this covenant without perfect love and perfect trust. I have that for you. I am not your girlfriend, and so we make love in the circle and raise power around us. But I *do* love you. The Hart loves you. The Swordmaster loves you more than both of us combined." At the mention of their names, a curtain parted in Wayne's mind and he saw Judith's instruction, their first time making love, her gift of the necklace that he had lost. He heard all Rebecca's stories and legends, even some of them from the classes he had slept through.

He rose toward his climax as did Lissa. They locked eyes in the moonlight and Wayne whispered.

"I come with perfect love and perfect trust." And they did.

WHEN HE AWOKE, his clothes were folded neatly next to him. He sat and looked up the hill at the glow. He must not have been out long, but where was Lissa? He started to pull on his pants when a voice spoke.

"Don't bother. You'll just have to take them off again." Wayne spun to see a black-robed figure standing behind him.

"Uncle? Bound One? What are you doing here? How…?"

"It's hard to sleep when you make a psychic racket like that," his uncle laughed. "You still have a connection to the spirit plane and I am dreaming."

"There's so much going on and I'm overwhelmed with the memories. But there are still dark spots and…" He looked up the hill again. "Bound One, I'm afraid. I don't want to go up there."

"Think of your oath, Unbound."

"What?"

"Ah. I lift the geas I placed upon you. Think and remember all." His uncle made a gesture and Wayne felt another layer of gauze removed from his memories.

"It's true. It's all true," he whispered.

"Now. Your oath, Promethean."

"I, Promethean, do of my own free will most solemnly swear to protect, help, and defend my sisters and brothers of the Art." Wayne repeated the words first spoken in the dark of his uncle's sanctuary. "I will keep secret all that must not be revealed. This do I swear on my mother's womb and my hopes of future lives, mindful that my measure has been taken in the presence of the Mighty Ones."

"Good."

"But what will I do?"

"Just what you've sworn. Up there." His uncle pointed and when Wayne looked back, he was gone.

Wayne stuffed everything in the shoulder bag except his knife and his walking stick. Then he set his face to the hill and smiled. He could not help himself.

He believed in magic.

WAYNE COULD SEE the silhouettes of the stone pillars against the fire-light long before he could see the people who had been dancing, but as he crested the hill and looked in from the North, his heart stopped. A man held a knife at Rebecca's throat. Not just a man. That evil doctor. Everything else went dark before him. Screaming like a madman, he charged toward the circle headlong between the giant stones that stood on the northern side. Enceladus and Asia. He could feel the heat of his own anger flaring in his temples.

When he shot between the two mammoth stones, the world suddenly slowed to a halt. He felt himself stopping, his momentum eaten at the gate. It was not like hitting a brick wall. More like diving into a bowl of gelatin. Even his scream died before it reached his ears.

No one had seen him or seemed to notice, they were so wrapped up in the battle that was taking place near the low stones on his left. He saw the two fall over the rock; saw the bounce on impact of Rebecca's body landing on top of the man. How that must have hurt her already bruised back and shoulders. Then he saw the missile launched and sailing toward where he stood, trapped by the unseen force between the rocks. And he couldn't move.

Rebecca had instructed him in self-defense and found him a slow learner. But her lessons were still there. Never duck and roll if just turning your head would save you. But in the mass, he couldn't even turn his head. And there was no doubt the knife would hit him as squarely as if it had intentionally been thrown at him. His own knife, made with his own hands. His anger burned in him. With one supreme effort he twisted his hands to bat the object out of the air with his staff.

It struck. The stick was ahead of the knife and the knife struck it squarely and stuck in the wood with a jolt that seemed to loosen the fabric of the mass holding Wayne. He knew without seeing that it had struck squarely in the heart at the center of the circle. Without his conscious will, the flames carved above the heart blazed into the fire, fueled by his anger. Flame leapt from the staff to his knife and he ripped the blade upward, severing the blockage and releasing him to charge through like a flaming meteor into the circle.

THE COVENERS FOLLOWED the flight of the blade toward the northern gate of Carles with their eyes and only then did they see the naked man between the stones. When the knife struck, sparks burst from the impact and the intruder disappeared behind a sheet of flame. Two men had already jumped to pin The Barber's arms as Rebecca crawled from his grasp, but only Judith moved to save Wayne. She grabbed the sword he had made for her and rushed toward the gate. She had no time to open a gate.

As if the door of a blast furnace had been opened, the flaming man burst into the interior of the circle and charged across it toward where Rebecca had fought her battle. Judith grabbed a ceremonial robe, intent on wrapping him to smother the flames, but there was no question what the goal of the flaming form was. He might as well have been Hyperion blazing through the sky in superhuman form as he covered the ground between the gate and the spot where The Barber stood pinned between two coven brothers. The flaming god descended and from The Barber a second figure emerged, bent on attacking the attacker.

"*Exorcizo te, omnis spiritus immunde,*" Wayne called as the demon separated itself from The Barber. The words had come from his uncle's book, all of which, Wayne found, was fresh in his memory. But getting the demon out of the man was only half the problem. Disposing of it before it found another victim was the other. This time, there were no words. Wayne raised the knife and a blade of wind extended from it, slicing through the form as it gained substance. The wailing shriek as the demon vaporized echoed in the sudden stillness of the moor.

Turning, Wayne leapt upon the altar stone with the knife still raised and his staff still flaming. He stood above the terrified doctor on the rock. The flame died on his staff leaving only the glowing blade of the stage prop hanging from it, but Wayne's naked body glowed as if at any moment it might again burst into flames. As he began his striking descent from the height of the stone, the knife he bore connected with the solid reality of a knife raised to challenge it. In that instant he saw the winking diamond eye of Elhin, Rebecca's *Athamé*. He followed the hand that held it to Rebecca's eyes where he gazed with such pained intensity that both clouded with tears.

"That is not our way of punishment, my friend. Let the circle handle it." He took in the totality of the situation for the first time. Rebecca stood naked in front of him and he realized with a heightened flush that he, too, was without a single stitch of clothing.

"Is it really you?" he whispered, his voice hoarse from the scream he had uttered.

"It is," she answered simply. Then for the first time she let her own vision widen and follow her arm to the touching blades. "Creüs," she whispered into the stillness of the circle.

Silence veiled the air as the gathering absorbed the meaning of the word that Rebecca had uttered. Even the High Priest sank to his knees as he realized he had nearly come under the sacrificial blade of the First Face of Carles. Rebecca knelt at the altar and kissed Wayne's feet. The entire coven knelt at the cue. Then she rose and kissed his hands. Then she kissed… *Oh my God!* Wayne's knees buckled as Rebecca's lips touched the crown of his cock. Rebecca caught him on one side as Judith caught the other. Rebecca planted a fourth kiss in the middle of his chest and finally invited his lips into a deep union with her own.

Ecstatic cheers burst out all the way around the circle. Wayne was suddenly down from the stone and caught up in the double embrace of Rebecca and Judith with his head buried between theirs.

"Is it too late to be embarrassed?" he asked. The two women laughed out loud.

"You have nothing to be embarrassed about, babycakes," said Judith, kissing his ear and cuddling close to both him and Rebecca. "Believe me," she finished.

"You are hot, though," Rebecca exclaimed, pulling back a fraction. "You could light a match on your skin."

"I'm glad I'm not wearing anything," he said. "I don't think I could stand it. What's this all about?"

"You just happen to have made your spectacular entrance into our circle bearing one of the four sacred symbols of Carles, slew a demon, and defeated a dark magician. The knife you brought. It's been missing for fifteen years," said Judith.

"This?" Wayne asked, looking at the knife still in his hand.

"Yes," answered Rebecca. "Remember I told you that the staff and cup were part of a set of artifacts that were used to focus psychic energy? The knife that you have is part of that set."

"And the leather pouch the old woman gave me was the fourth part of the set, wasn't it?" Wayne asked. Things were finally making sense. With his memories cleared, he could tell the difference between what he dreamed and what was real—most of the time.

"The old woman was my mother, the High Priestess of our coven," Judith explained. "In the bag was the Fourth Face of Carles." She reached up and kissed Wayne deeply. Not just a coven kiss, but the kiss of lovers. "My love, after everything you've been through, I hate to ask you this, but…"

"You want the knife," he finished for her. "I guess it was never mine anyway. I was told that it chooses its own." He held the handle of the blade out to her. She hesitated a moment then dropped her hand.

"Not me. Her." Wayne turned toward Rebecca.

"You are the Hart within the circle," Wayne said.

"Also, the Huntress of Carles," Rebecca continued. "I was tasked a year ago with summoning the Four Faces of Carles together here tonight."

"Then take this with my blessing," Wayne said, extending Creüs toward her, flat across his palm.

"It seems that I have received three of the four tools from your hand," Rebecca answered. "On behalf of Threlkeld into whose hands the First Face of Carles is ever entrusted, and for the cildru of the great circle Carles, I accept it from your hand." She took the knife from him. A faint thrill emanated from the blade. Rebecca knew its origin. She had bonded herself to the bearer of this knife in a fire ritual years before. It was a sensual, sexual thrill. Rebecca could feel her body tightening in response to the sensuality of the blade as she pressed her thighs together.

With both their hands clasped over the handle of the knife, she slipped into his embrace and felt the heat of his body pressed hard against her own. When they parted from the intimate kiss, both were flushed and Rebecca tried to speak twice before she finally held the blade high in her hand to show the circle.

"Behold, Creüs, Windmaster, Ruler of the Eagle, First Face of Carles."

The coven cheered.

24

Cauldron Dance

Sunday, 22 June 1969, very early in the morning

THE CHEERS died and the priestesses gathered beside Rebecca and Wayne.

"We should take care of our criminal priest," Judith said to Rebecca. "His presence in the circle is disharmonizing at best." Rebecca turned her attention back to The Barber behind the altar stone where he was still held.

"And what shall we do with him?" she asked as he was brought forward.

"Geld him and send him ball-less into the night like Saturn sent Uranus and was himself deposed," said the Priestess of Braithwaite. The Barber held his silence.

"Since he finds such solace in silence, let him keep it," Rebecca said. "Hear me, Doctor McBride. You have bent yourself in pursuit of power over the *cildru* of Carles. You have exhibited that drive in attempting rape in the midst of the circle to forge a bond that was not rightfully yours. You brought an evil presence into our circle. Nothing is less in keeping with the tenets of our fellowship. As reward for your lust for power, I strip you of your priesthood, your crown, your sacred tools, and your name. Henceforth you shall be called 'Silence' for the power your voice shall have." Rebecca raised her red staff as she faced him. "In the presence of the goddess, the cildru, and the Four Faces of Carles, I lay this geas upon you."

"So mote it be!" affirmed the gathering. And so, the tools and ceremonial robe of the priest along with the string that held his measure were gathered and cast on the fire at the center of the circle. The Barber, now Silence, was led by his guards to the Northern Gate and was expelled from the circle. Judith closed the gate behind him with the ritual sword.

"Oh, goddess, I'm glad that's over," Rebecca sighed as she leaned against the older priestess. "We can get on with it now. Whatever *it* is."

268

"There is still a small matter to be taken care of," the priestess said. "There is a stranger in our circle. An uninitiate. Dare we proceed with even the most minor ritual with him here?"

"I will vouch for him, Counselor," Rebecca answered.

"But will he prove himself?" the priestess asked. They looked over where Wayne had retreated to the altar stone as the former priest was expelled. His staff lay on the South. On the East, he had placed the former prop knife he had made. On the West was a coffee cup heavily inscribed with runes. He held a leather thong in his hand. Judith went to him.

"I think you need this," she said, lifting the pentacles she had given him at Christmas from around her neck. He looked at her and smiled, relief on his face.

"Thank you, Swordmaster. It must have been very difficult for you without this for the past few months."

"Yes. But it's yours now. I told you. Forever."

"Then you must take this," he said lifting the leather thong to place it around her neck. Judith looked at the medallion and gasped.

"Oh, my Goddess. Do you realize what this is? How can you just give this to me?"

"I made it for you. Is it okay?"

"Okay? You overwhelm me, love." She fell into his embrace and they held each other.

"Swordmaster," Rebecca said softly. "You must give him formal challenge." Judith separated herself from Wayne and looked into his eyes.

"Hang in there, lover. I think you know what comes next." Wayne stood and moved to the opening between the stones from which he initially entered the circle. Rebecca stood beside him and Judith picked up the ritual sword. For the first time, Wayne looked at it and smiled. It was the sword he had crafted for her and given her at Christmas. He was ready for this.

Judith raised the sword and pressed it against Wayne's chest. He knew how sharp this sword was; he'd whetted the edges himself. Judith was all business and Wayne realized he could still become a sacrifice. But he trusted them. In spite of their ups and downs, he trusted both Rebecca and Judith. He remembered his own recent, or distant past. He was not sacrifice, but Vagabond.

"Who stands before the gate of the dread Mighty Ones?" Judith demanded. The response came to Wayne as if he had rehearsed for this like any other play. It had been written in his uncle's *Book of Shadows*.

"A child of earth."

"Do you have the courage to make the assay? For know that it is better that you should fall on my sword here and perish than to assay the gates with fear in your heart." He thought it was vaguely ludicrous to ask him if he had the courage to do it. What worse could happen than he had already been through? He looked aside at Rebecca and spoke his response directly to her, rather than to Judith.

"I enter the circle of your friendship with perfect love and perfect trust."

"Who speaks for you?" Judith asked next. Rebecca stepped forward to pronounce her sponsorship before the Goddess, but Wayne raised a hand and held her back.

"There need none speak for me," he said softly. There was a gasp among the coveners gathered behind Judith. "I claim sanctuary in this circle as Vagabond in your midst, a priest after the order of Merlin. I come as a messenger of the Goddess."

There was a palpable silence in the circle. Judith looked questioningly at Rebecca but she was equally as surprised. It was Counselor, the Priestess of Braithwaite, who stepped forward to lay a gentle hand on Judith's and point the sword away from Wayne's chest and into the ground.

"It is written in the earliest of our records that the Vagabond is a priest without heritage. Thus it was when The Vagabond Poet came to us and others over the years. Truly, as he has brought to us the *Athamé* Creüs, he may be said to be the messenger of the Goddess. Your heritage, therefore, must stand unquestioned. But tell me, young Vagabond. By what name should we know you?"

"I am Promethean, The Unbound, heir of Prometheus, The Bound, a Vagabond Priest and Toolmaker."

The old priestess stepped up to him and kissed him.

"Welcome to Carles Castlerigg."

Judith, too, took him in her arms and kissed him. Perhaps it was less passionate than he had known her to kiss before, but at the same time, it was warmer and touched him more deeply. A third priestess, to whom he had not been introduced, kissed him in greeting. Then Rebecca was in his arms. He recognized her touch and the taste of her lips, before his eyes had opened to look into hers.

"Come then, Vagabond Priest. Meet the cildru of Cobhan Carles." Suddenly the circle was moving, passing him from one to another, spinning him around and kissing him. They chanted, they yelled and they screamed. He was caught up in the dancing and celebration. At last the celebrants collapsed around the fire and Wayne lay between Rebecca and Judith.

Judith heaved a deep breath which raised her breasts delightfully in front of Wayne. He felt himself responding to her. She stood and faced the coveners.

"The Hart, The Huntress of Carles, was selected as High Priestess at Litha last year. She was challenged. She has fulfilled all aspects of this challenge, even beyond what the challenger intended. She has gathered into our circle the Four Faces of Carles from the places they were concealed. Therefore, as Swordmaster and as Priestess of Threlkeld, I declare the challenge fully met and declare that Threlkeld recognizes Sadb, The Hart, The Huntress as High Priestess." The older priestess stood then.

"Braithwaite acknowledges that The Hart has succeeded in her challenge and by all rights of the Great Circle, Braithwaite recognizes Sadb, The Hart, The Huntress of Carles, as High Priestess." She looked pointedly at the third priestess. The mousy woman stood.

"High Lodore acknowledges the fulfillment of the challenge and recognizes Sadb, The Hart, The Huntress as High Priestess," she said. "But please. I ask of my circle to begin selection of a new priestess, for I have failed in keeping our former High Priest in check. As priestess of High Lodore, I must fulfill my duties, but as a wife and mother, I must excuse myself and follow my husband. There may yet be salvation."

With that, she dropped her tools, her robe, and her measure into the fire with her husband's and moved to the Northern Gate. Judith rose and opened the gate with her sword.

"Merry meet and merry part and merry meet again," the circle intoned. The priestess stepped through the gate and Judith sealed it as the woman walked away from the circle. Everyone was silent. Finally, Judith faced the remaining members of the circle.

"Who speaks for Skiddaw?" she asked. A man about Rebecca's age stood.

"Skiddaw accepted Sadb, The Hart, The Huntress as both priestess and High Priestess when it was announced last year. We have not wavered in our acceptance. We further ask that the High Priestess accept the Fourth Face of Carles, the pentacles Enceladus, as a sacred trust from her brothers and sisters and that she hold it on behalf of our circle for the Great Circle of Carles."

Rebecca bowed to the man and the members of his circle voiced in unison, "So mote it be."

DEVON LAYNE

"By consent of the lesser circles, we accept and affirm The Hart as High Priestess of Cobhan Carles," Judith declared.

"So mote it be," shouted all those gathered.

"It remains," said the Priestess of Braithwaite, "for our new High Priestess to gaze into the Cauldron Ops. However, we are without a High Priest and need a champion for this ritual." She looked pointedly at Wayne. Before he spoke, he turned to Judith.

"Um… this is a little outside of what I've been taught. What am I supposed to do?"

"Unbound…" she began and then dropped her voice to a whisper. "Wayne, do you love me?" There was so much yearning in her voice that Wayne nearly broke down in tears to hear it. Because he knew that in the circle they only used ritual names, he dropped his voice to a whisper as well.

"Judith, when I look at you I know that all I want for my future is in your arms. When I saw that priestess leave the circle because the asshole was her husband, all I could think was that if it was you who had been expelled, I'd do the same thing. It wouldn't make a difference to me what you had done or why. I would want… I would need to be by your side. I love you, babe, and if you walked from here right now, I'd be right beside you."

"I don't plan to share you," she said. "Not unless it's really good for me, too. But our High Priestess needs a champion. I want you to be with her."

"With her?"

"In any way that is needed," Judith clarified. Wayne hemmed.

"What am I supposed to do?"

"Help her. Raise the power she needs to descry the cauldron. Support her. Protect her. Once the scrying ritual begins, no one else in the circle will be able to do more than feed it power."

"But if I'm supposed to… you know… have sex? How can I do that to you? How can I do that in front of all these people?"

"Darling, don't you love her?" Wayne stopped his response short. Did he love Rebecca Allen, the professor who nearly flunked him? Perhaps not. But the woman who saved his life? The woman he sat beside when she was injured? The woman who shared her tools with him? Yes. He loved her. He nodded.

"Do what is necessary," Judith whispered. "And you'd better be damned sure she enjoys it!" she laughed. Wayne turned red and then faced Rebecca.

"High Priestess." He bowed. "As Vagabond Priest after the order of Merlin and Melchizedek, I am sworn to protect, help, and defend my brothers and sisters in the Art. As Promethean, The Unbound, I offer myself as your champion, yours to command in this ritual."

Rebecca rushed to him, but instead of embracing Wayne, she embraced Judith.

"Thank you. Thank you."

"Hey. There's nothing saying you can't enjoy this," Judith smiled. She caught Wayne in her arm and pulled him into the hug. "We might have to explore this further one day," she whispered. Both Wayne and Rebecca looked at her sharply and then began to laugh.

"In my dreams," Wayne said. "In my dreams."

REBECCA AND WAYNE placed their tools around the fire, joining the Four Faces of Carles. With three sets of tools arranged, they moved to the East and Wayne picked up Creüs, the *Athamé* that had been in his care for six months. Rebecca joined him and he raised the knife in his right hand. She placed her left hand over his and both felt the tingle of power and sexual energy that coursed through them. Rebecca invoked the powers of the East as the circle of dancers moved around them.

Holding the blade was like holding the tail of a cyclone. They made a full circuit of the fire, following the dance, and Wayne could feel the wind picking up as they passed each quadrant. The wind whipped through their hair and against their naked bodies. It tore around the circle in the wake of the dancers building into a towering cone of power around them. From each direction, the wind blew as it would in its season, but the four winds met at the tip of Creüs and mounted up from there to a point high above them. It seemed only slightly out of place to Wayne that the winds of all four corners of the earth should blow at the same time on the same point where they focused the energy of the knife.

Stranger still was the sweet seductive pull of power. They ruled the wind. Wayne was caught in the vortex of its power and scarcely felt Rebecca tug his arm down until the point of the knife touched the ground and the wind settled into a pattern of swirling around them. They were in the eye of the storm.

They moved to the south and Wayne picked up the staff, Iäpetus. In a repeat of the first circuit, Rebecca invoked the Powers of the South. At the mention of Iäpetus, the rod burst into flame in their hands. As they circled the compass, the fire came with them and when they reached the

South again, a wall of fire surrounded them. They moved to the West and picked up the cup Cottus. Wind and fire were things that Wayne could comprehend. Somehow it seemed natural that a knife could call wind and a staff could call fire. But when the cup became heavier with water and it began spilling over their hands as they completed another circuit, Wayne was a little freaked out. There was no rain, no stream to dip it in, not even a bucket. Yet the cup spilled water out all the way around the circuit.

As soon as Wayne touched the black disk, Enceladus, with its numerous magical inscriptions, the ground shook. Rebecca made her invocation and as they moved around the circle, a crack opened in the ground. When they completed the circuit, they were on an island, a fire blazing in the center and between it and a ring of fire surrounding them was a channel filled with water. The wind whipped around the circle, fanning the flames. At last, they continued to the East and each grasped the knife again.

The experience was a surprise to both Wayne and Rebecca.

Years before, she built a bond between the bearer of this knife and herself in a fire ritual. The bond went forever unconsummated. But the sexual and sensual charge that remained in this instrument was as strong as the day it was generated. In Wayne, it awoke a deepened sensual awareness that was new to him. It did not seek its own gratification but extended a caring and concern that he had demonstrated in sitting by an invalid's bed throughout the night, only a few days before. It awoke a willingness in him to be whatever the woman would have him be because he cared for her as the companion of his passage to adulthood.

As he turned to Rebecca, the first thing that he noticed was the still-blackened, over-exercised bruise that had resulted when she saved his and Judith's lives. His left hand reached to her shoulders as he drew her to his embrace and all his energy focused on easing that pain. As he touched her—as she came willingly into his loving embrace—the blackness lightened, faded, and disappeared.

IN REBECCA, THE same force was working in a different way. It awakened within her an inconsolable longing for a love she was unable to put behind her. It aroused her in a way that only a lifetime of that longing could do. Every sense in her body, her touch, her smell, her sight, all told her that Wesley Allen was near her. She could hear the strains of his music and the joy of his voice as he sang in the wild whirlwind surrounding them.

She did not—could not—lose sight of the fact that the man in whose loving embrace she was locked was not J. Wesley Allen. She knew Wayne and felt the tenderness that he gave to her; felt the bruises fade as he touched her. But it did not seem to make a difference here, behind the inner sanctum of Cobhan Carles. Such was their magic that here, behind this ivory veil, they were who they were, released to vent the passion they had felt building all along.

But they were so much more. As he laid her on a robe on the ground, she held herself open for him and guided him into her. In that moment, he *was* Wesley.

He was also the great horned god and she the goddess working the magic of Litha beneath the canopy of the heavens. Her Sun King was at the peak of his glory. They were all the lovers of the world who dared to indulge their fantasy on the shortest night of the year.

WAYNE KNEW THAT when Rebecca looked at him, she was not seeing the awkward student who slept through her classes. In fact, as he looked at her, the now familiar sensation of other eyes joining his own crept in on him. This time he knew what to expect; it no longer frightened him and he gladly invited the visitors to join him over whatever ages they might have traveled for release on this night. He recognized the Vagabond Poet who saw in Rebecca his own beloved Mari. He felt different, like he was more than Wayne Hamel, when a voice sang through his mouth inviting a longed-for and separated wife to his mountaintop. He knew this was what Rebecca drew from him and felt a kinship with the man. In that instant, he vowed to find her husband and reunite the couple.

And they were The Lady of the Rake and her husband, Lord Derwentwater, Ishtar and Tammuz, Arthur and Guinevere, hundreds of others to whom he could give no name but welcomed nonetheless.

It didn't matter.

For even in this crowd, Rebecca accepted and loved Wayne for what and who he was.

Each stroke burst from the two lovers hidden behind the impenetrable curtain of power around them and left them with more rather than less energy. Each climax sent them into a dance, holding each other as they spun around the fire, building the power higher and higher. Each peak was just a step up and not the mountain itself. They spun like the particles of an atom around the nucleus of Ops, the great black cauldron at the center of Carles. The knife had long since found its place at the Eastern edge of their circle. Now, hands joined, they danced around the undying fire on which the ancient cauldron boiled. The cauldron called them both inward and soon they were as engrossed in its depths as they had been in each other's. Their perspectives changed and they were now engaged in the deepest scrying that the powers of Carles could raise.

REBECCA THE HIGH Priestess knew the purpose of this dance, even though she gladly lost herself in its passion. As they circled the cauldron, each time she passed one of the Four Faces of Carles, she felt the prickle of it in her back, like passing through the spray of a hose. She gathered this power—the power of the greater circle dancing outside their sphere, the power of her sex act with her Vagabond Priest, the power of the tools and the watchtowers—and focused it on the black cauldron. Here she would find the answer; how would she find and rescue her husband?

This was the cauldron of Ceriddwyn where the dead come to life; a broth that imparts all knowledge and understanding; the womb of the goddess. And in its depths, Rebecca scried the lives of a thousand people who were remade and brought to new life as Wayne channeled the energy of the circle into it. In that instant, she could not separate the spirits of the cauldron from the ghosts of her own past. She stood in a different world. Behind her were a dozen paths leading to this single crisis point. She saw herself approaching from each of those directions. The Rebeccas that came were each different. One was an old and embittered woman. One was a lonely and frightened pregnant mother. One was the High Priestess of Carles and another the lover of the young man that orbited around her still.

Ahead lay a hundred other paths, fanned out like the points of a compass. On each path was a different Wesley and a different Rebecca walking away from her. But which was the one that would lead to her happiness and to the recovery of her beloved? It was the point of decision. If she would have her husband back, she must decide what path to take. All these futures closed in on her and down each path she saw a hundred other paths that might also branch off. The curse of controlling the future was choosing which of the many paths she should take.

She stepped out, forcing herself along any path, and her eye was caught by paths in more directions, a starburst of futures exploding around her like some awful nova. She was breaking up. The solid flesh that she had felt when she struck this point was disintegrating.

This is what had killed Mari and the Vagabond Poet. It was not the forging of the tool, but scrying the cauldron Ops, brought out only when all four tools were present in the Great Circle. The choices of futures were too much for the priestess to bear. The power of the great circle was more than the priest could hold and direct. Bits of what had been Rebecca floated off down one avenue after another like fallout in the aftermath of her own internal explosion. And one-by-one, the separate paths began to fade from before her eyes—fade as the futures became no longer feasible and the moment of choice passed. In their absence, she could see only a circle of faces holding before them the Four Faces of Carles and in their midst, in place of the black kettle, Rebecca saw the figure of her daughter, as oblivious to the roaring flames as the iron kettle.

It was not for Rebecca to free her husband.

Blackness surrounded her.

WAYNE, TOO, WAS caught in the world of visions as he scried in the cauldron and hovered over Rebecca. He knew other eyes would join his here and he would see their experiences. He no longer feared the intrusion but stepped back to watch objectively as The Vagabond Poet stepped out of the past.

"Learn," he whispered.

He stood in a mammoth sanctuary canopied above with the dark starless night. Right and left extended the ancient pillars after whose image the rugged circle of druid stones must in some distant age have been fashioned. Behind him stood the darkened, unopening gate of sunrise, sealing him in unending night. Ahead lay the altar upon which burned a waning sacrifice of fragrant leaves. This he all but ignored, mounting the steps to part the veil that separated him from the Priestess there. Her eyes held his in fatal fascination like a cobra staring its victim to submission before the strike.

The eyes went unblinking, staring past him, through him into a secret world that he could not share.

The Poet, caught up in his own unfolding vision as energy tore through him, did not understand what to do. No one told him. She was deep in trance, her eyes wide open and staring, unseeing and unblinking. He found the answer in her eyes. By some magic he scried their depths for a reflected image of what they saw. For a long time, they knelt, thus.

Wayne carefully and objectively analyzed the scene. Mari seemed gradually to be fading from his sight and he blinked his eyes to bring her back into focus. It was not a trick of his eyes. She was breaking up, dissolving in fragments and floating into the kettle before her. Disappearing. But what could he do?

The Vagabond Poet was a crazy man, a charging bull, rolling the cauldron from the fire, throwing the sacred tools right and left. Calling, screaming in panic after his vanishing priestess. He charged the wall of light, shattering the wards, but for Mari, the mother of his unborn child, it was too late.

Wayne snapped back into his own time/place with the painful fear of what he would find and a panic rising in uncertain response. He found himself kneeling across the cauldron, not from an image in his mind, but from Rebecca. There was a stark terror in her eyes. *You promised. Protect The Huntress.*

Comprehension flooded in on Wayne. Immense knowledge could be had from the cauldron Ops, but it exacted a heavy price. The collected energies of the circle were flowing through the Four Faces of Carles and into Rebecca. As she fed them on to the vision before her, they took bits of her with them in ever-increasing portions.

Wayne realized what he must do. It was not the ivory veil, but the cauldron itself. This was the same energy that caused the explosion and fire when the knife had struck his staff. He reached out with his mind and collected the streams of energy, refocusing them into himself. He spun, wrapping himself in the four ribbons of power like a maypole dancer. He felt his body temperature rise with the resistance of the energy flow. He could see his skin glow with the red heat.

And then he stepped into the flames. The cauldron was heavy as he wrapped his arms around it and lifted. Strange that he should notice its weight and not its heat, he thought absently. With a superheated body and what must have equaled superhuman strength, Wayne stood with the great black kettle embraced in his arms and held against his chest. Then he charged forward.

An explosive impact met him when he hit the surrounding wall of light—not the gelatinous mass he first encountered. The impact jarred his teeth, but the force of his blow was stronger than the barrier. It shattered. He stumbled through the circle and tripped over a covener lying on the ground at its perimeter. He fell, loosing the great kettle as he went, watching its momentum carry it on beyond him through the air. The last that Wayne saw was the ancient cauldron striking the low-lying altar stone in the East and the geyser of liquid that erupted from its broken form.

25
Fifth Circle

WHEN WAYNE awoke seconds later, Judith already cradled him against her breasts, her hand stroking his hair. A bird chirped somewhere in the distance, the only sound breaking the silence, and Wayne's first clue that the night was far advanced and dawn would soon break.

He looked up, searching for Judith's eyes, but found that they were focused on a spot beyond him. He followed her gaze to the broken cauldron and the fountain of steam that was still rising from it. It rose only some six feet above the altar stone and was not dissipating. Wayne craned his head around to find Rebecca also staring at the cauldron's remnants. She was in the care of the other priestess. He scrambled to sit upright next to Judith, finding that he needed her support. That last effort drained him.

"Oops," he whispered, looking at the broken kettle.

"Shh," whispered Judith. The entire circle stared at the relic and Wayne focused on the shifting steam rising from the cauldron. There in its midst, he saw a shape solidifying as if it could will the molecules of escaping steam into a form. And then he recognized her.

"Chameleon!" He struggled to his feet and lurched toward her.

"Unbound. You did it," she answered. She hugged Wayne to her, supporting his weight.

"Wait! How do you know her?" Judith demanded.

"It's the... uh... doughnut lady."

"It's me," Lissa said simply. "It gets harder to surprise you blokes every time."

"Theatre person?" Wayne asked Judith.

"The best."

The entire circle broke into applause and laughter and a dozen people moved to hug her in welcome. Rebecca joined Wayne and Judith.

279

"Is there something I should be doing about this?" she whispered to Judith.

"No. She belongs here," Judith answered. "Though how she got in through the wards, I don't know."

"They all fell apart when The Unbound cracked the pot," Lissa said.

"Damn, it's good to see you, sister," Judith said hugging the newcomer. "But you have a lot of explaining to do. You were training him?"

"Someone had to. You and The Hart were bollixing things up royally."

"That means you taught him... You bitch! With my boyfriend!"

"Uh... Swordmaster," Rebecca whispered. "Maybe we should hear the story first. Not that I'm one to speak..."

"Sister, it was for the circle. I'm going to assume this was, too."

"It was, love," said Lissa. "You can't imagine how hard it's been to be so close to the two of you and not be able to reveal myself. I was tracking what The Barber was doing and trying to protect the three of you as best I could."

"Protect us?"

"Have The Unbound tell you about the tornado on Oester," Lissa laughed. "I taught him every defense I knew and then he kept coming up with things I'd never taught him. I'd like to know who else was teaching. I thought it was you two!"

"Only when we realized he was being taught," Judith said.

"Uh... He's right here, you know. He might even have one or two answers," Wayne said.

"Sorry, babycakes. I didn't mean to be condescending," Judith said.

"Have you all been naked all night? It's freezing up here," Lissa said. She reached behind the stone for her robe and pulled it on. The rest of the coveners took that as their sign to do the same. Wayne pulled his shoulder bag open and got his own black robe out of it.

"Now that I've got most of my memory at my command, the three of you and my uncle all assumed way too much. And assume makes an ass out of u and me."

"Your uncle?" Rebecca asked.

"I know the wards are down, but I think we should have them before I talk further," Wayne said. He gestured and the gathered celebrants were wreathed in light as the dome took shape.

"Whoa!" Lissa said. "Who taught you that one?"

"If any of you had let me have all my wits about me, this might have been easier," Wayne began. "As it was, The Swordmaster gave me a gift of pentacles and swore me to secrecy with a blood oath. When I was puzzling this out while visiting my uncle at New Year's, he thought that meant she was training me. He had things to give me—pass on to me—and couldn't wait, so initiated me and gave me the knife that everyone's been so crazy to get. My uncle is a solitary called The Bound, initiated by the Vagabond Priest you all once knew as The Firebrand. Others of us found his name in certain rare manuscripts." He looked at Rebecca and Judith, knowing that they understood this was Benjamin Wilton.

"So, your uncle, The Bound, was training you?" Rebecca asked.

"Indirectly. He gave me the *Athamé* and his *Book of Shadows*. I've been learning from it."

"From what I've seen, The Bound's *Book of Shadows* should be entered in the records as a grimoire," Lissa said.

"I thought it was The Swordmaster who was training you," Rebecca said. "So, when I realized you were a toolmaker, I thought I'd help with some of the lore. I didn't attempt to train you beyond that."

"And I thought it was either you or The Swordmaster, so I was just going to supplement with the secrets of Ops," Lissa said. "I'd figured out it wasn't the tool-making that killed great-grandmother, but the scrying."

"Mari was your great-grandmother?" Wayne asked.

"Well, there's a couple more greats in there," Lissa answered. "But like you inherited your uncle's *Book of Shadows*, I inherited Mari's."

"That brings us to tonight," Judith said. "For such a bunch of fuck-ups, we seemed to have come out okay. Are you all right, sweetie?" Wayne hugged Judith to him.

"Yeah. I still need to get used to all this, though. I've only been getting it together since earlier this evening. Chameleon managed to get through most of the barriers you two set. Losing the pentacles was disorienting. Then The Bound appeared on the spirit level and released the last geas. He told me I had taken an oath to protect my brothers and sisters in the craft. And I'd sworn to Chameleon to protect The Huntress. I came up over the hill and saw that priest fellow with a knife at Re…The Hart's throat and went crazy."

"You did the right thing. Slaying the demon was unbelievable."

"It was like the knife took control and told me what to do."

"But… if I may interrupt," the other priestess said, moving closer to the four, "the circle is gathered to know the substance of The High Priestess's vision. Can you tell us what happened? We participated in the visions that were occurring in the cauldron and frankly were all passed out by the time The Unbound broke the spell."

"And the kettle," Wayne muttered.

"You're a toolmaker. You can make another," Judith giggled. Wayne groaned.

"The visions were coming too fast for me to separate," Rebecca began. "I was being overwhelmed until one image solidified."

"Your daughter," Counselor said.

"Yes. But I don't know what it means other than she apparently is the one to release my husband."

"That is undoubtedly a part of her mission, but our lore holds another answer as well," the old priestess said. She walked over to the broken cauldron. Wayne stepped behind Judith and made himself as small as possible.

"What other answer, Priestess?" Rebecca asked.

"The great cauldron Ops is broken," the Priestess intoned. "It requires that the circle dedicate another to take its place. Alas, that is where this evening began and is not where any of us wish for it to end. But the absence of a tool is not unknown to us. Over the centuries tools have been lost, hidden, and broken. Each time, a toolmaker has come into our midst. And each time a new tool has been forged. But these tools have not always had a physical manifestation as knife, wand, cup, and pentacles, or even cauldron. That is why there are four circles that make up the Great Cobhan Carles Castlerigg. In the absence of the tool, the lesser circle can be dedicated as the embodiment of that spirit, just as Threlkeld has functioned as the *Athamé* for these past fourteen years. The same is true of the cauldron. But we have no circle dedicated to Ops. It is my opinion that there must be a new circle with your daughter as its center, as the vision showed us."

"No!" Rebecca gasped. "She's too young."

"Agreed, but things take time. Has she apprenticed yet?"

"I have raised her in the ways of the circle."

"This is as it should be. It is time to take that a step further. A representative from each of the lesser circles should surround her and take her into their care and training." Judith immediately stepped forward and raised her hand, Lissa just a step behind her. Two other women from the other circles also stepped forward. "That was easy," the Priestess said. "But there is one more thing. A toolmaker." She looked directly at Wayne. "Vagabond. Can we commit this circle into your care to forge it into a tool of the coven? This has ever been the role of a vagabond in our midst—one who is not a part of any circle."

"I don't know what to do," Wayne responded. "How can I help?"

"I think you will figure it out," Rebecca laughed. "You seem to have figured everything else out this evening. But…" Rebecca came up close to Wayne and whispered into his ear. "Wayne. Can I trust you with my daughter? She is only fourteen. Please…" Rebecca was silenced when Wayne dropped to his knees and placed one hand under his foot and the other on his head.

"All between these hands I commit to the Goddess. I, Promethean known as The Unbound, do of my own free will most solemnly swear to protect, help, and defend my sisters and brothers of the Art. I take this vow as Vagabond Priest and as champion of the High Priestess… and her daughter. So mote it be."

"So mote it be," echoed the circle.

The four volunteers knelt before Rebecca as well and placed a hand on Wayne.

"High Priestess," Judith spoke for them. "You we know as The Hart and The Huntress. We of the fifth circle, known henceforth as the Circle of Castlerigg, accept the task of training your daughter, protecting her from all ill, and in league with your champion will forge the cauldron Ops of our own bodies, souls, and spirits. So mote it be."

"So mote it be." And with that, the ritual was over. Wayne dismissed his wards and the coveners went about gathering their tools, their clothes, and whatever other items they brought within the circle. The fire was doused and covered with soil and sod. The small stones were moved to the outskirts and into places next to the standing stones. In half an hour, the moor was pristine. Everyone was dressed in their street clothes again and Wayne threw his cape over his shoulders as he put an arm around Judith. Rebecca put an arm around him from the other side, careful to avoid his walking stick with her own.

"What happened to Chameleon?" he asked casually. "I didn't see her leave."

"That's the fun thing about Chameleon," Judith said. "You never know exactly where she is or when she will show up."

"Oh, come on," he said exasperatedly.

"Well, you tell me. She's a star. She likes to be cloaked in illusion."

"I'll say," Wayne chuckled.

"What?"

"Nothing." He looked up the hill. He was sure she was there, just at the crest watching them leave in the dawn's half-light. He smiled as words came to him from some remembered passage.

If we shadows have offended.
Think but this and all is mended.
That you have but slumbered here
While these visions did appear.

He yawned. For all he knew, he could be asleep now. He walked toward town with Judith and Rebecca.

Monday, 23 June 1969

THE TROUPE BOARDED the bus for London. They would see a show at Stratford-upon-Avon by the Royal Shakespeare Company, then in London they would see at least two more shows. All day Sunday, he and Judith had stayed in his room—naked. Between lovemaking and running out to get food, they talked about what they wanted to do and see in London.

"London Bridge," Wayne said. "I just have to walk across and look up at those towers."

"Okay. Well, two problems with that. First, London Bridge doesn't have towers. That's, appropriately enough, Tower Bridge by the Tower of London. Second, London Bridge was not falling down, it was sinking into the Thames. The City sold it to some Yank who is moving it out in the desert in America someplace. Right now, there is no London Bridge."

"How can you deflate my hopes and dreams so cavalierly?"

"So far, babycakes, I haven't seen anything deflate since we came to bed."

WAYNE BOARDED THE bus and passed Dr. Allen seated in the front making notes in a small book. She looked up and smiled. Wayne was about to speak when she winked at him. He lost the words.

While he was stopped in the aisle, Glenn ran into him from behind. Wayne turned around and pushed him playfully backwards.

"Who's there?" he demanded. Glenn charged forward, rushing the smaller man down the aisle where he slid swiftly and silently into a seat beside Judith. Glenn jumped into the seat in front of them knees first. He turned Gail's head back to see Wayne.

"Would you look at this?" he said. "I think the boy has gone Republican on us."

"My God, Wayne! What did you do to your hair and beard?" Gail asked.

"I always figured I'd try shaving after the show was over," he answered lamely. The bus lurched and began moving out of town by a circuitous route.

"You've got such a babyface!" Gail laughed.

"Hey, don't knock it till you've tried it," Judith responded. "I like it this way. It's sort of naked and it doesn't scratch when he gets it between... Oops."

"Oh, I get it," Glenn said. "You two finally found yourselves a hide-away, didn't you? Come on, old man, you can tell me. Where have you been for the last two days?"

"In bed."

"Whose?"

"In my room, you numbskull," Wayne said.

"I'll vouch for that," Judith said, adding fuel to the fire. "He was in bed the *whole* time."

"Oh! Hothothothot!" Gail said, hauling Glenn down next to her.

"And I think it's a good idea to keep that arrangement," Judith whispered.

"You're incorrigible," Wayne said as he kissed her.

"I hope that means sexy and available," she said.

The bus driver announced various sites and they settled back to watch the scenery. Wayne nodded off a little, but each time he closed his eyes, visions of the past two days swam into his conscious. Had he really made love to Rebecca? And Lissa? And Judith? All in the same waking period? It just seemed too fantastic to be true. Like picking up a kettle of boiling water right out of the fire. He glanced down at his arms. He had to have imagined some of it. Just not all of it. He was sure.

A SMILE STILL played on Rebecca's lips as Wayne was rushed down the aisle by his friend. She would have to talk to him about what had happened Saturday night. But there was time for that. It was too bad he and Judith were students and she was faculty. Then again... well there was always Lughnasad.

"WAYNE!" HE JERKED his attention back to Judith who was waving a hand in front of his face. "Hey! Where you at?" She followed his line of sight to where Rebecca was sitting. "I see. Come back to this plane for a while, would you?" She planted a sound kiss on his lips. "Look. You've got to pay attention up here. Now watch."

The bus rounded a curve in the road and Judith pointed at a stone cottage just below the roadway at the north end of Thirlmere Lake. It was a little cottage that looked like it was right out of a storybook.

"What is it?" he asked. She gave him a playful shove away from her.

"It's my home," she said. "I told you I had a cottage out here."

"You left that to come to Indiana? How could you?"

"It wasn't easy." He watched out the window until the cottage disappeared behind them.

"Wow."

"Like it?"

"Love it."

"Play your cards right and you could get an invitation to visit."

"When?"

"Oh, I don't know. When does this tour end?" she asked.

"You mean…?"

"It wouldn't be hard to get your ticket changed. You want to stay till after August first, don't you?"

"August first? You mean…?" he pointed his thumb vaguely back over his shoulder toward the stone circle.

"Lughnasad. The commissioning of the new circle," she said. He thought for a moment and cocked his head to one side.

"Classes don't start until after Labor Day."

"Then you don't have to hurry, do you." She kissed him again.

"Think you can keep me occupied that long?"

She grinned as wickedly as he could ever have fantasized. This was going to be one hell of a trip to England.

"Well, if all else fails, we could take a walking tour north, over to the Isle of Man and up into Scotland," she said.

"Walk to Scotland?" he asked. "Can that be done?"

"It's been done before," she said. "And you already have a walking stick." His arms slid around her and they didn't hear anything else until they reached Stratford-upon-Avon.

Ritual Reality

Wednesday, 19 August 1818—Mrs. Dilke's Diary

John Keats arrived here last night as brown and as shabby as you can imagine; scarcely any shoes left, his jacket all torn at the back, a fur cap, a great plaid, his knapsack, and a thick stick in his hand. I cannot tell what he looked like—such a vagabond!

The End

But the story continues in

The Props Master 2: A Touch of Magic

www.ingramcontent.com/pod-product-compliance
Lightning Source LLC
Chambersburg PA
CBHW070725280626
47159CB00023B/2724